'THE VAMPYRE' AND OTHER WRITINGS

JOHN WILLIAM POLIDORI was born in 1795 into a distinguished Anglo-Italian family. He was educated at Ampleforth College and the University of Edinburgh, where in 1815 he was awarded a degree of doctor of medicine, at the age of nineteen. In 1816 Polidori entered Lord Byron's service as his personal physician, accompanying him on his travels through Europe. It was while staying with Mary Wollstonecraft, Percy Shelley and Claire Clairmont at Byron's rented house by Lake Geneva, that Polidori began to write his most famous work, *The Vampyre*. The novel was published in 1819, originally attributed to Byron. Polidori and Byron parted company later in 1816; for a time Polidori continued to travel through Europe alone, before returning to England in 1817. He settled in Norwich, where for some years he practised as a doctor and pursued his literary career, until a serious accident damaged his health and made it impossible for him to work. On 21 August 1821 he died at the family home in London after accidentally taking poison.

FRANKLIN CHARLES BISHOP is a writer and journalist, and tutor for the University of Nottingham Continuing Education Department. He is the author of a life of Polidori and numerous articles on the Gothic.

FyfieldBooks aim to make available some of the great classics of British and European literature in clear, affordable formats, and to restore often neglected writers to their place in literary tradition.

FyfieldBooks take their name from the Fyfield elm in Matthew Arnold's 'Scholar Gypsy' and 'Thyrsis'. The tree stood not far from the village where the series was originally devised in 1971.

> *Roam on! The light we sought is shining still.*
> *Dost thou ask proof? Our tree yet crowns the hill,*
> *Our Scholar travels yet the loved hill-side*

from 'Thyrsis'

JOHN WILLIAM POLIDORI

'The Vampyre'
and other writings

Edited with an introduction by
FRANKLIN CHARLES BISHOP

Fyfield*Books*
CARCANET

First published in Great Britain in 2005 by
Carcanet Press Limited
Alliance House
Cross Street
Manchester M2 7AQ

A CIP catalogue record for this book is available from the British Library
ISBN 1 85754 787 X

The publisher acknowledges financial assistance from Arts Council England

Typeset by XL Publishing Services, Tiverton
Printed and bound in England by SRP Ltd, Exeter

Contents

Introduction

1

> There was no colour upon her cheek, not even upon her lip;
> yet there was a stillness about her face that seemed almost as
> attaching as the life that once dwelt there: – upon her neck and
> breast were blood, and upon her throat were the marks of teeth
> having opened the vein –
>
> from 'The Vampyre: A Tale' by John William Polidori,
> published 1819

On 1 April 1819 the *New Monthly Magazine* featured a short story entitled 'The Vampyre: A Tale by Lord Byron', which started a literary sensation. The public had seen nothing like it before and rushed to buy copies: thus it inaugurated a whole new genre of popular vampire fiction that continues to fascinate generation after generation of readers.

The proprietor and editor of the magazine, Henry Colburn, was delighted with his literary coup and even more pleased with the huge increase in sales it brought to his ailing literary magazine, which was to become the leading publication of macabre stories during the 1820s and 1830s. Almost immediately he issued *The Vampyre* in book form as a novella to cash in further on its popularity, followed later by other publishers eager to satisfy the enormous public demand. Five English editions of *The Vampyre* appeared during 1819. On the continent it proved even more popular and was rapidly translated into three editions in French. 1820 saw a bastardised version expanded into a two-volume novel by French author Cyprien Bérard, entitled *Ruthwen ou les vampires.* In 1824 a critical essay by A. Pichot insisted *The Vampyre* had more to do with Byron's popularity in France than all of his poetry. Even the celebrated German author Johann Wolfgang von Goethe (1749–1832) declared the work to be Byron's masterpiece. By 1830 editions were available in German, Spanish, Italian and Swedish translations. Further editions even appeared in America. Stage productions of *The Vampyre* quickly followed in the early 1820s with theatres in Paris showing several dramatic adaptations by the notable playwrights Charles Nodier (1780–1844) and Eugène

Scribe (1791–1861). James Robinson Planché translated Nodier's *Le Vampire* into English and in 1820 successfully performed it at the English Opera House in London. William August Wohlbruck and Heinrich August Marschner produced an opera based upon Polidori's tale entitled *Der Vampyr* in 1828 to much acclaim. Channel Four television produced a stunning version of *Der Vampyr* in 1993 in a contemporary London setting.

The publication of *The Vampyre* was, however, a literary deception and *succès de scandale* on a grand scale entirely perpetrated by Henry Colburn's unprincipled business acumen. He acquired the original manuscript from an unnamed correspondent and then falsely attributed the work to the most famous living poet of the time, Lord Byron, which he shrewdly and correctly judged would guarantee great public interest and huge sales; but even Colburn could not have foreseen the extent to which it would create a publishing phenomenon. In 1819 readers were profoundly shocked and titillated by a story in which the vampire was believed to be an accurate self-portrait of Lord Byron.

Byron, when informed of his name being falsely assigned to *The Vampyre*, irately declared he was not the author of the work; he had, however, written an unfinished vampire story entitled *A Fragment*, which his publisher later printed as an appendix at the end of his poem *Mazeppa* (published in 1819). Byron's vampire tale is a doleful piece of prose completely lacking the power of Polidori's work. The public still continued to believe that *The Vampyre* was indeed a self-portrait of Byron, a sensational if illogical extension and projection of the tortured Romantic hero evident in poems such as *Childe Harold's Pilgrimage* (1812–18) and *Manfred* (1817). To add further weight to this popular misconception Byron recently had been sharply caricatured by one of his spurned and angry ex-lovers, Lady Caroline Lamb, in her novel *Glenarvon* (1816) as Clarence de Ruthven, Lord Glenarvon. In *The Vampyre* it is the villainous Lord Ruthven who is the vampire – understood by astonished readers as a clear reference to Lord Byron.

The real author of *The Vampyre* was John William Polidori, an Anglo-Italian physician. Polidori was effectively cheated by his devious publisher Henry Colburn; immediately upon seeing his own work in print under Byron's name, he wrote to Colburn, demanding that his name appear as the rightful author of *The Vampyre*. The publisher prevaricated, protesting that it was he who had been compromised over the affair. He knew it was to his advantage to sustain the illusion of Byron as the author as long as possible, thereby maintaining its appeal, instead of admitting that it was the work of an unknown literary figure: consequently, he had done little to redress the matter, despite strong protestations from Polidori. The *New Monthly Magazine*'s sub-editor, Alaric Watts, resigned in protest at Colburn's deception thereby confirming that Polidori was indeed the real author. Despite this, the name of Polidori only appears in Colburn's second edition of the novella, described as *The Vampyre; a tale related by Lord Byron to Dr Polidori.* All other editions attribute it to Byron or simply omit an author's name altogether. By this time it mattered little to readers, who preferred to believe that Byron was the author. Polidori lost out financially through fear of losing a threatened court case over the dispute: he accepted the paltry sum of £30 from Colburn in full settlement, when he should have received enough from the huge sales to have made him a rich man.

John William Polidori, M.D. (1795–1821) was the oldest son of a distinguished Italian scholar and translator.[1] He had a classical education at the Catholic college of Ampleforth, near York, and later qualified as a Medical Doctor at the University of Edinburgh at the exceptionally young age of nineteen. Thomas Medwin,[2] a contemporary, described Polidori as 'a tall, handsome man, with a marked Italian cast of countenance, which bore the impress of profound melancholy; a good address and manners, more retiring than forward in society'. Polidori was a keen academic with interests in art, literature, architecture and history, who owned a collection of books in Latin, Greek, German, Italian, French and Spanish. His sister Frances married Gabriele Pasquale Giuseppe Rossetti in 1826, thus linking two highly cultured Anglo-Italian families. Frances became the mother of the celebrated Rossetti children; Gabriel[3] who, along with his sister Christina,[4] made substantial literary and artistic contributions to the Pre-Raphaelite movement.

In the April of 1816 Polidori (aged twenty) was appointed as Lord Byron's private physician and travelling companion. The famous poet was about to leave England, a self-imposed European exile to escape debtors. His wife thought him mentally unbalanced, and society was rife with rumours of an incestuous relationship with his half-sister, Augusta Leigh. Byron's publisher commissioned Polidori to write a journal of his travels with the poet.

Polidori travelled with Byron to Geneva where he met Percy Shelley, Mary Wollstonecraft Godwin (later Mary Shelley)[5] and her step-sister Jane 'Claire' Clairmont[6] (Byron's eighteen-year-old besotted lover). It was in the Villa Diodati by Lake Léman (Geneva) that the famous ghost story sessions took place, resulting in the genesis of Mary Shelley's masterpiece, *Frankenstein; or, The Modern Prometheus* (1818), Byron's *A Fragment* (1819) and Polidori's only published novel, *Ernestus Berchtold; or, The Modern Oedipus* (1819). Polidori also produced his seminal *The Vampyre: A Tale* (1819) based upon Byron's abandoned and unfinished piece.

Polidori was ill at ease with Byron and Shelley: after several petty rows and disagreements, they parted company late in the summer of 1816. He continued to travel through Italy, meeting Byron again in Milan and finally in Venice, before returning to England in the spring of 1817; he attempted to settle in Norwich, where he opened a dispensary treating the poor. He knew William Taylor (1765–1836), a well-known and philanthropic literary figure living in Norwich who was a close friend of the poet Robert Southey[7] (1774–1843) and correspondent of Walter Scott (1771–1832). Taylor introduced Polidori into the literary and social circles of Norwich, where he met the physician Thomas Martineau and his family, including his niece, the young (then aged thirteen) and future famous author, Harriet Martineau (1802–76). He continued to pursue his literary career, but after he sustained cerebral damage in an accident at Costessey Hall near Norwich, his mental and physical health deteriorated over the next four years with increasing rapidity. By 1821 he had abandoned both his medical and his literary careers. An attempt to study at Lincoln's Inn Fields for a career in Law was also discarded. He died in the family home in London in the August of 1821 after accidentally overdosing himself with a self-prescribed pharmacopoeia concoction. The Coroner memorably recorded 'Death by the Visitation of God'.

The Vampyre is a pivotal and extraordinary influential work combining elements of both Gothic and Romantic sensibilities, in which Polidori radically transformed the vampire of Eastern European mythology from an animated, rotting corpse that periodically rose from the grave to feed restrictedly on living relatives in the locale, into a travelling, handsome, amoral, aristocratic lethal seducer perfectly at home in high society and the London salons. The work broke with the explained supernatural school of Gothic[8] literature promulgated by Ann Radcliffe,[9] littered with hysterical anti-Catholicism,[10] and took it into the unexplained supernatural where the vampire exists intrinsically, without banal apology or theatrical illusion. Polidori secured for himself (though he was never to know it during his lifetime) a unique place in literary history with a tale he had originally written in 1816 whilst with Byron in Switzerland and dismissed as 'a mere trifle', never intending it for publication and indeed leaving his original manuscript with a lady friend near Geneva.

For an English readership generally lacking in knowledge about vampire mythology, Colburn had cleverly prefixed *The Vampyre* with a clarifying introduction and a fictitious 'Letter from Geneva'. Interest in vampire literature was embedded in Northern Europe, particularly Germany, with Goethe's *The Bride of Corinth* (1797) and Bürger's *Lenore* (1774). The first brief and speculative attempts to introduce vampiric elements into English appeared in poetry – Robert Southey's *Thalaba the Destroyer* (1801), John Herman Merivale's *The Dead Men of Pest* (1802) and later in John Stagg's *The Vampire* (1810), Byron's poem *The Giour* (1813) and Samuel Taylor Coleridge's *Christabel* (1816). Although these pre-date Polidori's *The Vampyre*, they did not deviate from the standard vampire folklore of Arabia and Eastern Europe. Metaphorical vampiric aristocrats are found in Gothic fiction of the eighteenth century as family usurpers, usually taking the inheritances from the rightful owners rather than their blood. Vampirism was also utilised in a political context to define economic exploitation of the working class by politicians sucking the life out of them via punitive taxes and debts even after death by burdening their surviving relatives with their financial demands.

The Vampyre remains, along with Mary Shelley's novel *Frankenstein; or, The Modern Prometheus*, of all the prose of the Romantic period the most republished and enjoyed by successive generations. Polidori created a new anti-Romantic icon; his drastic redefinition and introduction of the vampire as a lethal aristocratic seducer into English literature has had a continuing influence upon writers since 1819. He originated the powerful consciousness of the vampire as a mobile, evil force, undetected and cunning, unscrupulous, a dangerous predator yet seductively attractive. It has through successive imitations and development established an iconic literary motif that continues to fascinate and horrify. The mobility of Polidori's vampire added to its potency for exciting terror since, prior to his Lord Ruthven creation, the vampire of folklore had been a static monster trapped in its own foreign locale. Before the appearance of *The Vampyre* even English nineteenth-century readers would still have been in agreement with Voltaire's earlier sentiments: 'What? Vampires in an eighteenth century? Yes... in Poland, Hungary, Silesia, Moravia, Austria and Lorraine – there was no talk of vampires in London...'[11]

Polidori's archaic spelling of 'vampyre' alludes to the works of Joseph Pitton de Tournefort (1656–1708) and Dom Augustin Calmet (1672–1757). It was Calmet, a leading authority on vampires in the eighteenth century, who published in 1746 a treatise detailing more than 500 cases of documented vampirism. French botanist Tournefort wrote an eyewitness account of the dissection of a Greek *vrykolakas* (vampire). Vampire mythology originated from the East, especially Arabia and Greece after the establishment of Christianity and the later division of the Latin and Greek churches. The idea that a Latin body would not corrupt if buried in their territory gained credence with lurid tales of the dead rising from their graves and feeding upon the blood of the young and beautiful (Polidori utilises this aspect in his tale by having the vampire seduce Aubrey's sister). In parts of Greece (Polidori's tale significantly also has scenes located in Greece), vampirism was considered as punishment after death for heinous crimes committed whilst alive: the vampire was condemned to prey upon those he had loved most in life. Vampire folklore spread with variations to Hungary, Poland, Austria and Lorraine. Lurid accounts of Arnold Paul – the most famous 'vampire' of the eighteenth century – appeared in the *London Journal* of March 1732, relating how he had been turned into a 'vampire' whilst in Turkish Servia. Sporadic forays into vampire folklore appeared in English literature with Robert Southey's *Thalaba the Destroyer* (1801), which introduced the vampire to English readers in the female form of Oneiza, an Arabian maid, and Byron's poem *The Giaour* was steeped in Oriental mythology but none of the authors broke with the conventional vampire folklore.

Many writers of the Romantic Movement[12] in the early nineteenth century indulged in the rejuvenation of folklore and crude traditions by attempting imaginatively to reinvent and permeate them with perceptive and intellectual emotional responses. Other prominent literary works appearing in 1819 when Polidori's *The Vampyre* was published included Walter Scott's *Ivanhoe*, Byron's *Mazeppa* and *Don Juan* Cantos I–II and, interestingly, a three-volume set entitled *Anastasius; or, Memoirs of a Greek* by Thomas Hope, which like Polidori's *The Vampyre* was widely attributed to Byron on publication. Percy Shelley's *The Cenci: A Tragedy* and William Wordsworth's *Peter Bell: A Tale in Verse* were other notable publications.

Published in 1819, Polidori's only full-length novel, *Ernestus Berchtold; or, the Modern Oedipus* – like Byron's *Manfred*, Percy Shelley's *Laon and Cythna* and M.G. Lewis's *The Monk* – explores the then popular theme of incest. Polidori's novel also contains an historical account of Napoleon's 1798 invasion of Switzerland, one of the significant moments in the political development of Romanticism. As the literary critic James Rieger puts it: 'England lost a... novelist who, had he fulfilled the promise of *Ernestus Berchtold*, might now hold a place in the nineteenth-century hierarchy slightly above Charlotte Bronte...'[13]

Polidori's collection of poetry and his only published dramatic tragedy were contained in a volume entitled *Ximenes, The Wreath and Other Poetry*, also in 1819; the sonnets were especially well received. *Ximenes: the Modern Abraham* is his only published dramatic tragedy.

The philosophical essay 'Upon the Source of Positive Pleasure', published in 1818, was the result of a near-death-experience, when Polidori was in extremis after suffering concussion from his accident at Costessey Hall. An essay entitled 'Upon the Punishment of Death' arguing forcibly and eloquently against the judicial use of the death penalty for petty offences was published in 1816 in *The Pamphleteer*, the editor commending it as 'a very ingenious and valuable little tract'. In King George III's reign there were over two hundred capital offences, many for petty crimes, although in practice the courts were often reluctant to implement the death penalty in most minor cases. Cesare Bonesana, Marchese Beccaria's most famous work *On Crimes and Punishment*, published in 1764, which advocated penal reform in Europe, was a clear influence on Polidori's treatise.

Polidori, in collaboration with the artist Richard Bridgens, wrote the text for *Sketches Illustrative of the Manners and Costumes of France, Switzerland and Italy*, published in 1821. An epic Miltonesque style poem entitled *The Fall of The Angels; A Sacred Poem* was Polidori's final work; it appeared posthumously, also in 1821.

His other work includes the medical thesis, published in 1815, *Disputatio Medica Inauguralis, Quaedam De Morbo, Oneirodynia Dicto,*

Complectens, on the subject of sleepwalking and its suggested treatment. The source of Polidori's thesis was the *Encyclopédie* by Jean-Jacques Mènuret de Chambaud (1733–1815). Somnambulism had been defined by a treatise written by François Baissler du Sauvage de la Croix in 1768, which classified it with hallucinations of nightmares or night terrors and an accompanying inability to breathe; sufferers experienced weird creatures sitting on their chest – Henry Fuseli's painting *The Nightmare*[14] captures the horror perfectly. Also published were various literary reviews and in 1911, ninety years after his death, *The Journal of John Polidori*, detailing his time with Lord Byron. A very short story entitled *A Story of Miss Anne and Miss Emma with the Dog – Carlo* was also published posthumously. Apart from these works, the collected letters of Polidori and his family have remained previously largely unpublished. Polidori offers an inimitable and previously unheard voice, enriching our understanding of the Romantic period from a unique standpoint of both an observer and intimate of the Romantic dramatis personae yet precluded from personal success by his literary failures, his non-aristocratic status and by the religious prejudice of his peers. Polidori's professional rank as a physician with literary aspirations placed him in an uncomfortable position of peer rivalry against the aristocratic Byron and Shelley. His visceral understanding of the human condition contrasted vividly with his quixotic literary ambitions. As with his contemporary, John Keats (1795–1821), his intrinsic Romanticism was anchored by the prosaic necessities of life, Polidori as a medical physician and Keats as an apothecary, both constantly seeking expression through literary ambitions.

II

In 1816 Byron travelled through France, Belgium and into Switzerland before settling upon a summer's residence near Geneva at the Villa Diodati by the lakeside of Lac Léman. Nearby in a cottage called Maison Chappius was the *ménage à trois* of Percy Shelley with his lover Mary Wollstonecraft Godwin (later Mary Shelley) and her step-sister, Claire Clairmont, pregnant after an affair with Byron in London.

The group dynamics were complex: the members of the Shelley ménage were practising advocates of free love and radicalism;

Byron was a cynical Romantic patronising Catholicism with mocking humour; and Polidori was a Catholic with fierce literary ambitions. Byron, irritated by the demands of Claire, used the presence of Polidori to frustrate her intended amorous nocturnal visits to the Villa Diodati. Many years later, when Byron was dead and Claire was able as a middle-aged woman to examine her teenage obsessive love she described Byron as 'the merest compound of vanity, folly and every miserable weakness that ever met together in one human being... never was a nature more profoundly corrupted than his became, or was more radically vulgar than his was from the very outset'.[15]

During that fateful summer tensions within the group would manifest themselves in petty rows and irritations, especially between Byron and Polidori. Initially relations between Polidori and Percy Shelley seemed very amiable – both shared a common enthusiasm for chemistry and medicine although only Polidori held professional status. Shelley's radicalism, atheism and embracing of Godwin's philosophy of free love were at odds with Polidori's Catholicism and belief in an afterlife. After one incident he challenged Shelley to a duel, which was laughed off. In his diary for 4 June 1816 Polidori wrote: 'Went on the lake with Shelley and Byron, who quarrelled with me.' Polidori's vanity, sensitivity to criticism and religious psychological tensions proved a highly volatile mixture, although his friendship with Mary always appears harmonious if we read his diary – he gave her Italian lessons on a regular basis, went boating out on the lake with her until late at night and took her son William to be inoculated in Geneva. She was eighteen and he twenty, so flirtation cannot be ruled out. Certainly Polidori was not averse to the pleasures of the opposite sex: he records visiting a brothel in Geneva and he had female admirers at the numerous *soirées* he attended at the villas of the rich aristocrats. With Claire the situation was diametrically opposite – she found him a nuisance and an obstacle to her intended amorous liaisons with Byron.

Byron's immediate rapport with Percy Shelley increasingly led to the exclusion of Polidori – the most notable occasion being when Byron and Shelley went on a tour of the lake in Rousseau's footsteps, leaving the physician behind in the company of Mary and Claire. Polidori even tired of visiting the famous bluestocking intellectual, Madame de Staël,[16] at the Château du Coppet although he was a regular visitor to many other aristocratic households around Geneva; indeed, Byron actively encouraged him to partake of the local high society. Polidori, with his good looks, was not short of ardent female admirers in the wealthy villas and châteaux surrounding Geneva; he also made numerous male friends both in the medical and literary circles. He delighted in giving friends a copy of his medical thesis to read and even Madame de Staël made complimentary remarks about it. Except for his friendship with Mary, it was Polidori who was increasingly made to feel the male outsider of the group. Thomas Moore[17] (a friend of Byron) wrote that Polidori was the 'constant butt for Byron's sarcasm and merriment'.

Once when out in a boat, Byron was hurt by Polidori, who accidentally struck him on his knee with an oar; instead of apologising, the physician reportedly said, perhaps in retaliation for the many slights he had received from the poet, 'I am glad you can suffer pain.' Thomas Moore, a biographer of Byron, records that Polidori was 'in a constant hectic of vanity, he seems to have alternatively provoked and amused his noble employer.'

On 15 June Polidori records in his journal that he and Percy Shelley, a keen but amateur chemist, had a '…conversation about principles, – whether man was to be merely an instrument'. The reference to principles concerned the then popular scientific theory of man being nothing more than a kind of animated machine. Experiments in galvanism were well known and Polidori would have been familiar from his time at medical college in Edinburgh with the work of its discoverer Luigi Galvani (1737–98) and the gruesome experiments on cadavers by Giovanni Aldini (1762–1834) which suggested life might be restored. Polidori's Catholic sensibilities would be offended by this concept, but Percy Shelley as an atheist would have no such inhibitions. Mary Shelley overheard these conversations and they became a significant catalyst for her *Frankenstein; or, The Modern Prometheus*.

The summer of frequent storms and rain often confined Byron, Polidori and the visiting Shelley ménage to evenings spent in the Villa Diodati. With conversations often extending into the early hours of the morning and subjects growing more obscure and macabre the group (most probably on 16 June, a night of particularly heavy storms and rainfall), agreed each to write a ghost story, as a direct result of Byron's suggestion after readings of German ghost stories translated into French from a two-volume set ornately entitled *Fantasmagoriana, ou Recueil d'Histoires d'Apparitons, de Spectres, Revenans, Fantomes, &c.* (1812). The flickering fire in the grand salon of the Villa Diodati provided a suitably ghostly atmosphere for the group late into the night. Percy Shelley and Claire Clairmont soon gave up on their efforts at prose, while Byron wrote only a desultory fragment of an unfinished vampire tale. Mary began her *Frankenstein; or, The Modern Prometheus* and Polidori, *Ernestus Berchtold; or, The Modern Oedipus* (1819) his only novel.

Polidori, besides writing *Ernestus Berchtold*, was inspired to write up a vampire tale based upon the idea suggested by Byron's uncompleted fragment. Later, in a letter to Henry Colburn, Polidori explained the origin of the tale in Geneva in 1816: 'the Vampyre which is not Lord Byron's but was written entirely by me at the request of a lady... which I did in two idle mornings by her side'.[18] It was with her that Polidori carelessly left his original manuscript and apparently forgot all about it until he saw the story published in the *New Monthly Review* two years later.

Comparison with Byron's piece of dreary prose confirms that it was without doubt Polidori who breathed life into the vampire tale and made it into a genre of literature that continues to fascinate, horrify and intrigue. Polidori, by basing his vampire upon the character of Lord Byron, deftly transformed the monster of distant Eastern European tradition, giving it an immediate menace and potency.

The physician turned for his inspiration to the one man he had known intimately during that summer, the famous poet who had shown to his physician that he was a mere mortal, subject to the same foibles and bodily complaints as any other. Transposing the aspects of Byron that were less than meritorious, Polidori imbues his vampire with great presence. Polidori perhaps used the tale even as a wickedly humorous kind of exorcism to release his own feelings of anguish against Byron. His description of the vampire, Lord Ruthven is highly perceptive – a portrait drawn from his intimate observations of Byron: 'He gazed upon the mirth around him, as if he could not participate therein. His peculiarities caused him to be invited to every house; all wished to see him – in spite of the deadly hue of his face...' The intense, anxiety-filled, claustrophobic yet restrained prose of Polidori weaves a dreamlike intimacy throughout the tale. The companion of Lord Ruthven (the vampire) is a young man called Aubrey, enticingly something of a self-portrait of the physician. Polidori unmistakably demonstrates some acute knowledge of his own failings and inclinations: 'He thought, in fine, that the dreams of poets were the realities of life. ... the daughters – by their brightening countenances when he approached, and by their sparkling eyes, when he opened his lips, soon led him into false notions of his talents and his merit...'

Polidori belatedly tried to revive the vampire tale when he wrote, in November of 1819, to the publishers Longman to see if they 'would undertake to buy a second part of *The Vampyre* from me – as I must have something to engage my mind', but they refused his offer perhaps because the publishing furore and sensationalism of the original vampire tale had passed by.

Also published in 1819 was his only full-length novel, *Ernestus Berchtold; or, The Modern Oedipus*. The novel uses military, political and domestic themes, interwoven with supernatural events. The character of Olivieri may be modelled on Byron – not this time as vampire but as a corrupting aristocrat who excels in all vices and delights in debasing Ernestus. The *Literary Gazette* observed the novel to be, 'well constructed and ably written...' whilst the *Monthly Review* said the 'considerable powers of imagination... proved [Polidori] capable of writing in a higher and purer strain'. However, sales of the novel were miniscule and did nothing to establish Polidori as an author.

Byron and Polidori's ill-fated relationship during their brief period of intimacy during the summer of 1816 concluded in reflective vitriol from the physician and ambivalence from the poet, who saw only the annoying vanities of youth in his physician. Ironically, it was this failed relationship with Byron that provided Polidori with his most successful literary work, *The Vampyre*, casually yet cathartically written while at the feet of a female admirer. The petty rows and Polidori's indiscretions tried Byron's patience while the perfidy of Byron dismayed the physician. Polidori's Catholic sensibilities and insecurities placed him constantly on the defensive in religious and spiritual debates with Byron and Shelley. Neither did his literary pretensions impress since they induced ridicule whenever he attempted to bring any of his writings to their attention. Byron relinquished with Polidori's company in September of 1816 after just a few months. 'We have parted, finding that our tempers did not agree. ...There was no immediate cause, but a continued series of slight quarrels. I believe the fault, if any, has been on my part...' wrote Polidori to his father.

Polidori's historic transformation of the hideous, village

vampiric ghoul of the Orient and Eastern Europe mythology into an aristocratic, travelling seducer in *The Vampyre* began a unique genre of vampire literature. J. M. Rymer's *Varney the Vampire* (1847) reincarnated the aristocratic vampire as Sir Francis Varney whilst J. Sheridan Le Fanu's *Carmilla* (1872) features a female aristocrat – the Countess Mircalla Karnstein; Bram Stoker's *Dracula* (1897) brings his vampire Count from Eastern Europe to England. Anne Rice with her best selling novel *Interview with the Vampire* (1976) and sequels thrilled yet another new generation of readers. The fictional vampire is constantly being re-energised for new audiences. Polidori is responsible for creating a literary vampire figure that has become part of the popular imagination and perhaps it is entirely appropriate that both he and his iconic vampire figure have achieved immortality – in a literary sense.

Notes

1 Gaetano Polidori (1764–1853): an Italian writer and scholar, son of Agostino Ansano Polidori (1714–78) a physician and poet. Gaetano was onetime secretary to the great Italian tragedian Vittorio Alfieri (1749–1803). He came to settle in London from Paris in 1790 after resigning as Alfieri's secretary. He translated various literary works into Italian, notably John Milton's *Paradise Lost* and Horace Walpole's *Castle of Otranto*. He married in 1793, an English governess, Anna Maria Pierce.

2 Thomas Medwin (1788–1869): see his *Journal of Conversations of Lord Byron* ed. Ernest J. Lovell (Princeton University Press, 1966).

3 Gabriel Dante Rossetti (1828–82): a co-founder of the Pre-Raphaelite Brotherhood in 1848.

4 Christina Rossetti (1830–94): poet famous for *Goblin Market and Other Poems* (1862).

5 Mary Shelley (1797–1851): only daughter from the marriage of philosopher and novelist William Godwin (1756–1836) and Mary Wollstonecraft (1759–97) author of *A Vindication of the Rights of Woman* (1792).

6 Clara Mary Jane 'Claire' Clairmont (1798–1879): daughter of Mary Jane Vial Clairmont (1766–1841).

7 Robert Southey (1774–1843): Poet Laureate and one of the first generation of writers in the Romantic Movement. Celebrated as one of the Lake Poets along with William Wordsworth (1770–1850) and Samuel Taylor Coleridge (1772–1834).

8 Gothic novels were a style of writing popular in the late eighteenth century, which produced stories set in lonely frightening places usually with ghosts, apparitions and hauntings and lost inheritances. Supernatural events were invariably explained away in the dénouement by prosaic means. Major authors include Ann Radcliffe, Horace Walpole, William Beckford and Robert Maturin amongst many others.

9 Ann Radcliffe (1764–1823): author of *The Mysteries of Udolpho* (1794) the first 'best seller' gothic novel in English literature.

10 Anti-Catholicism in England and general prejudice against Catholics was common until the campaign for Catholic Emancipation succeeded in 1829.

11 *Questions sur l'Encyclopédie* (1772) by Francois-Marie Arouet de Voltaire (1694–1778).

12 The Romantic Movement developed in the late eighteenth century in opposition to the Enlightenment and its emphasis upon reason and science. The term Romantic was to do with the importance of emotions and individual experience.

13 *Dr Polidori and the Genesis of Frankenstein* from *Studies in English Literature 1500–1900* (1963), p. 471.

14 Henry Fuseli (1741–1825): artist and author famous for the often nightmarish contents of his paintings.

15 Claire Clairmont in a letter to Mary Shelley dated 15 March 1836.

16 Madame de Staël (1766–1817): French novelist and intellectual, a pioneer of French Romanticism. Her most famous novels are *Delphine* (1803) and *Corinne ou I'talie* (1807). She held notable soirées at her Château de Coppet near Geneva.

17 Thomas Moore (1779–1852): see his biography of Byron (1830).

18 Letter to Colburn, 2 April 1819.

Further Reading

The Diary of Dr John William Polidori, 1816, ed. William Michael Rossetti. Elkin Mathews, 1911

Franklin Bishop, *Polidori! A Life of Dr John Polidori*. The Gothic Society at the Gargoyle's Head Press, 1991

D.L. Macdonald, *Poor Polidori: A Critical Biography of the Author of 'The Vampyre'*. University of Toronto Press, 1991

Derek Marlowe, *A Single Summer with Lord B*. Viking Press, 1970

Angela Thirlwell, *William and Lucy: The Other Rossettis*. Yale University Press, 2003.

Henry R. Viets, *The London Editions of Polidori's 'The Vampyre'*. Bibliographical Society of America, 1969

The Vampyre
A Tale

(1819)

It happened in the midst of the dissipations attendant upon a London winter, that there appeared at the various parties of the leaders of the *ton* a nobleman, more remarkable for his singularities, than for his rank. He apparently gazed upon the mirth around him, as if he could not participate therein. It seemed as if the light laughter of the fair only attracted his attention, that he might by a look quell it, and throw fear into those breasts where thoughtlessness reigned. Those who felt this sensation of awe, could not explain whence it arose: some attributed it to the glance of that dead grey eye, which, fixing upon the object's face, seemed not to penetrate, and at one look to pierce through to the inward workings of the heart; but to throw upon the cheek a leaden ray that weighed upon the skin it could not pass. Some however thought that it was caused by their fearing the observation of one, who by his colourless cheek, which never gained a warmer tint from the blush of conscious shame or from any powerful emotion, appeared to be above human feelings and sympathies, the fashionable names for frailties and sins. His peculiarities caused him to be invited to every house; all wished to see him, and those who had been accustomed to violent excitement, and now felt the weight of *ennui*, were pleased at having something in their presence capable of engaging their attention. Nay more in spite of the deadly hue of his finely turned head, many of the female hunters after notoriety attempted to win his attentions, and gain, at least, some marks of what they might term affection. Lady Mercer, who had been the mockery of every monster shewn in drawing-rooms since her marriage, threw herself in his way, and did all but put on the dress of a mountebank, to attract his notice: – but in vain: – when she stood before him, though his eyes were apparently fixed upon hers, still it seemed as they were unperceived; – even her unappalled impudence was baffled, and she left the field. Yet though the common adultress could not influence even the guidance of his eyes, it was not that the sex was indifferent to him: but such was the caution with which he spoke to the virtuous wife and innocent daughter, that few knew he ever addressed himself to females. He had, however, the reputation of a winning tongue; and whether it was that this even overcame the dread of his singular character, or that they were moved by his apparent hatred of vice, he was as often among those females who adorn the sex by their domestic virtues, as among those who sully it by their vices.

About the same time, there came to London a young gentleman of the name of Aubrey: he was an orphan left with an only sister in the possession of great wealth, by parents who died whilst he was yet in childhood. Left also to himself by guardians, who thought it their duty merely to take care of his fortune, while they relinquished the more important charge of his mind to the care of mercenary and negligent subalterns, he cultivated more his imagination than his judgement. He had, hence, that high romantic feeling of honour and candour, which daily ruins so many milliners' apprentices. He believed all to sympathise with virtue, and thought that vice was thrown in by Providence as by authors in Romances merely for the picturesque effect of the scene: he though that the misery of a cottage merely consisted in the vesting of clothes, which were as warm, perhaps warmer than the thin naked draperies of a drawing room, but which were more pleasing to the painter's eye by their irregular folds and various coloured patches. He thought, in fine, that the dreams of poets were the realities of life. He was handsome, frank, and rich: for these reasons, upon his entering into the gay circles, many mothers surrounded him, striving which should describe with least truth their languishing or romping favourites: many daughters at the same time, by their brightening countenances when he approached, and by their sparkling eyes, when he opened his lips, soon led him into false notions of his talents and his merit. Attached as he was to the romance of his solitary hours, he was startled at finding, that, except in the tallow and wax candles flickering not from the presence of a ghost, but from a draught of air breaking through his golden leathered doors and felted floors, there was no foundation in real life for any of that congeries of pleasing horrors and descriptions contained in the volumes, which had formed the occupation of his midnight vigils. Finding, however, some compensation in his gratified vanity, he was about to relinquish his dreams, when the extraordinary being we have above described, crossed him in his career.

He watched him; the very impossibility of forming an idea of the character of a man entirely absorbed in himself, of one who gave few other signs of his observation of external objects, than the tacit assent to their existence, implied by the avoidance of their contact: at last allowed his imagination to picture some thing that flattered its propensity to extravagant ideas. He soon formed this person into the hero of a romance, and determined to observe the offspring of his fancy, rather than the individual before him. He became acquainted with him, paid him attention, and so far advanced upon his notice, that his presence was always acknowledged. He gradually learnt that Lord Ruthven's affairs were embarrassed, and soon found, from the notes of preparation in _____ Street, that he was about to travel. Desirous of gaining some information respecting this singular character, who, till now, had only whetted his curiosity, he hinted to his guardians, that it was time for him to perform the grand tour, a tour which for many generations had been thought necessary to enable the young to take some important steps in the career of vice, put themselves upon an equality with the aged, and not allow them to appear as if fallen from the skies, whenever scandalous intrigues are mentioned as the subjects of pleasantry or of praise, according to the degree of skill shewn in their conduct. They consented: and Aubrey immediately mentioning his intentions to Lord Ruthven, was surprised to receive from him a proposal that they should travel together. Flattered by such a mark of esteem from him, who, apparently, had nothing in common with other men, he gladly accepted the invitation, and in a few days they had passed the circling waters.

Hitherto, Aubrey had had no opportunity of studying Lord Ruthven's character, and now he found, that, though many more of his actions were exposed to his view, the results offered different conclusions from the apparent motives to his conduct. His companion was profuse in his liberality; – the idle, the vagabond, and the beggar, received from his hand more than enough to relieve their immediate wants. But Aubrey could not avoid remarking, that it was not upon the virtuous, reduced to indigence by the misfortunes attendant even upon virtue, that he bestowed his alms. These were sent from the door with hardly suppressed sneers; but when the profligate came to ask something, not to relieve his wants, but to allow him to wallow in his lust, or to sink him still deeper in his iniquity, he was sent away with rich charity. This was, however, attributed by him to the greater importunity of the vicious, which generally prevails over the retiring bashfulness of the virtuous indigent. There was one circumstance about the charity of his Lordship, which was however still more deeply impressed upon his mind: all those upon whom it was bestowed, inevitably found that there was a curse upon it, for they were all either led to the scaffold, or sunk to the lowest and the most abject misery. At Brussels and other towns through which they passed, Aubrey was surprised at the apparent eagerness, with which his companion sought for the centres of all fashionable vice; there he entered into all the spirit of the faro table. He betted, and always gambled with success, except when the known sharper was his antagonist, and then he lost even more than he gained; but it was always with the same unchanging face, with which he generally watched the society around. It was not, however, so when he encountered the rash youthful novice, or the luckless father of a numerous family; then his every wish seemed fortune's law – his apparent abstractedness of mind was laid aside, and his eyes sparkled with vivid fire. In every town, he left the formerly affluent youth, torn from the circle he adorned, cursing, in the solitude of a dungeon, the fate that had drawn him within the reach of this fiend; whilst many a father sat frantic, amidst the speaking looks of mute hungry children, without a single florin of his late immense wealth, wherewith to buy even sufficient to satisfy their present craving. Yet he took no money from the gambling table; but immediately lost, to the ruiner of many, the last gilder he had just snatched from the convulsive grasp of the innocent. This might but be the result of a certain degree of knowledge, which was not, however, capable of combating the cunning of the more experienced. Aubrey often wished to represent this to his friend, and beg him to resign that charity and pleasure which proved the ruin of all, and did not tend to own profit; – but he delayed it – for each day he hoped his friend would give him some opportunity of speaking frankly and openly to him; this, however, never occurred. Lord Ruthven in his carriage, and amidst the various wild and rich scenes of nature, was always the same: his eye spoke less than his lip; and though Aubrey was near the object of his curiosity, he obtained no greater gratification from it than the constant excitement of vainly wishing to break that mystery, which to his exalted imagination began to assume the appearance of something supernatural.

They soon arrived in Rome, and Aubrey for a time lost sight of his companion; he left him in daily attendance upon the morning circle of an Italian countess, whilst he went in search of the memorials of another almost deserted city. Whilst he was thus engaged, letters arrived from England, which he opened with eager impatience; the first was from his sister, breathing nothing but affection; the others were from his guardians, these astonished him; if it had before entered into his imagination, that there was an evil power resident in his companion, these seemed to give him almost sufficient reason for the belief. His guardians insisted upon his immediately leaving his friend, and urged that such a character was to be dreaded, for the possession of irresistible powers of seduction, rendered his licentious habits too dangerous to society. It had been discovered that his contempt for the adulteress had not originated in hatred of her character; but that he had required, to enhance his gratification, that his victim, the partner of his guilt, should be hurled from the pinnacle of unsullied virtue, down to the lowest abyss of infamy and degradation: in fine, that all those females whom he had sought, apparently on account of their virtue, had, since his departure, thrown even the mask aside, and had not scrupled to expose the whole deformity of their vices to the public view.

Aubrey determined upon leaving one, whose character had not yet shown a single bright point on which to rest the eye. He resolved to invent some plausible pretext for abandoning him altogether, purposing, in the mean while, to watch him more closely, and to let no slight circumstances pass by unnoticed. He entered into the same circle, and soon perceived, that his Lordship was endeavouring to work upon the inexperience of the daughter of the lady whose house he chiefly frequented. In Italy, it is seldom that an unmarried female is met with in society; he was therefore obliged to carry on his plans in secret; but Aubrey's eye followed him in all his windings, and soon discovered that an assignation had been made, which would most likely end in the ruin of an innocent, though thoughtless girl. Losing no time, he entered the apartment of Lord Ruthven, and abruptly asked him his intentions with respect to the lady, informing him at the same time that he was aware of his being about to meet her that very night. Lord Ruthven answered, that his intentions were such as he supposed all would have upon such an occasion; and upon being pressed whether he intended to marry her, merely laughed. Aubrey retired; and, immediately writing a note, to say, that from that moment he must decline accompanying his Lordship in the remainder of their purposed tour, he ordered his servant to seek other apartments, and calling upon the mother of the lady, informed her of all he knew, not only with regard to her daughter, but also with regard to the character of his Lordship. The meeting was prevented. Lord Ruthven next day merely sent his servant to notify his complete assent to a separation; but did not hint any suspicion of his plans having been foiled by Aubrey's interposition.

Having left Rome, Aubrey directed his steps towards Greece, and crossing the Peninsula, soon found himself at Athens. He there fixed his residence in the house of a Greek; and was soon occupied in tracing the faded records of ancient glory upon monuments that, apparently ashamed of chronicling the deeds of freemen, only before slaves, had hidden themselves beneath the sheltering soil or many coloured lichen. Under the same roof as himself, existed a being, so beautiful and delicate, that she might have formed the model for a painter wishing to portray on canvas the promised hope of the faithful in Mahomet's paradise, save that her eyes spoke too much mind for any one to think she could belong to those beings who had no souls. As she danced upon the plain, or tripped along the mountain's side, one would have thought the gazelle a poor type of her beauties, for who would have exchanged her eye, apparently the eye of animated nature, for that sleepy luxurious look of the animal suited but to the taste of an epicure. The light step of Ianthe often accompanied Aubrey in his search after antiquities, and often would the unconscious girl, engaged in the pursuit of a Kashmere butterfly, show the whole beauty of her form, floating as it were upon the wind, to the eager gaze of him, who forgot, in the contemplation of her sylph-like figure, the letters he had just deciphered upon an almost effaced tablet. Often would her tresses falling, as she flitted around, exhibit in the sun's ray such delicately brilliant and swiftly fading hues, as might well excuse the forgetfulness of the antiquary, who let escape from his mind the very object he had before thought of vital importance to the proper interpretation of a passage in Pausanias. But why attempt to describe charms which all feel, but none can appreciate? – It was innocence, youth, and beauty, unaffected by crowded drawing-rooms and stifling balls. Whilst he drew those remains of which he wished to preserve a memorial for his future hours, she would stand by, and watch the magic effects of his pencil, in tracing the scenes of her native place; she would then describe to him the circling dance upon the open plain, would paint to him in all the glowing colours of youthful memory, the marriage pomp she remembered viewing in her infancy; and then, turning to subjects that had evidently made a greater impression upon her mind, would tell him all the supernatural tales of her nurse. Her earnestness and apparent belief of what she narrated, excited the interest even of Aubrey; and often as she told him the tale of the living vampyre, who had passed years amidst his friends, and dearest ties, forced every year, by feeding upon the life of a lovely female to prolong his existence for the ensuing months, his blood would run cold whilst he attempted to laugh her out of such idle and horrible fantasies. But Ianthe cited to him the names of old men, who had at last detected one living among themselves, after several of their near relatives and children had been found marked with the stamp of the fiend's appetite. When she found him incredulous, she begged of him to believe her, for it had been remarked, that those who had dared to question their existence, always had some proof given, which obliged them, with grief and heartbreaking, to confess its truth. She detailed to him the traditional appearance of these monsters, and his horror was increased, upon hearing a pretty accurate description of Lord Ruthven. He, however, still persisted in persuading her, that there could be no truth in her fears, though at the same time he wondered at the many coincidences which had all tended to excite a belief in the supernatural power of Lord Ruthven.

Aubrey began to attach himself more and more to Ianthe, her innocence, so contrasted with all the affected virtues of the women amongst whom he had sought for his vision of romance, won his heart; and while he ridiculed the idea of a young man of English habits, marrying an uneducated Greek girl, still he found himself more and more attached to the almost fairy form before him. He would tear himself at times from her, and, forming a plan for some antiquarian research, he would depart, determined not to return until his object was attained; but he always found it impossible to fix his attention upon the ruins around him, whilst in his mind he retained an image that seemed alone the rightful possessor of his thoughts. Ianthe was unconscious of his love, and was ever the same frank infantile being he had first known. She always seemed to part from him with reluctance; but it was because she had no longer any one with whom she could visit her favourite haunts, to whom she could point out the beauties of the spots so dear to her infantile memory, whilst he was occupied in sketching or uncovering some fragment which had yet escaped the destructive hand of time. She had appealed to her parents on the subject of Vampyres, and they both, with several present, affirmed their existence, pale with horror at the very name. Soon after, Aubrey determined to proceed upon one of his excursions, which was to detain him for a few hours; when his hosts heard the name of the place, they all at once begged of him not to return at night, as he must necessarily pass through a wood, where no Greek would ever remain, after the day had closed, upon any consideration. They described it as the resort of the vampyres in their nocturnal orgies, and denounced the most heavy evils as impending upon him who dared to cross their path. Aubrey made light of their representations, and tried to laugh them out of the idea; but when he saw them shudder at his daring thus to mock a superior, infernal power, the very name of which apparently made their blood freeze, he was silent.

Next morning Aubrey set off upon his excursion unattended; he was surprised to observe the melancholy face of his host, and was concerned to find that his words, mocking the belief of these horrible fiends, had inspired them with such terror. When he was about to depart, Ianthe came to the side of his horse, and earnestly begged of him to return, ere night allowed the power of these beings to be put in action; – he promised. He was, however, so occupied in his research that he did not perceive that day-light would soon end, and that in the horizon there was one of those specks which, in the warmest climates, so rapidly gather into a tremendous mass, and pour all their rage upon the devoted country. – He at last, however, mounted his horse, determined to make up by speed for his delay: but it was too late. Twilight, in these southern climates, is almost unknown; immediately the sun sets, night begins: and ere he had advanced far, the power of the storm was above – its echoing thunders had scarcely an interval of rest – its thick heavy rain forced its way through the canopying foliage, whilst the blue forked lightning seemed to fall and radiate at his very feet. Suddenly his horse took fright, and he was carried with dreadful rapidity through the entangled forest. The animal at last, through fatigue, fell and he found, by the glare of lightning, that he was in the neighbourhood of a hovel which hardly lifted itself up from the masses of dead leaves and brushwood surrounding it. Dismounting, he approached, hoping to find some one to guide him to the town, or at least trusting to obtain shelter from the pelting of the storm. When near the door, the thunders, for a moment silent, allowed him to hear the dreadful shrieks of a woman mingling with the stifled, exultant mockery of a laugh, continued in one almost unbroken sound; – he was startled; but, roused by the thunder which again rolled over his head, he, with a sudden effort, forced open the door of the hut. He found himself in utter darkness: the sound, however, guided him. He was apparently unperceived; for, though he called, still the sounds continued, and no notice was taken of him. He found himself in contact with some one, whom he immediately seized; when a voice cried, 'Again baffled!' to which a loud laugh succeeded; and he felt himself grappled by one whose strength seemed superhuman: determined to sell his life as dearly as he could, he struggled; but it was in vain: he was lifted from his feet and hurled with enormous force against the ground. – His enemy threw himself upon him, and kneeling upon his breast, had placed his hands upon his throat – when the glare of many torches penetrating through the hole that gave light in the day, disturbed him. – He instantly rose, leaving his prey, he rushed through the door, and in a moment the crashing of the branches, as he broke through the wood, was no longer heard. The storm was now still; and Aubrey, incapable of moving, was soon heard by those without. They entered; the light of their torches fell upon nothing but the mud walls, and the thatch loaded on every individual straw with heavy flakes of soot, though at this moment it was apparently untenanted. There was one spot slippery with blood but it was hardly visible on the black floor. No other trace was seen of human presence having disturbed its solitude for many years. At the desire of Aubrey they searched for her who had attracted him by her cries; he was again left in darkness; but what was his horror, when the light of the torches once more burst upon him, to perceive the airy form of his fair conductress brought in a lifeless corpse. He shut his eyes, hoping that it was but a vision arising from his disturbed imagination; but he again saw the same form, when he unclosed them, stretched by his side. There was no colour upon her cheek, not even upon her lip; yet there was a stillness about her face that seemed almost as attaching as the life that once dwelt there: – upon her neck and breast was blood, and upon her throat were the marks of teeth having opened the vein of the neck: – to this the men pointed, crying, simultaneously struck with horror, 'A Vampyre! A Vampyre!'

A litter was quickly formed, and Aubrey was laid by the side of her who had lately been to him the object of so many bright and fairy visions, now fallen with the flower of life that had died within her. He knew not what his thoughts were – his mind was benumbed and seemed to shun reflection, and take refuge in vacancy – he held almost unconsciously in his hand a naked dagger of a particular construction, which had been found in the hut. They were soon met by different parties who had been engaged in the search of her whom a mother had missed. Their lamentable cries, as they approached the city, forewarned the parents of some dreadful catastrophe. – To describe their grief would be impossible; but when they ascertained the cause of their child's death, they looked at Aubrey, and pointed to the corpse. They were inconsolable; both died broken-hearted.

Aubrey being put to bed was seized with a most violent fever, and was often delirious; in these intervals he would call upon Lord Ruthven and upon Ianthe – by some unaccountable combination he seemed to beg of his former companion to spare the being he loved. At other times he would imprecate maledictions upon his head, and curse him as her destroyer. Lord Ruthven chanced at this time to arrive at Athens, and, from whatever motive, upon hearing of the state of Aubrey, immediately placed himself in the same house, and became his constant attendant. When the latter recovered from his delirium, he was horrified and startled at the sight of him whose image he had now combined with that of a Vampyre; but Lord Ruthven, by his kind words, implying almost repentance for the fault that had caused their separation, and still more by the attention, anxiety, and care which he showed, soon reconciled him to his presence. His Lordship seemed quite changed; he no longer appeared that apathetic being who had so astonished Aubrey; but as soon as his convalescence began to be rapid, he again gradually retired into the same state of mind, and Aubrey perceived no difference from the former man, except that at times he was surprised to meet his gaze fixed intently upon him with a smile of malicious exultation playing upon his lips: he knew not why, but this smile haunted him. During the last stage of the invalid's recovery, Lord Ruthven was apparently engaged in watching the tideless waves raised by the cooling breeze, or in marking the progress of those orbs, circling, like our world, the moveless sun; – indeed, he appeared to wish to avoid the eyes of all.

Aubrey's mind, by this shock, was much weakened, and that elasticity of spirit which had once so distinguished him now seemed to have fled for ever. He was now as much a lover of solitude and silence as Lord Ruthven; but much as he wished for solitude, his mind could not find it in the neighbourhood of Athens; if he sought it amidst the ruins he had formerly frequented, Ianthe's form stood by his side – if he sought it in the woods, her light step would sound wandering amidst the underworld, in quest of the modest violet; and often she would, suddenly turning round, show, to his wild imagination, her pale face and wounded throat, while a meek smile played upon her lips. He determined to fly scenes, every feature of which created such bitter associations in his mind. He proposed to Lord Ruthven, to whom he held himself bound by the tender care he had taken of him during his illness, that they should visit those parts of Greece neither had yet seen. They travelled in every direction, and sought every spot to which a recollection could be attached: but though they thus hastened from place to place, yet they seemed not to heed what they gazed upon. They heard much of robbers, but they gradually began to slight these reports, which they imagined were only the invention of individuals, whose interest it was to excite the generosity of those, whom they defended from pretended dangers. In consequence of thus neglecting the advice of the inhabitants they travelled on one occasion with only a few guards, more to serve as guides than as a defence. Upon entering, however, a narrow defile, at the bottom of which was the bed of a torrent, with large masses of rock brought down from the neighbouring precipices, they had reason to repent their negligence; for scarcely were the whole of the party engaged in the narrow pass, when they were startled by the echoed report of several guns, and by the whistling of bullets close to their heads. In an instant their guards had left them, and, placing themselves behind rocks, had begun to fire in the direction whence the report came. Lord Ruthven and Aubrey, imitating their example, retired for a moment behind the sheltering turn of the defile: but ashamed of being thus detained by a foe, who with insulting shouts bade them advance, and being exposed to unresisting slaughter, if any of the robbers should climb above and take them in the rear, they determined at once to rush forward in search of the enemy. Hardly had they lost the shelter of the rock, when Lord Ruthven received a shot in the shoulder, which brought him to the ground. Aubrey hastened to his assistance; and, no longer heeding the contest or his own peril, was soon surprised by seeing the robbers' faces around him – his guards having, upon Lord Ruthven's being wounded, immediately thrown up their arms and surrendered.

By promises of great reward, Aubrey soon induced them to convey his wounded friend to a neighbouring cabin, and having agreed upon a ransom, he was no more disturbed by their presence – they being content merely to guard the entrance until their comrade should return with the promised sum, for which he had an order. Lord Ruthven's strength rapidly decreased; in two days mortification ensued, and death seemed advancing with hasty steps. His conduct and appearance had not changed; he seemed as unconscious of pain as he had been of the objects about him: but towards the close of the last evening, his mind became apparently uneasy, and his eye often fixed upon Aubrey, who was induced to offer his assistance with more than usual earnestness – 'Assist me! You may save me – you may do more than that – I mean not my life, I heed the death of my existence as little as that of the passing day; but you may save my honour, your friend's honour.'

'How? Tell me how? I would do anything,' replied Aubrey.

'I need but little – my life ebbs apace – I cannot explain the whole – but if you would conceal all you know of me, my honour were free from stain in the world's mouth – and if my death were unknown for some time in England – I – I – but life.'

'It shall not be known.'

'Swear!' cried the dying man, raising himself with exultant violence, ' Swear by all your soul reveres, by all your nature dreads, swear that for a year and a day you will not impart your knowledge of my crimes or death to any living being in any way, whatever may happen, or whatever you may see.' – His eyes seemed bursting from their sockets:

'I swear!' said Aubrey; he sunk laughing upon his pillow, and breathed no more.

Aubrey retired to rest, but did not sleep; the many circumstances attending his acquaintance with this man arose upon his mind, and, he knew not why, when he remembered his oath a cold shivering came over him, as if from the presentiment of something horrible awaiting him. Rising early in the morning, he was about to enter the hovel, in which he had left the corpse, when a robber met him, and informed him that it was no longer there, having been conveyed by himself and comrades, upon his retiring, to the pinnacle of a neighbouring mount, according to a promise they had given his Lordship, that it should be exposed to the first cold ray of the moon that rose after his death. Aubrey was astonished, but taking several of the men, he determined to go and bury it upon the spot where it lay. When however he reached the summit he found no trace of the corpse, nor could he discover any remnant of the clothes, though the robbers assured him that they pointed out the identical rock on which they had laid the body. For a time his mind was bewildered in the conjectures, but he at last returned, convinced that they had secretly buried his friend's remains for the sake of the dress in which he died.

Weary of a country in which he had met with such terrible misfortunes, and in which all apparently conspired to heighten that superstitious melancholy which had seized upon his mind, he resolved to leave it, and he soon arrived at Smyrna. While waiting for a vessel to convey him to Otranto, or to Naples, he occupied himself in arranging those effects he had with him belonging to Lord Ruthven. Amongst other things there was a case containing several weapons of offence, more or less adapted to ensure the death of the victim. There were several daggers and ataghans. Whilst turning these over, and examining their curious forms, what was his surprise at finding a sheath apparently ornamented in the same style as the dagger discovered in the fatal hut – he shuddered – hastening to gain further proof, he found the weapon, and his horror may be imagined, when he discovered that it fitted, though peculiarly shaped, the sheath he held in his hand. His eyes seemed to need no further certainty – they seemed gazing to be bound to the dagger; yet still he wished not to believe his sight; but the particular form, the varying tints upon the shaft and sheath were alike, and left room for no doubt; there were also drops of blood on each.

He left Smyrna, and on his way home, at Rome, he inquired concerning the lady he had attempted to snatch from Lord Ruthven's seductive arts. Her parents were in distress, their fortune ruined, and she had not been heard of since the departure of his Lordship. Aubrey's mind became almost broken under so many repeated horrors; he was afraid that this lady had fallen victim to the destroyer of Ianthe. He became morose and silent; and his only thought seemed to be how to urge the speed of the postilions, as if he were hastening to save the life of some one he held dear. He arrived at Calais; a breeze, which seemed obedient to his will, soon wafted him to the English shores. He hastened to the mansion of his father, and there, for a moment, he appeared to lose, in the embraces and caresses of his sister, all memory of the past. If she before, by her infantine caresses, had gained his affection, now that the woman began to appear, she was still more attaching as a companion.

Miss Aubrey had not that winning grace which gains the gaze and applause of the drawing-room assemblies. There was none of that ephemeral brilliancy which can only exist in the heated atmosphere of a crowded apartment. Her blue eye was never lit up by the levity of the mind beneath. There was a melancholy charm about it which did not seem to arise from misfortune, but from some feeling within, that appeared to indicate a soul conscious of a brighter realm. Her step was not that light footing, which strays where'er a butterfly or a colour may attract – it was sedate and pensive. When alone, her face was never brightened by the smile of joy; but when her brother breathed to her his affection, and would in her presence forget those griefs she knew destroyed his rest, who could have exchanged her smile for that of the voluptuary? It seemed as if those eyes, – that face were then playing in the light of their own native sphere. She was yet only eighteen, and had not yet been presented to the world, her guardians having thought proper to delay her presentation at court until her brother's return from the continent, when he might be her protector. It was now, therefore, resolved that the next drawing-room, which was fast approaching, should be the epoch of her entry into the 'busy scene'. Aubrey would rather have remained in the mansion of his father's, to feed upon the melancholy which overpowered him. He could not feel interest about the frivolities of fashionable strangers, when his mind had been so torn by the events he had witnessed; but he determined to sacrifice his own comfort to the protection of his sister. They therefore soon arrived in town, and prepared for the day, which had been announced as the one on which a drawing-room was to be held.

The crowd was excessive – a drawing-room had not been held for a long time, and all who were anxious to bask in the smile of royalty, hastened thither. Aubrey was there with his sister. While he was standing in a corner by himself, heedless of all around him, engaged in the recollection that the first time he had seen Lord Ruthven was in this very place – he felt himself suddenly seized by the arm, and a voice he recognised too well, sounded in his ear – 'Remember your oath.' He had hardly courage to turn, fearful of seeing a spectre, that would blast him, when he perceived, at a little distance, the same figure which had attracted his notice on this spot upon his first entry into society. He gazed till his limbs almost refusing to bear their weight, he was obliged to take the arm of a friend, and forcing a passage through the crowd, to throw himself into his carriage, and be driven home. He paced the room with hurried steps, and fixed his hands upon his head, as if he were afraid his thoughts were bursting from his brain. Lord Ruthven again before him – circumstances started up in dreadful array – the dagger – his oath. – He roused himself, he could not believe it possible – the dead rise again! – He thought his imagination had conjured up the image his mind was resting upon. It was impossible that it could be real – he determined, therefore, to go again into society; for though he attempted to ask concerning Lord Ruthven, the name hung upon his lips, and he could not succeed in gaining information. He went a few nights after with his sister to the assembly of a near relation. Leaving her under the protection of a matron, he retired into a recess, and there gave himself up to his own devouring thoughts. Perceiving, at last, that many were retiring, he roused himself, and entering another room, found his sister surrounded by several gentlemen, apparently in earnest conversation; he attempted to pass and get near her, when one, whom he requested to move, turned round, and revealed to him those features he most abhorred. He sprang forward, seized his sister's arm, and, with a hurried step, forced her towards the street: at the door he found himself impeded by the crowd of servants, who were waiting for their lords; and while he was engaged in passing them, he again heard that voice whisper close to him – 'Remember your oath!' – He did not dare to turn, but, hurrying his sister, he soon reached home.

Aubrey became almost distracted. If before his mind had been absorbed by one subject, how much more completely was it engrossed now, that the certainty of the monster's living again pressed upon his thoughts. His sister's attentions were now unheeded, and it was in vain that she intreated him to explain to her what had caused his abrupt conduct. He only uttered a few words, and those terrified her. The more he thought, the more he was bewildered. His oath startled him; – was he then to allow this monster to roam, bearing ruin upon his breath, amidst all he held dear, and not avert its progress? His very sister might have been touched by him. But even if he were to break his oath, and disclose his suspicions, who would believe him? He thought of employing his own hand to free the world from such a wretch; but death, he remembered, had been already mocked. For days he remained in this state; shut up in his room, he saw no one, and ate only when his sister came, who, her eyes streaming with tears, besought him, for her sake, to support nature. At last, no longer capable of bearing stillness and solitude, he left his house, roamed from street to street, anxious to fly that image which haunted him. His dress became neglected, and he wandered, as often exposed to the noon-day sun as to the mid-night damps. He was no longer to be recognised; at first he returned with the evening to his home; but at last he laid him down to rest wherever fatigue overtook him. His sister, anxious for his safety, employed people to follow him; but they were soon distanced from him, who fled from a pursuer swifter than any – from thought. His conduct, however, suddenly changed. Struck with the idea that he left by his absence the whole of his friends, with a fiend amongst them, of whose presence they were unconscious, he determined to enter again into society, and watch him closely, anxious to forewarn, in spite of oath, all whom Lord Ruthven should approach with intimacy. But when he entered into a room, his haggard and suspicious looks were so striking, his inward shudderings so visible, that his sister was at last obliged to beg of him to abstain from seeking, for her sake, a society, which affected him so strongly. When, however, remonstrance proved unavailing, the guardians thought proper to interpose, and, fearing that his mind was becoming alienated, they thought it high time to resume again that trust, which had been before imposed upon them by Aubrey's parents.

Desirous of saving him from the injuries and sufferings he had daily encountered in his wanderings, and of preventing him from exposing to the general eye those marks of what they considered folly, they engaged a physician to reside in the house, and take constant care of him. He hardly appeared to notice it, so completely was his mind absorbed by one terrible subject. His incoherence became at last so great, that he was confined to his chamber. There he would often lie for days, incapable of being roused. He had become emaciated, his eyes had attained a glassy lustre; – the only sign of affection and recollection remaining displayed itself upon the entry of his sister; then he would sometimes start, and, seizing her hands, with looks that severely afflicted her, he would desire her not to touch him. 'Oh, do not touch him – if your love for is aught, do not go near him!' When, however, she inquired to whom he referred, his only answer was, 'True! True!' and again he sank into a state, whence not even she could rouse him. This lasted many months: gradually, however, as the year was passing, his incoherences became less frequent, and his mind threw off a portion of its gloom, whilst his guardians observed that several times in the day he would count upon his fingers a definite number, and then smile.

The time had nearly elapsed, when, upon the last day of the year, one of his guardians entering into his room, began to converse with his physician upon the melancholy circumstance of Aubrey's being in so awful a situation, when his sister was going next day to be married. Instantly Aubrey's attention was attracted; he asked anxiously to whom. Glad of this mark of returning intellect, of which they feared he had been deprived, they mentioned the name of the Earl of Marsden. Thinking this was a young Earl whom he had met in society, Aubrey seemed pleased, and astonished them still more by expressing his intention to be present at the nuptials, and by desiring to see his sister. They answered not, but in a few minutes his sister was with him. He was apparent again of being affected by the influence of her lovely smile; for he pressed her to his breast, and kissed her cheek, wet with tears, flowing at the thought of her brother's being once more alive to the feelings of affection. He began to speak with all his wonted warmth, and to congratulate her upon her marriage with a person so distinguished for rank and every accomplishment; but he suddenly perceived a locket upon her breast; having opened it, what was his surprise at beholding the features of the monster who had so long influenced his life. He seized the portrait in a paroxysm of rage, and trampled it under foot. Upon her asking him, why he thus destroyed the resemblance of her future husband, he looked as if he did not understand her – then seizing her hands, and gazing on her with a frantic expression of countenance, he bade her swear that she would never wed this monster, for he – But he could not continue – it seemed as if that voice bade him remember his oath – he turned suddenly round, thinking Lord Ruthven was near him but he saw no one. In the meantime the guardians and physicians, who had heard the whole, and thought this was but a return of his disorder, entered, and forcing him from Miss Aubrey, desired her to leave him. He fell upon his knees to them, he implored, he begged of them to delay but for one day. They, attributing this to the insanity, they imagined had taken possession of his mind, endeavoured to pacify him, and retired.

Lord Ruthven had called the morning after the drawing-room,

and had been refused with every one else. When he heard of Aubrey's ill health, he readily understood himself to be the cause of it; but, when he learned that he was deemed insane, his exultation and pleasure could hardly be concealed from those, among whom he had gained this information. He hastened to the house of his former companion, and, by constant attendance, and the pretence of great affection for her brother and interest in his fate, he gradually won the ear of Miss Aubrey. Who could resist his power? His tongue had dangers and toils to recount – could speak of himself as of an individual having no sympathy with any being on the crowded earth, save with her, to whom he addressed himself; – could tell how, since he knew her, his existence had begun to seem worthy of preservation, if it were merely that he might listen to her soothing accents. – In fine, he knew so well how to use the serpent's art, or such was the will of fate, that he gained her affections. The title of the elder branch falling at length to him, he obtained an important embassy, which served as an excuse (in spite of her brother's deranged state,) for hastening the marriage, which was to take place the very day before his departure for the continent.

Aubrey, when he was left by the physician and his guardians, attempted to bribe the servants, but in vain. He asked for pen and paper; it was given him; he wrote a letter to his sister, conjuring her, as she valued her own happiness, her own honour, and the honour of those now in the grave, who once held her in their arms as their hope and the hope of their house, to delay but for a few hours that marriage, on which he denounced the most heavy curses. The servants promised they would deliver it; but giving it to the physician, he thought it better not to harass any more the mind of Miss Aubrey by, what he considered, the ravings of a maniac. Night passed on without rest to the busy inmates of the house; and Aubrey heard, with a horror that may more easily be conceived than described, the notes of busy preparation. Morning came, and the sound of carriages broke upon his ear. Aubrey grew almost frantic. The curiosity of the servants at last overcame their vigilance, they gradually stole away, leaving him in the custody of an helpless old woman. He seized the opportunity, with one bound was out of the room, and in a moment found himself in the apartment where all were nearly assembled. Lord Ruthven was the first to perceive him: he immediately approached, and, taking his arm by force, hurried him from the room, speechless with rage.

When on the staircase, Lord Ruthven whispered in his ear – 'Remember your oath, and know, if not my bride today, your sister is dishonoured. Women are frail!' So saying, he pushed him towards his attendants, who, roused by the old woman, had come in search of him. Aubrey could no longer support himself: his rage not finding vent, had broken a blood-vessel, and he was conveyed to bed. This was not mentioned to his sister, who was not present when he entered, as the physician was afraid of agitating her. The marriage was solemnised, and the bride and bridegroom left London.

Aubrey's weakness increased; the effusion of blood produced symptoms of the near approach of death. He desired his sister's guardians might be called, and, when the midnight hour had struck, he related composedly the substance of what the reader has perused – and died immediately after.

The guardians hastened to protect Miss Aubrey; but when they arrived, it was too late. Lord Ruthven had disappeared, and Aubrey's sister had glutted the thirst of a VAMPYRE!

from *A Medical Inaugural Dissertation which deals with the disease called Oneirodynia, for the degree of Medical Doctor, Edinburgh 1815*

(translated from the original Latin)

This thesis, which I am writing on the very obscure disease oneirodynia, I will divide, for the sake of clarity, into several sections. For in medicine I hardly think it is open to doubt that only clinical practice can be the basis of theories. In fact all that exists in the physical body, the feelings and the activities of external bodies are so obscure that, it seems, the task of understanding the fundamental causes still lies before us.

On Oneirodynia. A general overview

The expression oneirodynia is a composite of the Greek words oneiros and duno and means walking while one is dreaming. If I were seeking to define the disease, I would say that these patients exhibit a certain tendency to do while sleeping, that which more commonly occurs in those who are awake.

Cullen divides the disease into two types: one, as activity and the impulse towards walking and various movements, and the second, the patient's being burdened by the sensation that the chest is being compressed by a dead weight. For the type arises not from a disorder of the mind but from a physical lesion of the heart, as a result of water pressing on a particular part of the thoracic viscera.

Many are the kinds of actions which this disease impels people to do. Some discuss everything that has happened on a particular day. Others reply to the questions of their friends and they discourse on a given topic in its appropriate context. Others draw their swords and clash them. Others discharge their firearms as if attacking bandits, not without great concern to bystanders and at great personal risk. Others again light lamps, put on their clothes, look for their keys, take wine and drink uproariously. Others rise from their beds and wander over roofs, fall into rivers, find themselves in difficult places or at great heights, from where no sane person would dare to follow them without compelling reasons, and do all this as if the danger were minimal. Such people return safely unless they are woken up. But if anyone is so rash as to wake them up, or if they were in the process of waking from sleep, they die headlong by their own hand.

For those who suffer from oneirodynia, I grant that all the channels have been opened to various senses. Nevertheless, it seems that they do not possess any sensations apart from those that relate directly to the action they are performing. Many seem to have their eyes open all the time but the majority do not make use of them. However, others have their eyes closed all the time as if in sleep. But what is more remarkable is that they retain all their memory of whatever they had done up to their last paroxysm, and yet, when they wake up, they remember nothing of it. Hence the process of cognition and of conscious memory appears to be dual, one faculty sleeping while the other is awake.

On the cause of oneirodynia

It is possible to state, if you will, three causes for the disease, namely proximate, remote, and predisposing causes. The proximate cause is that from which the disease itself arises immediately. The remote cause is that which comes before it. The predisposing cause is that which makes human beings susceptible to a particular illness.

The predisposing or determining causes are alcoholism, excessive eating, foodstuffs causing flatulence, an excess of clothing, poor posture, lying supine, study, the usage of opium, and everything, which propels blood to the brain.

Preface to two case histories of the disease

There are many remarkable accounts of those who suffer from oneirodynia. So I will choose just two examples, one with the authority of the Bishop of Burgundy as published in the French methodical *Encylopaedia*, and the other from my paternal uncle Aloysius Polidori, MD, PhD, which was delivered to the Royal Society of Medicine in London.

First case report. Description of raging convulsive oneirodynia, by Aloysius Eustace Polidori, MD, Ph.D

A twelve-year-old boy, whose mother was afflicted by recurrent headaches, and whose aunt was susceptible to epileptic seizures, was admitted at the beginning of February 1793. He would be overcome by chronic convulsions, or tremors, of the knees.

After bloodletting had been instituted and cathartic medicaments administered, he received baths from communal water-source and anthelmintic remedies, and each day ate Peruvian bark in water. From that time his condition improved intermittently. The symptoms often and uncontrollably recurred and receded, immediately to be followed by constriction of the throat, obstruction of swallowing, with the boy turning spasmodically, leaping, singing, behaving aggressively, and crying out in fear even when he was touched very gently.

Once again, on the 25th day of June I was called out to the boy just after nightfall and found him lying in bed. He recognised me just as he did the other people who were present. When I asked him how he was, he replied that his hips and thighs were hurting a good deal, and that this was most severe when palpated. I made further examination and two or three times observed that when his pulse faded and became muffled, the lower limbs would knock against each other. After a very brief kind of sleep he began to gesticulate and emitted babbling words with a gentle sound and happy expression. A servant was present, and when the boy became aware of his presence he began to throw punches at him. After a while he belaboured all who were in the way with a cushion and with punches. The symptoms of hysteria and spasm invariably would precede oneirodynia.

So much for Aloysius Polidori. It now remains for me to make a number of remarks on this case history. In the case of the boy the illness clearly arose from an affection of the brain, since they were attacked by spasms from the outset. On the one hand, the nature of this affliction of the brain is beyond our current knowledge. I consider that the illness has its origin not in an organic lesion of the brain but from a serious over stimulation of the brain and nervous system. Treatment of this illness is agreed to be left to nature. Indeed I believe that the sick person recovered when camphor was used as symptoms of excitability began to occur, with acquiescence of nature.

The Second Case History, from the French Encyclopaedia

When the Archbishop of Burgundy was at the seminary, he reports that he saw a certain priest who was suffering from oneirodynia, and who often used to go into his bedroom and to this and other things, and thus he became curious to ascertain the manifestations of this disease.

The priest would wander from his bed, take up a piece of paper, write sermons, and read over each pages as soon as he had written it – if with closed eyes can be said to be reading. The archbishop averred that one of his sermons was reasonably elegant and well composed.

Observations on the second case history

It is possible to argue that he had such a vivid imagination that he indeed retained the things imprinted on his imagination without the use of his eyes.

The rationale of the symptoms

The first thing which is self-explanatory is the state of mind and body of the patient suffering from oneirodynia, which I will explain, beginning with a definition of sleep. Sleep is that state of mind in which there is no conscious thought or, if there is such, it proceeds only from memory or from a connexion of ideas, with the physical senses almost entirely displaced.

Oneirodynia differs from sleep in this respect only, namely that the mind is in operation with a more vivid memory and that the other physical organs are predisposed to gain impressions, while others are switched off. And, if one may say so, oneirodynia is identical to the sleeping state, as anger or some other disturbance is to the waking state, for in both the mind and body are applied to one thing so that external stimuli arouse no sensory input. It is easy to explain how it happens that the mind is affected only by those things pertaining to the matter being thought about, if we keep in mind that the mind cannot proceed on two tracks at the same time, and that, when the patient does think about a particular thing he is nevertheless distracted from it by a stimulus to the mind. Thus, when the patient does something, he does it with such care that the mental affliction increases by the use of the faculties. Thus when the patient does something, he does it so attentively that the affliction of the mind is superior to ordinary stimuli. The senses whose work it is to explore the object of thought, however, are open to the smallest influences, which also happens in waking states when the mind is occupied, for we see that the more intent we are on something, the more the senses we have used to examine it are sharpened, and our other senses are more and more benumbed.

We see sleepwalkers who, as soon as they see something, retain such a memory that they are able to retrieve it readily even when it is displaced. But how can one explain the fact that they have a dual memory? Even though I have no real facts, I shall offer a hypothesis. Perhaps those who suffer from oneirodynia fall into that which is connected with the other preceding paroxysm, and fall victim again. If I may put it, you inhabit during sleep a state of imagination, which does not last longer than sleep itself, and the cause of which people remember nothing when they are awake.

We do not find it difficult, if we turn it over in our mind, to explain how someone can feel the cold so acutely that he believes himself to have been plunged into icy water, because this phenomenon is an everyday occurrence. As the mind is capable of concentrating on one matter at the same time, it does not feel the cold except when the mind is focussed on it. But if one thinks a great deal about it, one is troubled by cold very acutely indeed. Neither is this refuted by the fact that sufferers from oneirodynia are able to write and correct without the use of sight, but the sense of sight can be replaced, as in blind people, by the sense of touch. Oneirodynia is caused by hyper excitability.

Treatment of the condition

The general good health of most patients who suffer from oneirodynia is unimpaired, and there is no risk from this disease except when it leads patients into hazardous situations. Some authorities state that this disease sometimes induces catalepsy and mania. For this reason we do everything we can, but, as often happens, we do not know what makes the condition to become florid.

There are two procedures, which ought to be implemented:

1) to stop the presenting paroxysms, and
2) to dispel the underlying symptoms

In order first of all to fulfil the first of the criteria, we can remove only the predisposing factors. In the sleepwalker, intoxication, mental exertion, and other things that stimulate and then weaken the mind should be avoided. Perhaps a tonic should be administered, such as Portuguese bark, iron, and similar things.

First of all, when the paroxysm occurs, the doors and windows should be shut, and other people should be kept out of the way. Then the patient should be roused from sleep fearfully. Whipping, electricity, and cold baths, if they are so placed that the patient falls into them when he wanders from bed in his sleepwalking state, may inhibit the return of the paroxysms.

from *On the Punishment of Death*

(originally published in *The Pamphleteer*, 1816)

For though, without doubt, England is the nation the most fortunate in its domestic government it is now the time to look to our laws of punishment and guilt, in those cases where death is ordained by our criminal code. A subject which every one must perceive requires strong attention and gradual reform. The multiplicity of crimes, the great number of those yearly condemned to death certainly point out the existence of some radical error in the very foundation of our criminal laws.

Is it right to inflict death as do our laws for every petty offence? What hurt can one man inflict upon another, except murder, that can in justice require he should receive the most dreadful punishment man has in his power to ordain? No one will deny that punishment is necessary, but is it necessary that the punishment should breathe a spirit worse than the crime itself? Is it necessary that society should have murder on murder arranged in formidable array against it, for the smaller crimes of individuals of robbery and swindling? Let us consider the proportion of the punishment to the guilt, before we inflict the sentence. Acting as Christians, let us consider how great is our crime, if as the English law directs, we send men unshrived by repentance of their sins into another world in despair. They will step from this world into the next despairing and cursing their fellow-creatures, and we should have thoughts, which like corroding poison would work upon our peace, of having sent them for an eternity of pain into the deep, unconsumed, unconsuming abyss of fire. Even leaving out all religious views does it not strike us as out of all proportion? For having deprived another of a small sum we tear one from the bosom of his family for ever; we cast an unredeemable stain upon him, nay upon his innocent family, which if more mercy had been shown, he might have lived to wash away by tears and by deeds; but we rend him from all, consign his family, his posterity to ignominy, to shame, to want.

To thieve from the person a few shillings is a crime, which by our laws nothing can expiate but the death of the guilty. Yet to set fire to a field of rip corn is but a misdemeanour entailing some petty punishment. Can this be justice, can this be equity?

Examining the punishment of death, what is the result? Can we pretend that it improves the man? The question seems ridiculous because from the form whose every motion, gesture, glance of the eye, seem to breathe a divinity, we change him into a corpse; the sparkling lustre of whose eye is gone, the graceful motion of whose limbs is changed into rigidity, and which at last gradually becomes fit but for the food of worms. In what other view can they pretend it improves man? For they cannot suppose they improve his morals by hanging him. But if a different course had been followed, then we might have hoped to see the man improved, his heart might have opened to nobler sentiments, his mind might have been rendered capable of feeling the value of virtue.

Let us consult the criminal records of every country, and every line will contradict those who maintain that by the dread of death, men are hindered from pursuing the path that leads to crime. That the dread of death does not even deter men from the commission even of the smaller crimes, have we not every day demonstrated to us? Does not every day bring to our newspapers and increase of crimes? It has been found that the numbers of executions every year increase; that the populace of great towns are become now so accustomed to the sight of death that they attend the execution of a felon, as a farce at which they laugh or applaud. Need we wonder that when we daily see so many go with a firm tread and an unchanging eye to execution, that man should lose all fear of it? Man, we think, does not naturally fear death, – having the certainty of death always before his eyes; seeing his friends, his relatives, drop one after another into the grave; forgetting, neglecting, nay, laughing at every religious feeling, as man in these cases generally does, he grows gradually accustomed to the thoughts of death, at last divests it of all its terrors; and hence alone will not fear to increase the chance one in a hundred of his dying within a certain time, by stealing, to gain some important end. What serves to preach to men on eternity? They have no religious feeling, and they are not capable of imagining any other state than the present for the future. Conscious that eternity has already begun its reign, that they are under the wings of that monster, whose extremities are hid in the interminable abyss of night, capable from the degradation of their minds, of imagining no different state from the present, they will not grieve to part from their friends, for they must know, that the few years they may survive, will be but as the passing of a cloud before the firmament, and that when it has flitted from their gaze, their friends, if friends they can have, will be joined to them for an immortality.

If it is our wish to make vice shrink and virtue flourish, let us show we pay some attention to honesty; let us not punish various degrees of vice with equal infliction, let us appreciate what little virtue there is even in the wretch amenable to our laws.

Has not the experience of ages shown us the insufficiency of capital punishments? Does not Asia, Europe, Africa, American, every people, every nation, nay every village of this sublunary world, demonstrate the insufficiency of this punishment?

from *An Essay Upon the Source of Positive Pleasure*

(1818)

To the Reader

In September last I met with an accident which confined me to my bed. As I was in danger of death, I naturally revolved many speculative subjects in my mind. Amongst others, it happened that I took up that of Pleasure. I fell asleep while it still occupied my mind, and seemed to be conveyed, by unknown means, to a place, where many of the friends of my past life were assembled to discuss the same subject. One amongst them maintained that positive pleasure could not exist independently of the imagination. When I awoke, a confused remembrance of the chain of arguments, my friend had gone through, remaining with me, I thought them, to say the least, so specious, that I attempted to write them down, by what my own ingenuity supplied; the result is this Essay, which yet preserves the form of a speech. That these are the sentiments of another person I hope none will attempt to deny; for if the opinion of a certain philosopher be true, that sleep is for the convenience of souls having converse with dead or distant friends, there is not the slightest improbability in my statement. Nor can it be supposed that the experience of so young a man as myself would enable him to assert so many things in utter contradiction to all that has hitherto been felt and believed on this subject. I therefore trust that I shall not be made responsible for every sentiment in the book, so as to have it supposed, that any herein inserted are my own private opinions.

J.W.P.

Norwich, May 28, 1818

What would we say of a chemist, who in forming a certain salt, should attempt it, not by making the ingredients analysis had shown him to be its component parts, but by mixing every thing in his laboratory till blundering chance threw the salt into his hands? This is, however, the conduct pursued by almost all, in the search of pleasure – not knowing, and generally not enquiring, whence it arises, they seek what they know of but by name, and then complain of their stars and of providence when they do not find it: – whereas if it were known where to seek it, and what excites it, they would find that providence has thrown some flowers upon this desert of life, which, though not ever enduring, still may be obtained at little cost, and renewed with little fatigue.

I have therefore chosen PLEASURE as the subject of debate. But even supposing we gain the knowledge of its nature, when we consider the weakness of our minds, which cause us with childish impatience to snatch at every object that passes by us, the fickleness of our wishes, irritability of our nature, and morbid sensibility to the slightest shadow of pain, I fear we shall not be very sanguine in putting an end to the universal cry against fate, whom we accuse of having so unequally divided the light and shade of this moving picture.

It is, however, my intention to give my opinion upon the Source of Positive Pleasure, in hopes of coming, by our united endeavours, to a sure path in the search of this feeling. But the plans individuals may form are untried: we see disappointments so constantly attend every attempt which hopes to gain something new, when founded upon the reasoning of one individual only, that we are rather content to repeat the same unvarying round of amusements (though each time that they are repeated greatly diminishes the quantum of pleasure reaped from them) than waste our short span, on what, though it may vest the colours of the rainbow, like it, may never be grasped. I shall not therefore be disappointed if I persuade no one, for I can be conscious but of the feeling of my own individual self. – I am liable to error; I do not therefore give my opinion on Pleasure as a certain one; – it may be, that I alone have felt disappointment in every pursuit – a vapid nullity in every object. Others may have found that positive absolute Pleasure existed in the search of virtue – others that it dwelt with vice. I have found it in neither. – The first excites indignation and contempt of the human race, and the second of self. In starting this theory I am led by my own experience and by my own observations; but many may be convinced by a life of even longer duration, that Pleasure does exist as a positive active feeling. To these I will bow with envy, and listen with hopes of instruction.

I have chosen this subject as one I deem of the greatest importance. For pain is so predominant, that any means by which it may be encroached upon, and Pleasure increased, would be a blessing to the human race. Pain pursues us from our birth to the grave. We come into the world weeping, and pass from the bed of sickness to our tomb. Many philosophers have considered the avoiding of pain as the great motive for action: – amongst others, Locke, who asserted that the search of Pleasure was the avoidance of pain.

Pain and Pleasure are simple ideas, says Burke and I think that all who reflect without having a system to defend will agree with him. All that can be added to this is useless; for we cannot understand the nature of the soul, and cannot therefore explain what is a simple feeling.

Pleasure, in the common acceptance of the term, should be considered in two views, as a relative sensation, and as a positive feeling. Those feelings which arise from the body purely, are merely a discontinuance of pain, or relative pleasures; and secondly, that all positive pleasure depends upon that action of the mind which combines images of past or future objects together, either alone, or with those actually passing; so that in fact, there is no positive active pleasure depending upon an uncombined stimulus, and that we must not look for positive pleasure from the senses, or reason, except inasmuch as they may afterwards cause the imagination to act.

Eating is one of those animal gratifications most commonly sought for by Epicures, yet on what does this depend, but upon the want of materials to supply the losses by the constant friction of our living machine? This want is intimated to us by the pain called hunger, which is so violent that it causes any danger to appear trifling, so that it may be gratified. It is not because there is a positive pleasure in the taste that we sit down to our meals; but because we either have that pain upon us, or that we know by experience that it will come on if we do not take a proper nutriment.

The sight gives no pleasure independently of its exciting the imagination. But if the sight were perfect we should see every thing in its decaying and decayed state; we should see the reptile instruments of destruction upon every leaf, the effects of the weather and time upon every blade of grass, constant decay, and irreparable destruction.

If there is one arrived at an age, when he can look back upon childhood and manhood; let him excite in his mind the pleasant feelings of memory: – what pictures he raises up! The boy, educated in a town, will remember, in his old age, the lime-shaded play-ground, and the hoary antique church. He will paint in more vivid colours than the painter's pallet will afford, the mellowing tints of eve, which threw a rosy glow upon the steeple's top, and softened the harsh tints of his own manufacturing town. He does not bring to his remembrance, how the plain before the school often received him, harassed by the pedantic rule of his pedagogue, to give him up to the more tormenting tyranny of an infant Hercules. He may tell you of a college life, where, in the heyday of youth, with all the openness and rashness, attendant upon that age – wrapped in alternate study and pleasure, he quizzed, or received kindness from professors, staid up whole nights to drink wine, or the more intoxicating draught of poetry. He will tell you of his companions – of the one who held the secrets of his breast, who was, as it were, part of his own head, part of his own heart, – so completely were all his projects open to his discussion, his feelings exposed to his sympathy. But he will not tell you of the profession he was studying, being one he abhorred; of the hankering he had after history, poetry, and literature, while he was obliged to study mathematics, medicine, or theology. He will not tell you how he was forced either to sacrifice his reputation, and meet disgrace before his companions, or to forego the bliss of touching that more than heavenly lyre – poetry; which gives not insensate sounds, but, with its harmonious notes, breathes into vivid flames the irritable sparks of enthusiasm and hope.

Indeed, I know of no pleasures of memory, if they do not arise from the power the mind has of exciting pictures of the past, in which we leave out the bad, vest the moderate with the shading hues of Rembrandt, and colour the beautiful with the richest colours of Rubens. If indeed we were to raise up true pictures of the past, and were without a veil or colouring-glass to look upon our own actions, our friends' proofs of friendship, and our varying fortunes, we should look with disgust at the scenes of meanness, perfidy, and disappointed hope, which have formed the drama of our life.

Nor is the present more fruitful in active positive pleasure. I see, sitting around me, many buoyant with youth, and strong with hope. I see some around me, calm, for the hurricane of youth has subsided to the breath of maturer age, yet rest upon hope as their prop, and envy not those who have yet to go through that fiery ordeal, youthful manhood. Pleasure is their object; but where do they seek it? They have sought the pleasures of the past in imagination, and the present only receives its pleasing colouring from the same inexhaustible source. For Pleasure is never present except when the imagination acts. If we seek present pleasure, we take to the bottle, to opium, to dancing, or yield to enthusiasm, the mere ravings of folly; all of which have but one action upon the mind – that of banishing reason, and letting the pictures of the imagination pass rapidly before us.

Let us examine a few of the sources of our present pleasures. – I mean those which each can command, and which are sought by most.

Novels: – they give us pleasure by abstracting us from our own plans to the pleasures and pains of others.

History, – that causes us to excite in our minds visions of the past; which, if they had been painted by a poet instead of an historian, would have been equally true, for 'a mixture of a lie doth ever add pleasure'.

Scenery, is another source of pleasure to some: – but what is this pleasure? Does it not generally arise from the colouring the imagination gives it? Do we not people the mountains with fairies and dew-fed spirits? Do we not gaze upon the ocean as the emblem of man, always or ruffled with a breath, or torn by a storm? Do we not gaze upon the setting sun, and image him the emblem of a glorious and great man passed the meridian of his glory, sinking into rest, and though covered by the foul mists of calumny, yet sinking glorious and majestic into quiet, and going to illuminate, perchance, another world?

Rank in life is the ambition of many; but it is a wish for torment and pain. He who mounts to rank, is obliged by his pride to disown those whom he once loved – whom he once called by the endearing names of brother, father, sister, friend; or else he must expose himself to see them, cut by his acquaintance, and sneered at by his high friends.

Love, is perhaps the most universal passion that exists, and I should think there is no man, who has passed through life, without at some time or other, feeling its influence. But does not its constancy depend more upon the imagination of the lover than upon the merits of the beloved? Is it not a proof of this, that poets deify their mistress, and make heaven lament as over an inhabitant of its brighter spheres, and the earth grieve as at the misfortunes of a guest, when she is ill or dead? Is it not another proof of it, that lovers discover in the objects of their affection, charms which others cannot see, and seldom remain lovers beyond the honeymoon? After the lover's passion is over, esteem may take its place, and happy if no worse; but what positive pleasure does that afford? Were we not as well when alone? We had then no cause to fear that our secrets would be betrayed.

Children are generally considered to be synonymous with blessings: – but what are they except causes of vexation and trouble, tormenting us with their cries when in swaddling-clothes, with their obstinacy and stupidity when breeched, and with their follies and vices when men?

The love of power is another feeling almost universal; the schoolmaster and the tyrant are but types of each other, and of all mankind. Even Cato is made, by Cicero, to say – 'What pleasures are to be compared with the gratification of authority?' But does not all the pleasure here consist in anticipation? Can there be pleasure in attending levees, and bowing, with flattering words upon our lips, to the higher parasite of kings? But imagination can give us all the pleasures of power without our incurring the risk of pains. Fame and immortality: – how futile the one, how undefined the other! And yet fame is sighed for by the hero, immortality speculated upon by the sage.

A future state and immortality, perhaps the greatest sources of pleasure that man has ever found, depend entirely upon the imagination for their stimulus. The certainty of a future state would be horrible, if while completely ignorant of its nature, we were also without the power of speculating on what it may be. But our imagination acts, and vests it with such brilliant colours that we almost sigh to leave this world of pain, in the hope of realising our visions in the next. But how wretched should we be if we were to succeed in realising our own ideas of Paradise! They are but the plans of man, and we should find the same prophet's curse on man most poignant and terrible. For who could bear a life like ours if it were no longer to be measured by the lapse of minutes, days, or years? – if it were to be absorbed into eternity, where time cannot exist, for no measure could tell its lapse – no events could record its epochs; even death would lay aside his scythe and hour glass as things gone by, and we should have no joy at the death of an enemy, no grief at the decease of a friend, to mark the slipping by of the millions of years that are not even a definite portion of such a state. What would then be the variety of pleasure we can imagine, – eating, drinking, each one and all would produce but the same dullness when absorbed in eternity.

I shall therefore end with this, my examination of the different pretended sources of positive active pleasure, after saying a few words upon the consciousness of existence, which some maintain to be the source of this feeling. The futility of this assertion must, however, be acknowledged by all who reflect maturely upon the subject. For how can this consciousness of being give pleasure, unless from the colouring of the imagination? If it were really a positive active feeling, as we are always conscious of existence, we should always be in a state opposite to pain. The value set upon life by the savage amidst all his privations, and the care with which the prisoner endeavours to preserve existence, though it be to pass on to its end within the walls of a dungeon, are brought forward to prove that this simple consciousness has a charm in itself which binds us to maintain it. But are not the savage and prisoner induced to remain attached to their mortal corpse more by the dread of something in that unknown abyss which surrounds life, than by any pleasure derived from existence?

I hope, therefore, that though I have not been able either to go fully into the general bearings of my theory or to exhaust even a part of its illustrations, that I have at least traced the way to lead you in the right road in the search of pleasure; and that, by destroying the illusion of positive pleasure, I have put a guiding thread into the hands of some, by pursuing which, they will find that pleasure, depending entirely upon the imagination, depends upon ourselves, and cannot be shut out by the doors of a dungeon, or lost under the immense vault of heaven. I hope, also, that I may induce some to be content with seeking for happiness merely in giving way to their imagination, and never attempting to grasp those pleasures which will prove but phantoms, brilliant indeed to the eye, but unsubstantial, and sinking into airy nothing at the touch.

Ernestus Berchtold;
or,
The Modern Oedipus
A Tale

(1819)

The gods are just –
But how can finite measure infinite?
Reason! alas, it does not know itself!
Yet man, vain man, would with this short-lin'd plummet
Fathom the vast abyss of heavenly justice.
Whatever is, is in its causes just,
Since all things are by fate, but purblind man
Sees but a part o' the chain, the nearest links
His eyes not carrying to that equal beam
That poises all above.

Dryden's *Oedipus*

Leila – each thought was only thine! –
My good, my guilt, my weal, my woe,
My hope on high – my all below.
Then deem it evil what thou wilt –
But say, oh say, *hers* was not guilt. –

The Giaour

Introduction

The tale here presented to the public is the one I began at Coligny, when Frankenstein was planned, and when a noble author having determined to descend from his lofty range, gave up a few hours to a tale of terror, and wrote the fragment published at the end of Mazeppa.* Though I cannot boast of the horrible imagination of

---

* The tale which lately appeared, and to which his Lordship's name was wrongfully attached, was founded upon the ground-work upon which this fragment was to have been continued. Two friends were to travel from England into Greece; while there, one of them should die, but before his death, should obtain from his friend an oath of secrecy with regard to his decease. Some short time after, the remaining traveller returning to his native country, should be startled at perceiving his former companion moving about in society, and should be horrified at finding that he made love to his former friend's sister. Upon this foundation I built the Vampyre, at the request of a lady, who denied the possibility of such a ground-work forming the outline of a tale which should bear the slightest appearance of probability. In the course of three mornings, I produced that tale, and left it with her. From thence it appears to have fallen into the hands of some person, who sent it to the Editor in such a way, as to leave it so doubtful from his words, whether it was his Lordship's or not, that I found

the one, or the elegant classical style of the latter, still I hope the reader will not throw mine away, because it is not equal to these. Whether the use I have made of supernatural agency, and the colouring I have given to the mind of Ernestus Berchtold, are original or not, I leave to the more erudite in novels and romances to declare. I am not conscious of having seen any where a prototype of either; yet I fear that whatever is original, is not always pleasing. Nor is this my only apprehension. A tale that rests upon improbabilities, must generally disgust a rational mind; I am therefore afraid that, though I have thrown the superior agency into the back ground as much as was in my power, still, that many readers will think the same moral, and the same colouring, might have been given to characters acting under the ordinary agencies of life; I believe it, but I had agreed to write a supernatural tale, and that does not allow of a completely every-day narrative.

THE AUTHOR

some difficulty in vindicating it to myself. These circumstances were stated in a letter sent to the *Morning Chronicle* three days after the publication of the tale, but in consequence of the publishers representing to me that they were compromised as well as myself, and that immediately they were certain it was mine, that they themselves would wish to make the *amende honorable* to the public, I allowed them to recall the letter which had lain some days at that paper's office.

Part First

Upon the left side of the lake of Thun lies the small village of Beatenberg, which, under the care of a simple pastor contains no individual above the rank of a peasant: it was in this village that I was born. Misfortune seemed to be anxious at my very birth to stamp me for its own. – Just at the termination of the short war between Austria and Prussia, of the year 1778, my mother arrived at this village in company with a gentleman severely wounded, as he said, in the slight skirmishes, which had alone formed the military display of this campaign. There was a mystery about them, which they seemed to wish should not be unravelled. The worthy pastor, therefore, whom I have since called father, did not make any inquiries of his guests, though it appeared to him very singular, that the most difficult and steep roads should have been preferred for the route of an invalid towards his home. The tender care of my mother towards this gentleman was exemplary; it seemed as if that courage and firmness, which was wanting in his breast, had taken refuge in hers. They were not Swiss, for the language they spoke was unknown to Berchtold the parish priest. They apparently understood German and French; but they said so very little, and that with such evident embarrassment, that nothing could be learnt from their conversation. There being no inn at the solitary Beatenberg, the pastor, with his usual kindness, on hearing of the arrival of strangers at the close of the evening, had immediately waited on them to offer his services and house. They were to have been his guests, only for the night; but the fatigue of the journey again forced open the wound in the gentleman's side; determined, however, to proceed, he attempted to walk to the litter prepared for him; the exertion proved too great, he fell into my mother's arms, and almost instantly expired.

My mother was distracted; already far advanced in pregnancy, she fell upon the body, no longer capable of that firmness and resolution, which she had shown, when her companion's safety depended upon it. She listened to no one; but frantic, she sat by the dead body, alternately shedding tears, and bursting into a loud laugh. Berchtold urged those soothing doctrines of which he was minister, but in vain; he spoke in vain of another world, of future hope; none could like him, soothe the pillow of the dying peasant,

but here were miseries no hope could assuage. She at last fell
exhausted upon the ground, she was conveyed to bed, and in a few
hours I and a sister saw the light. But this did not allay her grief,
she sunk into a silence that nothing could induce her to break; her
eyes were fixed, and she at last died without a struggle. She was
buried by him, whom Berchtold imagined, in spite of the disparity
of his years, to have been her husband; and over their grave were
placed those simple crosses, which you must have seen in the
neighbouring church-yards. The pastor could not place any
inscription upon their tomb, for he had been so engaged in
attendance upon my mother, that he had not noticed the departure
of her only servant, who took with him every thing of value
belonging to his former mistress. He knew not what to do, there
was no clue in his hands by which he could restore us to our family;
for there was nothing to be found, except some linen and a locket,
with my mother's portrait.

Berchtold was a man whose humble endeavours had always
been engaged in the attempt to fulfil those duties his profession
imposed upon him. In these mountainous districts, the office of a
parish priest is extremely arduous; he is often called up in the
middle of the night, while the snow is falling, to go many miles
over the frozen glaciers, to administer to the dying peasant the
sacraments of the church. Berchtold never allowed the most distant
hamlet to want religious comfort; he was old, yet often has he
crossed to the foot of the Holgaut, merely to help the unfortunate
in their attempt at resignation, under domestic calamity. He was
not, therefore, likely to cast us from him; he immediately had us
conveyed to the cottage of a married sister, and caused us to be
brought up as luxuriously as an Alpine village allowed.

I remember little of my early years, it seems, that I have vague
visions of an age, when were spent whole days in gathering
flowers, to adorn my sister's head and breast, from the precipitous
bank that descends to the lake, when, at night, I was lulled half
trembling, to sleep by the tales of my foster-mother concerning
ogres and spirits from the dead. But all this is indistinct. When
about six years of age, I was removed to the house of Berchtold. He
called me son, and if the tenderest care and the greatest sacrifices
could entitle him to the name of father, which I gave him, it was
not wrongfully bestowed. One of the first circumstances which I
can remember, is that one day, while sitting with him upon a bank,
near the church-yard, gazing on the scene around, and watching

the white sails which gleamed upon the lake beneath our feet; I threw my arms around his neck, and asked him, 'Why they called me orphan?' He told me that my father and mother were dead. Retreating from him, I started, and trembling, asked him if he were then dead? He did not at first understand me; but upon my calling him by the name of father, he remembered that I had never heard the history of my birth. He took me to his breast, and weeping, told me, that I was indeed an orphan, that I was not his child. He then took me to the church-yard, and pointing to the raised sod, he told me my parents were there. I did not clearly understand him. I had then no idea of death; my mother, for so I called his sister, had told me tales of the dead, but these terrified without being understood. All the graves, save those of my parents, were adorned with flowers; upon my remarking this to him, he told me that they having died strangers there, none were bound to love them. I was hurt to see those flowers, which though faded, showed the attention of some living being, refused to my mother's tomb; it sunk deeply on my mind. And for years after, I felt a vague pleasure in strewing their graves with the fresh flowers that formerly were employed in adorning my sister's head. Often have I laid myself down looking upon their grassy covering, as if I expected that some of those tales of my mother would be realised with regard to myself, and that I should see them rising from their grave. My sister soon joined me in these meditations, and almost the first infantile communications which passed between us, rested upon another world. She would sit by me, and often the worthy pastor surprised us, after the sun had set, calling to our memory those tales we had heard when with our foster-mother.

We did not mingle with the other children of the village, for we delighted too much in each other's company; we spent hours together in talking about what had in a most unaccountable manner taken possession of our minds, or else we gamboled round Berchtold. He, debarred by his religion from the enjoyment of a domestic circle of his own children, had formed so strong an attachment to us, that his greatest delight was, when not engaged in his parochial duties, to join us in our games and infantile occupations. With all the simplicity of old age, he would lie down and allow us to play with his white locks, or tell us stories, which, though of a different nature from those of his sister, did not interest us the less. He was a good classical scholar, and was well versed in the history of his own country. From these sources he drew his tales, and at an early age he inspired me with an ardent love for independence and liberty, at the same time that he instilled into my heart, a burning thirst for the means of asserting a superiority over my equals. The anecdotes of Themistocles, Alcibiades and others, upon whom the fates of their country had depended, rested on my mind. Berchtold described to me the fallen glories of Rome, of that nation which once held sway over the known world. In short there was a material defect in my education, which is not uncommon, my imagination was stimulated, while my judgement was not called forth, and I was taught to admire public instead of private virtues. I rested upon those situations which one in the million attains, and in which the passions of others are to be guided, while I was not shown how to conduct myself, when my own inclinations and feelings might attempt to lead me astray in the common occurrences of life. With a strongly susceptible mind I imbibed deeply these first impressions, and throughout life this defect in my education has followed me. As I advanced in age, I gradually became acquainted with the Latin and Greek historians. Berchtold rashly, though innocently, took advantage of my thirst for relations of battles and deeds of renown, to induce me to learn. I consequently had Plutarch and Livy in my hands, long before I read any book tending to give man the power of regulating his passions.

I joined the villagers only in those military exercises, which are constantly performed after the day's labour in every hamlet. Sometimes I would go with the chamois hunter, and reaching the higher ridges of the Alps, whose snowy summits were visible from the lake, I forced myself to follow him in his venturous pursuit. But it for a long time required a strong exertion of my mind to induce me to venture amidst the vast solitudes of eternal snows. I always felt an inward shuddering and awe at the sight of my native wildnesses. Even now I cannot bear to listen to those, who, amongst our magnificent scenes, which man has not yet overcome, and which mock his power, can talk of pleasure, and dwell upon the beauty of the scenery. I cannot feel this. I seem always to crouch beneath some invisible being whose power is infinite, and which I am conscious I cannot resist. It seems that I hear him laughing audibly at our vain attempts to encroach upon his dominion. It appears to me as if the avalanche were but the weapon of his impatience, while he insidiously steals upon those habitations he has covered with his snows, by the silent, gradual approach of the glaciers. Let mankind labour for ages upon these ribs of the world, and their work shall not be seen. The pyramids might rise unnoticed upon the rocks before my view, undistinguished from the fragment that falls unperceived with the passing torrent. I cannot bear that human strength should be unable to stamp its hand upon these towering memorials of convulsions we could not influence, could not hope to control. This morbid feeling may have been excited by my foster-mother constantly pointing to the Jungfrau, whose white peak forms so prominent a feature in the view from her house, while she related the peasant's tale of those mischievous spirits who dance upon its glittering icy coat, decked by the moon's ray. I gained, however, health and vigour from these excursions, and I became at last one of the most noted for activity in all the canton.

I rapidly arrived at my twentieth year. My kind friend the pastor could not be induced to part with me. I was the only prop of his old age, I latterly always accompanied him in his visits amongst the mountains, often joined him in his prayer over the dying, and frequently have I supported him at the brink of that grave, over which he was calling down the mercy of God, and which was soon to be his own refuge. My sister increased in beauty, and each day added some new charm to her person, and some additional accomplishment to her mind. I often represented to my father that I was of an age when I should begin to do something, and attempt to take the burden of myself and my sister off his hands. He would agree with me in my arguments, but when the moment came, he was always so overpowered with sorrow, that I could not induce myself to leave him for the few remaining days he had to live.

I seldom visited Thun or Interlaken; I did not feel pleasure in the society of men. I there found them engaged in all the petty interests, which pervade human breasts in the narrow sphere of a miserable provincial town. I found they could not sympathise with one whom they looked upon as a wild romantic mountaineer. About this time the French revolution began to exalt my imagination even more than the history of nations gone by, and I burnt with the desire of viewing nearer those actions, which in our solitary village, echoing only a softened sound of their horrors, seemed to wear a certain air of grandeur and glory. I ardently wished to join those soldiers who had driven back the foreign invaders from their native plains. I little thought then how soon I was to be engaged in resisting these very men, amidst my own native mountains.

When the discussions between Berne and the French concerning
the Pays de Vaud arrested the attention of all, anxious to be
amongst men in action, and tired of my total want of employment,
I again begged my friend to let me depart to the capital; but still,
at his prayer, I remained with him. I laid myself down upon the
snow, shining as it then was in the first rays of spring, and
abandoned myself to visions of battle and renown. My spirits
gradually left me, there was a craving for exertion about me, which
I found it impossible to overcome. I seized my gun, and going
amidst the eternal glaciers and rocks, I sought by forcing myself to
exert my body, to lose this feeling of vacuity. But I often lost sight
of the chamois, engaged in the thought of my country, and
bounded from rock to rock, no longer occupied with what I
imagined was before me. My sister would endeavour to soothe me
by her caresses. I told her of my visions with regard to my country's
cause, and at moments excited even in her breast the sparks of
enthusiasm. But she generally echoed Berchtold's sentiments with
regard to the indecision and incapacity of the government.

Tired one evening of listening to Berchtold, who attempted to
repress my ardour, by representing to me that the country was
betrayed, and that, in consequence of the tardiness and imbecility
of the rulers of Switzerland, in spite of the courage and daring of
its peasantry, it was doomed to become an easy prey to France, I
left him determined again to seek refuge in the chase. I accordingly
set out the next morning, intending to remain several days amongst
the mountains; but I grew listless, and at the close of the second
day, I still found myself upon the Wengern Alp. I issued forth from
the chalet where I had taken some refreshment, and soon lost
myself in reflection. I now looked with pleasure upon the
Jungfrau's white head, glistening on the blue canopy of Heaven.
All the horrors of the Grindewald at my feet, the high summit of
the Schrechorn, with the echoing thunders of the numerous
avalanches, no longer appalled me. It seemed as if they now put
on their terrors against a presumptuous foe, in defence of their
children. There was no cloud upon the dark blue sky, – there was
no mist upon the rocks; and though the snow still covered the
whole surface of the mountains around, still there was a genial
warmth and splendour in the sun's reflected ray, that vivified and
strengthened. There was no sound, save that of the distant cataract,
and falling avalanche. I stood a long time leaning upon my musket,
to look upon this scene. How could avarice hope to find a resting

place in the minds of those nursed amidst such objects? How could slavery expect to find its votaries resident amidst such fortresses? The tyrant could not dare to add these horrors of nature to those already revelling in his breast. A slave who shrinks before the frown of a despot, could not stand erect amidst these awful monuments of a power that mocks at human prowess. Upon this occasion, it seemed as if the sun threw its proudest ray upon these rocks; they had seen, might hope to see, men worthy of gazing upon that nature which, lifting unappalled its head amidst the thundering clouds, had snatched their weapon from their grasp, and had thrown it at its feet, while, with its snowy head, it struck in defiance the arching canopy of Heaven. I was thus engaged in thought, which but served to increase my indignation at the conduct of men, who sacrificed to personal interest the safety of their country, when I was suddenly struck with the sound of a voice, which I shall never, never forget. In unison with my feelings at that moment, the notes sometimes broke out into the wildest tones of defiance; at others, suddenly sinking, they seemed uncertain and soothing. I dared not look around; I felt as if entranced, and I imagined I heard the voice of these mountains, mocking the invaders, then sinking into despondence. Gradually the voice approached, – I could distinguish words. – I heard footsteps. I suddenly turned round, and beheld a figure; I cannot describe it to you. Arrayed in a dress foreign to these mountains, her white drapery, breathed on by the wanton breeze, now betrayed the delicate form of her limbs, – now hid them from my sight. Her dark eye seemed exultingly to gaze upon my native rocks, while the wild notes of defiance played upon her lips. She suddenly saw me, and was silent. She looked around, as if for some one; and I then perceived, at a little distance, a man worn down more by grief than by age. I approached, and re-assured her. She blushed, and in that language which, in its very sound, breathes love, told me that she did not understand me. I could not answer; but, gazing on her, I seemed to be fascinated by her words. The old man approached, and we soon entered into conversation. I spoke Italian fluently; her surprise and pleasure cannot be painted, when she heard me address her father in her native language. I walked by her side, and I was often so lost in thought, that I was obliged to answer, by an unmeaning yes or no, the questions of the old man. Our conversation at last turned upon Switzerland; he seemed to be perfectly conversant with its situation. She entered with enthusiasm into its cause, and asked me, why I was idling amidst these valleys, when my country called me to the post of danger. These simple words from her lips caused an emotion in my breast that drew the blood to my cheeks. She thought of me. I at once promised to join my countrymen to-morrow. She then told me, that orders had arrived at the neighbouring towns for an instant levy to join the army of d'Erlach, which it was expected would be immediately brought into action.

I was yet walking by her side, when we arrived at Lauter-brunnen. At the gate of a small cottage, after having asked me to take some refreshment, which I declined, they bade me farewell. There was a carriage waiting at the door. The thought rushed upon my mind that I might never see her again. I know not by what impulse, but, ignorant of the forms of the world, I summoned courage, at the moment of parting, to ask of her a ribbond with which she was playing; that, as I said, I might wear it in remembrance of her who had made me decide upon joining the patriots. Blushing, she looked at her father, who smiled consent, and she bound round my arm the scarf which she had worn during the morning. I have often heard that song again; I have often seen that form; and many are the years I have worn that scarf: – they have been years of misery and grief. Memory has no moment to look back to between the present and that happy day. Yet, for such another moment of enthusiasm I would undergo all my miseries afresh. I revert to it as the Arab, in the midst of the rising sands, turns to his visions of the green speck upon the desert's sandy ocean; amidst dangers, that is his hope; in anguish, that is his refuge. That moment seemed to bestow upon me the happiness which my fancy had so long pictured in the future. But every moment since has only served to weave closer round me the meshes of that net, which has shut me out from joy. I then, however, felt as if time no longer weighed upon me; and I was grieved, when arriving at my father's door, I found that the joys of hours had passed as those of a minute.

I found my sister in tears; Berchtold, with his grey locks hiding the hands covering his face. Hearing my footsteps, my aged father rose, and taking me in his arms, with tears in his eyes, he told me, that he could no longer take upon himself to hinder me from joining my countrymen in the sacred cause of independence. He bade me take leave of my sister, and, while my courage remained, to surmount the pang of bidding her farewell. He told me, that he had caused my sister to prepare every thing for a parting, which he feared was to be our last. He embraced me, and rushed out of the house. My sister's eyes, wet with tears, now turned upon me, anxious to show the same resolution as my father had displayed, she hastened my departure. She gave me my gun and powder flask, – bound round my waist more than half the savings of Berchtold; and kissing me, bade me farewell. Bewildered by the rapidity of my different emotions, I hurried to the side of the lake, looked once more up the steep mountain, on the ascent of which Beatenberg raised its white cottages, and, turning the point of land which encroached upon the lake, I was soon wafted, in company with many others, towards the town of Thun. I did not heed the white sails hurrying along the blue rippling waves. I could not gaze upon the rich cultivated scenery of the lake. My mind was straying midst those wild glaciers, that once had been my horror, – which to-day had shown me the unknown. Why does fate cause the approaches of misery to be decked with all the show of promised happiness? From this moment begins my eventful history; till now I had only been in the hands of the foul fiends that have tormented me, as plastic clay, which they formed in that manner, best fitted to contain the miseries they were preparing to pour upon it. You may think I have rested too much upon my early years, which passed without action; but those years saw deposited in my breast the seeds which have brought me to the state of apathy and misery you witness. That vision has proved to me the harbinger of more woes than it promised pleasures, and that scarf, which you see is yet bound round my heart, has felt it beat more violently through anguish, than it did even through hope, at the moment it first encircled my arm. My life till now had passed in dreams. I had not known the rude blast of worldly interests; I had been unconscious of the activity of the bad passions, and had only viewed man in the shape of my foster-father, breaking by his presence the shackles of grief that restrained the energies of his children, as the sun destroys the icy bonds that bind the vital powers of the spring. In the cause of charity and virtue, I had seen employed those powers and that activity which, exerted in a less degree, have often excited the admiration of the multitude, and concealed follies, nay, crimes, from even the philosopher in that halo of fame they bring around them. The earliest impressions, I received, were those from my foster-mother's tales, and they have not left me even at present; how much less, when but entering on manhood. I had so often gazed upon my mother's picture, which my sister wore round her neck from her earliest infancy, that, while sitting by her tomb, it seemed as if her image had haunted me in my sleep, for I frequently found myself arguing as if I had had actual proof of the existence of beings superior to ourselves.

The evening had closed before I arrived at Thun. The town was crowded with the peasantry of the neighbouring mountains; there were fires throughout the streets, around which stood the aged and the boy, the mother and the virgin. They were all come to offer their arms in defence of their country. I approached the town-house; the door was crowded with petitioners, who were attempting to induce the sentinel to give them precedence in the enrolment of their names. I stood for some time watching the earnestness with which the aged laid hold of their very weakness and uselessness, as a reason why they should be preferred in the cause of death; while the young, elate with the hopes of youth, showing their sinewy limbs, appealed to their expectations of victory from their strength, as a reason why they should first be put upon the lists for battle. Their arms were more various than their ages; an iron wedge, sharpened and fastened to the end of a stick, served some as the substitute for a hatchet; burnt stakes and the chamois hunter's rifle mingled with the scythe rounded into a sabre, and the sickle straightened to a sword. While thus silently gazing upon the scene, a magistrate, a friend of Berchtold, going to his post, recognised me, and approaching, led me through a private entrance into the council chamber. My proffered services were immediately accepted, and I was directly ordered to put myself at the head of those villagers, who could be found in the town belonging to Berchtold's parish, avoiding, however, as much as possible the burdening myself with the infirm and women. I received orders to reach Berne in the shortest possible time, and to depart with the earliest dawn. I went out into the streets, a great part of the peasants had retired under the arcades which are on each side of the streets of Thun; they there formed one promiscuous mass, in which it was impossible to distinguish between man and woman. All was silent, save the dead sound of heavy footsteps and the hoarse voice of individuals like myself, treading amidst these sleepers, and calling out the name of that place, whose inhabitants they sought. The night was damp and dark, there was no light in the Heavens, and often as I went, I stumbled over the body of some unseen person, who, uttering a note of impatience, again turned himself to sleep. Imitating the example of the others, I called out the name of Beatenberg at every step, and soon mustered almost the whole population of Berchtold's parish. I had a painful task, the old pointed to their children, and with tears in their aged eyes, asked me if I intended to hinder them from setting the example to their children, of dying for their native soil. The women, pointing to their lovers, would take no refusal; they seemed determined to witness their conduct on the day of battle, and see if they were worthy of the love they claimed. I spoke separately to the young men, and advised them to steal from their companions and meet me at a certain hour about a mile from the town.

They retired to rest, and I laid myself down in the street to sleep; I was soon lost to all external objects, and I again saw hovering at my side, her, who had seemed in the morning but a vision. She smiled upon me, again urged me by those words; – but suddenly it seemed as if the earth parted between us, and a huge chasm opened at my feet; we seemed to stretch our hands towards each other; I threw myself into the gulph, and awoke. Finding it but a dream, I again attempted to compose myself to sleep, but in vain; her image still stood before me, and the moment I rested upon it, the idea of my orphan state and her apparent affluence startled me. I had not asked her name. I knew nothing of her; her form, her face, her voice, and her words already began to appear to my memory as the recollections of an unsubstantial, supernatural vision; but at this moment my hand fell upon the scarf, which I had now bound round my chest. The touch roused me from my painful reveries, and hope pervaded my breast. I started from the ground convinced that she did exist, I fell upon my knees, and uttered aloud a prayer to the Divinity to make me worthy of her. Hardly had the words passed my lips, when a loud hoarse laugh sounded on my ear. It was but a drunkard laughing at some wild imagination of his own; but it made me shudder. I left the town; a heavy thick rain was falling, there was no wind, nothing seemed stirring, the shape of the distant mountains could be perceived by the white mass they presented on the dark canopy of night; every thing else was of one dead hue. I leant myself against the trunk of an old tree, and the dawn had, unperceived by me, risen in the East, when I found myself roused by the salutations of many of my comrades.

I had in vain attempted to dissuade the old and the women from joining us; they were all with us at the appointed hour. I again as fruitlessly endeavoured to show them the embarrassment they would prove to our march; they would not listen, and I gave orders for the men to proceed. In consequence of the exercise the peasants had been accustomed to in their native villages, I found no difficulty in forming them into something like a regular body. Towards night, as I had purposely pressed the march throughout the day, I was glad to perceive that the number of the old and infirm had much diminished. Next morning I again proceeded; it was with great difficulty that I could restrain myself and comrades from stopping to assist the women and old men who fell by the roadside through actual weakness and fatigue. Their cries imploring assistance from lovers, from sons, were heart-rending. I shut my ears and dared not listen. The nearer I approached Berne, the more deserted I found the country, all had flocked to the town or to the posts of danger. At last, with a body of two hundred men, not even yet entirely deserted by the women, I entered the capital. I read dismay and horror upon every face, even the peasantry, which here, as at Thun, crowded the streets, were silent; there were no signs of enthusiasm, but the glance of suspicion fell from every eye. Just as we were approaching the great place, we met a party of soldiers with their bayonets wet with blood. They seemed with hasty steps to be hurrying from a spot that brought something horrible to their mind. They did not speak, but we soon learnt that they were the murderers of Stetter and Ryhiner. They washed the blood of their countrymen from their weapons in the blood of their invaders, and at last bathed them with their own. Posterity may then spare their names the brand of infamy, for a momentary fit of rage against those they imagined traitors to their country.

We were ordered immediately upon our arrival to reinforce the army at Frauenbrunnen, and were joined upon our departure by other militias, and by the venerable Steiguer, who had just thrown up the insignia of civil office in the determination of dying for his country. We arrived at a critical moment, the French having an advantage in cavalry and artillery, which the Swiss could not resist, were upon the point of surrounding the small army, the only impediment in their road to Berne. Steiguer immediately perceived the danger; ordering us to follow, he rushed forwards, and attacked the troops which, having already passed the right flank of General d'Erlach, were upon the point of gaining the road on his rear. The combat was obstinate, our chief attack was upon the artillery, with which the enemy was attempting to cross the road. Our women did not shrink, they rushed forward, threw themselves upon the wheels of the guns, and allowed themselves to be hewn to pieces ere they would quit their hold.

The army under d'Erlach had in the meantime began its retreat to Grauholtz. We found ourselves surrounded and engaged amidst the very carriages of our enemy's guns, which we had taken. By great exertions at last we formed ourselves again into a compact body, and suddenly, as if by one impulse, falling upon our knees, we offered a prayer to the God of battle. The enemy thinking we were about to throw down our arms, checked themselves for a moment; we arose; the officers placed themselves at the head of the column, which set up a loud shout, ran upon the foe, and bearing all opposition down, soon reached Urteren, where we made a momentary stand, and then reached Grauholtz.

The troops were immediately employed in raising an abbatis in front. While the men were thus engaged, Erlach and Steiguer met; at the instigation of the latter, the general came forward, and thanked my troop for the intrepidity it had shown during the whole combat. I was particularly noticed by them, and received from the aged general a medal he wore round his neck, as a token of his country's gratitude. 'I have seen,' he said, 'the sun rise to-day upon freemen; I shall not see it set upon my countrymen. Our country is lost; it cannot thank its sons; let me, therefore, who have directed its last efforts for freedom, acknowledge the few hours' respite you have obtained to its fate, by presenting you with this mark of honour, which I obtained from a free nation.' The loud roar of cannon burst upon our ears; he left me. I stood for a moment still; in one hand I held the medal, with the other I pressed the scarf of my unknown friend closer to my heart. Again we fought, but again their numbers enabled them to turn our flank, and, in spite of the strength of our position, we were obliged to retreat. One more struggle at the gates of Berne, and all was lost. The slaughter was horrible. Determined to sell my life as dear as I could, I rushed into the thickest of the fight; but my peasants followed me; they snatched me from danger, and bore me struggling through the town. I reproached them with having deprived me of an honourable death; one approached with aged steps; looking me in the face, he merely mentioned the name of Berchtold. I understood him; and, leaving Berne, we turned our steps towards Thun.

Unfortunately, the slaughter by the enemy's sword was not the only horror that attended the dispersion of our troops. The peasants and soldiers never, in their legendary tales, having heard of a defeat accompanied by a retreat, on their native soil, imputed the whole to the treachery of their officers. The French had from the very beginning spread papers to this purport amongst them. As we proceeded, we therefore found the bodies of many of their officers hacked to pieces by the infuriate stragglers. Upon our arrival at Musingen, we found General d'Erlach in the hands of some of these men, who had determined to convey him to Berne. With him was his wife, who had accompanied him in his flight, and a young officer, whom I had remarked earnestly engaged in looking at my scarf, at the moment I was receiving the general's thanks at Grauholtz. I remonstrated with the soldiers, but in vain. I gradually, however, contrived to approach the general, and, when I thought myself sufficiently near to shield him, drawing my sword, I called upon the Beatenbergers to assist me, and instantly attacked them. The young officer, possessing himself in the struggle of a sword, was soon by my side. The peasants joined us; we drove the soldiers through the village; but in the meanwhile some stragglers issued from the houses, and striking the defenceless old man with their hatchets, left him for dead in the arms of his wife. When I returned, I found him apparently reviving through her care; it was only for a moment, he could not speak; it appeared, however, as if he recognised me, for he pressed my hand, and turned his closing eyes, first on his wife, then towards me. Thinking he recommended her to my care, I promised that I would protect her to the utmost of my power; his eye glistened, and he expired.

At this moment I again heard the cries of the soldiers. As there was an unfrequented path over the mountains from this place towards Hoestetten, whence the young officer might easily get to Lucerne, I advised him to pursue it, and get immediately out of the canton of Berne. We parted. Gathering my peasants together, I directly set off with Madame Erlach in the cart towards Thun. She did not shriek or weep, she seemed stupified by the greatness of her loss, and, when arrived at the city, she without difficulty allowed herself to be taken from the body, and to be conveyed in a boat to Berchtold's, whence she retired in a short time to complete solitude, where she saw no one, and soon after died.

I cannot paint to you the joy of Berchtold when he once more held me within his arms. My sister's tears flowed now as profusely as at our parting, but from a different cause. I had only been away a few days, yet the crowded events that took place in that short period made it appear as many weeks. The first spot I sought with my sister was my mother's grave. There I sat with her silently engaged in thought; after some time we began to converse, and as I had nothing hidden from her, I soon told the whole of my history from the morning of that day on which I had seen the unknown. She seemed disturbed, and upon my pressing her to explain to me what passed in her breast, she advised me to beware, for that it was probably one of the spirits of the Jungfrau's eternal frosts that had accosted me. I laughed at what I deemed her folly; but I soon perceived that there was something more on her mind than she was willing to confess. In vain I besought her to disclose it to me; she told me she durst not, and asked me as a favour not to speak to her any more on this subject. Alarmed, I knew not why, I looked at her with earnest attention. She could no longer bear it, but throwing herself into my arms, informed me that while I was away she had seen our mother, who had appeared to her, arrayed in mourning, announcing, that I was in the greatest danger, and that she must guard me, but that unless she wished to share my peril, she must conceal it from me. 'Ernestus,' my sister said, 'I cannot obey, let your fate be mine, and I am content.' Saying this, she again pressed me to her bosom, and wept. I was moved, I sat down by her side; bound in each other's arms, we gazed upon the green sod in silence, unwilling to disturb those thoughts which we knew must be the same in the breasts of both.

Anxious to learn some tidings concerning the fate of my native country, I went every day to Thun. My indignation was excited by the recital of the cruelties and extortions of the French, and, when they dared to attempt disarming the inhabitants, determined not to submit to so base an insult, I was proscribed, and sought refuge amongst those mountains which had been the scenes of my prowess in the chase. I went and sat whole days by the rocks in the Wengern Alp, where I first saw that form which has since engrossed the whole of my thoughts. I made enquiries at Lauterbrunnen concerning the two strangers, but ineffectually; they had merely been there as other travellers, to view the sublime scenery of the mountains, and had not been heard of since. I remained a whole month amidst these rocks, only going to Beatenberg at night, when Berchtold and my sister would receive me, and supplying me with provisions for the ensuing days, tell me of all the insults that added to the shame of Switzerland. But at last they showed me the proclamation of Schwarenberg against the six eastern cantons. I immediately announced my determination to join them. Berchtold said nothing; my sister followed me out of the house, and begged to be permitted to accompany me. I refused, and upon her reminding me of her dream, told her, that, as it promised she should share my peril, it would prove impossible for me to go into any real danger without her, that therefore she need not follow me, or, if the fates decreed it, we should meet at that moment without any endeavours on our part to assist their fiat. I painted to her the horrors of the exterminating warfare that was carried on, and asserted that it was most likely not the peril of the sword in which she was to partake. In short, I forced her to promise me not to follow, by representing to her the misery Berchtold would undergo, if at once deprived of both of his adopted children. I led her back to the door, and left her in his arms.

It is useless for me to give you an account of this campaign. It is recorded in history with even all the unsuccessful struggles for liberty, as one of those gleamings of that noble spirit in men, which, though generally hidden under the pressure of vice and corruption, at times bursts forth like the volcano's fire. I was taken prisoner, and could find no means of escaping, till the French, towards the end of June, after the restoration of Rapinat, became more lenient in their treatment of their prisoners, and less careful in their watch over them. I once more joined the Underwalders, and was again witness to the defeat of my countrymen. I met the young officer I had saved from slaughter at Musingen. His name was Olivieri. We had no time for intercourse, always in action or on the march, we only saw one another in the field, where we often joined and tried to vie with each other in acts of daring and courage. We became at last noted in the army, and though only volunteers, we each soon found ourselves at the head of about ninety men, who always were ready to obey our commands.

In the midst of our struggles in the Underwald, intelligence reached us of an insurrection having taken place in the upper Valais; it was deemed necessary by the leaders of our army to send them assistance, and thus cause a diversion in our favour. They proposed that one hundred men should be given to each of us, and that with this force we should be sent to aid the Valisians in their attempt. It was a hazardous undertaking, we had to cross upon the flanks of the enemy, and should be obliged, it was supposed, to pass through the Grimsel, which was in the possession of the French. When it was proposed, no one was found to volunteer; no

Underwalder would leave his home in the hour of danger. I had however remarked a number of Schweitzers, who had joined us singly, having left their dwellings, though not countenanced by their countrymen who were ranged on the other side, to partake in the dangers of the patriotic Underwalders. To these men we applied, and in a short time, two hundred men were selected. We kept almost upon the summit of the high ridge that joins the Furca from the Lake of Lucerne, and crossing the glaciers by rocks, that even in the chase of the chamois would have startled me, we arrived at Realp, and soon crossed into the Valais. At Obergesteln we learnt that some French troops had that very night crossed from the Grimsel, while the whole body of peasants were engaged in the lower part of the valley, amidst the fastnesses attempting to stop that force which was advancing by the bridge of Hochflue. They had committed great outrages, and had caused those, who were able, to fly behind the glaciers of the Rhone.

Our undertaking now seemed desperate. The number of the French in the rear of our allies was greater than ours, and the end of the Valais through which we were to advance was flat and open, without any shelter, surrounded by steep mountains. Olivieri was however before me, we had each one hundred chosen men, and he seemed resolved on advancing. Not knowing how to procure intelligence of the enemy, I immediately offered to advance by myself and reconnoitre. As I well knew every part of this valley, I was certainly the fittest person in our body for such an undertaking; but my companion would not hear of ceding the post of danger to me; we were obliged to draw lots, and it fell upon him, and he departed.

In the mean time the women, hearing of our arrival, came from their fastnesses, and joined us. They seized upon every thing which offered the semblance of a weapon, and resolved to follow us. As my companion did not return as soon as I expected, fearful of a surprise, I determined to advance, and, if possible, gain some of the passes before the enemy knew of our arrival. I, however, previously sent forward a young woman, to see if she could obtain any intelligence of Olivieri. I then ordered the men to follow in silence, and marching all the evening, we at last, towards night, reached the village of Blizingen, where the valley straightens, and becomes more inclosed and rocky. The river here runs through a deeply-cut channel, more resembling a ravine, than a common bed. As I knew there was but one path, and that very steep and dangerous, I ordered my men to rest upon their arms, while I went along the river's channel to learn something concerning the enemy, who I thought could not have advanced much farther. At last, being arrived opposite the village of Vietsch, I heard a great noise, and saw many lights; making no doubt but that these proceeded from the point where the enemy was stationed, I returned. I found my men asleep; arousing them I ascended at their head the steep sides of the mountain, and making them march parallel with the path, but much higher, I brought them above the village, and hid them in a wood of pines that stretches along the steep. I now no longer feared the superior numbers of the enemy, the ascent was so precipitous that we could not be attacked, except to great disadvantage, while we could either join the Valisians, or fall upon the foe with every prospect of victory.

I determined once more to go and discover their exact position, giving the word that if I thought it a fit moment for an attack, I would fire my gun, and then sound my hunting horn, so that no mistake could occur from the firing of any drunken soldiers or guard. Wrapt up in my mantle I descended from the wood, and found the men lying securely asleep in the road between the houses. They were certainly all there; anxious to know something concerning my companion, I resolved, in spite of the risk, to awaken some straggler, and learn from him if any prisoner was amongst them. I accordingly approached one who, stretched along the edge of a precipice over the river, was sunk in a sleep that seemed that of the innocent. Putting my pistol to his breast, I awoke him. Alarmed, he was upon the point of calling out, when I threatened him with instant death. To my inquiries he answered, that a person had been surprised by some stragglers in the course of the day, and he added that he was then lying bound in a cottage in the very centre of the village, destined to be in the morning a butt for their muskets. It did not appear that his having been found armed had excited suspicion, as he was taken for a common peasant. Determined to save Olivieri, I knew not what to do with this sleeper, to shoot him would alarm the enemy, they might immediately dispatch my friend, and yet I could not leave this man to raise his comrades. I pushed him down the precipice, and directly entered the village. All were asleep, I found the cottage, there was a light in the window. I stole close to it, wrapping myself up in my mantle. I looked in; you may imagine my alarm when I saw two soldiers awake in conversation, while my friend, upon his back, was bound to a bench fastened to the floor. There were several soldiers at my feet, with their arms by their sides, a sudden thought struck me, I seized one of their guns and firing it, I instantly retreated to the other side of the cottage, where I had remarked a window close to the fatal bench. As I expected, the two soldiers went out to inquire about the report which they had heard; I took advantage of the few moments, leapt into the room by the window, roused Olivieri, who gazed upon me expecting death; I made a sign for silence, cut his bonds, and was again out of the cottage with my companion, when I heard the door open to admit the two soldiers. We hastened up the ascent, and when, amidst the rocks I fired my own fowling piece, and blew a national air upon my horn. Before the enemy, alarmed by the two soldiers, who missed their prisoner, could form, we were amongst them, and morn had hardly dawned before we had cut to pieces the whole of this detachment. I could have induced the men to give quarter, but the women were outrageous, they followed our soldiers, and dispatched the wounded, whom their more merciful companions had spared, while they excited the Schweitzers to slaughter even those who threw up their arms; none were saved. The Valisians who were making head against this body, hearing the report of so many guns, did not know what to believe; they however approached, and when they heard the Swiss war cry of liberty, they immediately joined us. Their joy cannot be expressed by words; Olivieri and myself had in the mean time met, and his thanks were profuse; but what was my sorrow to find that the young woman had been seized and bayoneted in cold blood, because she would not acknowledge the right of the French to a superiority over her nation; she had pretended not to know my companion, and thus avoided betraying us, by not being confronted with him.

We had gained a victory, but it only served to delay the subjection of this noble peasantry; they were obliged to come at last to a capitulation. We could not be included in it; the French asserted that the Schweitzers were deserters. We therefore determined to attempt once more a passage over the most unfrequented Alps. To avoid the Grimsel, where the French might pass to interrupt our passage, we crossed at once into the valley of Formazza. Hidden in the day amidst the woods, or upon the tops of precipices, my few companions, for our numbers had been greatly diminished, journeyed in the night by a circuitous route into the Vadi Bedretto, and thence over the St Gothard by the path we had come, towards the valley of Stantz. We had there expected to find our former companions yet struggling for life, if not for victory. We entered the valley, there was no living creature to be found, there was a silence unbroken by any sound of human labour, the hoarse ravens fluttered above us, as if they thought we also came to spread their banquet. We could find no one to guide us, no one even to tell us of our misfortune. Our imaginations pictured sufficient. The villages were burnt, the cattle lay slaughtered on the field, it seemed as if death, with one sweep of his scythe, had cut off the life of all. Creeping along the sides of the mountains, we approached Stantz, we expected to find the destroyers there; but when we were in sight, there was no town appearing. We found but sixteen straggling houses yet standing, all the rest were burnt; these also bore the Frenchmen's mark, they were billetted. We looked at one another in silence. The birds of prey were not disturbed by our presence, they continued feeding on the dead. While walking amidst these ruins, I at last heard the sound of a voice, it was the cry of sorrow. A mother had found words to call on Heaven for strength to bear her individual grief, heedless of her country's death. I saw her amidst these ruins, her hands were tearing up the soil to give the last refuge her country could afford to her child, – a grave. She did not at first perceive me, when she did, her hand worked doubly quick, while, with her eyes fixed upon the corpse, her hurried lips uttered, 'Hold your hand, hold your hand for a moment, I shall soon be ready to follow.' I dug her son's grave, and left her striking the sod as if she repented of having resigned the body to the earth.

We assembled our few remaining companions, Olivieri and myself addressed them, we advised them to separate and seek singly a refuge in their homes. While yet speaking one of them brought before us a man, who seemed to have risen from the grave. His grey locks, thinly scattered on his head, were entangled, his eyes were sunk so deep within their sockets, that their lustre seemed the last glimmering of life before it sinks. He had sought death from the foes, and they, in mockery, had bade him live. They had fastened him to a table in the open air, with several days' provision within his reach, and had placed before his sight the corpses of his aged wife, his children, and grandchildren, all marked with the wanton infliction of their barbarous cruelty, not even excelled by the voracity of the vulture or beasts of prey. This wretched being told us that the Schweitzers had troops placed the whole length of the other side of the lake, to hinder the fugitives from this valley escaping. Upon this intelligence our men became dejected; the thoughts of dying ingloriously by the hands of their treacherous countrymen, weighed upon their mind. They spoke some time amongst themselves, and then begged of us not to desert them, assuring us that if we enabled them to reach the upper part of Schweitz unbroken, they then could disperse to their families without danger. We could not refuse them. We ordered them to go along the shore, and see if they could find any boats; they soon got together more than enough to convey us over. But they had been observed by an individual, who had immediately put off in his skiff, and crossed to the other side. This rendered greater caution necessary, as he would undoubtedly inform the enemy of our neighbourhood. We offered to take the old man with us; he refused; determined, not even in ruin, to desert those spots which had seen his birth, and infancy, and manhood, he returned to the bodies of his children, threw himself upon them, apparently resolved to breathe his last sigh in defending these mangled remnants from further insult: all that we could do was to lay a fresh stock of provisions by his side.

Hoping to find the enemy unprepared, upon some point or other, we immediately entered our boats. They however watched us, and at the moment of our landing, appeared before us in a body so numerous, that it seemed impossible to escape. We formed our men in the very water into a wedge, and taking a gun and bayonet ourselves, we led them against the foes, determined either to cut our way through, or to fall upon the field of battle. After repeated charges we at last succeeded, but our numbers were reduced to fifty, and several were wounded. We mustered upon the very spot where the liberty of Switzerland had been sworn to by the three patriots; it was the valley of Brunnen. Fortunately the Schweitzers did not pursue us. Travelling night and day, we at last gained the higher parts of the canton, whence my companions came. We separated, and it was a proud moment when they brought their wives and children to thank us as the preservers of their husbands and fathers. Olivieri and myself were now alone amongst the mountains, as a reward was set upon our heads, and as we here depended entirely upon the fidelity of many who had shunned our cause, we determined to depart and seek some other refuge. My friend knew not where to go, being ignorant, as he said, where his family was; he having left it privately, while travelling, to join the

Swiss. He however determined to go into the Austrian dominions, and there seek for information. We parted with mutual protestations of friendship, and a promise from him of letting me know by means of Berchtold, when he had found safety. We had had little communication; I therefore scarcely knew more than that Olivieri was not his family name, and that he was an Italian. I had often remarked his eyes to be fixed upon my scarf, but his delicacy preventing him from speaking upon a subject, he perceived I was not willing to converse on, was the cause of our parting without further communication. He was indeed the brother of that object, which had never deserted my thoughts, which, sleeping and waking, my lips had often called upon. No night passed, though dangers surrounded me on every side, without her image rising to cheer for a moment my wearied heart; but the dreams always ended unhappily. It seemed as if the fates were determined to embitter even those moments, in which I was engaged in a noble cause, thus to prepare my mind for those pangs which follow guilt. You may think I rest too much upon these instants of my life; but I dread to narrate my miseries; the recalling to memory anguish and grief racks my heart; but I have begun, and you shall hear the whole.

Knowing the country well, and being acquainted with every pass, I found no difficulty in reaching the neighbourhood of Beatenberg, and I was soon locked in my sister's arms. Berchtold and Julia's anxiety about me had been great, they had heard by report of my being in action, and had seen in the papers the immense reward offered for my person. Seeing me safe they could not contain their joy; but morning came, and I was obliged to depart into the mountains, for who could be trusted? Treachery and avarice had proved at last the master passions in many breasts, though they had at first worn the mask of the noblest virtues. Promising to be back at night, I flew to the Wengern Alp, and there again visited the spot, which now began to appear sacred to my mind. At night I returned to the pastor's cottage; I only found my sister there, he was gone to Thun. Leaving the house, Julia led me to our mother's grave, and again begged of me to be cautious, for constantly while I had been absent the same admonition had been given. It did not seem to her to relate to a personal danger; it was a vague threat, that seemed the more terrific, because it could not be decidedly represented to the mind. She then begged of me to relate the dangers I had undergone; I gave her a minute account of the whole.

Amongst other things which she mentioned to me, was the arrival of a stranger, who had taken up his abode at Interlaken, and who excited the wonder of his neighbours by the account his servants gave of his riches, and by their intimation of his having communication with an evil spirit. The source of his riches was unknown. Many were the tales related concerning him, and if but half were true, she said, he must certainly be possessed of a wonderful power. He was old and apparently wretched. His only daughter accompanied him, her beauty was as much the subject of conversation, as the riches of her father. These were the only rumours my sister had heard, for they had only arrived a few days before. I wish that I had never known more. I did not laugh at the idea of the supernatural part of the report. We were both too strongly imbued with the tales of our foster-mother not to attach some credit to them. My sister's dreams, in which our mother visited her, my own which always portended misfortune, had enforced upon our minds the belief of the interference of superior beings.

For several nights I returned, but Berchtold was yet, as we imagined, at Thun. My sister and myself left entirely to ourselves, again talked over the feats of Olivieri, and she often asked me to repeat them, seeming with pleasure to rest upon every circumstance regarding him. Foolishly, I also took a pleasure in relating them, for though we had been constantly rivals, there was a frankness, a heedless daring about him, that excited admiration, at the same time, that the warmth of his expressions called forth a reciprocal feeling of love. I knew not then how to discover the sting protruding from the rich scales of the snake. We conversed upon our mother, and my inquiries were numerous about her person, her voice. I cannot explain it, but I wished even from Julia's dreams to aid the representation I had formed from her portrait of a being, who seemed even after life, to feel an interest in my fate. In the locket, there was a melancholy look about her dark blue eyes, that was rendered heavenly, by the soft smile playing upon her open lip. I had gazed upon it so often, that I had her image before me, even when far from home, but it was only distinct in the face, which appeared to be gazing on Heaven, with the consciousness of having obtained a prayer for me. Since my sister's dreams, it seemed as if I knew a mother's care, and I often sighed, to think, that though thus thoughtful of me even in Heaven, she did not think me worthy of enjoying her smile.

One morning I left my sister, and retired to the wild borders of the Brientz lake. The sun rose, and with its glittering ray painted on the water, the reflected images of the wild rocks upon the other side. There is a point which juts into the lake, and on it are the ruins of an old church; I did not feel inclined to exert myself to reach a more distant spot, but I laid myself down by an arching gateway, round which the ivy clustered, as if by its tenacious grasp, it would hold together the monuments of another age, upon which the breath of time was acting with a destructive power, unheeded by man. I seemed to feel this breath of time acting upon me as upon these works of man, the wild joys of youth seemed sunk into the melancholy uniform feeling attendant upon age, when all joy is passed, all hope extinguished by the consciousness of the presence of death. I gazed upon the mists as they rolled slowly along the hills, veiling successively the various beauties of the banks, and watched the cloud's shadow, depriving the lake of its glittering sheen. I rested upon their passing powers, but did not notice, that the glow of the bright sun invariably returned upon the spots, before darkened by a shadow. The peasants' barge, and the light skiff, passed rapidly before me, but unheeded they passed in silence, for it appeared, as if, even they sympathised in my grief. It was mid-day, I rose to shelter myself from the sun's ray, and sought that side of the point towards Interlaken. There was a small light skiff upon the water, and in it was a female figure. It was at some distance, it gradually approached; my heart fluttered, my breathing became difficult, my eyes were fixed upon a form I seemed to recognise. Her face was not lit up, as I had seen it, by all the fire of her indignant eye; carried along by her small latin sail, she approached. Her eye was gazing upon the rippling wave, cut by her prow, it seemed as if joy did not dwell there, her eye-lash veiled its splendour, while her black locks curling on the breeze, floated playfully around. Her breast at times would heave as if the sorrow in her bosom was loath to grieve her, but she seemed unwilling it should go, for she rested upon it. I stood intently gazing, it seemed as if my least motion would have at once destroyed an illusion. The current brought her heedless close to the shore, and the boat struck the bank; she looked around and saw me. It was plain she recognised me, for her eyes fixed upon her scarf. To paint to you, the varying expressions of that eye, and the varied colour of that cheek, is impossible. With slow hesitating steps she approached, our eyes did not dare to meet, and I stood by her for some moments in silence; at last with a trembling voice, she asked me if my name were not Ernestus Berchtold? 'If you own that name, fly instantly, you have been betrayed, and the blood-suckers are already, at Interlaken upon their way to Berchtold, do not go there to-night.' I could hardly acknowledge my name, I was so moved by her voice; she offered to convey me to the other side of the lake, if I thought myself safer there. Unconscious of what I was doing, I entered her boat, and taking the oars, tried by violent exertions to rouse myself; we did not speak; when upon the other side, I landed. Farewell fell from her lips, and it seemed as if the echoes mocking me, repeated farewell. I stood still, watching her as entering the current of the Aar, she was gradually borne down towards Interlaken; even when she had passed the bridge, I gazed, and seemed to see a white speck, that I imagined was her.

I turned away, and towards evening found myself upon the same spot on which I had first seen her. Again, she had appeared. At first, she had guided me into the path of honour, this day she ensured my safety. Was she then a vision? I asked myself. Was it my guardian angel, who invested that form? I did not think of pursuing my route to any place of greater safety, it seemed as if this spot where my protector had appeared, was secure, I laid me down beneath the rock, that had witnessed her presence, and offering up a prayer to Heaven, I gave way to all the visions my imagination offered. She had recognised me, she knew my name, my rank, and still felt an interest in my safety. If you have ever known, what it is to be in love, you may judge what my feelings were, if not, my words are useless, I hardly slept the whole night.

Next day I roamed restless over the Alpine heights around, I did not heed the horrors or the beauties of these solitudes. The cataract fell by my side, and yet I heard it not, wherever the valley wound, thither I followed; but as evening threw its stillness over nature, ere the light canopy of Heaven was darkened, I found myself upon the covered bridge of Interlaken, I had forgotten my danger. The open spaces between the beams supporting the roof, enabled me to see the different houses which skirt the river's side. Mine eyes however gazed upon that one, in which I had heard, the new inhabitants of this neighbourhood had taken up their abode. I had imagined my unknown was the beautiful daughter I had heard of from my sister; and I had not long been upon my station, when I saw her come forth, supporting upon her arm the feeble steps of the old man I had seen with her upon the Wengern Alp. Her eyes,

fixed upon his languid face, seemed anxiously to be watching the
features of her invalid father. There was a bush not far from the
door beneath the wide-spreading canopy of a lofty elm; she placed
him there, and I saw reflected on her face, the smile which beamed
upon the old man's, as he gazed upon the setting sun. I watched
her slightest action, her every glance, it seemed as if her words
soothed the pains of sickness, and lightened the languor attendant
upon an invalid's inactivity. Oh, if that smile had fallen upon
myself, as it then fell upon her father, if I had only felt its cheering
influence without that burning passion it has excited in this breast;
but I must not anticipate my narration. The sun sunk behind the
mountains, she carefully shielded her sire from the damp. I
watched her retiring steps, heard the door close after her, and at
last turned away.

Intending to depart again to some retired spot, I was advancing,
when I perceived that there was some one at the end of the bridge
apparently watching me, and then retiring as if to look up the road.
Alarmed, I seized my hunting knife and approached him: seeing
me advance, he came towards me, it was the servant of Berchtold.
He had seen me from a neighbouring height, and anxious, as he
said, for my safety, had immediately followed me, and finding me
on the bridge, had several times spoken to me without my paying
the least attention; perceiving at last how I was engaged in
contemplating the beautiful object before me, he had contented
himself with guarding the entrance to the bridge. I inquired about
the French soldiers, he turned pale, but at that moment I hardly
noticed it; he told me that they had been watching Berchtold's
house during the whole of the night, apparently aware of my being
in the habit of going there every evening. He informed me that
there were only two remaining, whom he had supplied so
abundantly with wine, that if I chose to venture towards the
cottage, he would inform Berchtold and my sister where they could
meet me, while he engaged the attention of my pursuers. How
easily I was deceived; I have since known the value of men's
professions; then I was young and confident in virtue. Berchtold
and my sister met me, but there were other soldiers in the
neighbourhood; those the servant led to a pass by which I must
descend on my return. It was but another instance of that venal
boasted honour which so much stains the Swiss patriotic history.

In the mean time I learnt from Berchtold that he had walked to
Berne, hoping to cause my sentence of outlawry to be cancelled;

that the French employers had lulled him with hope until he had been rash enough to acknowledge my being in this neighbour-hood; when they would listen to him no longer, but sent the soldiers I have mentioned. Even Ochs, who had formerly been his school-fellow, had laughed when he reproached him for so vile a breach of confidence. I spoke with my sister apart, and informed her of my discovery, she was surprised, and seemed downcast; but Berchtold, who had gone to listen, and reported all silent, joining us, we could not proceed in our conversation. I embraced them, and had begun to descend the steep, when I heard myself challenged; having my gun with me, I fired, and the challenger fell; but one leapt upon my back, it was my own servant, and I was surrounded. I struck upon every side, but it was in vain: determined, however, to be revenged, I threw myself upon the ground with the traitor; as we turned, I succeeded in getting him undermost, and plunged my hunting-knife up to the hilt in his chest. He groaned and died. I surrendered.

I was hurried to Interlaken, put into a boat, and before the dawn of day, was locked in the prisons of Thun. I expected to be immediately taken out and shot. I was not, however, disturbed till night, when I was awakened from a sound sleep, and, guarded by a company of soldiers, was ordered to be conveyed to the castle of Chillon, upon the lake of Geneva. Entering into conversation with the soldier who marched by my side, I heard from him that Berchtold and my sister had in vain applied for admission to my dungeon, upon hearing of my misfortune; that the reason I was removed at this late hour arose from the magistrate's fearing a rescue by the people, who once or twice in the day had seemed, by their tumultuous meeting, inclined to force the prison of him whom they called their only remaining patriot. From him I first learnt that my name was in every mouth; that there were romantic tales printed about me, and spread over all the country in spite of the police which endeavoured to suppress them. I did not feel any vain exultation at this; I was too near death; but I certainly experienced some satisfaction in the thought, that for Louisa, – that – that was her name. For years locked up within my breast, it has not passed my lips. I have not dared to utter that name, not even whisper it to my own ear; but it has been deeply engraven here. It is now a spell that conjures up horrid thoughts; once it did not.

But I must command myself. I had not visited this part of Switzerland yet, though beautiful, and perhaps richer than any I had seen, it passed unobserved before my eyes. The simple villagers, hearing my name, came round the inns at which we stopped, and looked upon me in silence. Mothers brought their children to me to kiss, as if my kiss could call down a blessing, or inspire heroism. I crossed the Dent de Jamanu, and soon saw the castle once the prison of Bonniva, now destined to be my own.

The draw-bridge was up, and the sentinels were parading as if they esteemed the castle of importance. Upon my name being mentioned the bridge was lowered, and I soon heard the clash of the chains employed in raising it after me. It seemed to be accompanied by a voice that bade hope to leave me. The rude stare of the soldiers, and the bustling scene of the officers, running to and fro, did not tend to relieve the sorrow that weighed upon me. I had dared danger in the chase upon the Alps; death in battle; yet here the thoughts of leaving all, oppressed me. I did not think of the pain of parting with existence; but Berchtold, my sister, the vision of the Wengern Alp, all seemed to press upon my imagination with eyes, that, by their look, seemed to denote a breaking heart. My head fell upon my breast, while, with folded arms, I walked along the vaulted passage. I was searched, all was taken from me, my knife, the little money I had. The rude jailor already had his hand upon the scarf, retaining it with a firm grasp, I looked at him, and seeing his daughter close by his side, 'If that child,' I said, 'should be far – far from thee, and thou couldst not hope to see her but in Heaven, couldst thou part with the only relic of her memory?' He looked upon his child, and let go his hold.

I was taken into a room where several officers were deliberating concerning me. I had stood before them some time, when one asked me my name. 'Ernestus Berchtold' was my answer. 'It is the traitor;' fell from the lips of one. I looked upon him; he could not stand my glance, but sunk into silence. They were considering whether they should lead me to instant execution, or whether I should be confined till the pleasure of the government at Berne should be known, as it was thought that they might wish to make a more public exhibition of the punishment of him they so gratuitously called a traitor. I was respited by one voice, and was instantly ordered to my dungeon.

To descend into the prison, which is below the level of the water, it is necessary to go down a narrow circular staircase. While descending it, we were stopped by that child upon whom I had rested my appeal to the jailor; to pass her we were obliged to go singly; when I came close to her, I felt something pressed into my hand, while at the same time she made a sign with her finger for silence. I put her present into my breast and followed her father, who was before me, while the others were at my back. I entered a long vault, its floor was the solid rock, and its high roof was supported by seven thick massy pillars. The waves of the lake dashed sullenly against the walls above my head, and the feeble light that pierced the high windows only showed me the damp black sides of this prison. There were the steps of a prisoner marked during a long imprisonment upon the very rock; I still heard the noise of bolts, but did not heed it, till I arrived at a narrow cell, partitioned off from the greater dungeon, which I had not perceived in the general obscurity. Into this narrow space I was forced to enter. It was not sufficiently long for me to lie down at full length, and the barred grating, which, far above my reach, was intended in mockery to represent a window, received no reflected light from the dark floor of Bonniva's prison. I heard the doors fastened one after another.

Beneath the slowly sounding wave I was cut off from humanity; the monotonous dashing against the castle's base alone broke the dread silence; it seemed like the loud note of the moments in nature's last hour. My spirits fled, and I leant against the stones to which I was chained, with hands clasped, and my eyes painfully straining, as if they sought at least to see the real horrors of my dwelling. Fatigued by my long journey over the steep Jamanu, I sought to sit and sleep, but the damp floor for a long time kept my racking mind awake to all the torments of thought, while it hoped for a momentary oblivion of woe.

At last I sunk into repose, and it was not until late the next morning that I awoke, but I awoke refreshed; I had seen the constant attendant upon my dreams, and I soon lost myself in thought upon her various appearances. The waves above me seemed silenced to a calm, and the sun's powerful meridian ray reflected upon the various sides of the greater vault, penetrated, though in a feeble glimmer, my solitary cell. Gradually stealing upon my ear, I heard a distant voice, which in melancholy notes seemed to sympathise with my sorrows. I listened; it approached; the measured strokes of an oar interrupted the heavenly strain; suddenly breaking into livelier notes it sung of hope; the voice was, they were Italian words, it was my vision's voice. It gradually sunk away into indistinct sounds. I seemed another being, hope breathed upon my heart, and Louisa wore the semblance of that enchanter; oh that I had died, that she had left me to myself to die! it was not the will of Heaven. Again I heard the splashing sound of the oar, and again that voice sounded on my ear; it was no longer the thrilling notes of an air, but in slow recitative it bade me hope, it told me that a boat should be stationed at two or three stone throws' distance from the castle, ready at all times to receive me if I could manage to get out, and that in the mean time endeavours were making at Berne, to gain a repeal of the sentence passed upon me. Again the song of hope sounded in my cell, losing itself gradually in the distance, it at last left me with nothing human within hearing.

I now remembered the child's present; feeling in my breast, it proved to be a file and a knife; I instantly began to work at the wall, dividing me from the great dungeon; while thus busily employed I heard the bolts of the vault withdrawn; my jailor entered, he spoke not, but threw me my pittance of bread, and laid down my pitcher of water. Hardly was he gone, when I resumed my work, the dampness of my cell aided me. The mortar was soft, and the wall built of small stones; when therefore I had scraped the mortar away from the crevices, I did not find any difficulty in forcing them out. One by one I tore away many, and I had already almost pierced the wall, when, fearful of penetrating entirely through, lest the jailor might next day detect my attempt, I managed to replace most of the rubbish in its situation, and to push the rest into a corner. I now began with my file to cut the chain that surrounded my waist. The jailor came next morning, and told me, that at the dawn of the ensuing day I was to be conveyed to Berne. This gave me additional strength, the hopes of liberty, of seeing Louisa, spurred me on, and in a few moments I was free from my chains. With what impatience I waited for the night. It came; I forced a passage through the wall, and I found myself in the great vault without a manacle. The moon's ray seemed with a smile to seek the ground on which I trod, for its cold beams pierced the grated apertures above, and illumined some dreary spots. I was not yet free, the window was high above my reach; but I did not despair, taking the whole length of the dungeon to give me power, I leapt, and caught with my hands at one of the bars. I raised myself, and resting my knee upon the shelving sill, I immediately began to employ my file, and the rusty bars soon gave way to my arm.

I paused a moment, the cool fresh air of the night, no longer poisoned by the noxious vapours of the subterranean dungeon, played amidst my hair; I seemed to inhale life. The moon's ray, decked with one glittering streak of light the whole breadth of the wide lake; it seemed the path of hope. Not far distant was a barge; in three or four hours my murderers would be at my prison door. The ground was covered with snow even to the water's edge; I leapt into the lake, and being a good swimmer I reached the boat numbed by the cold, I had hardly the strength to raise myself into it. There was no one to be found; there were some coarse provisions, a peasant's habit, and a letter; it had no direction, 'If safe,' it said, 'proceed to Milan, you will hear of us there. Your sister is well, Berchtold ill, but do not go to him, he knows we are attempting to save you, and he shall immediately be informed of your escape. The daughter of Olivieri's father.' It was now that I learnt that Olivieri was the brother of Louisa Doni. It was now explained why he so attentively examined my scarf.

I could not resolve on leaving Switzerland without seeing Berchtold, there was a western breeze, I hoisted the latin sail, and in a few minutes I was free from immediate danger, and on my way towards Beatenberg. It was necessary that I should keep amongst the mountains, and I only dared approach the most solitary chalets. They were generally deserted, and it was with difficulty that I procured sufficient to support nature during the three days I was upon my way. Arriving at Œschi, I took a boat from the side of the lake, and crossing, was soon at the foot of the steep, on which stands Beatenberg. The stillness of the night was broken by the sound of voices chaunting, which, stealing down the mountain, sunk upon the wave. Alarmed I knew not why, I rushed up the path; before the church porch, around the great cross that stood upon the green sward, knelt Berchtold's parishioners arrayed in white. Though the red glare of the pine torch fell upon their faces, it did not allow me to distinguish any one. Breathless I stood incapable of motion. The chaunt ended, the minister of peace arose, it was not Berchtold; 'He's dead,' I cried, and rushed forward; alarmed, the peasants rose, they recognised me and were silent; my sister took my hand and bade me pray for him who had died. Incapable of any longer bearing the anxiety attendant upon my fate, I knew not what I did, I knelt, I heard the solemn chaunt sing Berchtold's requiem, and could not join it. The earth closed over him, and the minister led me to my former home.

I was inconsolable, they talked to me of ensuring my safety; I was deaf to their remonstrances, and only listened to grief; my sister was left alone with me. She wept with me, and ere it was dawn, had persuaded me to depart. She told me that Louisa had been with her, had made her promise to join her, in case of Berchtold's death, so that I need not be under any anxiety on her account. She informed me that Louisa had walked with her over my haunts, had inquired after every minutes' circumstance about me. My sister said, she thought she loved me. I could listen to no more, embracing her, I issued forth, visited my mother's and Berchtold's grave, and soon lost sight of Beatenberg.

Louisa loved me! it was too true, if that love had fallen upon any one else it would have proved a blessing. On me; you see my withered lineaments, my sunken eye, my feeble step, think you, a common curse could thus blast the bloom of life? Berchtold was but the first victim to my love. My love has left me, a scattered pine amidst this desolate scene, but first it has destroyed all who were bound to me, my love has proved, but I must preserve my strength, – I have horrors to relate, – going through the Simplon, then a road only passable by mules or on foot, I soon arrived at Milan.

I was in safety, the city was in possession of the Austrians. I had hardly rested at the inn, at which I took up my abode and was making inquiries, in hopes of discovering the Donis, when Olivieri entered. We flew into one another's arms, he answered none of my inquiries, but leading me to his carriage, we arrived through the Corso at a palace close to the gates. We got out, I knew not whither he was leading me, the doors of the saloon were thrown open, and I found myself in the presence of his father, his sister. The old man advanced, and taking my hand, which hung by my side, he thanked me for having twice saved the life of his son. I knew not what to say; conscious I owed my life to Louisa's interference, I could not find words to thank her. The father at last led me towards his daughter, and bade her attempt to thank me. Her eyes turned upon me, suffused with blushes she had some words upon her lips, when I forced myself to stop her. 'Do not mock me, what do I owe to you? my life is nothing, when compared to that thirst of honour, you inspired in my breast.' Again, she blushed and was silent. At that moment, another carriage arrived, it was my sister attended by two faithful domestics of my friend; locked in my arms, she was at last taken thence to be clasped in those of my preserver.

After taking some refreshment, the father led me into another room, he there told me that Berchtold's last request was, that he should supply his place, and take my sister and myself to him, as his children. As he spoke, he showed me at the same time, the last lines which my foster-father had written a few moments before he died. They contained our history as far as he was acquainted with it; in them he bade me trust always in God, and recommended me to bow under that dispensation, which had made me an outcast on my native soil, and not to murmur at the will of him, who had deprived me of the feeble support a Swiss pastor could afford against the pressure of events, since he had raised me up a protector, so much more powerful in the father of him whose life I had saved. Doni took me by the hand, and perceiving the tear trembling in my eye, he begged of me to let him supply the place of Berchtold. He called me son; Louisa's father could not call me so in vain, I fell upon his neck, but could not speak.

Part Second

You have visited our alpine scenes and have undoubtedly been witness to the approach of one of those dreadful visitations of angry nature, which sometimes occur in the pent-up valleys. The black speck gathers upon the mountain's brow; amidst the silence and dead stillness of the air, it seems as if all were resting, in hopes of gaining strength to resist the desolating fury of the powers let loose against them. Only the lowing of the cattle, which, with its hollow lengthened sound, seems to give unheeded notice of the dread storm's approach, echoes upon the air, awed by the very stillness. Yet the sun shines brilliantly on the scene, doubled in the unrippled surface of the lake that seems proudly to bear the beauteous image, as if it were conscious how soon that smiling scene would be changed. – So passed the years, in which day succeeded day in unperceived succession, in which I lived under the same roof, partook innocently of the same joys and sorrows as Louisa. There was yet a weight upon my heart I could not explain; my dreams always terminated unhappily, and sleep, that refuge common to all misery, was to me like the waking hours of others. Immediately after our arrival, my sister was visited with a threatening appeal from our mother, who bade her depart with me once more to our native wilds, and never return. We could not understand the decrees of fate, lulled by the peace and apparent happiness around us, we were unconscious of what was in future, – we remained, and I am what you see – a spectre amongst the living.

Encouraged by Louisa, I again returned to my studies. All the morning engaged in the library of my benefactor, I followed them under his direction, chiefly reading the modern poets and historians, with whom I had little acquaintance. Louisa would often come, and, sitting by my side, read the same passages, and discuss the merits of a particular image, often directing my taste, and pointing out many beauties I had not before perceived, even in my favourite authors. You see those volumes; they are those we read together; they now form my whole library, but you cannot know the pleasure there is contained in a single one of those pages. I read them, and every word again sounds upon my ear, as if she spoke it. I turn round and am undeceived, Louisa is not by my side, though her voice seems speaking as when we were innocent.

In the evening we assembled in the saloon of the palace. Doni was distinguished from his countrymen by a state of affluence, which was apparently boundless, but which was the more extraordinary in this respect, that it did not excite the envy of his neighbours. His riches indeed seemed less for his own use than for that of his friends. He was of a noble family, but being the offspring of a younger branch, he had been early inured to hardships. Disdaining the mean idle life he was obliged to lead, in subservience to the will of a proud relation, he had left Milan at an early age, and had travelled into the East. He never, however, spoke of his journey, and always seemed anxious to direct the conversation into another channel, whenever it turned upon subjects in any manner connected with it. He had returned rich, no one knew whence; but there were whisperings abroad, that he had not gained his riches by commerce; though no one could trace where his riches lay; yet as his gold was poured forth with so liberal a hand, his wealth was deemed almost infinite. He had been strikingly handsome, and was extremely intelligent; but grief had weighed down his energies, and sorrow had broken his faculties. After his return he had married. Beauty was the mere casket, the riches were within; his wife was described as having possessed a mind, that without laying aside all that appealing delicacy and weakness, which binds woman to man; had all those powers and accomplishments, which unfortunately in her sex have generally been the panders to vice; but which, with her, were the handmaids to virtue. Her presence was commanding, but her voice was persuasive; its tones struck the heart and produced those emotions, which all remember, none can express, the feeling, as if we had been always virtuous, and were worthy of listening to the voice of a being superior to ourselves. The poor followed her steps, not with their usual boisterous cry for charity, but in silence; they seemed to watch the glance of her eye, as if the sympathy which shone there, had made them even forget their ragged miseries. Louisa was her counterpart, when I heard any one describing what her mother had been, it seemed that I could read the whole upon her daughter's face, and methought I could often perceive the speaker reading on the same page. Doni had loved her; nay more, had adored her, but she had married him by the persuasion of her parents, while her heart was engaged to another far away; he had returned, they saw one another, and fled together; Doni pursued them, fired at the carriage which was escaping and blood fell upon the road; – they did not stop. Doni then entirely lost all command of himself; he fell in the road, calling for mercy and relief from that curse, which had already begun to blast him. He had never recovered the shock; had retired from all those gaieties in which he had been once engaged, and devoted himself to the education of his children. For their sake he had, however, again entered into society, but in a very different style from his former magnificence. These are the circumstances which I heard of his history, from those friends with whom I spoke in the course of the two first years of my stay at Milan; besides this, I also found the reports of his supernatural powers to be believed and whenever I inquired concerning them, the speaker always looked round the room, before he ventured to speak, and would then only answer in whispers.

I have mentioned our evening assembly in the saloon of the palace; thither all distinguished by rank or science came – all visitors were alike welcome. There, no ceremony, which is but the vain-pointing of selfishness to its sacrifices, incommoded those, who, invited by the society they found there, chose to take a chair in this circle. Louisa's father always held the reins of conversation in his own hands, and instead of letting it fall upon the common place subjects of fashion, he turned the minds of his company to disquisitions that gave to each an opportunity of showing his information or judgement. At times, the existence and powers of the Deity were canvassed, – at times, the reality of beings intermediate between God and man; their qualities, and the facts related concerning them, came under consideration. Other evenings heard discussions upon the nature of virtue, whether it really were definite and felt, as is beauty, in every breast, or whether it were not merely an object of policy and self-convenience. The father and son generally took opposite sides, and under one or the other, each individual of the company enlisted himself, accordingly as it happened that he were either in a humour to be pleased with the general dispensation of providence throughout the day to himself, or was smarting under what he conceived to be an undeserved infliction of the evil spirit.

Olivieri made it a point to bewilder every one. He was a little older than myself; his head, though not perfect, had much beauty; a fine forehead, black hair, a dark, though small eye, united to a Grecian contour, formed, if not a pleasing, a striking physiognomy.

I soon found that he had read much. His body also had been exercised; though not graceful, he was active, and hardly any excelled him in a certain quickness of adaptation, both of mind and body, to any thing required. His opinions were paradoxical and singular. In religion he outwardly professed Catholicism, and strongly opposed those scribbling philosophers, who by sarcasm, attempt to overturn the religion of ages, though at the same time he allowed the absurdity and falsehood of the prevailing doctrines. This did not appear to arise from a spirit of opposition, but, if the motives he gave were true, from a chain of thought that did honour to his heart, not head. He asserted that Catholicism was the only religion affording to the poor and to the sick of heart, a balm for their evils. Calvinism, deism and atheism, were by him called the professions of the northern nations, cold as their native rocks. Professions to which enthusiasm, and the feeling of a certain refuge, so heart-soothing in Catholicism, were unknown. He maintained that it was not for individuals, who had the advantage of education and imagination, to shelter them from the over-whelming force of mental miseries, and unlooked for misfortunes, to attempt under a real, though vain pretence of the love of truth, to deprive the poor and uneducated millions forming the mass of mankind, of the consolation always offered by this religion, which instead of shunning the poor, gladly seeks their miserable hovel, in the hope of administering present comfort and future hope. Indeed he was inconsistent in his principles. He had not mingled much in general life, but while at Padua, where he had been sent to study, he had sought the acquaintance of all. From the knowledge of man he had there acquired, whether it were that he had constantly met with mean and weak companions, or that conscious of his own bad qualities, he had thence estimated the value of man's professions, he always seemed to view the human character in a darker hue than was warranted by truth, and to have formed his mind into a general contempt for mankind as a mass, and a determination, if ever an occasion offered, of rising at their expence, considering them but as tools to work with. His manners were at first always engaging, and rather pleasing, but this seemed irksome to him, and he gave way to an imperious, assuming air in conversation, which soon disgusted his friends. His ideas of a life after death seemed strangely childish, he did not believe in an immortality, yet he had so strong a love of fame, that there was no reputation he did not covet. He sometimes formed visions of a throne raised upon the blood of his countrymen spilt in civil war; at times, of the fame of a benefactor to debtors and galley slaves. He sought at the same time for the applause of the philosopher and the drunkard, the divine, and the libertine. Things, of which, even at the moment of action he was ashamed, were often done by him in the view of proving himself capable of excelling even in vice. It was hard to say, whether he owed a certain frankness and easiness of attachment, to his weakness, or to seeds sown in his breast by nature. But whether it were from his incapability of constancy acting up to his system, or to the overpowering force of nature, it was strange to hear him express himself a follower of a doctrine that has proved the leech of human blood, and at the same time refuse to tread upon a worm. The evil was, his riches induced the young to pander for him, the old to flatter him, on account of his specious talents and handsome appearance. He was a student, a gambler, and a libertine.

This man became my companion, his father often pointed me out to him, as the model for his conduct, and when he had to reproach him for the losses at the Ridotto, or when Olivieri sought an excuse in the plea of youth, for the ruin his libertinism had brought on many families, he would speak of me as an example of strength, resisting all the temptations of vice. I was a reed when the storm came, Olivieri had watched me at the meetings in the saloon, I was generally a mere listener, but my curiosity was alive, though silent; my mind had an insatiable thirst for knowledge. I was a Catholic, Berchtold had educated me in doctrines, without teaching me the foundation upon which they were built; he thought it impiety to question them. The conversation to which I was now present, seemed to rest upon the entire conviction, that all I believed was false. Yet this was not satisfactory. I heard arguments adduced in support of one assertion which seemed irresistible; but what was my surprise, on another evening to hear the same person adduce more than plausibilities in favour of the contrary hypothesis. I at last was bewildered, I was unwilling to believe the human mind incapable of truth, the more I examined, the more difficulty I found in the attainment of it. I heard the deist and the atheist contend; following but one of the chains of argument, I was convinced; looking at them together, I saw the lustre of truth equally on both; I knew not which to choose. I was a sceptic in fact, not in name. Night after night upon my sleepless couch, I called upon the God, whose existence I doubted, to visit me, as if God heeded the belief of an individual, as if the happiness of an infinite being like him depended on a man's faith in his existence. Olivieri perceived the state of my mind, I asked his assistance, he laughed at my attempt at knowledge, and bewildered me still more; I was restless, and seemed at length to be deprived of all motive for action. No superior being to smile upon our efforts, to whom we may show our gratitude, and whose approbation we may obtain; no virtue, but artificial trammels set up under its name, to lure the unwary into the toils of the wittiest knave. I wished I had never left those mountains, amidst which, I had thought, I felt the breath of a superior being, though he was clothed by my imagination in terrors. Nothing above man, and that man the sport of chance, of his own caprice. Yet within my breast it seemed as if aspirings dwelt which seemed to have been born with me. Were they but a mockery? I grew melancholy, whole days confined to my room, I meditated till my brain became a wilderness of various thoughts so entangled I knew not how to extricate myself.

My sister, fearing I was ill, would often sit by me, would bring Louisa, and they would together listen to my doubts. Julia seemed to be as much affected by them as myself, she listened with avidity, and echoed my own ideas. Not so Louisa, she talked of revelation, of a beneficent Deity, who had for a while left man in ignorance, to prove to him his own weakness, but had at last revealed himself, and announced a better state. While she spoke, she seemed like the first vision of the Wengern Alp destined again to save me, and set me free from these bewilderings, the first step towards vice. She soothed my mind, her lips quelled doubt into the peaceful certainty attendant upon Christianity. I no more paid any attention to the conversation of the evening, but set myself down by Louisa, and listened to her, while she was engaged in some work, which, though it employs the hands, leaves the mind at liberty. I sat by her, asking for some errand, some office, in doing which I might do her bidding; she was evidently gratified by my attentions, she would blush at my approach and smile; she would make room for me by her side. Oftentimes I gazed in silence upon her, and often our eyes met. Her breath at moments played upon my cheek, and sometimes her hand by accident touched mine. She would bid me read poetry to her, and often love was the subject of the poet's lay; my voice trembled, I dared not look upon her, for fear she should perceive the emotion upon my face. I loved her, but it was not a common love. I did not rest upon the hope of gaining her, she appeared a being superior to myself, of whom I was unworthy, yet it seemed, as if her smile were necessary to induce me to exert myself, and was a reward sufficient for the greatest deeds. She would sing to me, she would walk with me in the garden; but you must imagine, I cannot paint the charm, the magic, in her conversation. I have not described her person, for I could not, her mind was more heavenly than her eye, its expressions more delicately varying than the bloom on her cheek; there was meekness attendant upon power, softness upon strength.

If she had not left me for a moment, I might have been spared much guilt; but the sickness of a near relation was a call she could not resist. I had often followed her, when masked, she attended upon the sick in the hospitals. It is an Italian custom: often have I, disguised in the covering gown of the Misericordia, stood by her, whom it was impossible not to recognise. The dying called for her, though they knew her not; they soon distinguished her powerful tones which pierced through the bond of grief around the most withered heart, and poured upon it those precious consolations afforded by her religion. Her manner, her voice, her gestures, seemed at such moments to be those of a being who was conscious of the truth of what it announced; not from the testimony of man, but from having witnessed the presence of the very Deity. The loud groan, the stifled sigh, were silenced in her presence; pain seemed to have no power; conscience no sting. She left me to visit her relation.

For some days I felt lost; I knew not to whom to apply; my sister seemed always occupied; she spoke with me; but I was sorry to find she had imbibed those doctrines so easily eradicated, as I thought, from my own mind. I observed Olivieri paid her particular attention, and often conversed with her. He at last perceived how restless I was; he seized the opportunity, determined to gain an object, which I did not think him capable of attempting. During my stay at Milan, I had hardly ever been out in the evening, for, as it is not customary for unmarried females to go into society, I should have lost the pleasure of sitting by Louisa. Now I had no inducement to remain at home. Olivieri persuaded me to accompany him to the theatre of La Scala. I was induced by the splendour of the scenery, the beautiful dancers, the exquisite singing, to return. I was led into the boxes of our friends, and behind the scenes. I found my companion was every where well received. The dancers and actresses crowded around him: their conversation was lively and various. Gradually, the freedom in their discourse, which had at first disgusted me, grew indifferent; then pleasing by the wit sometimes shown even upon such subjects. One of these women, to whom Olivieri introduced me, was a mistress in her art, and well understood the artifices by which the young and unwary are misled: she was beautiful, and though her eye was never free from a certain look of confidence, the characteristic of this class, she could soften its expression, and cause it, in the presence of him she intended to inveigle, to send forth such glances as it was impossible to resist. By Olivieri's desire she attached herself to me, and I gradually took pleasure in her company; I saw her neglect the attentions of the first nobles in Milan to gain mine; in the midst of the rapturous applause of the whole theatre, she would turn her eye upon me to see if I approved; she seemed to sacrifice herself for me. When the opera was over, she would take my arm and lead me to the saloon of the theatre, where all were engaged in gambling. Sitting at a window, she drew me into conversation, gradually she approached the table; we at first stood merely as spectators; at last she tempted me to try my fortune: I consented, laid down my stake, it was soon increased to an enormous amount, for I was successful: I threw it into her lap, and we parted. For several nights I was equally fortunate; but at length I lost. I was so profusely supplied with money by the kind friend who called me son, that I did not at first heed my losses. I had given all I gained to the syren, who still urged me on: I lost every franc I had. She then supplied me; I was ashamed to take it of her, though it was what I myself had gained; but I hoped my luck would change; I lost the whole. She then began to exert her more baneful powers, she led me from folly to vice, in search of what she assured me was an antidote to memory; I joined the libertine and the desperate. I was ashamed of letting Doni know that he, whom he had pointed out as a model of virtue to his son, had sunk into the lowest debauchery. Louisa's image often – often was before me; but how dare I name her in conjunction with my vices. She had thrice been a ministering angel, guiding my steps, but then I was innocent. I dared not now rest upon the thought; and often I threw myself deeper into the sinks of vice, in hopes that such reflections would not pursue me thither

The syren, instigated by Olivieri, led me into every excess; while he plied me again with insinuations against religion, and sneers upon my credulous conscience that pictured a future state. I was now glad to seek refuge in unbelief; and I strove to lose myself in those thoughts which I had before fled, and from which I had been saved by my protecting angel. He also excited me to gamble, lent me money himself when I had none, and gathered round me every incentive to vice. He had been mortified at his father's holding me up as a pattern of strength against temptation; he was revenged, he exposed my weakness. I had hardly resisted the first approaches of vice, and had, in a short time, sunk below the lowest frequenters of its haunts.

One night I was desperate, every thing of value that I had was gone. Olivieri himself had been unsuccessful; and I knew not where to seek for the money I wanted to satisfy my creditors. I rushed out from the house, and found myself in the Piazza del Duomo. My brain was hot, my hair dishevelled; I rushed along, not knowing what I was about. I knew not where to apply. To destroy at once Doni's opinion of my virtue by telling him my situation, seemed worse than my present feeling. I stood still holding my head with my hand; I lifted my eyes from the ground on which they had been fixed. It was night, there was no light save from the glimmering stars and the newly risen moon, upon the dark canopy of Heaven. The white façade of the Duomo raised its huge mass in contrast with the night; shining even upon its dark veil, it seemed to awe the mind by its indistinct mass, which, weighing on the earth, forced itself upon the eye when all else was lost in the shading darkness. All was still and sunk to rest; I alone seemed waking midst sleep; in anguish, midst repose. I stood, I know not why, for some time gazing upon the marble statues and forms which gained a certain charm from the moon's silvering light. The mats, spread like a curtain before the doors, being raised by the dying breeze, struck with a measured impulse the wall: unconsciously I entered. Save where the light of the moon fell upon the heavy columns, vesting them with the faint hues of the coloured glass that adorned the windows, it was all darkness that seemed sensible to the touch. I walked towards the high altar. There is a subterranean chapel dedicated to St Borromeo, which receives its light through the flooring of the dome. The silver lamps, hung over the shrine, sent up a column of light to the very roof. I descended the stairs, and found myself within the chapel. The lamps were almost failing, and the silver walls darkened by the torch of the devotees absorbed the little light they emitted. I approached the shrine; the dried corpse of the saint, arrayed in his pontificals, seemed, by its repose, to invite me to seek peace where he possessed it. His eye, which once might also have known anguish, was now sunk in the socket, and presented but a mass of blackened mould in the corner of its former throne. I gazed upon it until I thought I saw it move; methought there was a smile upon its lips, as if it mocked my thoughts of peace. I repose with him, a benefactor to the poor, a saint! A laugh was almost playing upon my lips, when the words, half stifled with emotion, 'Intercede my patron, intercede for Berchtold,' sounded on my ear. – I turned; a female figure, I had not observed, was kneeling near the wall in earnest prayer. I approached, 'Who prays for Berchtold? your prayer is mocked.' Alarmed, she raised her head; it was – you know whom I would say – it was Louisa. She looked upon my face convulsed with the violence of my emotions, upon my dishevelled hair. – 'Is it you? Ernestus,' she said, rising, 'are you come to pray; Heaven has then heard even me, and has not left you. Break not my heart.' I could not utter more. She took my arm, we passed through the long nave; I dared not look around, methought some other form would burst upon my eyes in spite of the circling darkness, and blast me. A carriage was waiting at a little distance; she had left the gay dance to pray for me. I had handed her into her carriage, and was going; 'Berchtold,' she said, 'will you leave me?' She wished me, the wretch, to be still near her. I jumped into the carriage, and blessed the darkness that hid my face; we spoke no more. Every one had retired at Doni's. She took my hand when leaving me, and pressing it in hers, whilst she gazed upon my face; she bade me think – she would have said more; a tear fell from her unwilling eye, and she hastily turned away.

I returned to my room, I had not entered it for many days. Louisa knew my guilt; sleep would not refresh me, my thoughts revelled in a maddening breast. Whither could I turn for refuge from their power? Religion I had cast from me, as a foul fiend's mock; Louisa! rest upon purity, I dared not; then my native mountains rushed upon my sight, I seemed bounding along the crags, Berchtold smiled upon my innocence, I laughed aloud – innocence? it was but the want of temptation. I threw myself upon my bed, and though not asleep, I became so stupified by the very excess of pain, that even the phantoms of conscience no longer passed with distinctness before me. The night seemed to hang suspended over my head, as if in pity it would hide me from the day, so slow was its progress; morning at last returned, but with it were the same thoughts as had visited me during the night.

It was hardly day before I heard some one at my door, I opened it, it was Doni. I turned away my head ashamed to look upon him, he did not reproach me, telling me that he knew my present way of life needed a more abundant supply of money, than he had given me, he bade me to apply to him for any sum I wanted. I could not speak, I had expected he would have attempted to show me my vices in all their native horror; he pressed his offer upon me; ashamed to tell him the whole amount of my folly, I at last named a sum not half sufficient to satisfy my creditors, but I thought it would stop the mouths of the most clamorous, and that in the mean time, by economising my allowance, I might clear the rest. He asked me repeatedly, if it was the entire sum I owed; I answered yes; he left me, and in a few minutes returned, with gold to the amount required; 'Take it' he said, 'it is no loss to me, but your wonted happiness I see is fled, that grieves me. Believe one who is older than yourself, Vice is not the path of happiness.' I was silent. I intended immediately to pay my debts as far as I could, and at once to free myself from the life of a gambler, and a libertine.

My sister came to see me in my room, for I was ashamed of appearing at the breakfast table. I observed that the colour in her cheeks was gone, that she no longer was the open-hearted girl I remembered; attributing this however to the effect of my own follies upon her mind, I said nothing. She remained with me some time, but I no longer felt that pleasure I had always known in her company upon former occasions. We seemed both afraid of touching upon any thing relating to ourselves, and both evidently with minds deeply occupied about other important objects, talked of the most trivial circumstances.

When night came, I issued forth, determined to pay my debts, as far as was in my power; I entered the saloon of the theatre; there were only the banker and the punters arrived; they had arranged every thing for the faro table, and immediately they saw me, they began talking of the various successes of the last night. They told me how Olivieri had regained every thing at the very close of the evening. One or two gradually stepped in; amongst them was my friend, he was in high spirits; I took him aside, and told him that I was weary of this kind of life, and was determined to pay every one as far as I had it in my power. He would not let me finish, he laughed at my intentions, and told me, that as our good luck was now returned, it would be a folly to throw it away, that as I acknowledged myself incapable of paying the whole, it would be as well to owe a greater as a lesser sum. His companions soon perceived the subject of our conversation, and joined us. They all ridiculed my intention, and I was persuaded to venture once more. I at first lost, but suddenly the rouleaus poured upon me; one more stake, and I had regained even all my enormous losses; it was soon too late to retire, I almost lost all I had that morning received from Doni. It was now quite useless to think of retreating, I fell again into my former life, with more than double energy. I was at times surprised to find that great sums were paid to several of my creditors, I could not learn by whom; I imagined it was by Olivieri's father; this did not stop me. My vicissitudes were great, but I could never entirely extricate myself, so that I was always either lured by hope or urged by despair.

I need not describe to you the progress of my other vices; debauched women, men of whom one is ashamed, and wine, are generally the attendants upon gambling. I could not seek the house of Doni, nor of virtue; I threw myself into every haunt of desperate characters like myself, and learnt to boast alike of the smile of the prostitute, or of the tear of the debauched virgin; when losing, I stupified my mind with wine, and was glad to fall from my chair, provided memory failed with my senses. Noted cheats, and men proscribed from society for their low dissoluteness, often seized upon my arm on the Corso, as if I were one of their equals, and I dared not repel their familiarity, for I was in their power. Once Louisa saw me in this situation, she never again rode out on the Corso; I had the maddened impudence to bow to her. I at last became mad, and once, was induced to aid in depriving a young novice of all his wealth, by means of false dice. I could not however stand by and see his horrible despair, he had beggared a wife and two lovely babes. I had just then been lucky, I confessed my participation to him, and gave him the whole amount of his loss; it became known, and I was laughed at; but for once I could withstand ridicule.

At the Doni palace in the mean time, the same outward appearance was preserved; there were still the same evening assemblies, but they were less frequented, for Olivieri was almost always with me. He was apparently afraid I should escape him; he was constantly stifling all thoughts that arose in my breast, tending towards a return to virtue. He never left me but when I was deeply engaged in play or debauch; then he constantly went I knew not whither. I have since found it out, and that discovery has not been the least of those pangs my guilt has brought upon me. I entered so little into society, that I heard nothing of what was passing there. I was, however, one day standing on the Corso with Olivieri, speaking to some ladies who had drawn up their carriage close to a shop, when the conversation turning upon the number of foreigners, who were moving about in consequence of the peace which had just been concluded, a lady turning, asked me if I had seen the stranger who excited so much the curiosity of all circles. Upon my saying I had not, she began expatiating upon his singular character, rested upon his powers of fascination, and told me that all the ladies were in love with him. I did not pay much attention to this, thinking it but the foolish prattle of a young girl. She however continued; she wondered that I had not seen him, as he was a constant attendant upon Louisa, she having engrossed the whole of his attention, much to the mortification of all Milan.

Now I was roused. I let go Olivieri's arm, and wandered about alone. I dared not hope that Louisa could resist one whom all seemed to admire. The whole weight of my guilt fell heavily upon my recollection, and one after another all my vices presented themselves, arrayed against me. I did not return that day to any of my usual haunts. Towards evening, I found myself, fatigued with wandering, at the gate of the Doni palace. I know not what inspired me, it seemed as if I wished to gain the certainty of my fate. My steps, which till now had been slow and measured, suddenly quickened. I found myself at the entrance of the saloon; all was silent; the red purple glare of sunset pierced the windows. I stood for a moment still; a sigh burst upon my ear – I entered – Louisa was sitting looking upon the setting sun. It was her sigh. She did not turn: 'Is it you, my father?' I did not speak, she turned her head, her face was pale, but a blush mantled her cheek at the sight of me; her eyes were sunk and dim, but they brightened at my presence. She spoke my name, she rose, and with faltering steps attempted to reach a door leading to her apartments. I murmured audibly, but with a stifled voice: 'She flies me, she flies, she hates me!' She turned. 'Oh no: I do not, Ernestus, do not believe it.' She fell upon the floor; I approached, knelt by her side, but dared not touch her. I attempted it, my hand retreated; there seemed to be pollution in my touch; I dared not. The cool air played upon her face, and the chill of the marble floor gradually recovered her; she opened her eyes, I was now near her, I could see the marks of a suffering mind upon her face; her cheek now had no colour, save that reflected from the red light of the illumined West. Her tresses were disordered and neglected; her eyes sunk deep in their socket, how changed from the vision of the Wengern Alp! Her subdued voice could hardly articulate, when she again assured me with earnestness that she did not hate me, that she forgave me. Tears flowed down my cheeks, and I did not try to stop them. She looked upon me: 'It is too late,' she said, smiling with the smile of a broken heart; 'it is too late, Berchtold; I wish that I could weep, but my eyes are dried up.' The sounds of approaching footsteps were heard; she rose with difficulty; trembling, I offered my arm, she took it. I thought she would have spurned it. I could hardly support my own weight. I saw her to her door, and threw myself upon the staircase near it; but I soon heard strange voices in the saloon; the thought of its being his voice, who, I had heard, was my rival, at once made me start. I rose, retired for a moment to my room, and then entered.

The apartment was now lit up. The company were in greater numbers than I had ever seen before. My rival, I said to myself, is then so attractive. No one observed my entry; they all seemed engaged around one man. It was my rival; I never saw so singular a figure. His bust and head were handsome, and bore the signs of strength. His black hair was in ringlets; his face was pale with a blueish tint that diminished even the colour of a naturally pale eye. His hands were joined with their palms turned towards the ground; his eyelids almost covered his eyes, which turned upon the floor, while his head erect, bore in its general expression the marks of contempt. He was speaking with elegance upon the fallen glories of some sunken nation; when he had ended, and the conversation had became more general, he raised his eyes, and affecting surprise, he seemed ashamed of having attracted so much notice, though he did not blush, for the hue of his features seemed invariable. He retreated to a corner of the room, left vacant by the pressure of the company towards the spot he had just occupied. He there bent down his head, as if abstracted in thought; but looking under his eyebrows, he was evidently engaged in remarking the effect he had made upon the company. He again gradually got a circle round him, and again was apparently carried away by the great powers of his mind, and held forth upon some subject, and then once more retreated. I was tired of watching such acting, and looked round for my sister. She was at that moment entering; she immediately addressed Doni, who seemed alarmed, and went out. I approached – Louisa was ill and could not appear. Julia looked upon me as if she knew it had been my presence which had thus affected her friend; I could not bear that look: 'Do not reproach me, I feel all the shame of my crimes.' 'I reproach you!' she answered, 'You mock me, I! it is not for one like me to do it.' She turned away, I did not understand her; I asked her why she rested upon one like her. 'Oh! do not ask me, my shame must not be spoken.' The noble stranger approached, and broke off our conversation by asking after Louisa. I could not stand by him, but joined some of my former acquaintances; for though my heart was breaking, I dared not leave the room, determined to watch minutely every action of him I fancied my rival.

I entered into conversation, and forced myself to inquire about this stranger, who thus engaged the attention of all. There was a certain affectation of mystery about him, which induced all to seek him, in hopes of penetrating the veil he threw round his actions. I met with one who had known him intimately in his own country. From whom I learnt several traits of his character; it appeared that this German was much distinguished amongst his countrymen for his talents, – that he was generally esteemed a hater of all the vanities of the world, but that he passed many hours at his toilette; that he was deemed broken-hearted from having been crossed in love; but that he was incapable of feeling that passion, being wrapt in selfishness, that made him sacrifice every thing around him to the whim of the moment: that he was deemed irresistible, and that no woman upon whom he fixed his eye could withstand the fascination of his tongue, but that he had never dared to tempt any woman, who was not of the most abandoned character; that even they were never addressed with boldness, but were always made to compromise themselves by some folly with him in public, before he would give them the least marked sign of attention; that in fine he was a confirmed coward with women. In society he was playing off a strange coquetry with the whole world, affecting to be modest and diffident, whilst he protruded himself into notice. He was, however, rich, handsome, and noble by birth, I was an orphan dependent upon charity. He was every where received with great attention, no where with greater than in Doni's palace.

Perceiving that Louisa's father did not return, I became alarmed, and anxious to gain some information, I sought for him. He was walking with hasty steps before her door. Upon seeing me, he was turning away, but moved by my broken voice, he stopped, looked upon me, and addressed me, 'You saved my son, Berchtold, but my daughter, my beloved daughter dies; it is, however, useless to speak to you, leave me, go to your room, Louisa's better.' Every thing seemed confused to me, I could not believe that I was the cause of Louisa's illness, I could not believe that she could love such an outcast as myself. I was several times in the course of the night by her door, listening for some sound that should assure me of her existence. I fell asleep at last upon the sofa in my room, and I saw her in my dream as when she first appeared before me, glowing in health, buoyant with spirits; suddenly I thought she ran towards me, but ere she reached me, she faded like a flower, and fell to the ground. I awoke, all was still, but my heart beat violently. It seemed as if this were the fulfilment of my former dreams, my vices were the evils, the warning voice of my mother commanded my sister to fly, for they were doomed to be the death of all I loved.

Morning came, my first inquiries were concerning Louisa; she was very ill, and in a state of great weakness. Doni was not yet risen, and was apparently quite overcome. During the whole day, I was not one moment at rest; I wandered from one room to another, and sent every instant to inquire concerning my protector's daughter. I stood by the door watching all who came from her room, and begged them to tell me every change they observed. Towards evening a packet was put into my hands; it contained receipts from every one of my creditors. There was no explanatory paper. Imagining it to be the gift of Doni, I determined to thank him; I went to his room; I found him lying upon his couch very much fatigued and exhausted; he was courting repose, but it was in vain; anxiety was painted upon his face, and grief seemed to stamp him with its chilling furrows. My first question was concerning his daughter. I then showed him the packet, and had begun to thank him, when he interrupted me. 'Young man, thank not one, who wished that you should first have paid the price of your vices before he freed you from your embarrassments. I had resisted my daughter's entreaties, till last night, she offered to give up her allowance, every thing, to free you; I refused, but I could not long do so, to a child I thought dying.' I was thunderstruck, the packet fell from my hand; I thought I should have fallen through shame; but he spoke again, 'Would that your apparent shame were the least security against your follies, but I believe you to be incurable.' He motioned me away; I fell at his feet, and called

Heaven to witness that I would never again partake of vicious pleasures. He raised me from the ground, pressed me to his bosom, and with a blessing told me, that if I kept this promise, he might yet be happy; he bade me leave him to his hopes, again embraced me, and I left him.

For the first time during the last many weary months, I felt something like repose in my mind. It seemed as if the vow I had made to Heaven might be relied on, and as if I again might know the consolation of a conscience at rest. That night I slept quietly and soundly, for Louisa was announced to be much better, and my heart felt a little repose. It was but to give me strength to bear worse than I had yet endured.

Next morning Louisa saw me, she was upon the bed of sickness, but she had partly recovered the shock my abrupt entry had caused her. I shall never forget the moment I entered. I had expected she would have received me with marks of horror; she smiled; oh, no! she did not hate me. I sat by her, she allowed me to take her thin cold hand within my own; it chilled my heart with its touch. There was a clear whiteness that overspread her face, where it was not tinged by the hectic flush, her eye shone with a glassy brilliancy that seemed not mortal, it was the glance of death mocking my senses through a beauteous vizor, for there were the seeds of death sown deep in her broken heart. She spoke but little, what she did utter, however, were words of kindness, and they were all her weakness allowed her to say. She often turned her brilliant eyes upon me, and the soft smile upon her lip, I thought was excited by the gentle whisperings of hope, that I was snatched for ever from vice. The latter part of the morning was passed near her in a silence that was not mute, for there is a language which, though not addressed to the ear, still speaks the thought within. Her physician came and advised me to retire. I bade her farewell; an anxious look accompanied the words, 'Where are you going?' but when I intimated my determination of staying at home, I cannot describe to you the joy expressed upon her face as she repeated my farewell.

I had been so little at home, that I knew nothing of what had lately happened. I was, therefore, much surprised, when, upon desiring a servant, towards night, to see if Doni was in his apartment, he refused, saying he had not courage. Upon making inquiries, I found that their master's supernatural powers had been much talked of lately amongst the servants; for during the latter days, unusual noises had been heard in his room, and every morning, all his things had been found in a strange confusion while he was apparently so exhausted, that it was evident he had had no rest during the night. Thinking all this very explicable from the state of anxiety in which he had been kept, I tried to convince the servant, but he appeared firm in his belief, and refused to carry my message.

Louisa seemed rapidly to recover strength. As we were in the very middle of summer it was thought proper by her physicians that she should be removed to a cooler situation than the neighbourhood of a great city. We accordingly retired to the banks of the Lago Maggiore. The palace close to the lake was refreshed by the cooling breeze that passed over the water's vast expanse, and the playful fountains that sported with their noisy showers in the apartments towards the land, promised to shield the invalid from the noxious effects of an Italian sun; while the magnificent scenery of the varying basin before our view, seemed to promise relaxation to the mind. We arrived late at night, and immediately retired to our beds. I arose betimes, and issuing forth ascended the numerous terraces, which, one above another, seemed like the work of some enchanter. When viewed from the water's edge, garden seemed to be hanging above garden, as if man had acquired the power of piling nature's gifts even into the air. I did not heed this, for my native mountains were in sight; I did not gaze upon the rich islands, which seemed like fairy dwellings springing from the lake; I gazed upon Monte Rosa, which, high above the neighbouring hills, asserted the glory of its alpine birth. Though all around seemed burnt by the sun's ray, it mocked his power and bore its unvarying white vest, in defiance of his frown, upon its aged limbs. While yet engaged looking upon its high summit, with all the crowded images of infancy offered by my memory, my sister passed me. She seemed lately to have lost all her spirits, she did not appear to be attracted by the beautiful scene near us, or the sublimity of the alpine ridge beyond. She was gazing upon the ground, I joined her, she started, and with a trembling voice asked me, 'Why I was come?' I answered her; at that moment I saw Olivieri turn the corner of the alley and approach; but immediately he saw me he retired, and I at the same time perceived that my sister was violently agitated. I looked at her, and begged of her to tell me what I was to imagine; she hastily replied, 'Nothing, nothing;' and her colour, which had deserted her at the sight of Olivieri, returned with greater rapidity than it had fled the moment before. I insisted upon an explanation; she said she was unwell, weak, and made other excuses of the same nature. I now remembered her agitation a few evenings before, when we were interrupted by the Count Wilhelm. I threatened, if she would not satisfy me, to seek an explanation from Olivieri. She fell upon her knees before me, begged me not, assured me that it concerned a third person. I was moved, I had the weakness to promise that I would seek no farther.

I had not seen my friend till this moment, since the payment of my debts; he had never been home, and I had not sought him. He had not accompanied us, and I had not been aware that he was expected. I re-entered the house, hoping to find him; but no one had seen him, and he did not appear at breakfast.

Louisa made her appearance at that meal. You may imagine my pleasure at again seeing her out of her sick chamber. She made room for me by her side. I accompanied her into the orange-walk near the house, and I sat near her for two hours while she enjoyed the beauty of the scene. She looked at the Alps, then at me, it seemed as if the recollection of our first meeting passed through the minds of both. Involuntarily I opened the bosom of my vest and showed her the scarf, which I had constantly worn since that day. She smiled. 'I did not think of this at that time,' she said, 'I did not know your name, but when the fame of Berchtold, Ernestus Berchtold, was echoed by the wild rocks to the voice of every peasant, I sighed and wished he might be the chamois hunter of the Wengern Alp. It was I sent the saviour of my brother's life to battle. I sent the hero to aid in the rescue of his country; it was in vain, yet I was conscious of a feeling of pride whenever I thought of it.' She spoke of my former life, and passed in silence over that part, when every moment had been spent in shame. I cannot describe my sensations to you. The feeling of how little I deserved such praise, mingling with the pleasure of hearing it from Louisa's lips, embittered what else would have been the proudest moment of my life. Her father joined us, and seemed pleased at seeing us together; he seated himself upon the other side of his daughter, and we spent the whole morning together in conversation, till the sun becoming too powerful, Louisa was obliged to retire for shelter and repose, and we separated.

Day passed after day, and Louisa's health seemed rapidly to recover; but my sister evidently became more and more restless. She generally avoided, and very seldom sought our society. I knew not what to understand; determined however to force her to an explanation, I one evening, finding her alone, induced her to walk out with me. We wandered, without perceiving it, into the garden. She seemed determined upon silence. Wrapt in thought, the sun's red disk fast sinking in the West, the birds' evening carol, the varied light of the Heavens reflected from the soft silky clouds over the purpling surface of the lake, the cooling breeze which played upon her feverish cheek, were all unnoticed. Yet she was wont, in all that feeling of nature's charms which accompanies youth, to gaze upon that orb, and figuring it as the image of that Providence she adored, think the birds sang hymns of thanks to him for all he gave. But now she passed, and all was unheeded. There was a seat upon the river's side, which, shaded by the plants that crept entangled round the branches of a noble chestnut, formed a bower, whence all the beauties of the rich nature round could be viewed. I attempted in vain to enter upon the subject of what was causing this apparent misery in her breast; she was abstracted, and answered merely by monosyllables. I at last ceased to press her, and we both sunk into silence.

The spreading clematis of the bower hid us completely from the path near us, while its open leaves allowed us to see distinctly all that passed in the avenue. There was a wall of cypress which ran along one side of the gravel walk, fully exposed at this moment to the sun's rays. I saw at last approaching from the bottom, the Count our protector; he seemed in earnest conversation with some one, but I could perceive no one near him; yet his lips and hands certainly moved as if he spoke. As he gradually approached, I could even distinguish sounds. I motioned Julia to observe him; she did so and soon pointed to the hedge. I could not at first see to what she directed my attention; but at last I perceived the outline of a figure, through the shape of whose body the very leaves were visible; something in the manner that I have seen in the summer, a current of heated air, accurately defined by the wavering outline of the things between which and our sight it stands, only that this was even more sensible to vision. I could not distinguish its voice, but I at last caught some of the words of Doni. I had hardly time to make these observations, when the Count seemed to start, and the figured vapour went.

We did not move; we for some time seemed rooted to our seats; at last Doni disappeared amidst the trees, and we looked at each other. It was then true what we heard at the lake of Thun, our protector had communication with a spirit. My sister seized the subject of conversation with avidity. We related to one another several slight circumstances, which had come to our knowledge, many incidents which we could not explain. The reluctance of the servants to approach the chambers of the Count all pressed upon our minds. The immense wealth, which seemed inexhaustible, must, it appeared to us, be connected with this untenanting spirit. We resolved not to mention the circumstance we had just witnessed to any one. But it was not effaced from our own memory. We returned to the house and saw our protector there as usual, but his face was, or I imagined it to be, pale; his eyes wandered, and then seemed to fix their angry glance at times upon us; but whether this were imagination or reality, I could not decide. I went to bed, but not to sleep, the thoughts of having seen an unembodied being, the tales of my foster-mother, of power, of wealth, arising from the communication with beings of another world, arose before me. Obtaining such a power, it seemed as if I might learn the things hidden in the earth's deepest recesses, the ocean's depth; I even thought, that by such a power, I might tear away the veil which the first Cause has thrown over itself. Nor did these visions disappear with the morning's light, they were as distinct in the sun's brightness, as in the night's obscurity. I arose determined to speak on the subject with the Count. He met me with an affectionate embrace; I took his hand, had the words upon my lips, when, meeting his eye, I saw expressed therein such anxious fear, such meaning, that the words fell into inarticulate sounds; instantly his eye was as usual; nothing but brilliancy was there. We went together to fetch Louisa from her apartment, and descended to the breakfast table.

Louisa seemed to take a great pleasure in my society, and sought in every way to bring me near her; she seemed afraid of trusting me to myself in my first steps towards retracing the paths of virtue. She again resumed the subject which had formed the topic of conversation, before her fatal departure to visit her sick relation. She painted to me the charms of a religion, which taught us to look up to the infinite power above us, not as to an object of terror and fear, but of love and hope. Her mind, without losing the least of that delicacy which is the magic charm that spreads its influence round the footsteps of woman, was energetic and clear. Her simplicity was not misled by the winding, intricate sophisms of the deist and unbeliever; her belief was built upon persuasion, which, though it had at first depended upon faith, had not scorned the bulwarks of reason. The earnestness with which she spoke, did not make her appear bold or presuming; for the mild look of her dark eye seemed looking to Heaven to beg for inspiration from him, whose cause her lips were pleading. She would often lead me towards the chapel, and without affectation, would kneel down by my side motioning me to imitate her, and bending devoutly before her maker, would pray for me. I did not think of myself; but gazing upon that veiled eye, which did not seem to think itself worthy of looking towards the throne of God, while petitioning for strength against mortal weakness, a prayer would involuntarily rise from my heart for her. I did not feel the time long when near her, though it was even spent in prayer; to have communication with the Almighty in union with her, seemed to be an additional bond amongst those numberless ties which bound me to her. From the first moment that I had seen her, she seemed to visit this earth as my protecting angel; now it appeared as if such a being had led me to the throne of him of whose commands she was the bearer. I did not notice the lapse of months; and autumn had already vested the scene around with its checquered hues, ere this happiness was interrupted; I had even forgotten all my imaginations concerning the being attendant upon Doni. It seemed as if misfortune could no longer visit me; such is human foresight.

I have already mentioned to you the singularity of my sister's conduct; it grew more and more remarkable. She never came down in the morning, but, confined to her room, she spent the hours in solitude: when she did appear, it was but to retire to a corner, where, enveloping herself in her shawl, she apparently brooded over some thoughts that destroyed her peace. Her appearance was completely changed; her auburn hair, which once floated in ringlets of soft varying light upon her shoulders, was now entangled and neglected; her cheeks, on which was wont to play a hue more delicate than that of the white rose, were pale and sickly; her eyes no longer shone with sparkling lustre, they were now heavy and inflamed from the want of sleep. I often saw the silent tears fall from her eye; but it was in vain to question her; she wept bitterly at every inquiry I made, and seemed agitated to the most violent excess whenever Olivieri's name was mentioned. I was bewildered by the inquiries of Doni and Louisa, who constantly expressed their anxiety concerning her.

We were assembled together at the breakfast table as usual one morning, and were conversing about Julia, who had made her appearance the evening before at the supper table, which she had not done for a long time, when a servant came to tell us that her maid had applied several times in the course of the last hour for admission to her room, but that she could obtain no answer. Louisa offered to see if she could obtain admission; in vain, we went together; all, all was silent. We burst open the door, there was no one, every thing seemed in disorder, the bed had not been slept in the last night; upon the floor there were many pieces of paper torn into fragments; and upon the table there was a note addressed to myself. I took it trembling, I was afraid she had committed some desperate act. I could not open it, but gave it into Doni's hand; he read it

'My shame can be no longer hidden; I fly then to hide myself; curse not your sister, my own feelings are sufficiently bitter to satisfy even the injured honour of Berchtold. – Your degraded Julia.'

I sunk upon the bed; Olivieri immediately presented himself to my mind as the seducer of my sister. I could not speak, and my friends were silent, they looked upon me with pity. I dared not inform them of my suspicions, they would bring the old man's grey hairs to their grave, and would cut off the feeble thread of life in Louisa. She bore up against the shock; and while the tear trembled in her eye, she sat down by me, and strove to soothe, not console me, for that she knew was impossible.

Servants were sent in every direction. I searched all the neighbourhood. I determined instantly to go to Milan, and make inquiries directly from Olivieri, concerning the fate of my sister. I made a plausible excuse for my departure, and soon reached the Corso, Doni's palace. The servants had not seen him for some time. I forced myself to seek him in the places which had been my former resort. My late companions hailed my approach; but I turned from them in disgust. Olivieri had no where been heard of lately. Distracted by my suspicions, which now seemed to wear the semblance of certainty, after several days spent in the vain search, I returned to the Lake.

We soon fixed ourselves again at Milan. It was now impossible to keep his son's absence a secret from Doni. He learnt it, but did not seem to imagine any connection between the flight of my sister and his son's conduct. Perceiving this, I did not intimate to him my horrible doubts, but left him in entire ignorance. In the mean time

I made the most minute inquiries concerning both; but could learn nothing.

Louisa's health in the mean time gradually recovered; but she never lost the hectic flush upon her cheek; she gained strength, but the seeds of death were hidden, not destroyed. During her gradual recovery, I was always with her; and if you can picture the happy hours of one sitting by a being he loves – adores, at the same time, that his imagination paints her to him as a spirit of Heaven, you may imagine my happiness, when sitting by Louisa, whose smile, whose glance told me she loved. She had gained me fame; had saved my life, my honour; had restored to me the hopes of a future state, the belief in a kind God. I know not your belief, your principles; you may sneer at the feeling which dictates my ranking the two last with the former; but, young man! believe one who has experienced the whole of fate's wanton inflictions; he who can still rest upon futurity, confident in the goodness of his maker, may find a refuge in the greatest misery; he who cannot, may indeed despair, he has but the present, and that may indeed be dreadful.

Louisa's image was always with me. I loved her, but so did every one; I could not for that reason hope to gain her. I was an orphan, how often has the thought of that sunk my buoyant hope, which still would revive. I had no rank. Count Wilhelm had again renewed his addresses. It seemed dishonourable in me to continue any longer near her, endeavouring to gain her affections; it seemed as if the debt of gratitude I owed to Doni forbade my attempting to gain his daughter. The Count had rank and wealth. I could not hope that her father should prefer me, degraded by vice, my birth perhaps tainted with dishonour, to one whose name was a spell upon all Europe. I had determined to leave Milan, and to plead the necessity of further inquiries for my sister. Doni approved of my intentions, and in a few days I was to set off. I had been preparing for my departure, and had been talking to the servant about the trifles necessary for a solitary journey; it was not yet the hour for the company to assemble, and lost in sorrow I was slowly approaching the saloon, when those notes which had sung hope to me in prison, sounded on the air. They were falling upon the breeze broken, and in a melancholy tone; though the air was lively, it seemed as if Louisa sought to sing of hope, while her heart could not echo back the strain. I had not heard the song since I sunk into vice. The sound was silenced, I entered; Louisa was leaning upon her harp, her head was fallen upon her hand. There was no light, and the lowering clouds hid the little daylight that might have been afforded by the setting sun. I could just distinguish her form, almost lost in the obscurity; suddenly she moved, struck her harp in wild notes, and sung the words of a broken heart. I could not hear more; Louisa's name fell from my lips; 'Sing not so, Louisa; if you have not happiness, who shall possess it?' She sunk upon a chair, and I approached. 'You leave me tomorrow,' she said, 'I shall no longer have any one to cheer me, any one, whom I can' – She stopped and hesitated. I stood breathless by her side. 'I shall, I will return.' 'You will find me a corpse, I feel no power of life within me, it seems as if my soul still clung to life that it might converse with you, when you are gone.' I took her hand; I bade her, if she loved me, not to speak in words that pierced my heart. 'Love you,' she answered, 'you cannot know what I feel towards you, I am myself ashamed that any can divide my heart with God, but you –' I fell upon my knees. 'I will not go, I cannot, Louisa has confessed her love, she loves the orphan Berchtold, if that words could express the least part of what I feel, I would speak. I love you, let my silence speak the rest.' I felt her feeble hand press mine, she had fainted, her weak health had not given her strength to listen. We had not heard the storm which had burst over our heads, I had not seen the flashes of Heaven's anger, which had unobserved spread its lurid light around us. I lifted her in my arms, carried her to her chamber, and delivered her to her maid. She recovered.

I was alone; the thunders echoed still in the distance, and the horizon was lit by the forked lightning. But in my breast the convulsions were not subsiding. At the first moment it seemed as if happiness indeed were mine; but Doni's image came quickly across my mind, and all I owed him seemed to be imaged as so many reproaches for my having stolen the affections of my benefactor's daughter. The company assembled, but I could not join them. The tumult in my breast was too powerful to allow me to participate in the light frivolity of a drawing room. I retired to my chamber, and was soon lost in meditation upon that fatality, which made the very circumstance on which I had rested as the bourne of all my hopes, a cause of anguish and reproach. I determined to see the Count immediately after the company had retired. No malefactor, who is listening in expectation of hearing the lengthened toll, warning him of the executioner's approach, ever counted the moments with greater anxiety than mine. The clock struck, and each brazen sound seemed to vibrate through my body, as if it bore grief upon its sound. At last the carriages began to depart, and I entered the apartment of my friend. I had never dared to call him father, it seemed to my mind too sacred a title to be profaned by me; he was Louisa's father.

I had been some time in his apartment before he entered. He came, his face was full of anxiety. 'My daughter,' he said, 'I fear is going to relapse, something has agitated her strongly, and she will not tell even her father what it is. Berchtold,' he continued, 'you have never before seen a father in the agony that I endure, my daughter's life sinks visibly before me, and I cannot discover the cause. You have therefore no conception of the pain it brings.' I knew not what to say. 'Olivieri too is I know not where, perchance in the haunt of the lowest vice, perhaps acting again the hero, as when with you. You are not my child, yet you now form my only comfort, my only hope.' I could not hear more; – he praise me! who had, like the snake stinging the child enchanted by the beauty of its scales, robbed him of his treasure, insidiously won his daughter's love; I interrupted him. 'I am a wretch, not worthy of your affection, your daughter loves me, I have dared to tell her she was my only hope; spurn me from you, I expect it; but do not blame her.' I fell upon my knees, 'Do not blame her for loving such a wretch as me, she pitied me and my daring devotion changed pity into love.' My head was hid within my hands, I expected to be cursed by him I looked up to as a father. He raised me from the ground. 'Ernestus, this is nobly spoken, I will not reproach you with your former vices, Louisa shall be security to me, that you will always prove what you now show yourself.' I was amazed; I embraced him, but could not speak. Louisa was to be mine, – my guide, my wife. At that moment happiness seemed to be descending from Heaven to be our handmaid, while in fact despair and horror were preparing their flight from the lowest abyss to wait upon our nuptials.

Next morning I was admitted to Louisa's chamber; I told her that her father had consented to our union. A gleam of joy crossed her pale face, she said she was happy, but those words were in a broken and weak voice. I heeded it not, so great was my joy, I sat with her, she listened to my plans of happiness, and smiled; it seemed as if she were conscious of their being but to be imagined. I was at last called away by my own servant, who putting a letter in my hand, told me that he had found it thrown in at the door. It was my sister's hand-writing; fearful of agitating Louisa, I hastily put it into my bosom, and making an excuse left her. When in my chamber, I opened the note. The lines were few:

'A mother appeals for her child to your charity, she has but a short time to live, but her child has not a broken heart. Julia.'

Berchtold had been written, but a tear had effaced the characters. There was the name of an obscure street in the most retired part of Milan.

I immediately repaired thither, and soon found myself in an abode of misery I cannot describe. It was upon the highest story, the roof in several parts let in the hot ray of the sun, and the window was not glazed, but stuffed with dirty rags. It could not be called a shelter, for the floor bore on its black soft texture the marks of every cloud that had passed over it. In one corner there was a bedstead, over which was spread a blanket, that seemed not to have been removed for many years, it was so black and thick with dirt. A broken dish and rags, which I but too well recognised as the remnants of my sister's dress, were the only things upon the floor. I heard a difficult breathing, which proceeded from the bed. I approached, and found my sister. She was pale and squalid, her hair, entangled and loose, covered her face and bosom, and her clasped hands hung from the bed. She was apparently asleep, and her child was grasping her breast with its little hand, trying in vain to obtain sustenance from its fevered mother. I stood for some time gazing upon her; finding she slept soundly, I descended the creaking stairs, and sending some person of the house for clothes and food, I waited till they returned and carried them up with me. The noise I made awakened her, she shrunk from me; 'I did not call you for myself, but this child's cry pierced my heart, – do, do not therefore curse me, if I have even brought you to witness your sister's infamy. I could not die and leave my child sinking unaided upon my putrid corpse.' I spoke kindly to her, she looked upon me, and said, 'Ernestus,' with an incredulous voice, and burst into tears. I soothed her, spoke to her of her child, induced her to take a little nourishment, and saw her feed her little babe. She looked at its eager eye and face while feeding, at moments hugged it to her bosom, while a stifled laugh escaped her; she did not seem to notice me, and I spoke not. At last she fell exhausted upon the bed. I gave her the clothes I had brought, she did not heed me.

I hastened to Doni, related what I had seen; he ordered every thing to be got ready at the palace, and procuring a litter he accompanied me to the abode of my wretched Julia. At sight of him, she hid her face, and would not speak. I had her conveyed to the litter with her child, and we arrived at the palace. The physician of the family being sent for, announced to us, that from the state of exhaustion, into which she had fallen, there were but a few hours remaining of her life. I watched by her all night, she did not speak; I took Louisa for my model, and spoke to her of those hopes which had seemed on her lips to have the power of soothing sickness, and to still the fears of death. She was moved by what I said, for her cold hand pressed mine. I put questions to her with regard to her seducer; she was silent; but a convulsive motion seemed to seize her whole features. I urged her no more. She seemed to revive a little in the morning; auguring well from it, I began to speak to her of her child, talked to her of its health, said it should be named Ernestus, and promised that I would be its father. She raised her fallen head, and looking with tears in her eyes, blessed me, but hardly had the words fallen from her lips, when shuddering, she said, 'My blessing! that, that's a curse.' I took her to my breast, she shrunk from me, 'You know not whom you embrace.' 'It is my sister, whom I hold in my arms,' I cried, she burst into loud sobs, and fell again, upon her pillow. 'You shall hear,' she replied, 'what a sister!' She prepared to relate to me the whole of her late history; I advised her to repose awhile first. 'Well, well, I shall have the less time to feel the blush of shame, and to hear your reproaches, 'tis better so.' She fell asleep after uttering these words, but she was restless, her face was convulsed, and the twitching of her arms began to give the signs of the rapid approach of death.

I seized this moment of apparent rest to inquire for Louisa. She was much better; we had kept our discovery of Julia a secret, fearful of agitating her too much; I determined therefore to see her, lest, making some inquiry concerning me, she might hear how I was engaged. I entered her room, and staid with her for some time; she spoke of her love, and added, that all that she thought wanting was the presence of her brother and Julia. I could not answer, but rose, and again went to my unconscious sister. She was disturbed in her sleep, and was calling upon Louisa's name; she seemed to reproach her for not seeing her; but then she appeared to meditate and said; 'True, true, I am an outcast.' She awoke, looked wildly around, met my eye. She was lost some time in thought, and then addressed me; 'I know what you are waiting for but ere I unfold the whole of my shame, give me your solemn promise that you will grant your sister her last dying request.' I gave it her. 'You will then never mention to either of my former friends what I narrate, and you will let me die, certain that you will never injure him that ruined me, for still, still I love him.' I assured her, that I would leave it to Heaven to punish him, for I was conscious it was Olivieri, Louisa's brother. It was him, the account that I had given of his bravery in the Swiss war, the description I had made of his daring feats had gained an entire possession of her imagination. When, therefore, she met him at Milan, his beauty, his specious manner and apparent knowledge had completed her fascination. I myself, when bewildered by doubts, had sapped the foundation of her religious principles; and Olivieri, who was not blind to her partiality, had fanned the spark of scepticism, till he had destroyed all belief in virtue and a future state. I lost myself at the gambling table; and my conduct was but an additional proof in her mind, that the present was all that belonged to man. Before we left Milan, the seducer accomplished his criminal purpose. Though however, she had become a convert to his theories, she could not divest herself of all feeling of shame, much less could she entirely drive from her heart those doctrines which Berchtold had instilled at that age when the first impressions become part of our very nature; they hung around her, and haunted her day and night; she had sought for courage to apply to Louisa or myself in her difficulties, but had not dared.

Her mind being in this state, she described the effect upon it, at sight of that being almost lost amidst the ambient air in conversation with Doni, as wonderful. Her mind had immediately recovered its elasticity, for she hoped, if she could obtain communication with such a being, to be able to find some certainty amidst the horrid doubts that revelled in her mind, and to procure the means of hiding her shame, or daring to face the day, by means of its power. Determined to learn the spell which could raise a transparent, all-pervading being, she resolved to watch, without remission, the conduct of the Count; she learnt nothing for some time. He apparently differed in no habit from the others around. But the impression in her mind was not effaced: at last it appeared to her that upon certain days, the Count never touched animal food, and she found by observation that this happened on every combination of seven in the days of the month. Upon inquiry amongst the servants, she found that upon the morning of those days, the room of Doni was always in the greatest confusion, and she herself remarked, that upon the evening preceding, he seemed always more anxious, and the day after more fatigued than usual.

Julia resolved to watch the Count upon the next seventh night; she found that it was possible to look into his room through the wainscot of a closet for wood that opened into the passage leading to his apartment. The night came, meat had been avoided, all were gone to their rooms, only the footsteps of the domestics arranging every thing for rest, sounded on her ear; she described herself, as having listened apparently for hours, though only minutes elapsed, while these sounds continued. At last, all was silent; she said, that not even the vine leaves overspreading her casement were heard to rustle; for every breeze was hushed, all was so quiet, that the ear seemed to feel as it were the silence. She was awed, her heart beat quick, she held her breath; at that moment she thought a slow step sounded along the corridor; alarmed she knew not why, she seized her lamp, and was upon the point of rushing out, when the door slowly opened, and a figure clad in a white robe entered; its dark black eye was fixed; its grey locks seemed as if no breath of air could move their weight; no sign of life, save the moving feet belonged to it, for the face was pale, the lips blueish. It approached with an unvarying step; it was Doni! its hand took hers within its cold grasp, its eye shone, as if a tear had passed over it, its lips quivered as if it wished to speak, or thought it spoke. She stood still, motionless; while it approached, it seemed as if she had strength for any thing, but when it turned to go, the lamp fell from her hand, and she fell upon the floor. It was morn, ere her wildered senses returned, it was too late. Doni never noticed in any way the event of that night. She was bewildered, she knew not what to think, it seemed from his unchanged conduct towards her, that he was unconscious of the event. Yet she asserted that she could not have mistaken the features of him who had visited her in that awful manner; her imagination laboured, her judgement laid down the balance and became as dead. Her phantasy painted to her mind pictures of splendour and of power, more brilliant than those of the Arab tale-teller, or God creating Bramin. But more than all, it represented to her the means of ensuring Olivieri's love, which she could no longer flatter herself she possessed; he had not seen her, but for a moment, since she had left Milan dishonoured, and then it was but to laugh at her fears, which she was but too conscious were not in vain.

Day followed day towards the seventh. At times she caught Doni's eye fixed upon her, as if it sought to read her mind; but she

thought this might be imagination, yet it seemed to her as if her
intentions were divined, and that from some cause or other, they
could not be opposed, else why this silence? The fatal night came.
Julia, determined to brave every thing, went down that evening,
which she had not lately done, to supper. Her agitation was great,
but she forced herself to conceal it. She was conscious the Count's
eyes were fixed upon hers, yet she dared not to look up and meet
his. She rose to depart, he came to her to say good night, his voice
failed him, his hand shook. She retired to her room; she
determined, frightened by the awful silence of her protector, to
give up her intention. She threw herself upon her bed, but sleep
abandoned her, or if it for a moment came, it presented such
brilliant visions to her eye, that nothing mortal was to be compared
to it. She seemed to have spirits instead of pages to attend her, genii
instead of servants. It seemed as if at their bidding the very earth
would heave and show within its entrails, all its richest treasures.
Olivieri appeared joined with her in this state of power. She roused
herself. The clock with its solemn peal seemed trembling to intrude
upon the solemn night. One might have thought nature were dead,
for not even the owl shrieked, and the darkness and nocturnal sleep
that weighed on the earth, seemed no longer the type of the eternal
rest of the world, but its fulfilment, all appeared sunk into such
undisturbed repose. Julia alone seemed living, she looked in the
creation like the Arab in the sandy plain, animate amidst
inanimation, organised amidst unorganised matter. Even she must
have appeared as if she were some spirit of another more restless
sphere, for her hurrying glance, the fearful resolution breathing in
her face, must have made her bear the stamp of something more
than mortality. She seized her lamp, started, then advanced, and
laughed with that laugh which plays upon the lips, when the heart
ceases to beat through violence of feeling.

At last she reached the gallery of her protector's room; she
opened with a trembling hand, the door of the adjoining closet, and
entered. The dread silence still continued, it was only broken by
the loud breathing of her heaving bosom. She sat down upon the
pile of wood in the corner of the closet. She could not find courage
to pursue her undertaking; at last a deep groan made her start;
terrified she leant against the wall; as she gradually recovered
herself, she raised her eyes, and looked through a crevice that
opened to her sight the Count's room. I could not learn what she
saw, she however informed me that she discovered the means of

raising a superior being; but that startled at his appearance, she had
sunk to the ground. She found herself, when recovered, upon her
bed, but no one was near her. She determined to put her power
into effect the ensuing night. She would not join the family at
breakfast, but remained in her room all day. She did attempt to
raise a spirit, but what was her horror, when the walls of her
apartment echoed but scoffs and mockings, they seemed to say that
she needed not a greater price than the gratification of her passions,
and that they would not give her more; that she was theirs already,
and that to command them could only be obtained by one not
already damned. Unappalled she repeated her call, but it was in
vain, all sunk to quiet. Desperate, for her shame could no longer
be hidden, she formed at once the resolution of leaving the house
and seeking her seducer. She got out, and entering a boat, managed
by skulking along the banks of the lake throughout the day, to
arrive in the night at Sesto Calende; she thence easily obtained a
conveyance, and reached Milan.

She had sought refuge at a small inn, and sending to Olivieri, he
came to her, but it was only to make fully known to her the horrors
of her situation. It appears he treated her with brutality, though she
did not say so. He staid with her but a few minutes, and left her for
ever. He offered her no assistance, seemed even to have implied
that if unwilling to return to her brother, she might live by exposing
her shame to all, and boldly seeking whom she might inveigle. He
left her with only the small sum remaining from what she had
taken with her, and immediately left Milan to go she knew not
where. She had thence retired to the room where I had found her,
and had there managed to support life, and was delivered of her
child. Her money however failed her, and, at last, her poor
neighbours, tired of assisting her who could no longer pay them,
having refused to aid her any more, she had struggled with the
pains of hunger for two days in solitude, hoping for relief from
death. But her milk had failed, and her child's voice had pierced
its mother's heart; she could not resist such an appeal; she arose,
wrote the few lines to me, and staggering, in the morning while all
were at rest, to the gate of the palace, had thrown them under the
gate. From thence she had hardly found strength sufficient to reach
her miserable couch, when fatigued, she sunk into a kind of stupor
from which my approach had roused her.

This is the substance of what my sister told me. Her narration
was broken, and many were the pauses she was forced to make to

recover strength. Her feeble breath hardly seemed sufficient to allow her to end her tale. Night came, and she was delirious. She screamed for Olivieri, called on him to come and see her die. She held my hands, and looking on me asked me my name, denied it could be me, for I could not be more kind than Olivieri; but why rest upon such a scene? She died in the morning without a return of reason, but still calling, in the last moment, upon her lover.

My sister was dead. Her tale had unfolded to me the causes whence her misconduct arose. I was the source of all, my colouring of Olivieri's good qualities, my exposing to her the sources of doubt in those doctrines our sainted foster-father had taught us, my example in the career of vice were the causes of her fault – her death. It was yet but the second victim to my fate; there were two others wanting; I sat by the dead body reflecting upon the horrible fatality that had caused my virtues and my vices to prove alike mortal to the two beings who for many years had been the only companions I possessed in nature, the only sympathisers in my joys and sorrows. If the pangs of conscience could be depicted, I would, for your sake, young man, paint in its truest colours, the horror I then felt, the pangs I now feel; but the attempt would be vain. I had loved my sister with all that affection two isolated beings naturally feel towards each other. She had been to me as the weaker part of myself, which always needed protection and defence. To me she had been the holder of all my secrets, the partaker of all my sorrows; when an outcast, she had received me; when a wretch, she had not spurned me.

No one was with me when she died. The servant of Louisa found me many hours after her decease, extended upon her corpse. She came from her mistress to seek me. I rose; I knew not how to conceal the anguish of my mind. Louisa soon discovered it, and obtained from me the knowledge of my sister's illness and death. She did not inquire further; she perceived I was not willing she should know the rest, and was silent. I was astonished to see how firmly she bore the shock, she exerted herself to find some means of allaying my grief, but she did not know that it was conscience that worked within. I left her, and her pretended strength was gone. She had forced herself to assume an apparent calm to assuage my grief, but could not command her own.

My sister was interred privately. Doni and myself, were the only mourners, and a tablet, with merely the name of Julia Berchtold, marked the spot where my sister lay. Her child was put to nurse.

I gave him his mother's and my own name, that I might still have a bond between us. Every day I went to see the little orphan, and taking him from the fearful nurse, I gazed upon his infantile face, while a bitter tear fell from the eye of him who had been the cause of his birth being loaded with infamy and shame. While I looked upon him he would smile, but that smile brought to my mind my sister's; it was a melancholy playing of the lips, that seemed to mock at the pleasure that excited it; the eye was not lit up with the same feeling, but still appeared absorbed in its continued grief.

Part Third

I had already undergone more than falls to the lot of most men in this valley of miseries; but I was not allowed repose; from this moment my heart was torn piece-meal, by fiends each more horrible than the other. Not many days had elapsed since Julia's death, when Olivieri's father received an anonymous warning to prepare himself for the worst news. The letter was dated Strasburgh. Next day he read in another letter, that his son, under an assumed name, had been taken with several others of a band of robbers, who had for a long time infested the banks of the Rhine. Doni had now become aged and infirm, he was not capable of undergoing the fatigues of a long journey, yet it was hardly possible to hinder him from setting off, to attempt saving his only son. He blessed me when I insisted upon performing that office. 'You have twice saved his life in the field of honour, may you be as successful in snatching him from the death of infamy.' He gave me unlimited power, and rushed into his daughter's apartment to seek there for the comfort all else seemed to deny him.

I departed, travelled night and day, I saw Switzerland again, but did not even notice it, my mind was anxious, was alarmed; it seemed as if Heaven wished by repeated inflictions of its bitterest curses, to humble to the dust the family circle of my protector. I was so rash, that for a moment I dared to question Providence. So weak is all mortal knowledge; misery is but the fruit of vice, virtue never feels the world's infamy; there is a heavenly beam of certainty in the merciful justice of their God that enables the just to look upon all the inflictions of this life, but as the most lenient atonement due to a tender, though offended father, for those weaknesses belonging even to our nature.

I arrived at Strasburgh; its fretted spire, rising high above the houses, upon the far extended plain, for a long time marked the bourne to which I was tending, while the winding road that forms the approach, seemed to mock my endeavours to reach it. Justice had been summary, there had not even been a regular trial, but a court martial had been summoned, and instantly had condemned the prisoners to death. A respite had however been granted for a few days, in consequence of the hopes entertained of inducing some individual to betray the secret retreats of their comrades. I immediately proceeded to the prison and asked admission. Application being made to the governor, and it being evident that I was not one of the gang, I obtained it. I entered; bolt after bolt slowly sounded as they were forced from their rusty clasps, and I found myself in a low gallery, the damp was slowly falling in measured drops from the arched vault above, and the coldness of the chilly air made me shiver. The jailor bore a torch before me; its red light at last rested upon the strong fastenings to a narrow door. I gave him money, and seizing the torch, entered.

Upon a little straw, covering a few loose stones in a corner, lay a form, which seemed reckless of all. The light of the torch did not cause it to move, its hands were upon its face, clenched; its whole posture was strained, as if by the convulsive stiffening of its limbs it would harden itself against the inflictions of the mind. I could not speak; thrice I strove to utter the name of Olivieri, and thrice it stuck in my throat. 'Speak, I can listen to my fate,' Olivieri at last said in a hurried voice, 'Death they say silences all voices, if it can silence that which echoes through the chambers of my breast, scaring oblivion and repose, I shall be content to die, though on the wheel, waiting, when all my limbs are crushed, for that repose the iron bar may give.' He did not move, but seemed to mutter this, addressing himself as much as me. 'Olivieri,' at last fell trembling from my lips. He with one exertion stood erect; his eyeballs straining in their sockets, seemed to seek the horrid certainty they knew would blast them. Berchtold appeared before him. He threw himself upon the straw, and with a hand clenching with furious grasp his long black hair, he seemed to force his head upon the ground, fearing his eyes should again turn upon me. I sat upon the stones at his side, laid my hand upon him, bade him be comforted. He shrunk as if my touch froze him. I told him of my hopes of obtaining his release, of the wealth I could employ in bribing his judges. He looked up; 'You talk to me of mercy; Julia was seduced by me.' 'I know it,' I replied, 'it is your father, who acts by me, I am but my benefactor's agent. For him I am to attempt to save his son.' 'His son?' he echoed in a faltering voice, 'true, I was his son.' I in vain asked him for information on which to proceed; he would give me none. I left him.

I applied to the court which had passed his sentence. I saw the members who had composed it in private. They gave me an account of the desperate gang to which he had belonged, and painted in horrid colours the devastations they had committed in the French territory. It appeared that Olivieri had put himself at the head of these outlaws, and had with the most daring rashness and carelessness of life, always eluded the numbers that often seemed to surround him. I made those who appeared favourable to my pleading great presents, under the pretence of enabling them to aid the furtherance of my objects. Amongst the others, the governor seemed to have the most influence. I gave him immense sums, which he promised to expend for the prisoner's advantage. The next day was appointed for the execution. I had not seen Olivieri again, I was anxious not to encourage too much his hopes of life, while all seemed uncertain. I called early in the morning, upon the governor; I saw him. He raised my expectations very high, he said, that if I could but find the slightest pretence for a respite, that it was determined to grant it. 'If I were to judge by your riches, he and yourself must be of higher rank than you pretend.' I had concealed both our names. 'Now, if you can but show that some one of influence is interested in his fate, we will admit of an appeal.' Rashly I was induced to utter the names of Olivieri Doni, and Ernestus Berchtold. I was surprised at seeing the man before me turn of a most deadly pale. His limbs seemed to fail him, but he in an instant recovered himself; his voice alone betrayed an emotion I could not understand. He assured me that he would instantly occupy himself about it, and I left him. An hour afterwards I received a note from him saying, that I should prepare a carriage and post horses upon the bridge, and as the clock struck the first hour of the morning, that I should present myself at the prison door, where I should meet my friend. That this had been thought the best means of allowing his escape. Passports were enclosed, which would allow us to pass the bridge, and we should then be in safety. I immediately prepared every thing, anxious for the arrival of the moment when I was again to save the brother of Louisa.

Towards evening, restless, I issued out. I wandered up and down that part of the main street, which, covered by arcades, brought to my recollection the towns of my native country. Memory was rapidly crowded with the images of infancy, while the evening tints, and the stillness of nature soon enabled me to abstract myself entirely from the surrounding objects. I at last found myself in the cathedral. There was no one there, even devotion seemed for a while to have laid aside its pomp to enjoy the balmy freshness of an April evening. I had at last advanced into the most obscure part of the aisle; when turning round, a light figure dressed in the singular vestment of the neighbouring peasantry, caught my eye. Her step was hurried, and her head moved anxiously as if seeming to shun observation. Thinking that my presence might be painful, I was retiring, when she beckoned to me. I stood still, and she was immediately by my side. She hastily addressed me. 'You are a friend of Olivieri Doni's, you perceive from my knowing his name, that I am in his confidence. He once professed love to me, he has probably done so to many more, who are now like me ashamed of their name; but even if I told it you, it would be useless. Hoping to be of service, and anxious to hear of him who still possesses my affection, though he has broken the peace of her, who loves him; but I deserve it, for I am guilty, he cannot love guilt; I am so lowered, that I was not ashamed to gain my object, by seeking one of the prison guard. I have just left him intoxicated. From him I learnt, while he was blabbing all, that he was called upon to perform a service this night in the course of his duty, that he disliked. I gained from him that he was to belong to a party, who were to lurk in one of the streets and seize my lover and yourself, at the moment you thought yourselves secure of freedom, for that the police were anxious to take you, who, they suspected belonged to the same gang, and therefore had resolved to arrest you, while engaged in aiding the escape of your friend, which alone will ensure your condemnation.' I was astonished, could I then be so shamefully betrayed? I immediately remembered the sudden emotion of him, who had promised so much, when he heard our names, and it flashed upon my mind, that I had a faint recollection of his name as being that of an officer in the French troops opposed to us in the Underwald, who having been placed in a post of importance, had been surprised by Olivieri and myself, and had been, in consequence of his precipitate flight, broken and disgraced. It was now nearly dark, I could not think of deserting Olivieri without still attempting his rescue. The girl's information might be false. I spoke with her, she appeared sincere; I offered her money, she refused it; my case was desperate, I determined to confide in her, I got her to lead me to the neighbourhood of the prison, and show me all the turnings and secret cuts through the different streets. I soon gained a perfect idea of the plan of this part of the town, and I began to hope in consequence of the intricacy and number of turnings in this neighbourhood that I might elude the ambush, if I could at any point break through the guards. I did not entirely open my plan to my guide, but asked her if she knew of any certain place of refuge, whither I could retreat in case of need. She led me and showed me her apartment, it was miserable, but there was an air of neatness about it that seemed, in contradiction with the poverty, visible in every article. 'If you can arrive here without being observed, you are safe.'

To avoid suspicion, I immediately left her and returned to my hotel, which was close to the river. The hour approached, I armed myself with a sabre and a pair of pistols, and hiding under my large Italian cloak another sword and pair of fire arms, I sauntered negligently out of the inn door, and calling my servant, I told him in a loud voice to take care the horses were ready, as I intended to set off the moment I had fixed on. This I did to blind any one, who might be watching my motions. Then turning down some of the most abrupt windings, I first went whither I had learnt the different parties were to be placed. By means of keeping close to a shaded part of the walls of the streets, which being lit by a single reverberating lamp suspended in the middle between the houses, were rather dark, I could approach very near them without being perceived. I discovered one point which I thought weaker than the rest, for the number of the men seemed smaller, the silence being greater. I then returned, entered the main street leading to the prison, and soon found myself at its gate, without meeting any one. The high narrow windowed walls, were suddenly illuminated by the moon bursting in all its splendour from behind a cloud, and high above my reach I perceived some one watching me, he retreated and I heard the gates open. I could not perceive who was there, for the hollow opening was in the dark shadow thrown over it by a salient buttress. My heart beat violently. It might not be Olivieri, a person was pushed out, I heard the words, 'I am free,' spoken in a voice that denoted the despair within. I approached, it was Olivieri. Throwing off my mantle, I stood before him; he did not notice me, though the moon's ray was full upon us. I roused him, thrust the sword and pistols into his hand, and bade him follow me. 'We are not safe, we must baffle the traitors yet,' said I, 'be firm, we have escaped greater perils than these, follow me.' His broken voice, merely answered, 'To death.'

I hastened towards the point I thought the weakest. A shrill whistle sounded at our back, and we found ourselves surrounded. The first who approached, were dead at our feet. They retreated before us, we had broken their circle and were already free towards the street down which it was necessary to turn. 'Now to the right,' I cried to my companion. A shot struck him and he fell; I rushed to the spot hoping that he might rise. I struck on every side determined not to leave him in their hands, their numbers increased, but at the same time I heard a trampling of feet at my back; desperate, I rushed forward; a female shriek struck my ear, and at the same time I found myself joined by about twenty men. Their blows told, we caused the town-guard to retreat, I could not again find Olivieri's body. I rushed along the streets, and was soon at the young woman's door. I heard voices; alarmed, I listened, they were evidently from their conversation trying to console some one. I knocked, a female voice immediately exclaimed, ''Tis he,' and the door was opened. I entered, Olivieri was extended upon a couch, attempting to write a few lines; he had just finished. Around him were many men in a strange uncouth garb. They were his former companions, who having received the same intelligence from the girl as myself, had resolved to attempt a rescue, and had stolen singly into the town. Olivieri gave me what he had written, it was to his father; his pale face was turned towards me, his feeble arm could hardly support its own weight. 'Berchtold, I have not deserved the risking yourself for me; can, can you forgive me dying.' 'I do,' was my answer, and I held his extended hand. He threw himself upon his bed, and in a stifled voice, 'There is another, whose forgiveness I do not ask, but tell, oh! tell her, it was her shame that has damned me, that made me desperate, damned me.' 'She's dead, she too would have forgiven you; she died speaking of you, but not cursing you.' His limbs were instantly relaxed, and moved no more.

We were now aroused by the entry of another robber, the soldiers were approaching, I begged of them not to leave the body of my Louisa's brother to their insults; they lifted it from the couch, and placed it in a recess so artfully contrived, that it bid defiance to the most accurate search, and they promised me they would return and bury it. We took the young woman with us, and separating, we singly hastened to a spot by the river's side, where we hoped to find boats. Ten only reached it, we entered a small wherry. The town was in such confusion that the necessary orders had not been sent to the different boundaries. We let the boat float down the stream, and soon found ourselves beyond the fortifications. We landed on the German side, and presently reached one of the dwellings of the free-booters. I now learnt that it was this same girl, who had written the anonymous letter to her lover's father. I offered her a considerable sum of money, again offered to secure her an independence, she refused it all, and insisted upon remaining with those men amongst whom she had first known Olivieri. I remained with them a considerable time, anxious to see the body of my former friend secure against any insult, and before I left them, aided by the daring of these men, who managed to enter the town and take the body from its secret hiding place, I had the satisfaction of consigning him to the earth. I gave them all the loose money remaining with me, secure upon my letters of credit of having more than enough to convey me whither I liked.

I reached Inspruck, not deeming myself safe in any part of the French territory, I determined to remain here, and I wrote to Doni merely mentioning that I had been unsuccessful, and telling him where I had stopped. I thought it best not to tell him more for fear of my letter being intercepted, and hoping that when I saw him I should be able to break the fatal news to him. My last hope was vain, for all the papers and public prints contained a full account of the daring attempt I had made to save a robber from the ignominious sentence of the law. Our real names were also mentioned, and at the same time that many rested upon the courage, they pretended had been shown in this attempt, many took advantage of the connection of our names with a gang of robbers to throw discredit upon our former conduct in the cause of Switzerland. It was soon known through my banker, at Inspruck, that I was the notorious Ernestus Berchtold, and I was surrounded by people, who were glad to seek some refuge from their ennui, in gazing upon one, whose name seemed to have something like romance attached to it.

Count Doni arrived, Louisa too, though weak and feeble, still in better health than when I had last seen her, accompanied him. She had been forced to exert herself to support her father under his anxiety for his son, and then under the severe blow of seeing his own name in all the prints, known to all as the father of Olivieri, 'a captain of banditti'. The spring had given her the requisite strength, and I was glad, after so long an absence, to see her once more sitting by my side with renovated life. I could not take my eyes from her, and I rested upon her face so long, that I gradually forced myself to hope that her hectic flush was but her natural colour. We were constantly together, and tried in each other's presence to forget the griefs that weighed upon us both. I had given the last lines of my former friend to his father. He had read them in his own room, and though when we next met I remarked that his eye turned upon me wet with tears, as he evidently did not intimate the least inclination to expose to me what his son had written, I did not seek to learn the substance of Olivieri's note; though I was anxious to learn whether he had disclosed his conduct towards Julia. We never after mentioned his name, and we tried to keep the thoughts of his melancholy fate out of our minds, by resting upon our hopes of Louisa's welfare.

Count Wilhelm, whom I have before mentioned, found us on his way to his native country; hearing of our being at the same hotel, he sent in his name to my friend. Day after day he remained at Inspruck. The whole of the evening was spent with us in our apartment, and he seemed to seek more and more the means of showing attentions to Louisa. At first I was not disturbed by them, but at last I became fretful and irritable, for it appeared as if Louisa took a pleasure in his conversation. I had heard so much of his power of attaching women, that it seemed impossible for her to resist him. Every thing he did, though the most simple action, was perverted in my mind, to a covert sneer at my poverty and insignificance. I often answered him abruptly, and even insulted him. Louisa's meek eye turned upon me, but it seemed to have lost its influence. I one night found him by her side, he seemed to be earnestly pleading, he had hold of her hand, and she smiled. Stung to the quick by so slight a circumstance, I turned furiously away and retreated to my chamber. Had Berchtold taught me to command my passions, had he but shown me as models for my conduct, men, in the privacy of life, I might have escaped much. It is vain to rest upon it. I had thought that Louisa's influence over my mind, would have hindered me ever again losing myself, hurried away by any passion. But here Louisa's form arose in all the hideousness of jealousy's distorting mirror! I was mad. My clenched fist struck the table, I could not command myself. I remained some time in this state, when turning my eyes towards my bureau, I perceived an almanack; I seized it in mockery; I counted up the days since she had told me she loved me. I was suddenly struck, it was the 28th day of the month, it was a combination of seven. It seemed as if by one exertion I might free myself from doubt, and be at once lost in the horrible certainty, or be for ever blest in the knowledge of Louisa's heart.

I did not reflect; the hour struck; I seized my lamp, and rushing out was already close to the apartment of Doni, when wavering on the wick the flame suddenly sunk and expired. Yet nothing around was dark, it seemed as if I was surrounded by a mist formed by a dazzling light, too dazzling to allow me to view the objects round. I was a moment startled, but undismayed I strove to rush forward, my feet were bound to the floor. I strove but in vain to move. Gradually the light cleared, and gradually the features of that face, which I had so often gazed upon in my imagination, my mother's, appeared distinctly before me. Her form was majestic, but in her eye there was a softness, which was not even destroyed by the severity of her feeling. 'Ernestus,' were her words, 'Heaven has decreed at my prayer, that this crime shall be spared to you, you shall not act ungratefully.' – She seemed to vanish with an expression of sorrow upon her face, as if she were not allowed to continue, and felt the horror that burst upon me in consequence of the ignorance in which I was left. My senses forsook me, and the dawn of day had already pierced the thick clouds before I recovered.

I did not return to my room, I went into the open air, my thoughts were hurried; baffled, I was not subdued; jealousy still was not banished, I did not rest upon my mother's apparition, so strongly had the idea of Louisa's infidelity taken hold of me. While walking amidst the intricate windings of a public garden, I heard voices near me. One was Count Wilhelm, I heard him boasting of the favours of some lady, whom another thought loved him, and he suddenly presented himself before me; I grossly insulted him. He took a pleasure in torturing me with his pretended concern at my mistress's kindness to another. I struck him, we fought and he fell severely wounded. I stood by him and he was amply revenged. He told me that he had seen me entering the preceding evening, that being at that moment engaged in speaking about me, and Louisa having expressed her wish that I might be received into the Austrian service, he was offering his interest to forward my views, and that knowing how easily I was irritated, he had purposely taken her hand. He advised me to fly, I was obliged to do so for I was no longer safe where I was.

Louisa was then innocent. I cursed that fate which seemed to hang about me, always shielding me from death. I had fought in battle, but never yet had received the slightest wound: I had escaped from prison while the axe was falling. My rashness seemed to be incapable of hurting me; for there was a shield around me, that snatched me from peril. I was preserved from worse than death. Even this last act could not divide me from Louisa. She loved me indeed. Alarmed at seeing my antagonist brought in wounded, she did not shriek; she did not give herself up to loud and weak lamentations; but conscious, that probably my life depended upon the event of his wound, she sacrificed herself entirely to the care of the invalid. With unremitting attention she watched by his bedside. But when he was declared free from danger, then the cold hand of strengthened disease made itself felt. She was obliged again to return to her sick chamber. But first she begged her father to inform me of the favourable result. I returned. Doni met me on the stairs, – embraced me; but no joy was visible on his face. He announced to me the dangerous state in which Louisa lay, but did not reproach me; she had forbidden it. I was introduced into her room. Consumption was ruining her system; she was faint and weak; her continued cough and the marked colour on her cheek, but too well denoted the power it had acquired. I could not even ask her how she felt; but the tears fell down my cheek on the moist hand that held mine. She allowed me to stay with her. Talked to me of that power, whose pleasure it was to strengthen the weak and console the wretched, she said that he had soothed the agony of death's visible approach, and until she saw me, that she had found relief in the thought of the short time we should be separated. But now she saw my grief, she was sorry I should be left alone, even for those few moments, without a being, to whom I was attached; that she again wished for life, if amidst all its miseries she could but hope for the power of consoling me through these inflictions. In fine, she did not speak of herself, but of me – of the wretch who had gradually broken the weak threads which bound her pure soul to life. Count Wilhelm perfectly recovered, left us. I had seen him, and as the only atonement in my power, had acknowledged my folly, and had begged he would pardon it, though it had been so severely felt by him. He returned a vague answer, and I saw him no more.

Doni's interest was great; his wealth insured him friends, active in bringing back to their neighbourhood one whose riches fell in beneficent showers upon all. By their influence, he soon obtained a pardon for my resistance to the civil authorities in behalf of Olivieri, and I was granted permission to return to any part of the

French territory. As the cold Alpine air seemed to hasten the rapid steps of his daughter's decline, he determined upon having her conveyed again to the borders of the Lago Maggiore, which had seemed last year to have possessed such renovating powers. We departed, and soon found ourselves fixed in our abode. Nature wore the same aspect as the year before. Palanza, with its white walls and glittering columns shone as brilliantly in the sun's ray; the smile of Heaven seemed to play upon the fairy islets of the Boromei, and the rich woods of Belgirato reflected in the blue surface of the water, seemed to put the beauty of this in competition with the sublimity of the wild rocks of the upper part of this long lake. But Louisa's health had faded. She could hardly hope, if the disease continued its hasty steps to see these scenes again. But still that fairy enchanter, hope, acted upon me, and as each day she gained some slight addition to her strength, I pictured to myself years of happiness united with her I had long so ardently loved. She would not undeceive me, but left me the illusion. She was again able to enjoy the freshness of the air, and to walk out, amidst the varying scenery around. I supported her, and felt the light pressure of her feeble form resting upon my arm. She would stop, and draw some reflections on the bounty of God, even while in pain, from the various pictures before her; always attempting to turn my mind towards those thoughts, which she well knew could alone give me consolation, and a resting place in this vale of miseries. But still she seemed to recover strength. I entreated her to hope, and not to give way to such desponding thoughts. Her father, who was deceived as well as myself, begged of her to console herself; talked to her when alone of me, and spoke of his hopes of seeing us united, of her forming the only prop to his old age, and that I, how could he say it? was alone worthy in his estimation of receiving from a father's hand so great a treasure.

Unwilling to grieve her father, she yielded to my importunities, promised to be mine, if upon a certain day her acquired strength had not given signs of decay. You may imagine with what anxiety, with what hopes I watched each intervening moment. Every cold breeze made me shudder; every cloud that veiled the sun's ray caused me pain. I counted her breathings: whenever she moved, watched the firmness of her step. The day arrived. She was not weaker, but had seemed to find renewed energy in the thought of being mine. She was mine. I cannot paint to you the delirious state of mind, in which the next months passed over my head. I had a right to protect. I was something to that being; but I will not rest upon these feverish moments, you may imagine them; Louisa was mine – Louisa mine! But Heaven had not smiled upon our union – no, no. It was but the anger of a God veiled under the brightest hues. Louisa was my, – but I must relate the whole. Her health, as the winter approached declined again, and we returned to Milan. We lived with her father.

To engage my wife's attention, I resolved upon fitting up a part of the palace anew for our private use. Every thing was ordered, when it occurred to her that the best ornament we could add would be the portrait of her father. I had recovered from my sister our mother's locket, and showing it to Louisa, we determined upon having it copied and hung opposite the Count's. To give Doni, as we thought an agreeable surprise, we determined upon having them privately executed, and placed in their situation without his cognisance. I sought for a painter, and spent whole mornings with him at his eazel, directing him how to paint my mother. I described to him, as well as I could, her appearance to me at Inspruck, and pretending that I had seen her in a dream, I insisted upon his representing her in such a situation. He executed it, and by the magic effect of his pencil, excited a most extraordinary impression of awe in my breast, whenever I turned my eyes upon the picture. She seemed starting from the canvass; the outline of her figure was lost in the blaze of light, and her face, meek amidst splendour, severe, though with features naturally mild, seemed speaking those words I had heard. I took Louisa to see it; she felt the same awe as myself, though she could not assign a reason for it, but she continued gazing, till I perceived her eyes wet with tears.

The pictures were privately introduced into the house. We had succeeded in keeping them secret from Doni. In a few days was Louisa's birth-day, we resolved therefore to make him our guest upon that occasion in our new apartment. We invited several of our most intimate friends. Every thing passed in gaiety. At last, all the company were gone, and we remained alone. We then, taking him each by one hand, led him into what we intended should be our private sitting room, telling him he should then see our best friends, the one in Heaven, the other on earth. The door was opened; directly before him was his own portrait; he seemed surprised and pleased; he turned round; I had hardly announced to him that the one he then saw was my mother's, when he fell. Alarmed we raised him. 'Your mother! did you say, your mother?'

He threw himself upon the floor, and called upon God to free him from the consciousness of horror like to his. We knelt by him close together; he saw us, raised his aged hands, and with a fluttering voice bade us, if we dreaded Heaven's most dreadful curse, to separate. But again he fell to the ground, crying, 'It is too late, too late, the crime is consummated.' We raised him, he turned hastily away, for he was opposite the portrait, and besought us to take him thence. We led him to his chamber; he motioned us to leave him.

We retired in silence, we knew not what to understand; was it merely the greater effect of that portrait's power which had been exerted over us. We could not hope it, we were lost in conjectures. Louisa's health was so much broken that I was alarmed for the effects it might have upon her, and, therefore, strove to turn her mind from the subject; but in vain. She did not sleep the whole night, the anxiety concerning her father would not allow her to seek forgetfulness even for a moment. The effect may be imagined upon so weak a constitution. Her father refused to see us for several days, and each day I saw the mind acting upon my wife's health with alarming rapidity. When this reached the ears of her father, he could no longer resist our importunities, he saw us; but the sight of his haggard and wild countenance did not restore Louisa. He had evidently been engaged in writing. We pressed him to explain his conduct. He replied, I knew not what I wished to learn. 'It will blast you, as it has done your friend. You must learn it, but it shall be when I am in the grave, and before him who has thus punished my crime; then, then, I may intercede for you, if I myself am sufficiently purified by suffering. He may hear a father's, though it be a criminal's, prayer.' His words seemed almost incoherent, he at times called me son, but then with hurried impatience he corrected himself; he asked me whence I got that portrait, I put the locket into his hands. ''Twas mine, I gave it,' he hurried, pressed it to his breast, and bade us leave him. We did; he saw us daily, but in silence; he seemed absorbed in one thought, and to that he could not give utterance. He took little, too little, nourishment; but always occupied in writing; he seemed but to find strength for that; when we saw him, he was hardly capable of motion. His task was at last finished. We had been with him as usual, when we were suddenly recalled. He was dying; he bade us kneel down by his side, he blessed us. He took the papers from his table, and putting them into my hands, he bade me read them when he was in the grave, and know the horrors that awaited me; he commanded us to trust in God's mercy, and he sunk, blessing us, upon his couch, breathed no more.

I bore my Louisa from this scene, she was from this moment confined to her bed. I saw the Count laid in the vault of his ancestors, and then returned to my wife's chamber, whence I never issued till I had no longer a wife. It was evident that all art was unavailing. It was the undermining of a constitution, not by a common bodily disease, but by the griefs of a heart that had never lately found a moment's respite from the most bitter inflictions. Yet, even at this moment, she seemed to forget herself, in her attempts to console me. She alone broke the silence around; I sat in mute despair; I saw Louisa before me, and I was to be left isolated, scathed by divine anger, without consolation. She held my hand, spoke to me of another world; for a moment her words would even subdue my grief, and let me feel as if that hope were enough. At last, seeing the silent sorrow that was preying confined within my breast, she sought to rouse me, bade me read those papers; I did in a luckless moment; only hinted at the horrible mystery unfolded there, and saw the last convulsive throe I was destined to witness in any bound to me by love. I cannot tell you more; read that damning tale, and then you may know what I dare, nay, dare not rest upon. My history is quickly ended. I was dragged from the now lifeless Louisa; but I stole from my guards in the night, gained an entrance into the room, where death showed, as if boasting his beauteous victim, dressed in pomp. The wax tapers seemed to burn dimly, as if in unison with the solemn scene; the black walls, the felted ground, the corpse stretched out, arrayed in white, the stillness visible upon that beauteous face, stilled even the tumult in my breast. She did not seem dead but asleep, I had held her in my arms, upon my breast, looking as she then looked, I gazed upon her for moments, it seemed as if I believed the still appearance wronged my senses. I was about to press her to my heart, my lips were approaching hers, but I started; there were two flies already revelling on those lips, and she could not chase them. I hurried away, I could not remain any longer there. I followed her bier also, and I saw my dearest, my last bond to this earth deposited there, where peace seemed to invite me too. Religion, Louisa's words, however, had not lost all influence, I resisted that will, which would have led me to immolate myself a victim to the manes of those my love had slain. The hopes of a futurity, of Louisa in Heaven, upheld me.

I retired first to Beatenberg, there in the former house of Berchtold, I spent some time: it was too near the first scenes of memory. I left them and came hither; here, amidst these rocks, bound to me by no memory of the past, I spend the few hours allotted me by Heaven, in penance; here each day, my prayer is offered up, that in mercy I might be taken to Louisa. My life has been a life of anguish, of vice, of crime; but still amidst these there have been moments, there has been a being, which, if life could be renewed, would cause me to dare all again, once more to go through those few moments. Often in my dreams I see that form, but now, if when in this mortal life her beauty could not be described, how can I now, that her form, her face, are decked with the smile of him, who glories in the glory of his children. When she now appears in my dreams, there is no longer that hideous chasm opening between us; she is always decked as if for another bridal day, and I awake confident in that day's approach without guilt.

But leave me, depart to-morrow upon your intended journey, if that you stay, who knows but the curse which has attended me through life may yet be acting, and may fall upon you as well as all others whom I have loved. These papers will explain to you what I have withheld, the life of Doni. If that you return this way, you may find me dead. Drop not a tear over my grave, I shall be with Louisa. Farewell, but depart knowing that there exists a consolation, which man cannot take from you, which misfortune cannot destroy, the belief in a future state, in the mercy of a redeeming God. It is there I find refuge.

The Life of Count Filiberto Doni

The family to which I belong is one of the most noble in Lombardy; but I, being the son of the younger branch, did not enjoy many of those advantages which belong to high rank. I was sent at a very early age to a college of Jesuits, and soon distinguished myself so much, that all the allurements the society was in the habit of holding out to young men of promise, were employed to attach me to this community. I had, however, been educated amongst the mountains; and having been nursed by an old retainer of the family, I had conceived so high an idea of the importance and consequence attached to nobility, that I could not resolve upon putting on a dress, which bound me to forego all those advantages and pleasures, the early associations excited by my nurse, had taught me to believe, belonged to the entry of a nobleman into that very world, my venerable master endeavoured, in vain, to persuade me, was every thing horrible. In the mountains, a son of even the lateral descendants from the Lord, is always looked up to with so much respect and veneration by the poor inhabitants of these districts, that it is no wonder if I was deceived. When the religious began to flatter and distinguish me above my companions, as I was not conscious of any exertion in the acquisition of that mental superiority about which they talked, I attributed their attentions to the respect they felt for one of such exalted rank, as I imagined myself born to, having been left also for the whole of the time with the men, without having paid a single visit to my family, the distant memory of what I had seen at home, appeared to me in contrast with the plain life of my superiors, as something magnificent and passing comparison. My parents, hearing of the talents of their son, were anxious for his entry into an order, whose influence they well knew could be profitable in the greatest degree, not only to the individual, but to the whole of his family. When, therefore, they found that their son was determined not to bind himself by any bond which should hinder him from enjoying, what his imagination had pictured; they thought the best plan in such a case was to allow me to view nearer, that misery which attends nobility devoid of riches. I was accordingly sent for home.

I arrived – I was astonished at not being led to one of those numerous palaces I met on my way to my father's, in the streets of Milan. My guide and myself came at last into the Corso; I began to reconcile myself, seeing the end of the city before me nothing but palaces on both sides; when suddenly, we turned down a narrow street, and I came to the gate of an obscure house. I did not speak, but my feelings were hurt. I ascended a narrow staircase, and I found myself in the presence of my mother. She was lying on a couch covered with leather, dressed in all the dirty tawdry of one who glories in the past; she was playing with a dog with one hand, while the other was stretched over an earthenware brazier. A dirty servant, slip shod, with hair which had apparently never been touched by a comb, led me into the room, and announced me. My mother did not even move, she was too busily engaged by her puppy to notice me. At last, tired of seeing only the same jumps, turning round in the act of stretching her weary limbs, she saw my figure; imagining it to be that of her son, she addressed herself to me. 'Ah, Filiberto, so you are really come home to load your parents with your expences, when you might have become a Jesuit with every prospect of power. Well, we shall see how your father will bear it. For my part I will not sacrifice any more first representations for your follies. I had already engaged a box at the Scala, with the money I had spared from our very food; when your father, hearing of it, went and sold the tickets because you were expected.' These were the first words, I remember, my mother spoke to me. I cannot describe to you the various feelings they excited in my breast. I could not believe this to be my mother. I did not answer her; but engaged in thought, I sat down, and soon lost sight of the white cold walls and brick floor, in the bitterness of my imaginations. My father entered, throwing off his huge great coat, which, placed upon his shoulders, covered both his body and the clay vessel containing the heated charcoal; he embraced me, and seemed really pleased to see me.

I spent a miserable day, for it was the very one on which a new opera was to be brought out, and all the usual companions of my mother, having, by intrigue and what not, secured places, she was left alone without even her *cavalier servente,* in the company of her husband and son this was insupportable, and she did nothing the whole evening but vent her bad temper upon me, sneering at my foolish ideas of rank. My father, who seemed accustomed to these scenes, quietly took his seat in a retired part of the room, and with his great coat confining the warm air arising from his *scaldino* around his body, soon fell asleep. The servant came in after the Caffè, and spinning at my mother's side, for a time diverted her attention from me, by joining with the complete appearance of an equal in all that mean criticism of their neighbours, which is esteemed the more witty according to its ill-nature. I was at last glad to go to bed. You may imagine what was the bed room of the son, when the receiving room of the *Padrona* was such as I have described.

As I passed by a door upon the staircase, I saw two heads put out to look at me; they were my sisters; I cannot describe to you the sensation I felt, when I found no one had thought it necessary to bring them to see their brother, or even to mention them to him. I found them dressed in the most coarse clothes, and I had hardly been there a few minutes, before they began recounting to me the hardships and privations they had lately undergone in consequence of the anxiety of my mother to secure a box at the opera for this night. It is useless to paint more scenes of this nature; my mother was vain, and spent even what should have been given to feeding her children, in the most distant imitation of the rich, to whom she had the honour of being allied, and who condescended to laugh at her for her pains. My father loved quiet above all things; his income was small, very incompetent to supply the foolish vanity of my mother, he was therefore always in debt, and even obliged to be a mean hanger on upon the elder branch of the family.

Next day I went with my father to visit the head of our family, and I there saw what my imagination had represented to me. The numerous servants seemed bustling about, as if their wills were too rapid for their limbs. The rich liveries, which were almost reflected in the burnished floors of marble and precious woods, the porphyry columns, the fresco paintings, and the silken coverings to even the footstools astonished me. I followed in silence the officious servant, who seemed amazed at my astonishment at that splendour, in which he had always bustled, though but the son of a cowherd. We were conducted into the boudoir of our relation. He was at his toilette, every thing breathed effeminacy, all was luxurious, the delicately coloured curtains let in the enfeebled light of the noon day. When I entered I could hardly distinguish the objects around, for coming from rooms illuminated by all the powers of the sun, my eyes could not feel the weaker impressions of this veiled obscurity. My relation struck with the astonishment I displayed at such magnificence, amused himself with calling forth signs of wonder from me. I was invited to stay with him, and I accordingly went from my mother's, who was glad to get rid of the inconvenience arising from the addition I caused to be made to the daily expences, at the same time that she was proud of having to talk about the notice I had excited at the Palazzo Doni. My relation conducted me every where. I was introduced by him to the casino of the nobles, and was always in his box at the theatre of La Scala. He advised me to attach myself to an old Countess, whose *cavalier servente* was just dead. I did so, and soon had the honour of carrying her shawl, and whispering in her ear even to the exclusion of her superannuated husband, at all the places of public resort.

I was now initiated into all the magic enjoyments of wealth and splendour. Without any riches or merit of my own, I enjoyed all the luxuries, which were not a little heightened by the visits I paid my father's house, where I saw poverty in its most appalling state, accompanied by pretensions to rank. I was intoxicated. The Countess had several daughters, these I seldom saw, though they were approaching rapidly to womanhood. It however happened, that soon after I had obtained a footing in her house, that a birth-day of her eldest child occurred. She resolved upon celebrating it by a little ball, chiefly composed of the immediate connections of the family. I was admitted by virtue of my office. I had never before been in a ball-room. The splendid chandeliers, the gay dresses, and the beautiful women, surrounding me on every side, raised a scene before me, which even my most vivid fancy had never imagined.

I could not dance, I was therefore a mere spectator; but I was not idle, I had never been accustomed to see unmarried females, for they are not admitted into the society to which I belonged. There appeared a charm about them I could not define; they fixed my attention, and as each moved in the light dance, with all the agility and grace attendant upon youth, while their retreating looks seemed to denote a fear that they excited observation; I attempted in vain to discover what fascinated me. My heart beat violently, it seemed as if I had never before witnessed beauty. Towards the end of the evening, a party of foreigners entered; they had come to reside in Milan; with them was a young lady. She entered into the dances. She had not the light airy step of her companions, she had not the same brilliancy of eye, but there was something so powerful in her meek glance, in her measured graceful step, that enchained the senses. From that moment I could gaze upon no one else. She alone seemed to be moving, she alone seemed to be the object worthy of attention. I was yet gazing upon her, when the Countess called me to join her party at tre sette. I accompanied her, but it was in vain for me to attempt fixing my mind upon the cards before me. I saw nothing but that figure which had been that moment before my sight. I made blunders that called forth impatient exclamations from my partners, and I was at last allowed to rise upon the plea of a head-ache. I instantly entered the other room, but she was gone.

She had however left her image in my breast. For several days I did not see her again, but at last she began to appear in public, for being a foreigner, her parents did not confine her as is customary amongst Italians. I often left the Countess in the Theatre, and placing myself in the pit, near the box in which she was, watched her slightest motion. There was a melancholy look about her that seemed to indicate an acquaintance with grief, that was extraordinary in so young a person. Her dark blue eye was seldom unveiled; her long modest eyelashes generally hid their splendour, and her silence, and her uninterested glance, added a charm to her figure I cannot describe. Her goodness and charity were spoken of by all, her beauty was not envied or denied by her own, while her gentle manners and winning smile, seemed to gain the heart of all the other sex. I accompanied the Countess to her house. I sat by her, but could not speak with her. It seemed as if the emotion in my breast, stifled the words I was about to utter. She however noticed me, and her parents in repeating their compliments to the lady I accompanied, included me in a general invitation to the house.

As it was not the custom for ladies of rank to rise until a late hour, I had a great part of the day upon my own hands. I used generally to lounge about, and sometimes go to the Ambrosian Library, in quest of something to engage my attention. One morning I was there as usual, and I found the Ernachs there. Matilda was with them, they were just then occupied in viewing the manuscript of Virgil, with Petrarch's annotations. When the Cicerone pointed out the last note of this latter poet, in which he speaks of his love to Laura, I could not help remarking, a momentary emotion which passed across the face of Matilda. Her mother also observed it, and immediately taking her arm, accompanied her into the room containing pictures of several of the greatest masters. I followed them, and entered into conversation by pointing out the heads of the Milanese Raphael, which one cannot examine without feeling a stillness come over our senses foreign to our nature. There is so much beauty and heavenly quiet about them, that they indeed resemble representations of a poet's dream. Before we parted, I was accepted as the guide to the curiosities, which they had not yet seen, and my office was to begin the next day.

It is useless to describe to you the gradual steps of love. I at last neglected the attentions due to the Countess, while sitting by the side of Matilda. At last, no longer capable of enduring the feelings within my bosom, I confessed my love to the object I adored. She was not angry, nor did she seem surprised; but in a voice that betrayed inward agitation, she begged of me to lay aside all hopes of gaining her hand, and conjured me not to mention it to her father. I was confused and abashed. I retired and returned to the palace, where I confined myself to my chamber. Not having appeared for several days in society, and inquiries being made concerning me, I was soon sought for by my kind relation. He seemed so anxious about the ill health, which he imagined was the cause of my absence from those gaieties in which I always seemed to delight, that I was induced to lay open to him the whole of my heart. He tried to administer consolation, but could not succeed; my vanity was mortified, and reflecting upon my poverty, I had imagined that I was despised for some richer rival. He seemed to know Matilda better, told me he could not believe it, but I dwelt so much upon the subject, that he saw it was useless to oppose my opinion any longer. He attempted to induce me to accompany him into society, but I refused, and for some days remained alone in my chamber.

Sick with all the splendour around, which seemed to mock me, I determined in spite of the expected reproaches of my mother, to return to my father's house, where by long confinement I fell ill. My kind relation hearing of this came to me, and tried to represent to me the folly of my conduct; but disappointed love and mortified vanity, did not allow me to listen. Seeing me thus haunted by the idea of riches, he generously offered to advance me a considerable sum, and to give me letters to a friend at Alexandria, where I might he thought employ my capital to the greatest advantage in commercial speculations. I thanked him, and accepted his kind offer. I soon left Milan, determined never to return till those riches were mine, which should enable me to assert a rank equal to any in my native city. I arrived at Alexandria, and was soon engaged in mercantile speculations, with an eagerness that caused all my transactions to appear more like the ventures of a desperate gambler than the secure projects of a merchant. I found several Europeans established in this city, chiefly engaged in the commerce of grain.

Amongst the rest, there was one who seemed to form a particular attachment to me; he was several years older than myself, and was noted amongst us for a certain avoidance of pleasure which did not appear natural to his years. He was always engaged, when not occupied in his business, either in reading or in a solitary ramble through the burnt neighbourhood of this ruined town. I was the only person he sought; he seemed to place his confidence in me, and made many inquiries, at first vaguely, concerning those I had known at Milan. Happening to name the

Ernachs, his face immediately became anxious, and his questions evidently bore a stamp of interest they had not before shown. This excited my attention and caused me to make more particular inquiries concerning him. Little was known; he was a German, and it was thought he had been disappointed in love. He perceived the attention I began to show him, and one evening when we were alone, he told me that he had at first been induced to seek my society, from a letter he had received from Matilda. 'You must have perceived the interest, with which I listened to your account of the family of the Ernachs; know that I love Matilda, that I have reason to believe my affection is returned, but that owing to my poverty, I have never dared to confess even to her the feelings of love I bear within my breast. We were together from earliest infancy, all our pleasures were in common, and though, when I grew to manhood, I no longer dared to use the familiarity of my earlier years with her, who began to vest the charms of woman, still we partook in the pleasures of each other's occupations. Many things we studied together. I read the lighter authors of literature to her while she was engaged in those occupations attendant, in our country, upon every female member of a family. I at last opened Petrarch, and read those sonnets in which love is so delicately portrayed. You cannot conceive my emotions, when I perceived that she felt them as I did myself, and that she often raised her modest eyes, while a blush mantled her cheek, to gaze upon me, while my trembling voice seemed not to be reading the sentiments of another, but speaking the feelings of my own breast. We seemed, indeed, not to want to comment upon what we were both sensible expressed only those truths which echoed in the breasts of both. When, however, I retired, I always upbraided myself for thus exposing, though indirectly, that love, of which I had no reason to think her parents would approve, for I had no profession, and was not born to riches. When, however, I saw her, and she again asked for the author whose delicate pencil only traced the most fading hues of love, I again read. We were thus engaged, when we were interrupted by her mother, who had stood unperceived some time watching the emotions but too visible in our countenances. She did not then speak, but taking another opportunity, when I was alone with her, she gently intimated, that I had not acted honourably in thus engaging the attention of Matilda to such poetry, as was but too powerful a seducer of the mind. I was but too conscious of it. I acknowledged my error, and promised to take no further occasion of thus acting upon her daughter's susceptible heart. She placed entire confidence in me, and was not deceived. I applied to my father, who, at my desire, sent me hither to push my fortune, and I have succeeded as well as I expected.'

How shall I convey to you an idea of what passed in my mind? Before me stood the unconscious cause of my being rejected by Matilda. He had told me, he loved her, that she loved him. I was silent when he ended, I could not rouse myself to speak to him; he, thinking that his narration had tired me, made an apology, to which I could only answer by monosyllables; he retired and left me to my own thoughts. It was evident Matilda preferred another. My feelings may be imagined, – cannot be described. It seemed as if some demon actuated me, I fell upon my knees, and dared even to call God to witness my vow of obtaining the object of my affections, in spite of all obstacles. It seemed as if I felt more at peace after having thus resolved upon not yielding even to him she loved, the possession I ambitioned.

I sought Huldebrand, for so was my rival called, determined to worm into his confidence, and gain the whole of his secret. I told him not to impute my abstraction on the former evening to any thing but my mind being engaged in thought upon a circumstance, which I noticed at Milan, and which was now fully explained. I then mentioned to him the emotion I had noticed in Matilda's countenance, while listening to the memorial of Petrarch with regard to the duration of his love. This immediately secured his attention, and I soon learnt many circumstances with regard to their early years; and I became convinced, that there was really no engagement between them.

In the mean time my speculations, which had been begun rashly, had for the greater part turned out badly, and I found myself with a capital considerably diminished. Huldebrand who could not remain ignorant of my losses proposed to me, as I seemed ignorant of the best means of securing a profitable commerce, to join him. I did so; but growing tired of the slow advantages to be obtained by the regular channels, I at last induced him to join me in a speculation that seemed to promise a certain and at the same time immense profit. We ventured, and lost all we risked. My loss did not grieve me much, for it had reduced my Matilda's favoured lover to the same want as myself. He was not however dismayed, nor did he reproach me, but immediately exerting himself to recover all that remained of our property, he proposed, that we should join some Armenians, who were about to leave Alexandria and penetrate into the interior of Asia, in hopes of finding some opportunity of bettering our small fortunes. I consented, and we accompanied them.

We entered Persia, and travelled even into India. We soon found our capitals rapidly increasing, for, imitating the Armenians, we bought upon several occasions precious stones, which we resold almost immediately greatly to our advantage. It is, in no way necessary for me to give an account of these countries, towards the understanding the fatality that attended my life. I travelled through them careless about the scenery or inhabitants; the whole of my attention was engaged in my endeavours to acquire wealth. Matilda stood constantly before me as the bride of Huldebrand, and my father's house always appeared in contrast with the palace of the head of our family. I soon entered into the spirit of the traffic I was engaged in, and restrained as I was by Huldebrand's steadiness, we rapidly indeed accumulated an immense sum, which we carried always with us in precious stones.

I had been particularly struck by the venerable appearance of one of our companions, he was aged, his head was white with the numbered years that had passed since his birth. This was the more remarkable from the contrast it offered with the jet black hair and beards of his countrymen. He was never engaged in their occupations, he never seemed to be concerned in any mercantile transaction, yet he seemed to be careless of his money, which he gave profusely to all. He seemed to delight in the society of strangers, and therefore sought ours; but Huldebrand not speaking his language did not gain the same hold of his affections as myself; he indeed treated me completely as his son, and often directed me in the conduct of our concerns; his advice was always advantageous.

This stranger seemed to look upon me as his pupil, and he gradually turned my mind to the objects around me. But he did not improve my heart by the opening of my mind. He was himself extremely rich; when therefore he held forth upon the happiness of contented poverty, I thought he was but a mere visionary, imagining the Arabian delights of a sandy desert, while shaded by the canopying foliage of a grove, and surrounded by all the riches of a cultivated country. I looked around, and I saw the genius and the idiot both equally subservient to the will of the wealthy. I saw virtue trodden under foot, and vice, that monster in rags in the cottage, adored as a goddess in the temples of the gaudy palace. Wherever I went, it seemed as if gold, in the bustling of the whole of life, had the same effect as a few aspers thrown amidst the obstreperous crowd that immediately leaves off its hideous yell in haste to scramble for the miserable gain. Riches were a thirst upon me. I could not believe that Matilda or Ernach, her father, could resist the splendour of wealth. But Huldebrand was with me, half our common property was his. He loved, was beloved. Whenever I looked upon him, my heart did not beat quicker; it seemed for a moment to pause, as if his sight blasted its vital action, but it beat again with redoubled violence, when Matilda's image rose upon my mind, and my former vow was again repeated.

Though my appetite for riches was not sated, it was gratified; our speculations had been constantly doubling our capital, and we had already left the banks of the Euphrates, turning our steps towards Europe, when we gradually entered the vast desert that spreads its subtle sands from the Red Sea, almost to the Mediterranean. Having all our wealth about us in jewels and gold, we were anxious about our safety. Every night the cry of the watchful sentinel bidding us be upon the alert, while it called to the roaming Arab to depart, sounded on my waking ears, and often I arose in painful anxiety, to gaze upon the far spread horizon, lost sometimes in the misty light of the bright moon. I envied the sound sleep of the poor camel-driver, who lay extended by the animal entrusted to his care, as heedless of my wealth, as the brute about the fate of his burden. At last the ground seemed to acquire firmness to the foot, and the camel already began to browse upon the solitary stunted plants that here and there spread their parched growth to the no longer beneficent ray of an eastern sun. I thought myself secure, night came, and I was standing by my open tent, for I could not rest; I was gazing upon a long line which bounded the horizon, with a thin dark streak, indicating the palm boundary to our toilsome pilgrimages; there were slight clouds flitting before the moon, and as their shadows fled over the vast expanse, my heart beat quicker, for each, as it approached from the horizon, seemed to my hurried imagination, as the dark shadow formed by an Arab troop; one followed the other, always bearing deceit with it. At last from the long line of palms, a black speck seemed to move with great rapidity; I could trace no cloud upon the Heavens, which could throw its dark shadow upon this track; I breathless called a sentinel, the alarm was given, but we were surrounded; I went about like a madman, encouraged the men to fight, – fought. The circle was gradually straitened round us; the men fell by the distant arrows at first, but the work of death was not slower, when the sword clashed against sword, and the robber's foot trod upon his antagonist's. I struggled, my riches were lost; while yet struggling amidst our very tents, I heard the old Armenian cry for help, he was combating with a young Arabian, who had thrown him to the ground. I rushed forward, bade the robber defend himself; we fought, I succeeded in disarming him, and was upon the point of thrusting my sword through his body, when he begged of me to spare his life, promising that both the Armenian and myself should be safe. I saw all resistance was at an end, I gave him back his weapon, and approached the old man who was wounded. He took my hand, thanked me for my attempt to save him, but he thought his wound was mortal; he bade me at the same time console myself for the loss of my accumulated wealth, saying that he would, ere he died, make me ample amends.

Our lives, at the intercession of the Arab I had spared, who proved to be a man of rank amongst the robbers, were granted us. He conveyed the Armenian to his own tent, and I anxiously placed myself by the old man's side, watching, with the agitation of a desperate gambler, every various expression of his countenance; it was my last stake. Huldebrand I knew was not killed, but had been given, as part of the booty, to one of the robbers, in hopes of his ransoming himself; but he was ruined like myself, had lost every thing; I was however, if not deceived, to obtain riches as abundantly as before. Matilda might then be mine; I made no further inquiries about him who had partaken the vicissitudes of commerce and of life with me, who had been almost beggared by my rashness, and whose steadiness had enabled me to recover every thing, and to gain wealth. I sat by the old man; every sound that fell from his lips, seemed the announcement of his bequest, but he was silent on that subject.

Five days elapsed, at last the sixth was passing, and his strength was evidently rapidly failing, his breath became hurried, and his eyes began to take that lustre, which seems to be the last exertion of the departing soul; he then spoke, 'I wished,' he said, 'that my life had been spared but a short time longer, I could then have bestowed wealth upon you, without the conditions that may now startle you. Know, but how dare I tell it? you may look upon me with horror, and while I am wishing to bless you, may turn away from me. I have a power that is supposed to bring the curse of the Almighty upon it; I can, – I have the power of raising a spirit from the vast abyss, and make him lay at my feet, the infinite wealth enclosed within the earth's recesses. But if you would listen to one aged, who has borne this blasting power from early youth, you would refuse the dangerous gift. For there is a condition necessarily bound to that power, which will undoubtedly quell your ardent longing even for riches.' It was in vain that he addressed me thus, Matilda and wealth connected rose to my imagination. I pressed him to explain himself. He did. He told me that either I could only call for a certain sum at a time, and that at each time, some human domestic infliction, worse than the preceding, would fall upon me, or that, I at once, could gain unlimited power, and constant domestic prosperity, on the condition of giving myself up for ever to the will of a malignant being. He had chosen the first, had called but once for the exertion of the demon's power, but his happiness had been withered by that once. I did not hesitate, I laughed in my own mind at domestic happiness, I had lived only in Italy, and in the East, I begged of him to disclose his secret; he did. I bound myself to the first condition.

I impatiently rose, I left the old man upon his dying couch, and retreated to my own tent. I raised the spirit, his hideous form might have appalled a stronger heart than mine. I trembled, but his mocking laugh subdued my fears, and bending my knee, I acknowledged him as my superior through life. I cannot describe the scene, I could not without recording some part of the spells by which I raised this monster, and he has but too fully proved his power for me to be willing to put the least clue into the hands of any one which might bring the curse I have felt upon him. Besides riches, I gained other powers, but these are not connected with yours and my Louisa's fate, I shall not speak of them.

I returned to the sick man's tent, the Armenian was dead. I did not feel sorry, how could I at that moment; I was exultant, my wealth was so enormous, I did not see a possibility of spending it. The next day the robbers buried my benefactor in the burning sands. I proposed a ransom for myself to the Arab, he insisted upon my accepting my freedom. I did, and we eat together; no longer fearing treachery, I made him a present to an enormous amount. He was surprised, but did not make even the smallest inquiry.

I roamed about the encampment, for I was desirous of seeing these robbers in their native barren plain. While wandering about their black tents, I heard a voice of pain issuing from one of the most miserable. It was Huldebrand, he was calling, in the delirium of a fever, for a drop of water to allay his thirst. The well was close to me. The tent was open, no one was near, he was extended upon the sandy floor, with hardly any clothes to defend him from its hot touch. I, even I, could not resist this appeal, I seized a vessel lying by his side, and drew it from the well full. I was turning towards him, when suddenly his tones altered, he seemed to press his breast, while in the softest words he addressed some one. I approached, he was imagining Matilda stood by him. The words sounded on my ear, – 'I know, Matilda, that you love me.' The pitcher fell upon the sand, and the water was drank up by the burning dust, and I turned away with a raging heart, from the dying Huldebrand.

I instantly determined upon leaving the spot. The noble Arab escorted me to the utmost boundary of the desert, and I was safe from danger. I hired camels and horses, and proceeded to Aleppo, spreading every where that I was a merchant, who had been very successful in my speculations. This was easy to me, for I could refer to people with whom I had had transactions, and my name was known. I hastened to Italy, and soon reached Milan, I entered with all the pomp of riches; I will not describe my entry, it was foolishly splendid, nor will I attempt to paint to you the daily display I made of some new folly; they were produced by the intoxication of a madman. Matilda, for she held no less a powerful influence over me than my avarice, was the object of the whole. I found her health much decayed, she had not heard of Huldebrand for more than two years. Yet there was perhaps a greater charm in that pale cheek and languid eye, than I had found in the delicate colouring of the one, or the splendour of the other. If I could gain her love now, it would, indeed, be an ample compensation for her former rejection. I began by spreading the report of her lover's death, though I was not certain of the fact, yet I thought, at any rate, that he could not re-appear so soon as not to allow me time to accomplish my end. I then went to her father's, and in the course of the conversation announced it.

Matilda was inconsolable, but she took pleasure in my society, for I could talk to her of Huldebrand, I related indifferent particulars concerning him, the eagerness with which she listened reached my heart; I determined, however, to endure even these pangs, rather than lose the opportunities afforded me of sitting by her side. As in the course of narration, I introduced the relation of actions in which I had been his benefactor, she blessed me for it. I felt like a baffled demon. I gradually began to talk of myself. I sounded the father and mother with regard to a marriage; obtained their full consent and approbation. They gradually broke it to their daughter. She wondered at my seeking for a widowed heart; insisted upon my taking some months to consider of it, while she herself fulfilled the term of mourning she thought due to her lover's memory. I was anxious, and fearful of Huldebrand's appearance. I pressed my suit with earnestness; my relations, her father, her mother, used all the arts of persuasion to induce her to anticipate the day. She did, and we were married.

It now seemed as if I could dare the world. I had Matilda, had wealth, the only objects my mind had ever rested upon were mine. I had two children, Louisa and Olivieri. You cannot imagine the splendour in which I lived. Where could the mortal be found who had greater supposed sources of happiness than mine? yet I was miserable; Matilda was mine, my wife, but her affections still rested upon the image of my rival. I doted upon her; it seemed as if the price of guilt I had paid bound her the more to me, as if she were to form the only happiness I was to know, and she did not love me. She differed entirely from my countrywomen; she enjoyed her domestic circle, she was modest; and while she stood amongst the abandoned wantons, who formed the only society around her, she stood erect, as if she were sent by Heaven to show deluded men the beauties of the virtues they despised.

I had not enjoyed the society of my wife more than three years, when my momentary happiness was blasted. Matilda came home one day, as I imagined, from the Corso, flurried and violently agitated. She threw herself upon the sofa, and lost in thought, she did not perceive that I was near her. She drew from her breast a note: I could see over her shoulder; it struck me that it was Huldebrand's hand-writing. She seemed to look upon it as if she could not believe her eyes. She viewed it, her hands fell, and the movement of the eyelids over the fixed eyes seemed to denote the belief in a deceit of the senses. Her breath was still, her cheek pale, she did not move. I unavoidably discovered myself; she turned, looked at me, and the tears bursting from her eyes, rolled down her cheeks, as she rushed out of the room. I dared not follow her. Huldebrand might be stalking in my very house, might be close to me, his words of reproach might be already in the air, prepared to damn me with their sound. I should be proved in the world's face, a liar, a wretch without a spark of generosity, of gratitude, in Matilda's face – I hid myself in my chamber, for the consciousness of my guilt caused me at first to wish for concealment. But the thought of my rival roused me; was it not possible to remove him? I rushed out of my room, and was upon the point of going through the great gate, when I perceived a figure descending the staircase, wrapt closely in a large mantle. It was a woman – it was Matilda. Her hurried step and anxious glances thrown around caused me to watch her. She went out into the street, I followed her; there was an obstacle near the theatre, she cleared it, but I lost her in the crowd of carriages. In vain I tried every opening leading to the theatre, I could not recover a trace of her. At last I was obliged to lean exhausted against the wall, and Ernach, her father, coming from the theatre, discovered me. Perceiving my agitation at sight of him, he insisted upon escorting me home. He attempted to lead me to explain to him the cause of my trembling limbs, which weighed upon his arm. He did nor know that he sought to know my shame; I insisted upon his leaving me, and I at last fell exhausted upon a chair in my saloon.

I know not how long I had remained in this situation by myself; I at last heard Matilda's light step ascending the staircase. I did not move, my eyes remained still gazing on the ground when she entered. At sight of me she started, but she commanded herself approached me with a faltering step. I attempted to clasp her to my bosom, as if I know not what passed in my mind. She retreated. 'You have a right to know where I have been in this clandestine manner.' I hid my face with my hands, I was conscious she had been to see Huldebrand. She had been with him, she would say no more. I threw myself at her feet, she turned away. 'I can no longer even esteem you,' were the last words she said, when she left me.

She went out several times in the course of next day; once I attempted to follow her. She perceived me at the door: 'Filiberto,' she said, 'seek not to pursue my steps, I am but active in the cause of virtue. Retire and leave me. You must be aware of what hangs over your head. Would that Heaven may grant I could avert it from my husband, my children's father.' I was left in a state of mind that bordered upon phrenzy. I rushed out of the house, and turning my steps another way, I did not return towards my home till night. When I did return, I found every thing in the greatest confusion. There was a carriage with posthorses at the gate. The moment I approached, my valet came to me to tell me of my shame. Matilda had been seen leaving Milan, with a gentleman in her company. I jumped into the carriage, and followed upon the road they were reported to have taken.

I did not speak during the whole time; I did not listen, though my servant, having entered with me, was telling me more of the circumstances. Night and day I travelled in pursuit. I seemed to be gaining on them. I at last overtook them just as I was entering a village in Savoy. They were upon the point of leaving it. I sprung out of my carriage, and with the speed of a demoniac I ran after them. In my furious haste, I fell. I did not attempt to rise, but instantly fired; my wife's shriek was heard: they, however, drove on. When my carriage with fresh horses overtook me, my servant tried to raise me, I had dislocated my ancle. Blood, my servant told me, could be traced upon the road, as if it had fallen from my wife's carriage. I could but look upon myself as Matilda's murderer, the shriek was hers. My emotions and feelings were so violent and various it would be impossible to portray them. The demon's power was upon me, and his curse proved a bitter one.

I was conveyed home, where I was for a long time delirious; I became calm but not less miserable. My attendants then gave me a letter, which had been found upon my wife's dressing table, after my departure in chase of her. She was innocent, she had not fled with Huldebrand, but with her father. Huldebrand had upon that condition agreed to conceal my crime, my shame. She had left her home, her children; had sacrificed her own to shield my name from infamy. I did not at this intelligence relapse into the violent ravings I had undergone. I sunk into a state of apathy, whence nothing could rouse me. I refused even to see my children, and hardly ever leaving my chamber, I spent the night and day with short intervals to self-reproach in combating inflictions of the mind more dreadful than any corporeal penance of the holy anchorite.

Many years had thus passed, I had not once seen my children, not even heard of them, for I would speak with no one. I at last saw them by accident. You know Olivieri's violent character. He had constantly inquired after me, always baffled by the servants in his wish of seeing me; he at last seized his opportunity, but Louisa had watched him, and they both appeared in my sight struggling with one another; for she was trying to hinder his disturbing me. If Matilda herself had stood before me she could not have affected me more; for Louisa, though her features are different, her eye dark, has the expression that gave such power to her mother's looks, playing upon her face. She at last, no longer capable of resisting her brother, threw herself at my feet, and earnestly begged me not to be offended with her dear Olivieri. I took her to my arms. From that moment I was aroused. I could not leave my daughter, but gave up all my time to the education of my children; but I brought another curse upon my head, for I neglected Olivieri; except in his literary studies I did not assist him, his mind was allowed to be biassed by any one who chose to trouble themselves with acting upon him. Louisa on the contrary was my constant companion, she rewarded my care. You know her, if ever a wretch like me might have hope, it must be in the prayers such a being can offer up for me to the throne of Heaven.

After some time I proposed journeying through the different countries of Europe, to show my children the different peculiarities of nations. We had already entered Switzerland when my son left me. I had been accustomed to his often quitting me for days together, and hardly noticed his departure. Louisa and myself proceeded to the different spots remarkable for their beauty or sublimity. On the Wengern Alp we saw you. We soon after heard daily of the feats of Ernestus Berchtold and Olivieri. I don't know why, but the thought of the chamois hunter we had seen being this Ernestus, first struck my daughter, and I soon joined in the belief. A letter from Olivieri appointed Interlaken as the place of meeting; we went there. Events in which you were concerned brought us again to Milan.

The immense riches I had obtained from the spirit under my command, though much diminished, were yet more than sufficient to maintain us in sufficient splendour, not to fear any thing like a competition. But Olivieri and yourself were gamblers. Louisa forced me again to risk an infliction equally severe as the last, for your sake. I could not resist her prayers for you. I again called the spirit from his immortal haunts, and Olivieri's infamy was the consequence. Your debts had proved so enormous, that in my attempt at saving him from an ignominious death, I was again obliged, though I knew the horrible powers of the demon, to call upon him. I did so. He announced to me that I had exhausted my spells, and that after this infliction, as nothing round me would remain, on which he could breathe his pestilential breath, he would no longer obey my summons. I called upon him to take back his gold, he laughed and left me. I had no suspicion of Olivieri's seduction of your sister; when therefore his letter was put into my hands, you may imagine how your noble conduct affected me. I did not speak of it, for what could a father say? Must I even acknowledge it to you, I sometimes rested upon it with a feeling of consolation, for I hoped, that crime of my son's might be the infliction upon his father, meant by the demon as passing all others. Louisa I thought might then be spared, and you two might at least be happy.

But you married; I dreamt of happiness, on Louisa's birthday accompanied you to your room, and the demon's threat I found had indeed been fulfilled. Your mother's portrait was Matilda's. Olivieri had seduced, you married a daughter of Matilda, of Matilda's husband, and I was the murderer of her father.

from Ximenes,
The Wreath and Other Poems

(1819)

Sonnet

To the Night

O Starry night! thou art most beauteous fair,
And I could gaze on thee, till my sight ached –
Thy cooling zephyrs play amidst my hair,
And cool my fever'd brain, which long has waked –
Such stillness seizes on the ear – the beams
Of yonder galaxy steal on the eye
With such soft soothing power – the whole it seems
Would bid us seek for heaven above that sky –
And hope for peace beyond that bright'ning zone,
Which seems to keep her near yon heave'nly throne; –
But still thou pleasest more, 'cause thou canst show
The image of _ _ _'s pow'r when flow
Such magic words, as still man's stormy breast,
Such rays as sooth e'en mem'ry, future fears to rest.

Sonnet

On being told that I was changed

I'm changed, ay changed indeed! The festal board
Was wont to cheer – but nothing now can gain
A passing smile, or transient bliss afford –
For I _____'s love cannot obtain –
My comrades jeer and say a drop of dew,
From off the verge of midnight Hecate's broom,
Fell in my mouth, as grief those accents drew,
In which absorpt I wailed by saddened doom –
Some tell me that of late a poisonous tear
From bleared old maid fell in the merry cup,
In which I pledged her love – which drop would bear
My senses down and bring grim madness up –
But I'm not mad, tho' dazzled now by her lov'd face,
As by the sun's bright disk, on all, her form I trace.

The Wreath

To _____

O thou! For whom this humble Wreath is formed,
Not from the flow'rs that deck the lowly meads,
But from those flow'rs Apollo's ray has warmed,
On which the dance Thalia often leads.

Despise it not, because the flow'rs are dull,
Or ill arranged – my heart beat high with fears,
My eyes with love's despairing tears were full,
Looking to pluck the robe Parnassus wears.

For since thy image burst upon my sight,
My fancy paints but heaven as a meet place,
Where thou couldst dwell, and I a mortal wight,
But pine to see the spot, which thou may'st grace.
Despise then not my Wreath, they beauty blame alone,
And let thy lover's sufferings for the crime atone.

Written at the Grimsel

In Switzerland

In vain I seek these solitary rocks,
Which seem to leave no track upon their side
For man to tread upon. – These enduring blocks
Of the world's masonry, o'er which storms glide
Powerless, unmoved stern in their might yet stand,
And leave no room for man's destructive hand. –
Yet I am vainly hid within their breast,
They cannot breathe on me their quiet rest –
Man's passions will intrude, man's wants assail
E'en me – whose tongue is dead, save when the gale
Strikes on my ear with harsh but plaintive note,
Exciting words which mingling with it float,
And make the echoing rocks respond my grief,
As if I'd take from sympathy relief. –
But vain illusion! E'en fond hope is dead,

And all save angry passions hence have fled,
Angry with fates, who gave but visions' food
Unto my mind, when, foolish youth! I woo'd
Their smiles. – Oh why, tormenting fiend-like sprites
Thus let me go midst passion's, folly's flights,
Midst men in fine, with visions in my mind,
That I midst them might friendship, virtue find? –
Oh why still in my soul, those hopes of fame,
Which brought the sigh when busy morning came
Stealing from midnight lamp those studious hours
Midst which I cull'd the various fragrant flowers
That grow where'er the Muses' feet may tread,
And which I hoped enwreath'd might deck my head
And bright with glorious gleam, might shining there,
For ages show an undiminish'd lair –
Why make me strike the lyre as I felt
That happiness in some vale lonely dwelt,
Waiting for me, when from my sounding lyre
Such strains should flow as fit a poet's fire –
Why let me read th' historic page, where's told
In lying tales, that men could freedom hold,
That men in ancient times of Grecian sage
Gainst meaner passions constant war would wage.

But these, e'en these, I might forgive, forget,
But why that vision send? – Was it to whet
The point of all your stings? That vision sent
Of one so meekly bright, if the moon lent
Her soothing ray, she had not been more fair,
Nor could she be more light, if from the air
Yon blushing lovely cloud, that seems to lave
In the sun's western ray, ere in the wave
He sinks to rest; not if yon cloud came down
To vest around its lightness as a gown
Upon her limbs, could she appear more light –
And, as she pass'd, wending her air flight
To whence she came, methought I heard a sigh
As wafted on the breeze come from the sky,
Methough I saw grief passing o'er her brow
As she gazed on me, chance she wished to show
She felt my pains – But I awoke, and lo!

The morn, stealing upon the upland brow,
Had rayed herself in mist as if to hide
In pity her light rosy glorious pride
Seeming as tho' she wished me still to dream,
And not to break this only joyous gleam.

Fool that I was! I let that image rest
Upon my mind – I hugg'd it to my breast.–
Forgetting that such forms to heaven alone
Are given to hover round the Godhead's throne –
For oh! I vainly yet must seek this haunt,
Which solitude to make its dwelling's wont,
I cannot fly that beauteous form – one time
I saw her on yon beetling rock – I climb –
Bounding from crag to crag, I haste to clasp
Her airy shape – the mist has mock'd my grasp –
And high on tow'ry pinnacle I stand
Gazing on scenes subdued by man's foul hand,
To fly the sight of which I'd sought this cave
In hopes of rest their absence never gave –
Oft, oft, I'm wak'd from slumbers by her voice,
Which seems with her to call me to rejoice;
But all that strikes my ear is the harsh sound
Of the lone breeze that wanton beats around.

Oh! Why then fliest thou Time! With slacken'd wing?
Why not with thee old blear-eyed age e'en bring?
It's whit'ning snows would drop upon my head,
At last 'twould lead me to a quiet bed. –
Or if e'en years should pass, length'ning my age,
Ere death my foes in battle might engage,
Still hoping to begin my journey's toil,
I might with pleasure gaze, leaving this coil,
On all that once had reft me of my peace,
Conscious I went, where they'd no longer teaze.

Ximenes

XIMENES: Must I then once again call up afresh
             Sorrows past cure? – My memory alone,
             Ere my lips speak, renews my heart's anguish
             And maddens every thought, till I avoid
             With anxious care the very name of her
             Who wrought my woe; and in oblivion try
             To drown all traces of my wretched lot –
             Vainly I thought that time with lenient hand
             Would mitigate my grief's severer pangs –
             But still with age its poison seems to spread.

             When first we met in Florence, lively youth
             And buoyant hope spread o'er my future years
             Such brilliant hues, as if the magic wand
             Of old dames elf had been at pleasant work –
             My heart then opened to the sun of love,
             As the soft hare-bell, when Aurora's tints
             Glow in the east, expands its silken leaves
             To the life-giving orb. – The maid I lov'd
             Was then the pride of Florence, and excell'd
             In every grace, each rival's lessen'd charms –
             But why so fondly dwell upon the theme?
             She is not mine – the thought disturbs my brain –
             It burns with all the phrensy of despair. –

From a dramatic tragedy originally entitled *Count Orlando; or, The Modern Abraham*, Act I, scene ii.

The Fall of the Angels
A Sacred Poem

(1821)

Canto the First

Section 1
The Creation of the World

I

Through infinite, eternal space 'twas night
And darkness: scarcely the blue lightning shone,
As, flashing idly thro' it's harmless flight,
It lit discordant elements alone.
Oblivion spread its vast long limbs, with sullen pride,
Midst the loved, changeless shades, that every thing could hide:
No speck of beauty, sparkling there on high,
As some meek flower, that breaks the snow to shine,
No sun sail'd, like a ship, across the sky,
A startling show of pomp and power divine.

II

Then sounds alone, like Etna's breathings, broke
Upon the wilder'd ear of Seraphin,
And seem'd as if the presence they bespoke
Of one who mock'd at God and scoff'd at him.
For element 'gainst element was loudly warring,
And latent flames, and waves, and rocks, were broken jarring;
Then were unknown fair music's magic power,
The still soft sounding of the speaking wave,
The rolling crash of clouds, that proudly lower
As if the Almighty used the voice they gave.

X

Yet all was barren; nothing but a stream
Of splendent suns and stars attracts the sight:
Mingling, they deckt each other with a gleam,
Each caught its beauty from its brother's light.

But, by the grateful sight of seraph's joy beguiled,
Jehovah, pleased, look'd on his vast work and smiled:
Then suddenly they see the planets move,
They see, upon the barren glittering earth,
The bending corn, the forests, nodding grove,
And worlds and oceans teeming one great birth.

from *The Diary of*
Dr John William Polidori

(1816)

24 April   I left London at 10 in the morning, with Lord Byron, Scrope Davies, Esq., and J. Hobhouse, Esq.

The view from Shooter's Hill was extensive and beautiful, being on a much larger scale than the view from Stirling.

The plain, enamelled with various colours according to the different growth of the corn, spread far before our sight, was divided irregularly by the river. The Thames next, with its majestic waves, flowed in the plain below, bearing numerous fleets upon its flood. Its banks in many parts were beautiful. The chalky banks were alternated with the swelling hills, rising from the waves, of the pleasing green-brown, the effect of the first dawn of spring on the vegetable creation.

At Canterbury we saw the Cathedral. I know not how it was, whether my mind had been prepared by the previous sight of glorious nature to receive pleasing impressions, but the spot where the high altar and Thomas à Becket's tomb stood seemed to me one of the most beautiful effects that I had ever seen arising from Saxo-Gothic architecture; for, though it had not all the airiness and awe-inspiring height that I had seen in other cathedrals, yet its simple beauty pleased me more than anything I had yet seen.

Remounting, we soon arrived at Dover, where we slept, when the packet-boat captain had sufficiently disturbed us.

25 April   This day was spent at Dover. The greater part was occupied in procuring what had been neglected in London, and in seeing the carriage well packed up. After dinner, however, we went in search of Churchill's tomb, raised, we had learned, to his memory by his friend Wilkes. Arrived at the house of the sexton, he led us to a ruined church, passing through which we came into a churchyard, where children, heedless and unconscious of what they trampled on, sportively ran amid the raised turf graves. He pointed out to us a tombstone, undistinguished from those of the tradesmen near him, having merely, like them, a square tablet stuck into the ground, whereon was written, 'Here lie the remains of the celebrated Churchill.'

Life to the last enjoyed, here Churchill lies.

Candidate

The green turf was beginning already to decay upon his tomb, which when the sexton heard us lamenting he assured us that his grave, as well as the rest, would be newly decked as soon as Nature had vested its fullest green – for that was an old custom.

Churchill owed, then, only to a common hand what the pride of a friend refused – the safety of his burial-place. Wilkes only sought the gratification of his vanity. While he consigned his friend's last relics to the keeping of a tablet, he consigned his own pride in such a friend to the keeping of a column in his own grounds. Yet I do not know whether the scene was not more moving, though no vainly pompous inscription pointed out the spot where this poet was buried.

There were two authors; one, the most distinguished of his age; another, whose name is rising rapidly; (and a third, ambitious for literary distinction). What a lesson it was for them when, having asked the sexton if he knew why so many came to see this tomb, he said: 'I cannot tell; I had not the burying of him.'

We then returned home, where, having delivered my play into their hands, I had to hear it laughed at – (an author has always a salvo) partly, I think, from the way in which it was read. One of the party, however – to smoothe, I suppose, my ruffled spirits – took up my play, and apparently read part with great attention, drawing applause from those who before had laughed. He read on with so much attention that the others declared he had never been so attentive before.

I afterwards went out, and did a very absurd thing, which I told; and found I had not only hurt myself but might possibly hurt others for whom I cared much more.

26 April   We embarked at 9 o'clock, much hurried, with three servants.

When at a distance, we waved our hands and hats, bidding adieu. The wind was completely in our teeth, but we made the passage in sixteen hours. The coast of Dover is very striking, though miserably barren-looking. The cliff is steep, though not such as Shakespeare paints. The castle – at a distance, which is the only way I viewed it – is miserable. Sailing from England, I for a long time kept my eye upon its stern white cliffs, thinking on her who bade me join her remembrance with the last sight of my native soil.

They at last faded from my sight, and all on board looked dreary; the sea dashed over us, and all wore an aspect of grief. Towards night a most beautiful spectacle was seen by myself, who alone remained on deck. The stars shedding merely a twilight enabled me to see the phosphoric light of the broken foam in all its splendour. But the most beautiful moment was that of its first appearance: no sound around save the sullen rushing of the vessel, and the hoarse cries of the heaving sailor; no light save a melancholy twilight, which soothed the mind into forgetfulness of its grief for a while – a beautiful streak following the lead through the waves. We arrived at Ostend at 2 o'clock in the morning.

26 April   We passed through the gates, paying a franc a head, and went to the Cour Imperiale. We were astonished at the excellent inn and good treatment, except that I got a dreadful headache from the smell of paint in my bedroom, and that the tea was perfumed. As soon as he reached his room, Lord Byron fell like a thunderbolt upon the chambermaid.

Arising in the morning, I went upon a stroll round the town. Saw little girls of all ages with head-dresses; books in every bookseller's window of the most obscene nature; women with wooden shoes; men of low rank basking in the sun as if that would evaporate their idleness. The houses generally good old style, very like a Scotch town, only not quite so filthy. Very polite custom-house officers, and very civil waiters. Fine room painted as a panorama, all French-attitudinised. Went into a shop where no one spoke French. Tried German; half-a-dozen women burst out laughing at me. Luckily for myself, in a good humour; laughed with them. Obliged to buy two books I did not want because I let a quarto fall upon a fine girl's head while looking at her eyes. Coaches of the most horrid construction; apparently some fine horses, others small. Fortifications look miserable. Once stood a fine siege, when 40,000 on one side and 80 on the other fed fowls and manured the fields. What for? For religion? No – for money. *There* was the spring of all. As long as only religion and rights were affected, bigoted religionists and wild republicans were alone concerned; but a step too far, and all was ruined.

We set off at 3, with four horses. Postillion with boots to his hips, nankeens, leather hat with quaker brim, only neatly rounded with black riband; a blue and red coat, joined to which a most rascally face, with lips that went a few lines beyond the brim of this hat. A dreadful smacker of his whip, and a driver of four horses from the back of one of the hindmost. We were obliged to hire a calèche to send with our luggage. The rascal made us pay three times too much at each of his barriers; but, after having (on account of the horses not being ready at the next post) gone beyond his beat, he allowed the toll-keepers to be honest, and only take a few centimes instead of a franc. The country was very flat, highly cultivated; sand, no waste. Roads paved in the middle, with trees on each side. Country, from the interspersion of house, spires, cottages, etc., delightful; everything comfortable, no appearance of discontent.

We got out of our carriage at a place where the horses ate bread and hay, and walked on to a church-yard, where we found no tombstones, no funeral – pomp, no flattering eulogy, but simply a wooden cross at each grave's head and foot. On the side of the church-steeple, at a little height, was made a niche wherein statues formed a crucifixion, as an object to excite reverence and adoration of God in every passenger. We passed on, and arrived at Bruges at the fall of the evening. Our passports were dispensed with on our mentioning that we were not stopping. We entered one of the most beautiful towns I ever saw; every house seemed substantial – had some ornament either of fretwork or lines – all seem clean and neat. We stopped at the post. We were shown into the postmaster's parlour on our asking for something to eat – well furnished – better even than a common middleman's house in London. N.B. – Everywhere 6 francs for a bottle of Rhenish. Women generally pretty. Flemish face has no divinity – all pleasing more than beautiful – a sparkling eye in a full round. Their pictures of every age have the mark of their country.

As we went from Bruges, twilight softened all the beauty, and I do not know how to describe the feeling of pleasure we felt in going through its long roof-fretted streets, bursting on to spots where people were promenading amidst short avenues of trees. We passed on. At the gates I saw a boy with sand in his hand let it through his fingers laughingly, heedless of the myriads whose life hung upon each sand.

We passed on at 10. We came to a village where we heard the sound of music. The innkeeper, on our enquiring what it was, asked us politely in to hear a concert of amateurs. We descended, and were gratified and surprised at hearing, in a village of 5000 souls, a full band playing difficult though beautiful music. One march particularly struck us. But what was our surprise, when the door opened, to view the group: none apparently above the rank of labourers, yet they met three times a week. In our country the amusement is to reel drunk as many. There was one figure manifestly consumptive, yet he was blowing an enormous trombone.

Within a few miles of Gand, I was wakened from a pleasant fireside in England by my companion saying 'They have lost their way'; and, seeing a house near me, I jumped out to enquire, when to my great fear I saw it was deserted. I immediately suspected something, and went back for a pistol, and then thundered at the door; no one came. Looking round, I saw other houses; towards which upon my moving the postillion got off, and, telling me in French, as a consolation, that he could not understand it, went with me towards a house where there was light, and suddenly ran off. I immediately went to the carriage, and we gave sabres to the servants; when he ran back from out of sight, and knocked again at the door and roused two, who told us the way. By the by, we had crossed several times the bridge, and from the road and back again, whereas we had nothing to do but to go straight on, instead of which he crossed over and was going back in the direction of Bruges, when our servant stopped him. I cannot explain his conduct; he was dreadfully frightened.

We arrived at Ghent at 3 in the morning, and knocked some time at the gates, but at last, by means of a few francs, got through – passports not asked for. Got to the Hotel des Pays Bas, where Count Artois resided while at Ghent. We were ushered into a splendid room, got excellent Rhenish, butter, cheese, etc., and went to bed.

27 April   At Gand Charles the 1st of Spain was born. It was here he really showed the insufficiency of ambition and all the joys of manhood. After having at Brussels resigned to Philip his extensive dominions, he came here, and enjoyed many days while passing over the scenes of his youth, which neither the splendour attached to a European or an Indian crown nor to the conquests of his powerful and noble views could efface. He did not seek Pavia; no, it was at Gand that he sought for his last draught of worldly joy. The town was worthy of it, if beauty and antiquity, if riches and liberty with all their train, could render it worthy of him. This town has all the beauty of Bruges, but more extensive: finer houses perhaps, fine cathedral, fine paintings, fine streets, fine canal. The streets are perhaps the finest I have seen; not so unpleasantly regular as London, not so high, but more rich in outside.

We visited the Cathedral; and, after having been accustomed to

the tinselly ornaments of our Catholic chapels, and the complete
want of any in the Scotch and English churches, we were much
pleased with the Cathedral's inside dress: paintings that were by
the hand of masters; the fortune of a bishop expended in building
the part near the altar in marble and statues not contemptible,
united with the airy, high fretted roof and little light, impressive
of awe. Under this Cathedral is the first Belgian church that was
built in the reign of Charlemagne, 800 years, I think, after Christ.
It is low-roofed, but so strong it bears the weight of the Cathedral
upon it. There were several paintings preserved in it (before the
date of oil-painting), where the colours are mixed with white of
egg. Some curious tombs, where the different styles are evident. In
the earliest tomb some of the draperies on the relief are in a bold
fine style. One of the earliest has a bishop, where all his robes are
carved out, with almost the threads of his vest. Others, however,
are for general effect. We mounted 450 steps to the top of the
steeple; whence we saw a complete horizon of plain, canals,
intersecting trees, and houses and steeples thrown here and there,
with Gand below at our feet. The sea at a distance, bound by the
hands of man, which pointed 'So far shall ye go and no further.'
Bruges held in the horizon its steeples to our view, and many
hamlets raised from out their surrounding wood their single spires
to sight.

Treading again the iron-plated 450 stairs, we came into the
street; and, mounting into a fiacre, we went to the Ecole de Dessin,
where we found a well-provided gallery of paintings, with two
students, unmoved by the visitors around, painting with the
patience if not the genius of Dutch masters. They were rather a
nuisance on the present occasion, as one covered with his machine
a *chef d'oeuvre* of Rubens, the *St Roch amongst the Sick of Plague*. There
were two more by the same, of St Roch and his Dog, etc. They were
in a different style of colouring – sombre and grey; none of his gay
draperies that I, no connoisseur, thought were constituents of
Rubens. I saw – I do not remember whose, but – a picture that
struck me much, *The Beheading of St Jean*, where all the interest and
beauty consisted in a dog smelling the dead body. There were two
of Van Eyck, the first (according to the Flemish) who invented
painting in oil; where the colouring was splendid and very like the
stiffness of glass, but the faces were very good. Kruger had many
here in honour of Charles the Vth. Amongst the others, one rather
(though probably not meant as such) satirical: Charles, landing,

takes hold of Dame Africa, who quietly points to a lion at her feet. Query – to drive him away? There was a *Judgment of Solomon* by the same, where the child was painted dead with most perfect nature; so much so that my companion, who is a father, could not bear its sight. Teniers has here a *Temptation of St Anthony*: strange caricature – what a satire! If mere deceit is the acme of perfection, some Dutchmen may snatch the palm from either Apelles or Parrhasius. They paint boards with an engraving upon them, or a door, or aught else, so inimitably that it deceived my friend. We went into the Academy of Casts, of Design, etc. There are generally 400 pupils in this town: many fall off annually without great advancement, and are trod on the heels by others.

We thence proceeded to another (we might say) cathedral. The steeple is not yet finished: the model is exhibited, with the curses of the Flemish exhibitors upon the 'grande nation' for having taken the funds for its finishing. There are more good pictures than even in the Cathedral: the columns also please me more, being round, with a Gothic approach to Corinthian capital. The most beautiful painting I have yet seen is here (though I probably shall not be held out in my opinion by connoisseurs) – by Pollent, representing the trial of the true Cross upon a sick lady. The harmony of colouring, the soberness (without the commonly accompanying dullness) of the colouring, the good design and grouping, are, in my opinion, beautiful. Not even the splendid colouring of Rubens can make his pictures, in my eyes, equal to it.

There is one standing by it, of Vandyck, which has some sublimity in it, perhaps arising from indistinctness. It represents the effect of Christ's last sigh. By this altar stood twelve small pictures, hung out at this time for people to tread the 'way of Calvary', representing the different stages of our Saviour's sufferings. There were many more pictures, but I cannot remember; seeing so many crowded in the Gallery put others out of my head. But there were painted in the Cathedral of St Bavon, on the marble in the style of reliefs, different subjects of Scripture in a most masterly style; and so well were the shades managed that we could hardly believe the cicerone when he assured us they were paintings.

In the Gallery of Casts there were the statues of two English laides of London by an artist who resided thirty years there, and upon his return bestowed these as his finest works. The faces, though not perfect or Grecian, I must say for my countrywomen, pleased me almost as much as any Venus de'Medici.

I have found the people polite, so far as showing the way and then not waiting for a reward – taking off their hats as if *you* had done them the favour.

28 April   We set off at 8 this morning to go to Anvers; but, after having proceeded some way, one of the wheels refused to turn, and, after at the next village hammering a long while, I rode off in a passing calèche to Ghent, where I put a marechal with his assistant into a voiture, and, mounting myself on horseback, returned to the coach. My horse was particularly fond of the shade; and, a house being near one of the barriers, he kindly stopped there to cool me. I, after waiting some time, began to press him to go forward, when he kicked etc. We went, while the carriage was being repaired, into a cottage, where all was extremely neat, and we saw two pictures in it that certainly would not shame the collection of many of our *soi-distant* cognoscenti. The old man was sick of a fever; and, upon giving him medicine, his kind half sympathetically fell ill of a toothache. Never did I see such chips of the old block as his two daughters. They were very kind. It being Sunday, we saw all the women of the village – all ugly: indeed I have not seen a pretty woman since I left Ostend.

On proceeding on our journey, we stopped for our passports, and the fellow began bullying us, thinking we were French; but, when he heard we were English, he became cap in hand, and let us go: indeed, we have not yet shown our passports.

Having eaten, I issued forth in search of the Promenade and found the canal with walks called La Copeure. Many ladies, all ugly without exception – the only pretty woman being fat and sixty. It very much resembled the Green Basin, where our West-end cits trot on one another's heels with all possible care: not quite so crowded. Coming back, I toursed to the Roi d'Espagne, where, as in a coffee-house, I found a room full of disreputable women and card-tables. This, instead of the streets, is the lounge for such women. I went to the Café Grand, where by means of mirrors some excellent effects are produced. There also were billiards, cards, dice, etc. A cup of coffee, some centimes; a glass of lemonade, two sous: a woman presides at the end of the room.

'Lord Byron' was in the *Ghent Gazette*. Lord Byron encouraged me to write *Cajetan*, and to continue being a tragedian. Murray offered £150 for two plays, and £500 for my tour.

29 April   Looking from my window, I saw a native dashing about in a barouche and four. There is in the town a society of nobles, and another of literati. Mr Scamp has a fine collection of pictures, which I did not see. In Ghent, as well as in all other places where I have been, the barber's sign is Mambrino's helm. On the Sunday mornings there is a market for flowers in pot in the Place des Armes.

We set off at 11 in the morning, and passed through some fine villages: one of which, St Nicholas, the mistress of the inn told me Buonparte made into a town – 'mais il n'y a pas des postes'. The country is tiresomely beautiful. Fine avenues, which make us yawn with admiration; not a single variation; no raising ground – yes, one spot raised for a windmill, The landscape is as unchangeable as the Flemish face. The houses white-washed, with a row of trees before them; the roofs tiled, and the windows large. Indeed, the appearance of comfort in the places we have passed through is much greater than any I have seen in England. We have only seen one country-villa, and that very English: its pasture had the only firs we have yet seen.

The avenues are sometimes terminated by a church or a house – the church very ugly; and both very tiresome, as they always prove much farther off than is at first expected. The ground cultivated, and without a weed – no waste ground. The plough moves as if cutting water, the soil is so light a sand. Women work in the fields as well as men. No more difference is found in the face of the inhabitants than in the face of the country. Nothing striking, all avenues, no genius, much stupidity. They seemed to spend all their fund of cleanliness upon their fields and houses, for they carry none about them.

An oldish man wears a three-cornered cocked hat, capacious breeches, black or blue stockings, buckles, and a great-coat; young, fancy travelling-caps. The women wear enormous gold ear-rings, large wooden shoes. Their dress is a kind of bed-gown, like the Scotch. Young girls of eight in town have their hair dressed with a net or cap. In town and villages the better peasant-women wear a black silk mantle with a hood, that looks well. Multitudes of children everywhere, who tumble and run by the side of the carriage to gain a few centimes. In the larger villages the market-places are splendidly large, with a little square in the middle, with pollards and a statue. The houses seem comfortable everywhere.

Going into the house of a postmaster, we saw some English prints. At another, our servants having got down and comfortably seated themselves to a bottle of wine etc., the postmistress, on our getting out took *us* for the servants, and told us 'the messieurs Anglais were in yon room' and then made us a thousand apologies. At every posthouse place there is kept a book of the posts: many barriers – every 1½ mile.

At Gand they had told us we could not reach Anvers without passing the Scheldt at 2 o'clock – we passed it at 6½.

The town of Antwerp makes a good figure at a distance chiefly on account of its Cathedral, which has a very airy appearance, the steeple showing the sky between its meeting arches. About five steeples. The fortifications, which enabled Carnot to make such a defence, produce no great effect on the sight.

The Scheldt is a fine river, not so large as our Thames, and covered with ugly Dutch vessels. We passed our coach in a boat.

On landing, twenty porters ran off with our things to a cart. As they were passing, one in all the pomp of office stopped us, and asked for our passports, which (on handing to him) he detained, giving his directions to the police.

The older parts of Antwerp have a novel and strange effect by the gable-ends being all to the street, ornamented – very acute angles. The Place de Meer is fine. The old street, the finest I ever saw, has some fine houses. Many of the houses have English labels on them. In our sitting-room are two beds. Indeed, the towns are beautiful: their long streets, their houses all clean-stuccoed or white-washed, with strange old-fashioned fronts, the frequent canals, the large places and venerable cathedrals. Their places are much finer than our squares, for they contain trees, and are open without railing.

Went to the café, and saw all playing at dominoes. Read *The Times* till the 23rd. Fine furniture, everywhere of cherry-tree.

At Gand in the Cathedral the cicerone laid great stress on the choir-seats being all made of solid acajou. The master of the inn at Ghent assures me the carriage of Buonaparte was made in Paris – the body-carriage at Brussels: no English work. Plenty of Americans in the town.

30 April Got up late, and went to look at the carriage, and found that the back had been not of the best-made. Called a marechal, who assured me it could not be better. Breakfasted. Then looked at an old calèche, for which asked 60 naps. Refused it.

Got, with a guide, a calèche to see the lions. The town is large: apparently, not a proportionable quantity of misery. Women better-looking. At all the fountains, Madonnas – and upon all the corners of the streets, with lamps before them. Lamps with reverberators strung on ropes into the middle of the streets. Went to the Cathedral. Everywhere we have been, dreadful complaints of French vandalism. In this chapel it has been shameless: once crowded with altars of marble, now there are about five – only two marble, the others painted in imitation. Pictures were stolen – altars sold by auction – only one saved, bought by a barber for a louis. The others, with all the tombs, monuments, everything, broken by these encouragers of the fine arts. So great was the ruin that there were five feet of fragments over the church – even the columns that support the roof were so much defaced that they were obliged, in restoring it, to pare them all much thinner. Some pictures were carried to Paris, of which some are now about to be replaced. It was the feast of St Anthony, and many candles were burning about, and some relics were fixed above the doors. In many parts of the chapel were frames containing silver representations, very small, of bad limbs etc., offered by the devout. Many images over altars, dressed out in silk and taffeta: most common one, the Virgin Mary. Though the French acted with all the spirit of Vandals and true Gauls, yet to their very mischief is owing the greatest beauty of the Cathedral, the choir not being divided from the church, so that from one end to the other there is a complete perspective and one of the finest effects I have seen, the airiness and length being now proportionate. There is one great defect in the internal decorations – that they are Greek. What bad taste it is to ornament Gothic with Corinthian columns must be evident: to make it also more glaring, the marble is all coloured. There is here a fine marble altar-railing. Indeed, in all the churches we have here seen they are beautiful – especially where boys, called in Italian 'puttini', are sculptured. The confessionals are of wood, with evangelical figures, nearly as large as life, between each box – not badly carved.

We went to see another church, wherein is the tomb of Rubens.

It is in a chapel by itself, where annually a mass is said for his soul. It is worthy of him: ornamented by a painting, by himself, of St George, and a statue he brought with him from Rome of the Holy Virgin. The church in which he is buried was saved from pillage by the priests belonging to it revolutionising. It is crowded with altars and pictures – some Rubens, some Polenck, and others. There is a painting by Metsys, who originally was a maréchal, and who with his mere hammer formed the decorations to a pump, which was not bad. The Latin inscription on his monumental stone refers to a story related of him: that, upon courting the daughter of Francis Floris, the artist with indignation talked about the dirty rascal's impudence, he being merely a blacksmith; on which Metsys set off for Rome, and upon his return asked the daughter to introduce him to her father's room of painting: where, finding a picture not finished, he painted a bee – that excited the indignation of Floris's pocket-handkerchief, and gained him his daughter. I have seen the picture, and it might be true. The pump is not bad, being merely beaten into shape. On top is a giant who used to cut off merchants' gains by means of tolls, and their hands by means of axes. He used to throw an iron band into the scales of his tradesmen; and from thence, 'tis said, Antwerp got its name.

The sides of this church all along are lined with confessionals.

In the Church des Augustins we saw Rubens's *Assembly of the Saints*, from Paris; where he has shown how weak he could be in composition, and in vanity – for it is the third picture in which he has put himself in St George's armour. The composition is confused, without an object to fix the attention.

A Vandyck near him is much superior.

Here is also the famous picture of Jordaens, of *The Martyrdom of St Apollonia*. Colouring approaches Rubens; but abominable composition – crowded, large, numerous figures in a small place. There were some modern paintings of existing artists – meagre statue-compositions.

In the Musée we saw many Rubenses. The famous *Descent from the Cross*: the effect of the white sheet is wonderfully beautiful. Picture's drawing I do not like. The Christ seems not dead, as there is certainly action; but the colouring is splendidly rich. The *Crucifixion* near it, inferior in all. In a sketch near it he has not succeeded so well in the white sheet, it being not so splendidly white. We could only see the side-pieces of the great *Crucifixion*, as the large piece was being framed. In these there is much caricature drawing: a woman rising from the dead – surely a woman large as Guy Warwick giant's wife, if ever he had one: caricature physiognomies, and most hellish egregious breasts, which a child refuses, with horror in its face. His horses have much spirit – true Flemish size. Indeed, divest Rubens of his rich apparel, and he is a mere dauber in design. There is a *Mary going to Elizabeth*, looking more like a cardinal: indeed, my companion, Lord Byron, took her for one of the red-vested nobles. No divinity about his Christs; putrefaction upon his Gods; exaggerated passion about his men and women, painted not all-concealing. In his picture of *The Adoration of the Magi*, query did he not intend to play upon the people by passing off a caricature for a religious painting? The royal personage in green seems as if his eyes had grown big after dinner. He has no costume properly applied: the Virgin in the manger is dressed meretriciously in silks and lace. Then look at our blessed Saviour showing His wounds. His finest painting is his *Crucifixion* in which is the white sheet: but there are defects. What then must be the power of colouring which causes you to view his paintings with pleasure! It is like melodious music which makes you forget the absurd words of an old English song.

Vandyck, in my opinion, was much superior to Rubens. His colouring, near his, is sombre; but then his design is more perfect, his impressions remain longer in the mind distinct, and do not fade away into ideas of red and blue round white. A little *Crucifix* of his is worth his rival's largest paintings. His *Christ Dead* is beautiful, wherein are contained the Blessed Virgin, St Mary Magdalene, and St John weeping: the different expressions of grief, the unison of colouring with the subject, the composition all excellent.

From the Cathedral we went to see the works of Napoleon. We first saw the Basins. They are not so large as our West India Docks – square – but are capable of holding ships of the line; there are two. Between them is what was formerly the Hanseatic Hall, now magazines.

When the English were last here they threw bombs, but this was of no avail; dung was put upon the ships, and men were at hand in case of fire. From the Basins we went along the quays – very long, along the labouring Scheldt; then into the places for marine arsenals, where the vessels were on the stocks – the finest works I ever saw, now useless through our jealousy. The rope-house, quite finished, is enormously long, and is to be pulled down. The timbers for the ship were numbered, and carried to Amsterdam. The citadel was mean-looking, though so strong. The chief batteries are as old as Alva's time – there was one pointed out as erected by Colonel Crawford. Before Napoleon's time there was little done towards the formation of these basins and others; but, said our guide, 'he decreed they should be made, and they appeared'. They are all surrounded with high walls to hinder the escape of the employed. Carnot has commanded here twice. He was rather disliked, yet they had rather have him than any other. They all agree in his genius. In the time of the Walcheren business the English were expected with open arms: only three hundred soldiers – Bernadotte was general. The siege was not very strict on the last occasion, and no mischief was done on either side. In the Basins there have been twenty-six line. In the dread of a siege all the suburbs were destroyed and all the trees around. The suburbs rose immediately, the trees in years. In the citadel there are 1500 forcats. Sometimes the number exceeds 2000.

Having seen thus much, we returned, lunched, and rode off. Hardly gone a little way when our carriage broke down. The trees are more various – vegetation more advanced – more inequality of ground – more pollards – more apparent misery – more villas, some pretty – more clipped hedges – more like England – fine, large, town-like villages. Carriage broke again – walked to Malines – arrived there at ten. Women improve.

At Antwerp, in one church on the outside, saw a supposed exact imitation of the Sepulchre, though I do not know how it came seated 'in purgatory'; as there certainly is a place so called round it, full of the damned and flames. The place is grotto-work. Within there is a representation of our Lord swathed in linen. All over there are statues, so so. David is at a respectable distance from purgatory: this makes it the more remarkable that the Sepulchre is seated in purgatory. Indeed, indeed, there is much absurdity.

There is an academy for drawing and painting, with a museum. The Place is in a garden.

On arriving at Malines we found Mr Pradt gone from his bishopric amongst his brethen: and we are assured he was a 'vraiment français', and that he was not a 'Catholique', and that this town wanted a 'vraiment Catholique'.

The country from Antwerp to Malines becomes more and more like England: trees more various, not the same dead flat but varied with gentle swells, many pollards, and more miserable cottages.

There is in the Cathedral a painting by Floris – the one on which is the bee – where he has shown great imagination and fire in the devils. It is the victory of the angels when fighting against the devils.

1 May   As soon as up, I went to the Cathedral, which has a fine tower. On entering I saw many pictures. None that I saw seemed particularly good. The church was pretty full of people, who really seemed devout. They were not the old and weak, but there was of every age. The young maiden was seen by the side of decrepit age, beauty by deformity, childhood by manhood. The effects on the mind is contagious. Many masses were going on at the same time. A woman went round for money for the chairs. Here I saw the first Christian caryatides.

We soon set off for Brussels. Between V. and that town the road is beautiful; a canal on one side, fine trees forming a long avenue diversified with glimpses of a rich country. We passed the Castle of Lac, the former residence of Buonaparte. It has a fine front upon an eminence, but the dome stands forth in glaring ugliness. We entered Brussels by the Allée Verte, a fine promenade.

Brussels, the old town, is not so fine as Antwerp, Ghent, or Bruges. The Grand Marché is very beautiful, only the buildings seem to be neglected. Fine public offices, with a tall spire, on one side – the Maire opposite. The Place Royale is very fine; the fronts of the houses and hotels around seeming together to form parts of one great palace; and the church on one side, with the housy wings, has a fine effect in spite of the ugly tower at the top. The gardens are beautiful with green, and well laid out in walks, with groups and termites – the Palace opposite. The entrance from the Place Royale presents a fine front, and the suburbs round it are also good. We are at the Hotel d'Angleterre. Saw *Morning Chronicles*, which are again dutysied.

Brussels was not at all fortified in the Waterloo time. The Germans at one time had retreated as far as the gates, which were obliged to be shut against them. In case of a retreat there would have been a pleasant rush, almost as great as at a fashionable rout, as they must all have passed through Brussels.

The carriage was put under hand. Crowds of English.

2 May   We have seen many, many soldiers. No wonder they were light of foot when not more heavy of age, for none have beards yet except some few cavalry.

The English women are the only good-looking women in Brussels; though, with true English Bullism, they vest *here* a complete Anglomanian costume, preserving their French fashions for the English winds to waft. The women of Brabant and the

Netherlands are all ugly to the eye after the piquant begins to pall, for there are no regular beauties or beauty of expression, except that levity which tells of lightness of cares and youth.

It is not for a foreigner to call a thing absurd because it does not tally well with ideas, or the ladies' costume, except the black mantle, should be put down as such by me. The men also are short and bad-looking, either consummate impudence or complete insignificance – no individuality. The indelicacy of these Belgians is gross; all kinds of disgusting books publicly sold, and exposed to the eyes of all young damsels – beastliness publicly exhibited on the public monuments – fountains with men vomiting with effort a stream of water – and still worse. The town (Brussels) is situated on an eminence, and is really poor in comparison of the other Belgic towns by us seen.

After dinner, having dressed, I went, having written two letters, to the theatre. Mounting a voiture, I was soon there. Ascending some stairs, I came to a door where, after some knocking, a man took my money, and gave me tickets, which, changed twice, brought me to the first row of boxes. The first look at the lobbies was sufficient to give me an idea of all the rest – misery, misery, wherever one turned – to the floor, to the ceiling, to the wall, to the box-wall, all garret of the St Giles style. Most of the doors had *Abonnement* written on them. I got into one, and what a sight! boxes dirty with filth. One chandelier was sufficient for the pockets of a Brussels manager, hung from the middle. Pits divided into two parts of different prices, boxes into three, and a gallery. Chairs, not benches, in the boxes. Ladies came and sat and talked, and talked and sat and stood, and went away. Many English ladies. Orchestra began – all violins, seven in all. Curtain up – a farce: no – it did not make me laugh. How call that a theatrical amusement which only seems fitted to excite the pleasurable sensation of yawning? It was French. An actress, the best amongst them, spoke French like a base pig; another contorted the fine lady into one with a paralytic stroke after sitting up at cards; the gentlemen like purlieu-bullies: and high life was copied from the waiting-maids of butchers' ladies. I was a little surprised at the applause that a lady actress gained. It moved me astonishingly: not her acting, but the lookers-on acting pleasure. At last came the wind whistling through the reeds, the thunder-hurling cheeks, and lashing hands, to my great admiration. It moved phlegm.

One who was to act Blondel was vomiting at home. I went

behind the scenes, and saw dismay in every face, and terror in every limb. The curtain drew up, and the play began. Hisses hisses, hisses. It fell, and fear increased. Some time was spent in cogitation. The venturous gold-decked hero advanced, retired, was rebuked by the police and forced to advance. Hisses. He said to the audience he was forced to advance. They listened, and quiproquos commenced between the players and the audience, with the sonorous hiss of anger. The police saw all was in vain, and ordered the actors off the boards. I in the meantime, was chatting with two apparent goddesses, who very concisely explained the trembling of the actors, etc., by telling me of real showers of eggs, etc. As I left the house I heard groans and hollow sounds, and cries of 'Give me back my money: I am an *abonne*, and I have seen nothing.' I ran – I and the police pushing on, the mob pushing us back, etc. Going along the lobbies, what was my wonder to stumble on a bookseller's shop, where was an assemblage of delicacies fit for the modest, and wondrous delicate!

3 May   I saw in the street three dogs, of the bull-dog race, dragging up a hill at a good pace what I am sure two men would not have strength to drag. I saw also a goat fastened to a child's car. I went all over town for a calache – bought one for 75 louis. In the evening, having procured redingoes (which I did not use), we mounted a coach and drove to _____. Returned home, ate, and slept.

4 May   Having risen, foolishly paid 40 naps. to the coachmaker. My Lord and servant stepped into the calèche. I and a servant got on horseback, and went to Waterloo. We soon entered Soignies, which on both sides formed a beautiful wood (not forest, for it was not wild on either side) for several miles. The avenue it formed varied in length: sometimes the end was formed by a turn of the road, sometimes by the mere perspective effect of narrowing. The trees are all young – none of above thirty years' growth. We then reached Waterloo, where were the head-quarters of Napoleon. An officious host pressed us to order dinner. We ran from his pressing, and advancing came to St Jean, where the boys continued the offerings we first had at Waterloo of buttons, books, etc. This was the village which gave the French name to the battle, I believe, as it was the spot which Napoleon tried to gain. The view of the plain, as we advanced to the right, struck us as fields formed almost with

the hopes that spirit and war would make their havoc here. Gentle
risings, sufficient to give advantage to the attacked – few hedges –
few trees. There was no sign of desolation to attract the passerby:
if it were not for the importunity of boys, and the glitter of buttons
in their hands, there would be no sign of war. The peasant whistled
as blithely, the green of Nature was as deep, and the trees waved
their branches as softly, as before the battle. The houses were
repaired. Only a few spots with white plaster between the bricks
pointed out the cannon's ruin; and in ruins there was only
Hougoumont, which was attacked so bravely and defended so
easily – at least so I should imagine from the few killed in the
garden and the appearance of the whole, while so many French lay
dead in the field. In the garden were only 25 English killed, while
in the field 1500; and on the other side 600 French, not counting the
wounded, were slain. Indeed, the gallantry, the resolution and
courage, which the French displayed in attacking this place,
guarded from the heights by our cannon, and by our soldiers
through the loop-holes, would alone ennoble the cause in which
they fought. Before arriving at Hougoumont, the spots where Hill,
Picton, and the Scotch Greys did their several deeds, were pointed
out to us. The spot which bore the dreadful charge of cavalry is
only marked by a hedge. The cuirassiers advancing, the Scots
divided – showed a masked battery, which fired grape into the
adverse party's ranks – then it was the Scots attacked. I do not now
so much wonder at their victory. The cuirasses which we saw were
almost all marked with bullets, lance- and sabre-cuts. Buonaparte
and the French, our guide said, much admired the good discipline
and undaunted courage of the short-kilted Scots. Going forward,
the spot at which the Prussians, the lucky gainers of the battle,
emerged, was pointed out to us – and, a little farther on, we were
shown the spot where Colonel Howard, my friend's cousin, was
buried before being carried to England. Three trees, of which one
is cut down, mark the spot, now ploughed over. At Hougoumont
we saw the untouched chapel where our wounded lay, and where
the fire consumed the toes of a crucifix. We there inscribed our
names amongst cits and lords. We found here a gardener who
pointed out the garden – the gate where the French were all burnt
– the gap in the hedge where the French attempted, after the loss
of 1500 men, to storm the place – the field, quarter of an acre, in
which were heaps of Gallic corpses. The gardener and the dog,
which we saw, had been detained at Hougoumont by General

Maitland in case of a retreat. The peasants declare that from 4 to 5 the affair was very, very doubtful, and that at the last charge of the Imperial Guards Napoleon was certain of being in Brussels in *quatre heures*. Wellingon, after the defeat of the Prussians etc., on the 17th went to Waterloo, and determined where he would place each corps. This was a great advantage: but, in spite of the excellence of his position, he would certainly have been defeated had it not been for the fortunate advance of the Prussians. From Hougoumont we went to the red-tiled house which is the rebuilding of the house where was Buonaparte's last station and head-quarters. It was from this spot that he viewed the arrival of the Prussians, under the idea of their being the corps of Grouchy. It was here he felt first the certainty of defeat, just after he had led the old Imperial Guard, in the certainty of victory, to his last attack. La Belle Alliance next appreared along the road, here where Wellington and Blucher met. The name is derived from a marriage in the time of peace: it is now applicable to a war-meeting. Thence we returned to St Jean, after going again to Hougoumont. There we were shown cuirasses, helms, buttons, swords, eagles, and regiment-books. We bought the helms, cuirasses, swords, etc., of an officer and soldier of cuirasses, besides eagles, cockades, etc. Beggars, the result of English profusion. A dinner, measured by some hungry John Bull's hungry stomach. We rode off the field, my companion singing a Turkish song – myself silent, full gallop cantering over the field, the finest one imaginable for a battle. The guide told us that the account Buonparte's guide gave of him after the battle was that he only asked the road to Paris, not saying anything else.

At Hougoumont various spots were pointed out: amongst the rest the one where Maitland stood watching a telegraph on the neighbouring rise, which told him what was going on on both sides.

We rode together through Soignies forest – black. The twilight made the whole length of the road more pleasing. On reaching home, we found the coach was jogged; so much so that it would not allow us to put confidence in it, etc. At last we gave it into Mr Gordon's hands. My friend has written twenty-six stanzas (?) to-day – some on Waterloo.

I made up my accounts, and was not a little startled by a deficit of 10 napoleons, which I at last found was a mere miscalculation. Rode about thirty miles in all.

Forgot to say I saw Sir Nath Wraxall at Dover, who, having introduced himself to Lord Byron as a friend *de famille*, began talking, knocking his feet in rattattat, still all the while oppressed by feeling very awkward.

At Brussels, the people were in a great stew, the night of the battle of Waterloo – their servants and others waking them every minute to tell them the French were at the gates. Some Germans went there with mighty great courage, in flight. Lord W sent to a colonel to enquire whether he was going to fly from or to the battle, giving him his choice to act in either way. On hearing this, the said colonel boldly faced about, and trotted to Brussels with his troop. A supernumerary aide-de-camp, the brother of N., with two others, was riding between the ranks while the French were firing; when, ours crying out 'They aim at you', all three were struck in the jaw, much in the same place, dead. After the battle, a friend asking what was become of N., the serjeant pointed to his feet, saying 'There', which was fact. Dacosta, the guide, says that Buonaparte was cool and collected till the Prussians arrived; that then he said to Bertrand, 'That appears to be the Prussian eagle'; and, upon Betrand's assenting, his face became momentarily pale. He says that, when he led up the Imperial Guard, on arriving at the red-tiled house, he went behind a hillock, so as not to be seen, and so gave them the slip. Wellington acted the soldier when he should have acted the general, and the light-limbed dancer when he should have been the soldier. I cannot, after viewing the ground, and bearing in mind the men's superior courage, give Wellington the palm of generalship that has been snatched for him by so many of his admirers. Napoleon only took one glass of wine from the beginning of the battle to the end of his flight.

5 May Got up at ten from fatigue. Whilst at breakfast, there came a Mr Pryse Gordon for L[ord] B. I entertained him. He has been to Italy, and travelled a great deal – a good-natured gentleman. Took him to see the carriage: he introduced me to his son by means of a trumpet. After his departure we set off for the Chateau du Lac, where we found the hind front much finer than the other for want of the startling (?) dome and low windows. It has all its master-apartments on the ground-floor: they are extremely well laid out both with regard to comfort and magnificence – they were furnished by Nap. We saw the bed where Josephine, Marie Louise, and the Queen of Holland, must have been treading fast on one another's heels. The hall for concerts divides the Emperor's from the Empress' rooms – it has a rich appearance, and is Corinthian. The flooring of the Emperor's is all wood of different colours – checked – having to my eye a more pleasing appearance than the carpeted ones of the Empress. I sat down on two chairs on which had sat he who ruled the world at one time. Some of his eagles were yet remaining on the chairs. The servant seemed a little astonished at our bowing before them.

We returned, it raining all the while. After dinner Mr G came for us to go to coffee. We went, and were graciously received; Lord B as himself, I as a tassel to the purse of merit. I there saw a painting of Rembrandt's wife or mother by himself, which was full of life, and some verses by Walter Scott written in the hostess' album, where he says Waterloo will last longer than Cressy and Agincourt. How different! They only agree in one thing – that they were both in the cause of injustice. The novels of Casti were presented to me by Mr Gordon, which I was rather surprised at. We came over. Scott writes in M. G book –

> 'For one brief hour of deathless fame'
> 'Oh Walter Scott, for shame, for shame'

6 May   Mr G and son came whilst at breakfast; gave us letters, etc. Saw the little child again; B gave it a doll.

The *carrossier* came. Set off at two, passing through a country increasing in inequalities. We arrived first at Louvain, where we saw the outside of a beautiful Town-hall, which is one of the prettiest pieces of external fretwork I have seen. Thence we went to Tirlemont, where was a Jubilee. Saints and sinners under the red canopy (the sky dirty Indian-ink one) were alike in the streets. Every street had stuck in it, at a few paces from the house-walls, fir-branches 16 or 17 feet high, distant from one another 5 or 6 feet. Thence to St Trond, where we ate – and slept, I suppose. The country is highly cultivated, and the trees older. The avenues have a more majestic appearance from the long swells of ground and the straight roads, but there is more squalid misery than I have seen anywhere. The houses are many of them mud, and the only clean part about them is the white-wash on the external walls. Dunghills before some must be trodden on before entering the houses. The towns also fall off greatly in neat and comfortable looks. The walls round them look ruined and desolate, and give a great idea of insecurity. We put the servants on board-wages.

7 May   Set off from St Trond at 11. The country is highly cultivated; continual hill and dale; lower orders miserable in perfection; houses built of mud, the upper storeys of which are only built of beams, the mud having fallen off. Bridges thrown over the dirt they were too idle to remove. Dunghills at their doors, and ditches with black fetid water before their first step. Liège has a pretty neighbourhood, but the town itself is filthy and disagreeable. They visited our passports here at three different places. The hill above the town is enormously steep; and from some way beyond it has a beautiful view of Liège with its towers and domes – of the country with its many cots and villas – and of the Meuse. The road now lies through a scene where cottages are spread like trees, and hedges like furrows of corn, the fields are so minutely divided. A little farther still we had a most splendid view through many miles. From a valley we could see everything clearly, crowded in a blue tint, and in a river through it we could see the shadows of the trees. The cottages are improving, and the roads becoming the worst ever seen; paved still, but so horridly hilled and vallied that the rolling of the carriage is like the rolling of a ship.

We came at last to Battice; but before entering we passed by a village where beggar little cherubs came to the carriage-side, and running cried out, 'Donnez-nous quelque chose, Monsieur le chef de bataillon'; another, 'Monsieur le general.' And a third little urchin, who gesticulated as well as cried, perceiving the others had exhausted the army, cried, 'Un sou, Messieurs les rois des Hanoveriens!' We arrived at Battice, where beggars, beggars. There we found horses just come in.

After debate (wherein I was for Aix-la-Chapelle, LB for stopping) we set off; and such a jolting, rolling, knocking, and half-a-dozen etc., as our carriage went through, I never saw, which put LB to accusing me of bad advice; clearing however as the road mended. The rain fell into a pond, to be illuminated by sunshine before we reached Aix-la-Chapelle at half-past twelve.

8 May   Got up late. Went to see the Cathedral: full of people, lower ranks, hearing mass. Miserable painting, architecture, etc. Saw also a church wherein was no particular picture or anything. At Liège the revoluntionists had destroyed the fine Cathedral.

A German boy who led me about Aix-la-Chapelle, on my asking him in broken German about the baths, led me to a very different place. I was astonished to find myself in certain company. The baths are hot sulphuretted-hydrogen-impregnated water. The sulphur-beds are only shown to dukes and kings: so a kingdom is good for something. I saw the baths themselves: like others, not very clean-looking.

We left Aix-la-Chapelle at twelve, going through a fine country, with no hedges but fine woods in the distance. We arrived at St Juliers, strongly fortified, where they took our names at entering and at exiting. It is a neat town, and was besieged last year. We were at the post taken by a man for Frenchmen, and he told us we had been driven from Russia by a band of the Emperor. He seemed to be very fond of them, and gave as a reason that he had been employed by them for many years. And, I forgetfully saying, 'What! were they here?' – 'Yes, and farther.' I answered, ' Jusqu'a Moscou.'

'Oui, et presque plus loin.' That 'presque' means much. The French were not generally liked, I believe. The lower orders perhaps liked them, but the middle, I doubt. But I cannot say; I may perhaps be influenced by the opinion of a beautiful face of this town, who, on my asking her whether the *dames n'aimaient pas beaucoup les Francais*, answered, '*Oui, les dames publiques.*'

We find it a great inconvenience that the Poste is a separate concern, and generally pretty distant from the inn. The women are many of them very beautiful, and many of them, as well as the men, have fine dark eyes and hair. The men wear ear-rings, and curl their hair; which, if I remember rightly, was the custom in the time of Tacitus. Many of the women wear their hair combed quite back, and upon it a little square piece of linen. The French were particularly polite during the siege.

We entered the dominions of the King of Prussia a little beyond Battice. It causes a strange sensation to an Englishman to pass into one state from another without crossing any visible line. Indeed, we should not have perceived that we had, if we had not been stopped by a Belgian guard who asked us if we had anything to declare. The difference is, however, very striking. The men, the women, everything, improve – except the cottages. The people look cleaner, though everything else is dirty; contrary to the Belgians, they seem to collect their cleanliness upon themselves, instead of throwing it upon their cots, tins, trees, and shrubs.

We arrived at Cologne after much bad, sandy, heavy road, at 11. The pavement begins to be interrupted after Aix, but ends almost entirely after St Juliers. Cologne is upon a flat on the Rhine. We are groaning at having no sight of far-famed Cologne, when we came suddenly under its battlements and towers. We passed through its fortifications without question. After having found the gates shut, and feed the porter, we found inns full, and at last got into the Hotel de Prague.

9 May   Got up very bad. Sat down to breakfast. Just done, we heard some singing. Enquiry told us, buyable. Got them up. A harp played by a dark-haired German, pretty, and two fiddlers. She played and sang *The Troubadour*, which brought back a chain of Scotch recollections, and a German song; then a beautiful march, in which the music died away and then suddenly revived. After a waltz we dismissed them. We both mounted a voiture, and drove through the town to the Cathedral. Great part pulled down by the revolutionists, and the roof of the nave obliged to be restored with plain board – a staring monument over Gallic ruin. There is fine stained glass, and the effect of its being very high and variegated in the choir is beautiful. We saw a fine painting here by Kalf: vide *Taschbuch*. The tomb of the three kings said to be worth three millions of francs, and an immensely rich treasury wherein was a sacrament worth one million of francs. In falling down a step I broke a glass, for which they at first would not take anything – which at last cost me three francs. Kept countenance amazingly well.

Went to see St Ursula's Church, where we were shown virgins' skulls of ninety years old, male and female, all jumbled into a mass of 11,000 virgins' bones arranged all in order – some gilt, etc. A whole room bedecked with them. All round, indeed, whatever we saw were relics, skulls; some in the head of silver-faced busts, some arranged in little cells with velvet cases, wherein was worked the name of each. Paintings of St Ursula, etc. Asked for a piece out of the masses: only got a smile, and a point of a finger to an interdiction in Latin, which I did not read.

We went to see a picture of Rubens, *The Nailing of St Peter to a Cross*; the best design, though not very good, I yet have seen of his. A German artist copying it spoke English to us.

Returned home. Sent my name to Professor Wallraf: got admission. Found a venerable old man who has spent his life in making a collection of paintings and other objects of vertu belonging to his country, Cologne, which he intends leaving to his native town.

Many pictures were extremely good, especially painting of individuals. Kaft was a native of this town, who painted in oil before oil-painting was known. Saw some Poussins, Claude Lorraines. Some moderate. A Tintoretto of *Campavella* beautiful: colouring and drawing strong and expressive. A Rembrandt and a Teniers, etc. A master of Rubens. A copy in colours from the drawing of Raphael by one of his disciples. Cologne has stamped more coins than some empires, and has coined twenty-six kinds of gold. He had made drawings of them, but the revolution stopped it. The revolutionary Gauls, he said with a tear in his eye, has destroyed many very valuable relics of Cologne; and, pointing to a leaf of a missal with another tear, he said: 'Many like this once adorned our churches: this is all.' He had the original manuscript of Albert le Grand, *History of Animals*; Titian's four designs of the Caesars at Polenham, with own handwriting; the Albert Durer's sketch of Christ's head which belonged to Charles II; and a painting of Albert Durer's Master. He wishes for a copy of any of Caxton's printing in England.

Went to buy some books. Found Miss Helmhoft, a fine woman. Had a long confab. Bought more books than I wanted. Heard her spout German poetry that I did not understand; and laughed at the oddity of her gesticulation, which she took for laughter at the wit of a poet who was describing the want of a shirt – and was highly pleased.

The French destroyed convents, and made of them public places for walking.

Have been taken for servants, Frenchmen, merchants – never hardly for English. Saw the Rhine last night – fine mass of water, wide as the Thames some way below Blackwell; but no tide, and very deep. Town dirty, very decayed, badly paved, worse lighted, and a few marks of splendour and comfort.

10 May   We have seen crucifixes for these four days at every turn, some made of wood, some of stone, etc. Set off, after having defeated the imposition of a postman, to Bonn; the scenery not anything particular till we see the Seven Hills, a large amphitheatre on the right, glimpses on the left of the Rhine, and the Seven Hills. Bonn at last appeared, with its steeples, and on the neighbouring hills castles and cots, towers, and (not) towns.

I saw yesterday a picture of Rembrandt's with three lights in it very well managed, at Wallraf's.

Saw R. Simmons' writing in the police-book at Bonn, and wrote to Soane.

The innkeeper makes you put your name – whence – whither – profession and age – every night. Rogues all of them, charging much.

11 May We saw the first vines a little before entering Cologne some days ago. We left Bonn at eleven, the town having nothing in particular. The Seven Hills were the first that struck our sight on one of the highest pinnacles in Drachenfels, now a mere ruin, formerly a castle of which many a tale is told. There was by the roadside a monument raised upon the spot where one noble brother killed another. Crucifixes all the way. We had the river on one side when rose hills (not mountains) cultivated halfway for vines – and the rest, nuts, shrubs, oak, etc. Towers on pinnacles, in ruin; villages (with each its spire) built of mud.

Cultivation in a high degree; no hedges, ground minutely divided into beds rather than fields; women working in fields; ox and horse ploughing; oxen draw by their heads alone. Peasantry happy-looking and content. Two points particularly struck us – the Drachenfels, and the view at a distance before coming to Videnhar when the distant hills were black with the rain. But the whole way it is one of the finest scenes, I imagine, in the world. The large river with its massy swells and varied towered banks.

We changed horses at Bemagne, and passed over a road first cut by Aurelius, Theodoric, and Buonaparte. B's name is everywhere. Who did this? NB. – Who that? – He. There is an inscription to record this. Andernach – a fine entrance from Bemagne, with its massy towers and square-spired church. From Andernach we passed on. Saw on the other side Neuwied, a town owing its existence to the mere toleration of religion. It is the finest and flourishing we have seen since Ghent and Antwerp. We saw the tomb of Hoche at a distance; went to it. There was inscribed 'The army of the Sambre and the Moselle to its general-in-chief Hoche'. The reliefs are torn off, the marble slabs broken, and it is falling. But –

> 'Glory of the fallen brave
> Shall men remember though forgot their grave,'

and the enemies may launch malicious darts against it. Andernach the Rhine loses much. The valley is wider, and the beautiful, after the almost sublime, palls, and man is fastidious.

About a mile from Coblentz we saw Marceau's tomb – too dark. Crossed the bridge over the Moselle, entered Coblentz; asked of military, no pass; went to inns, rascals. Went to the Trois Suisses – well served; fine view of Ehrenbreitstein fortress in sight. When French besieged it, Marceau was here at this inn, and the canon-ball pierced it several times. – There were 84 French officers here, when they would not believe the Cossacks would pass; they had to fly as quick as horses could convey them, for the C, getting into boats, made their horses swim across. Cs rascals – ate and drank and never paid. The general of them mean into the bargain; for he sent the waiter in search of a louis he had never dropped, and went off. – A flying bridge in face of me.

12 May Got up. Looked at the fine view, and went to the bath, which was at a malster's – 30 sous. Thence entered a Catholic church – organ – children singing, which had a fine effect. A copy of Rubens – lineal. Breakfasted.

Mounted a calèche, and went to Marceau's monument. The tomb of heroes made into a certain place very much expressed the flickering flame of fame. Thence to the Chartreuse: deserted, ruined, window-less, roofless, and tenantless – with another in sight in the same state. Plenty of reliefs on the roadside belonging to the Road to Calvary, an oratory on the hillside, where were many peasants bowing in reverence. Thence to the flying bridge managed by boats fastened in the stream with a rope, and by the rudder.

Saw a motley group of peasants with their head-dresses of gold and crimson or green with the steel pin. Cocked hat, blue coat and stockinged heroes with a fork. Officers, artillery-men, etc; crosses given apparently with as profuse a hand to the soldiers as to the roadside.

Went to Ehrenbreitstein. Everything broken by gunpowder; immense masses of solid stone and mortar thrown fifty yards from their original situation; ruined walls, gateways, and halls – nothing perfect. Splendid views thence – Coblentz, Rhine, Moselle with its bridge, mountains, cultivation, vines, wilderness, everything below my feet. Mounted again. Passed the Rhine in a boat (rowed), looking very like the Otaheitan canoes. Into the carriage – set off. Scenes increasing in sublimity. The road raised from the side of the river without parapet; two precipices coming to the road headlong.

Indeed the river reaches foot to foot – splendid, splendid, splendid. Saw the fort belonging once to Muhrfrey, where he raised customs, and resisted in consequence sixty cities. Arrived at St Goar. At the first post saw the people in church; went to hear them sing – fine.

13 May   Left St Goar. Found scenery sublime to Bingen. Men with cocked hats and great buckles hacking at the vines. The scenery after Bingen gains in beauty what it loses in sublimity. Immense plain to the mounts, with the Rhine *in medio,* covered with trees, woods, and forests. Fine road to Mayence made by Nap; his name has been erased from the inscription on the column commemorative of the work. Insolence of power!

Mayence a fine town, with a cathedral raised above it of red sandstone. Bavarians, Austrians, and Prussians, all in the town – belonging to all. The best town we have seen since Ghent.

One of our postillions blew a horn. Saw yesterday a beautiful appearance – two rainbows, one on the top of trees where the colours of the foliage pierced the rainbow-hues.

Arrived at Mayence at 6½. Saw along the Rhine many fine old castles. This below is what LB wrote to Mrs Leigh some days ago: written May 11 on Rhine-banks. See *Childe Harold,* from 'The Castle Crag of Drachenfels' to 'Still sweeten more these Banks of Rhine'.

14 May   From Mayence, where I saw the spot where they said lately stood the house where printing was invented; it had been pulled down by the French. The gallery I could not see, because the keeper had taken it into his head to make a promenade. Saw the cathedral, pierced at the roof by bombs in the last siege the town underwent. The reliefs – some of which were in a good style – many decapitated. There was a German marshal who was represented as gravely putting forth his powdered head from under a tombstone he has just lifted up – with an inscription saying 'I am here.'

From Mayence we went to Mannheim through a fine country. Crossed the Rhine on a bridge of boats. Taken very ill with a fever at Mannheim – could not write my journal.

15 May   Being a little recovered, set off. Fine alleys of Lombardy-poplars and horse-chestnuts – neat villages. Entered Carlsruhe through a grove of Scotch firs and other trees that had a fine effect. Saw the Palace.

Entered the inn, and was very ill. Took ipecac.and op.gr.15. Headache, vertigo, tendency to fainting, etc. Magnesia and lemon acid – a little better, no effect.

Went a drive about the town. Saw the neatest town we have yet met with: the only objection is the houses stuccoed with white – bad for the eyes. Saw the outside of the Palace, and went into the garden laid out in the English manner.

Went home: dreadful headaches: ate some stewed apples; took some more magn and acid; had no effect; lay down; got up after two hours. Was just going out when LB came to take from my hand a plated candlestick, to give me a brass one. Got on a few steps; fainted. My fall brought the servants to me. Took 4 pills; going out again, when LB made the servant put down the plated candlestick, to take up a brass one; went to bed.

Medicine had violent effect: better on the whole, though weak.

Just as we were going out I met Sir C. Hunter at my chamber-door, who told me he had heard so bad an account of my positively dying that he came to enquire how I found myself. I asked him in. He took care to tell us he was a great friend of the Grand Duke, who had sent his groom of the stole (he called it stool) in search of lodgings for the worth Mayor; gave us a long sermon about rheumatism, routes, etc.; left us. In the evening he sent in the *Guide du Voyager en les pays del'Europe*, begging in return some of LB poems.

Went out. Saw a church. Columns like firs – Corinthian, golden capitals: loaded everywhere with gilt, perhaps tawdry, but fine-tawdry. The environs are beautiful. Drove a great deal about: fine trees and fine cultivation.

18 May From Carlsruhe to Offenberg; much better. Slept halfway: blinds down the other, so nothing to mention except fine trees, fine cocked hats, fine women, and yellow-coated postillions.

19 May Set off from Offenberg; saw some scenes that please me much; hills and clouds upon them; woods with mists. Passed through Freiburg, where we saw the steeple pervious to the top with trellis-work showing the light, which had to my eyes a beautiful appearance.

I think Charles, when he said, 'The German for his horse,' remembered the G postillions; for they talk to theirs, and the horses on their part listen and seem to understand. The greater part of to-day I have found the ladies in a strange costume of short wide red petticoats with many folds, and a hat of straw as wide as a wheel. Arrived at Krolzingen to sleep. Left Krolzingen: got to a hill. Fine view thence: the Alps, the Rhine, the Jura mountains, and a fine plain before us – fine country. Crossed the Rhine, and were in Switzerland. The town upon unequal ground – some parts very high, and some low; the greater part very narrow streets. After tea went to take a walk: went upon the Rhine bridge – upon a hill in the town.

21 May   Went to see a panorama of Thun, the first Swiss one: crowded foolishly with people, and too small. Saw a gallery that the artist had formed. A fine Raphael, not his; a good Rembrandt, the first I saw historical; a *Circumcision*; a head of the caricaturist David; two heads of Divinity; a *Christ and Virgin* – mere pieces of flesh and drapery. Went to a marchand d'estampes. Saw there *Nelson's Death*, Chatham's ditto, and other pictures of England. *The Dance of Death* has been destroyed: but it was not Holbein's, but his restorer's. The collection is dispersed, that once was here, of his paintings.

Agreed with a voiturier to take our carriages to Geneva in five days. Set off. Country increases from hills to mountains with great beauty. Passed through Lipstadt and came to ____. Went before supper to climb a hill where we found a goatherd who could not understand the French that asked for milk till it had the commentary, 'We will pay for it.' The scene was very fine: to the right, beautiful; to the left, it had a tendency to sublimity; on one side hills covered to the top with trees; on the other, mountains with bald pates. Came down. Found the servants playing at bowls. They were obliged to run the bowls along a narrow board to the men. Supper: read *Arabian Nights*; went to bed.

22 May   Left _____ at 9; passed the Jura mountains, where we saw some fine castellated scenery, and women ornamented strangely – amazingly short petticoats, not below the knee, with black crape rays round their heads that make them look very spidery. Soleure is a neat town with stone fortifications, and a clean church with fountains before it. The houses in this neighbourhood have a pleasing strange appearance on account of the roofs, which slant out on every side a great way. Immense number of Scotch firs – roads fine. Voituriers slow, and have eight francs of drink-money a day, being two; which being too much according to the *Guide du Voyageur en Europe*, where it is said 1½ fr., we showed it to our courier, who was in a passion. Came to _____, where we slept.

23 May Left _____: got a sight of some fine Alpine snow-capped mountains. Came to Berne; delightfully situated; beautiful streets with arcades all their length. Dined there. Saw a spendidly beautiful view coming down a hill, with hills covered with fir, ash, beech, and all the catalogue of trees; Morat at the bottom, and the Jura mountains behind, with snowy hair and cloudy night-caps. Arrived at Morat; neat with arcades. Stopped at the Crown inn. All the way had debates whether clouds were mountains, or mountains clouds.

24 May The innkeeper at Morat, being a little tipsy, and thinking every Englishman (being a philosophe) must be a philosophe like himself, favoured us with some of his infidel notions while serving us supper. Near Morat was fought the battle wherein the Burgundians were so completely thrashed. Their bones, of which we took pieces, are now very few; once they formed a mighty heap in the chapel, but both were destroyed by the Burgundian division when in Switzerland, and a tree of liberty was planted over it, which yet flourishes in all its verdure – the liberty has flown from the planters' grasp. Saw Aventicum; there remains sufficient of the walls to trace the boundaries of the ancient town; but of all the buildings, both for Gods and men, nothing but a column remains, and that only remnant for more than a hundred years. There are mosaic pavements, and even the streets may be perceived in a dry summer by the grass being thinner. The mosaic in a barn, probably once of a temple, was pretty perfect till the Gallic cavalry came and turned it into a stable. It is formed of little pieces of black, white, and red bricks; little now remains. There was also a copper vessel in the middle; that too has disappeared. The town is shamefully negligent of the antiquities of their fathers, for there is another more beautiful and perfect mosaic pavement discovered, but which they have allowed the proprietor to cover again with mould rather than buy it. We found in a barn heads, plinths, capitals, and shafts, heaped promiscuously. The Corinthian-column capital is deeply, sharply, and beautifully cut. A head of Apollo in all the rudeness of first art – a capital of a strange mixed order. There is the Amphitheatre, hollow yet pretty perfect, but no stonework visible; overgrown with trees; the size, my companion told me, was larger than common. In the town there were some beautiful fragments of ornament-sculpture incorporated in the walls; all marble. In the walls of the church we sought in vain for the inscription that Mathison mentions to Julia Alpinula.

I copied the one below on account of its medical tendency. The letters in this as well as in all the other inscriptions are formed like our Roman print, not in the least imperfect: 'Nvminib. Avg. et Genio Col. I. El. Apollini Sagr. 9. Postum Hermes lib. Medicis et Professorib, D.S.D.'

From Aventicum or Avenches we went to Payerne. We have seen in many places boys leading goats just in the antique style. Thence we went to Moudon – dirty town. Stopped for refreshments. One fine view we have had all the way, but nothing equal to the view descending to Morat.

Darkness came on. We saw the Castle wherein _____ defended himself against the French who besieged it for a month: looks so weak, it seems a wonder. The Swiss castles are not nearly so interesting as the Rhine ones. They are very conical-roofed and no battlements. We saw the lake, but for a long time doubted whether it was a cloud below, a mist before, or water beneath us. Entered Lausanne.

25 May Left Lausanne, after having looked at a bookseller's, who showed me a fine collection of bad books for four louis. Enquired for Dewar: name not known. We went along the lake, that a little disappointed me, as it does not seem so broad as it really is, and the mountains near near it, though covered with snow, have not a great appearance on account of the height [of the] lake. We saw Mont Blanc in the distance; ethereal in appearance, mingling with the clouds; it is more than 60 miles from where we saw it. It is a classic ground we go over. Buonaparte, Joseph, Bonnet, Necker, Staël, Voltaire, Rousseau, all have their villas (except Rousseau). Genthoud, Ferney, Coppet, are close to the road.

We arrived at Sécheron – where LB, having put his age down as 100, received a letter half-an-hour after from Inn Keeper – a thing that seems worthy of a novel. It begins again to be the land of the vine. Women, who till the Pays de Vaud were ugly, improving greatly.

26 May After breakfast, and having made up the accounts to-day, and having heard that the voituriers made a claim of drink-money all the way back, we ordered a calèche; but, happening to go into the garden, we saw a boat, into which entering, we pushed out upon the Leman Lake. After rowing some time, happening to come to the ferry, we found the waiter with a direful look to tell us that it was *pris pour un monsieur Anglais*, who happened to be _____. We got another, and went out to bathe.

I *rode* first with LB upon the field of Waterloo; *walked* first to see Churchill's tomb; *bathed and rowed* first on the Leman Lake. – It did as much good. Dined; entered the calèche; drove through Geneva, where I saw an effect of building that pleased me: it was porticoes from the very roof of the high houses to the bottom.

Went to the house beyond Cologny that belonged to Diodati. They ask five-and-twenty louis for it a month. Narrow, not true. The view from his house is very fine; beautiful lake; at the bottom of the crescent is Geneva. Returned. Pictet called, but LB said 'not at home'.

27 May   Got up; went about a boat; got one for 3fr. a day: rowed to Sécheron. Breakfasted. Got into a carriage. Went to Banker's, who changed our money, and afterwards left his card. To Pictet – not at home. Home, and looked at accounts: bad temper on my side. Went into a boat, rowed across to Diodati; cannot have it for three years; English family. Crossed again; I went; LB back. Getting out, LB met M Wollstonecraft Godwin, her sister, and Percy Shelley. I got into the boat into the middle of Leman Lake, and there lay my length, letting the boat go its way.

Found letter from De Roche inviting me to breakfast to-morrow; curious with regard to LB. Dined; PS, the author of *Queen Mab*, came; bashful, shy, consumptive; twenty-six; separated from his wife; keeps the two daughters of Godwin, who practise his theories; one LB's.

Into the calèche; horloger's at Geneva; LB paid 15 nap. Towards a watch; I, 13: repeater and minute-hand; foolish watch.

Went to see the house of Madame Necker, 100 a half-year; came home, etc.

28 May   Went to Geneva, to breakfast with Dr De Roche; acute, sensible, a listener to himself; good clear head. Told me that armies on their march induce a fever (by their accumulation of animal dirt, irregular regimen) of the most malignant typhoid kind; it is epidemic. There was a whole feverish line from Moscow to Metz, and it spread at Geneva the only almost epidemic typhus for many years. He is occupied in the erection of Lancaster schools, which he says succeed well. He is a Louis Bourbonist. He told me my fever was not an uncommon one among travellers. He came home with me, and we had a chat with LB; chiefly politics, where of course we differed. He had a system well worked out, but I hope only hypothetical, about liberty of the French being Machiavellianly not desirable by Europe. He pointed out Dumont in the court, the rédacteur of Bentham.

Found a letter from Necker to the hotel-master, asking 100 nap. for three months; and another from Pictet inviting LB and any friend to go with him at 8 to Madame Einard, a connection of his. We then, ascending our car, went to see some other house, none suiting.

When we returned home, Mr Percy Shelley came in to ask us to dinner; declined; engaged for to-morrow. We walked with him, and got into his boat, though the wind raised a little sea upon the lake. Dined at four. Mr Hentsch, the banker, came in; very polite; told LB that, when he saw him yesterday, he had not an idea that he was speaking to one of the most famous lords of England.

Dressed and went to Pictet's: an oldish man, about forty-six, tall, well-looking, speaks English well. His daughter showed us a picture, by a young female artist, of Madame Lavallière in the chapel; well executed in pencil – good lights and a lusciously grieving expression.

Went to Madame Einard. Introduced to a room where about 8 (afterwards 20), 2 ladies (1 more), LB's name was alone mentioned; mine, like a star in the halo of the moon, invisible. LB not speaking French, M. Einard spoke bad Italian. A Signor Rossi came in, who had joined Murat at Bologna. Manly in thought; admired Dante as a poet more than Ariosto, and a discussion about manliness in a language. Told me Geneva women amazingly chaste even in thoughts. Saw the Lavallière artist. A bonny, rosy, seventy-yeared man, called Bonstetten, the beloved of Gray and the correspondent of Mathison.

Madame Einard made tea, and left all to take sugar with the fingers. Madame Einard showed some historical pieces of her doing in acquerella, really good, a little too French-gracish. Obliged to leave before ten for the gate shut. Came home, went to bed.

Was introduced by Shelley to Mary Wollstonecraft Godwin,

called here Mrs Shelley. Saw picture by Madame Einard of a cave in the Jura where in winter there is no ice, in summer plenty. No names announced, no ceremony – each speaks to whom he pleases. Saw the bust of Jean Jacques erected upon the spot where the Geneva magistrates were shot. LB said it was probably built of some of the stones with which they pelted him. The walk is deserted. They are now mending their roads. Formerly they could not, because the municipal money always went to the public box.

29 May   Went with Mr Hentsch to see some houses along the valley in which runs the Rhone: nothing. Dined with Mr and Mrs Percy Shelley and Wollstonecraft Godwin. Hentsch told us that the English last year exported corn to Italy to a great amount.

30 May   Got up late. Went to Mr and Mrs Shelley; breakfasted with them; rowed out to see a house together. S went from Lucerne with the two, with merely £26, to England along the Rhine in bateaux. Gone through much misery, thinking he was dying; married a girl for the mere sake of letting her have the jointure that would accrue to her; recovered; found he could not agree; separated; paid Godwin's debts, and seduced his daughter; then wondered that he would not see him. The sister left the father to go with the other. Got a child. All clever, and no meretricious appearance. He is very clever: the more I read his *Queen Mab*, the more beauties I find. Published at fourteen a novel; got £30 for it; by his second work £100. *Mab* not published. – Went in calèche with LB to see a house; again after dinner to leave cards; then on lake with LB. I, Mrs S, and Miss G, on to the lake till nine. Drank tea, and came away at 11 after confabbing. The batelier went to Shelley, and asked him as a favour not to tell LB what he gave for his boat, as he thought it quite fit that Milord's payment be double; we sent Berger to say we did not wish for a boat.

31 May   Breakfasted with Shelley; read Italian with Mrs S; dined; went into a boat with Mrs S, and rowed all night till 9; tea'd together; chatted, etc.

1 June   Breakfasted with S; entered a calèche; took Necker's house for 100 louis for 8 or 365 days. Saw several houses for Shelley; one good. Dined; went in the boat; all tea'd together.
  Rogers the subject: LB thinks good poet; malicious. Marquis of

Lansdowne being praised by a whole company as a happy man, having all good, R said, 'But how horridly he carves turbot!' Ward having reviewed his poems in the *Quarterly*, having a bad heart and being accused of learning his speeches, LB, upon malignantly hinting to him how he had been carved, heard him say: 'I stopped his speaking though by my epigram, which is –

> '"Ward has no heart, they say, but I deny it;
> He has a heart, and gets his speeches by it."'

On LB writing a poem to his sister wherein he says, 'And when friends e'en paused and love,' etc., Rogers, going to some one, said; 'I don't know what LB means by *pausing*; I called upon him every day.' He did this regularly, telling LB all the bad news with a malignant grin. When LB wrote 'Weep, daughter of a royal line', Rogers came to him one day, and, taking up the *Courier*, said: 'I am sure now you're attacked there; now don't mind them'; and began reading, looking every now and then at LB with an anxious searching eye, till he came to 'that little poet and disagreeable person, Mr Samuel –' when he tore the paper, and said: 'Now this must be that fellow Croker,' and wished LB to challenge him. He talked of going to Cumberland with LB, and, asking him how he meant to travel, LB said 'With four horses.' Rogers went to company, and said: 'It is strange to hear a man talking of four horses who seals his letters with a tallow candle.'

Shelley is another instance of wealth inducing relations to confine for madness, and was only saved by his physician being honest. He was betrothed from a boy to his cousin, for age; another came who had as much as he *would* have, and she left him 'because he was an atheist'. When starving, a friend to whom he had given £2000, though he knew it, would not come near him. Heard Mrs Shelley repeat Coleridge on Pitt, which persuades me he is a poet.

A young girl of eighteen, handsome, dined within half-an-hour yesterday: buried to-day. Geneva is fortified – legumes growing in the fosses. – Went about linen and plate.

2 June Breakfasted with Shelley. Read Tasso with Mrs Shelley. Took child for Vaccination.

Found gates shut because of church-service. Went in search of Rossi. Saw a village where lads and lasses, soubrettes and soldiers, were dancing, to a tabor and drum, waltzes, cotillons, etc. Dr R not at home.

Dined with S; went to the lake with them and LB. Saw their house; fine. Coming back, the sunset, the mountains on one side, a dark mass of outline on the other, trees, houses hardly visible, just distinguishable; a white light mist, resting on the hills around, formed the blue into a circular dome bespangled with stars only and lighted by the moon which gilt the lake. The dome of heaven seemed oval. At 10 landed and drank tea. Madness, Grattan, Curran, etc., subjects.

3 June   Went to Pictet's on English day.

4 June   Went about Diodati's house. Then to see Shelley, who, with Mrs Shelley, came over. Went in the evening to a musical society of about ten members at M. Odier's; who read a very interesting memoir upon the subject of whether a physician should in any case tell a lover the health, or anything that, from being her physician, comes to his knowledge.

Afterwards had tea and politics. Saw there a Dr Gardner, whom I carried home in the calèche. Odier invited me for every Wednesday.

Came home. Went on the lake with Shelley and Lord Byron, who quarrelled with me.

5 June   At 12 went to Hentsch about Diodati; thence to Shelley's. Read Tasso. Home in calèche. Dined with them in the public room: walked in the garden. Then dressed, and to Odier's, who talked with me about somnambulism. Was at last seated, and conversed with some Génevoises: so so – too fine. Quantities of English; speaking amongst themselves, arms by their sides, mouths open and eyes glowing; might as well make a tour of the Isle of Dogs. Odier gave me yesterday many articles of *Bibliothèque* – translated and rédigés by himself, and to-day a manuscript on somnambulism.

6 June   At 1 up – breakfasted. With Lord Byron in the calèche to Hentsch, where we got the paper making us masters of Diodati for six months to November 1 for 125 louis.

Thence to Shelley: back: dinner. To Shelley in boat: driven on shore: home. Looked over inventory and Berger's accounts. Bed.

7 June   Up at ___. Pains in my loins and languor in my bones. Breakfasted – looked over inventory. Saw LB at dinner; wrote to my father and Shelley; went in the boat with LB; agreed with boatman for English boat. Told us Napoleon had caused him to get his children. Saw Shelley over again.

8 June Up at 9; went to Geneva on horseback, and then to Diodati to see Shelley; back; dined; into the new boat – Shelley's, – and talked, till the ladies' brains whizzed with giddiness, about idealism. Back; rain; puffs of wind. Mistake.

9 June Up by 1: breakfasted. Read Lucian. Dined. Did the same: tea'd. Went to Hentsch: came home. Looked at the moon, and ordered packing-up.

10 June Up at 9. Got things ready for going to Diodati; settled accounts, etc. Left at 3; went to Diodati; went back to dinner, and then returned. Shelley etc. came to tea, and we sat talking till 11. My rooms are so:

Picture-gallery	
Bedroom	

11 June Wrote home and to Pryse Gordon. Read Lucian. Went to Shelley's; Shelley in the evening with us.

12 June Rode to town. Subscribed to a circulating library, and went in the evening to Madame Odier. Found no one. Miss O, to make time pass, played the Ranz des Vaches – plaintive and war-like. People arrived. Had a confab with Dr O. about perpanism, etc. Began dancing: waltzes, cotillons, French country-dances and English ones: first time I shook my feet to French measure. Ladies all waltzed except the English: *they* looked on frowning. Introduced to Mrs Slaney: invited me for next night. You ask without introduction; the girls refuse those they dislike. Till 12. Went and slept at the Balance.

13 June Rode home, and to town again. Went to Mrs Slaney: a ball. Danced and played at chess. Walked home in thunder and lightning: lost my way. Went back in search of some one – fell upon the police. Slept at the Balance.

14 June   Rode home – road almost all day. Dined with Rossi, who came to us; shrewd, quick, manly-minded fellow; like him very much. Shelley etc. fell in in the evening.

15 June   Up late; began my letters. Went to Shelley's. After dinner, jumping a wall my foot slipped and I strained my left ankle. Shelley etc. came in the evening; talked of my play etc, which all agreed was worth nothing. Afterwards Shelley and I had a conversation about principles, – whether man was to be thought merely an instrument.

16 June   Laid up. Shelley came, and dined and slept here, with Mrs S and Miss Clare Clairmont. Wrote another letter.

17 June   Went into the town; dined with Shelley etc. here. Went after dinner to a ball at Madame Odier's; where I was introduced to Princess Something and Countess Potocka, Poles, and had with them a long confab. Attempted to dance, but felt such horrid pain was forced to stop. The ghost-stories are begun by all but me.

18 June   My leg much worse. Shelley and party here. Mrs S called me her brother (younger). Began my ghost-story after tea. Twelve o'clock, really began to talk ghostly. LB repeated some verses of Coleridge's *Christabel*, of the witch's breast; when silence ensued, and Shelley, suddenly shrieking and putting his hands to his head, ran out of the room with candle. Threw water in his face, and after gave him ether. He was looking at Mrs S, and suddenly thought of a woman he had heard of who had eyes instead of nipples, which, taking hold of his mind, horrified him. – He married; and, a friend of his liking his wife, he tried all he could to induce her to love him in turn. He is surrounded by friends who feed upon him, and draw upon him as their banker. Once, having hired a house, a man wanted to make him pay more, and came trying to bully him, and at last challenged him. Shelley refused, and was knocked down; coolly said that would not gain him his object, and was knocked down again. – Slaney called.

19 June   Leg worse; began my ghost-story. Mr S etc. forth here. Bonstetten and Rossi called. B told me a story of the religious feuds in Appenzel; a civil war between Catholics and Prostestants. Battle arranged; chief advances; calls the other. Calls himself and other fools, for battles will not persuade of his being wrong. Other agreed, and persuaded them to take the boundary rivulet; they did. Bed at 3 as usual.

20 June   My leg kept me at home. Shelley etc. here.

21 June   Same.

22 June   LB and Shelley went to Vevay; Mrs S and Miss Clare Clairmont to town. Went to Rossi's – had tired his patience. Called on Odier; Miss reading Byron.

23 June   Went to town; apologised to Rossi. Called on Dr Slaney etc. Walked to Mrs Shelley. Pictet, Odier, Slaney, dined with me. Went down to Mrs S for the evening. Odier mentioned the cases of two gentlemen who, on taking the nitrate of silver, some time after had a blacker face. Pictet confirmed it.

24 June   Up at 12. Dined down with Mrs S and Miss CC.

26 June   Up. Mounted on horseback: went to town. Saw Mrs Shelley: dined. To Dr Rossi's party of physicians: after at Mrs S.

27 June   Up at Mrs Shelley's: dined. No calèche arrived: walked to G. No horses: ordered saddle-horse. Walked to Rossi's – gone. Went to the gate: found him. Obliged to break off the appointment. Went to Odier's. Met with Mr _____, a friend of Lord Byron's father. Invited me to his house: been a long time on the Continent. Music, ranz des vaches, beautiful. Rode two hours; went to Mrs S; Miss C talked of a soliloquy.

28 June   All day at Mrs S.

29 June   Up at 1; studied; down at Mrs S.

30 June   Same.

1 July   Went in calèche to town with Mrs S and C for a ride, and to mass (which we did not got to, being begun). Dined at 1. Went to town with Rossi. Introduced to Marchese Saporati; together to Mr Saladin of Vaugeron, Countess Breuss, Calpnafur; and then to a party of ladies. Found Lord Byron and Shelley returned.

2 July   Rain all day. In the evening to Mrs S.

5 September   Not written my Journal till now through neglect and dissipation. Had a long explanation with S and LB about my conduct to LB; threatened to shoot S one day on the water. Horses been a subject of quarrel twice, Berger having accused me of laming one.

LB went to town in pursuit of thieves who came to steal the anchors after stolen my sail. Was refused permission to go out. I went to the Syndic Saladin, and told him I begged his pardon for our servants, who must have said something insulting, or else he could not have refused permission to leave the port. Thieves attempted to break into the house.

An apothecary sold some bad magnesia to LB. Found it bad by experiment of sulphuric acid colouring it red rose-colour. Servants spoke about it. Appointed Castan to see experiment; came; impudent; refused to go out; collared him, sent him out, broke spectacles. Laid himself on a wall for three hours; refused to see experiments. Saw LB, told him his tale before two physicians. Brought me to trial before five judges; had an advocate to plead. I pleaded for myself; laughed at the advocate. Lost his cause on the plea of calumny; made me pay 12 florins for the broken spectacles and costs. Magnesia chiefly alumina, as proved by succenate and carbonate of ammonia.

Dined twice at Madame de Staël's; visited there also; met Madame de Broglie and M; Miss Randall; two Roccas; Schlegel; Monsignor Brema; Dumont; Bonstetten; Madame Bottini; Madame Mongelas; young de Staël.

The society I have been in may be divided into three sets: the canton of Genthoud, Coppet, and Geneva. The canton is an assemblage of a neighbourhood of about seven or eight families, meeting alternatively on Sundays at each other's houses, and every Thursday at the Countess of Breuss's. The Countess Breuss lives at Genthoud in a villa she has bought. She has two husbands, one in Russia, one at Venice; she acted plays at the Hermitage under Catherine. Not being able to get a divorce, she left Russia, went to Venice for six days, stayed as many years, married (it is said), bought villas, etc. in the Venetian's name, and separated. Her family consists of Madame Gatelier, a humble friend, a great lover

of medicaments etc, Abate _____, her Almoner, an excellent
Brescian, great lover of religionists. A mania in the family for
building summer-houses, porticoes, and baths; neatly planned; an
island with a ditch round it; a Tower of Babel round the trunk of a
chestnut; a summer-house by the roadside of a Moorish
construction. The Countess is very good-natured, laughs where
others caluminate and talk scandal with prudish airs, kind to all.
The society is extremely pleasant; generally dancing or music. It
was the birthday of Charles Saladin, who, having been four years
in Nap's army, knew nothing of the matter. She asked to have the
fêting of him. They acted first a charade on the canton of Genthoud.
She acted with Mr Massey junior, with others, and myself as a
woman – the words to blind. Then came a kind of farce, in which
Charles was dressed as the C.B., Gatelier as the Abbé, and Miss
Saladin as Gatelier: each took one another off. Written by C.B.
When at last another of the society brought a letter announcing it
to be Charles' birthday. Then they, while he was in his amazement,
sang a song to him, presented him with a bouquet and purse. Then
an elegant supper, and afterwards a ball on the arrival of Madame
Toffettheim with her son. A great party was invited; and after tea
two plays were acted – Le Pachà de Suresne and Les Ricochets. There
were an immense number of spectators. The actors were, in Le
Pachà de Suresne, Madame Dorsan, la Comtesse Breuss; Laure,
Madlle. Brelaz; Aglaé, Clemann; Nathalie, M.; Madlle. Remy,
Madame Gatelier; Perceval, Alexia Saladin; Flicflac, Polidori;
Joseph, C. Saladin. – Les Ricochets – I do not remember the
characters. The actors were Alexia, Charles, Auguste Saladin,
Massey le jeune, La Comtesse Breuss, Madame Mathilde Saladin.
The rehearsals before were frequent.

I got a discretion from the Countess, which I took in the shape
of a Swiss, in consequence of a wager that I could not go straight
home.

La Toffettheim is a nice, unpretending, lady-like woman,
pleasing and affectionate. Her son full of liberty-ideas. It was here,
in consequence of Massey junior dancing extremely well, that
being defied, I danced a pantaloon-dance, by which I made
enemies; for, upon my refusing it at the Saladins', they thought it
was a personal refusal. Saladins of Vaugeron, father and mother.
Father deaf, good-natured: said to me upon reading my thesis,
'Mais, Monsieur, il n'y a pas de paradoxe.' The mother pretended
to play shy on account of Madame B.

The daughter – because, the first night I saw her, knowing her by particular introduction, I stuck to her – thought me in love and said so – fool! Madame Mathilde pretended prude in mine and Madame B.'s case, while she herself has got Mr Massey junior dangling, not unheard, after her. Charles a good boisterous soldier, at Leipzig, Nassau, and 13 ingwen Waterloo business. Makes up for wit by noise, for affection by slaps on the back. On his birthday I addressed him with (after supper) –

> 'Jeune guerrier dans l'armée du premier des héros,
> Dans la cause de la France dédaignant le repos,
> Que la chute de vos ans soit tranquille et heureuse,
> Comme fut l'aube de vos jours éclatante et glorieuse.'

Auguste, a simple neat fool, despising learning because he is noble and has enough to live upon; content to dangle, with a compliment and a sentiment, after a woman's tail. Alexis, so so, good-naturedly ignorant husband to Mathilde. Massey senior, active pleasant man, excellent fencer and dancer – been secretary to Bertrand. Massey junior, confident, impudent, insolent, ignorant puppy. Saladins of Maligny, neither good nor bad, rich: to gain a little more, let their villa to Lord Breadalbane, and retired to a cottage, though both old and only one ugly vain daughter. Lord Breadalbane, and excellent, good-sensed though not quick man: answered – when the Duke of Bedford said to him, 'What would you give to have the Breadalbane estate in Bedfordshire?'.– 'Why, your Grace, I should be sorry if my estate would go to Bedfordshire.' Gave a very good ball at which I was. His son Lord Glenorchy, good, shy, not brilliant young man. His lady not spoken to. His daughter excellent dancer, rather haughty. Mr Evans, a good sensible man, biased in his thoughts by his cassock. At the society he took up the immortality: Lord Glenorchy gave a positive No. Saussure, Mrs, a wax talkative figure. Mr, a would-be scientific gentleman: thought me a fool because I danced pantaloon, and himself a wise man because he knows the names of his father's stones. Jacquet, Madlle., got half in love with her, – no, her 8,000 a year: her face and bad-singing exposures cured me. Foncet, officer of the Piedmontese troops, jealous of him. Brelaz, Portuguese lady, – in love with her; I think fond of me too; imprudent; her daughter also against me on account of it; shows it too much publicly; very jealous; her daughters, sprightly good-looking girls. Clemann – got half in love with her; nice daughter. The Cavalier pleasing. Had a dispute in a public ball with her two fools. One of the Saladins, Auguste, courts her, and she laughs; she excites love in every young man's breast. Miss Harriet is rather too serious for her age, pretty and well-informed in novels and romances, and rather too sentimental. Cavalier's Marianne is a fine hoydenish creature: applies when studying, and romps when playing.

Madame de Staël I have dined with three times; she is better, those who know her say, at home than abroad. She has married poor Rocca. She talks much; would not believe me to be a physician; presented her my thesis, which she told me she had read with pleasure. Talked about religion, and puts down every of Rocca. Ugly; good eyes. Writng on the French Revolution; polite, affable; lectures, and tells all to LB. Madame de Broglie, her daughter, a beautiful, dirty-skinned woman; pleasant, soft-eyed speaker; dances well, waltzes. Schlegel, a presumptuous literato, contradicting *à outrance*; a believer in magnetism. Rocca, a talkative, good-natured, beautiful man, with a desire for knowledge; the author of *Walcheren* and *Espagne*; excellent at naïve description. Rocca, the judge, very clever and quick, rising; know little of him. Been seven years in the courtship of Miss Saladin; she neither refuses nor accepts him, but keeps him in her train. Miss Randall, sister to Mrs Norgate. Monsignor Brema, friend of Ugo Foscolo, enthusiastic for Italy, encomiast in all, Grand Almoner of Italy, hater of Austrians. Dumont, a thick, heavy-thoughted body, editor of Bentham. Bonstetten, friend of Gray.

The first time LB went, there was Mrs Hervey there; talkative, sister and a great friend of the Noels; she thought proper to faint out of the house, though her curiosity brought her back to speak with him.

Bonstetten told me that, upon his saying to Gray that he must be happy, he took and read to him the criticism of Johnson, which happens to have been written after Gray's death; he used to go in the evening to tea, and remain all night reading the English authors with him. Gray introduced him to society; and, one of the professors having asked him if he understood what he said, he replied he thought so, but very diffidently – 'So you think so only!' Gray, hearing this, showed B some passages to ask *him*, which B did in a public company, complimenting him upon known knowledge; when all the company, one after the other, began contradicting the Professor's opinion. Then B, turning to him, said, 'You perhaps thought *you* understood Shakespeare.' Gray told him that there was none who could *perfectly* understand him.

Rossi, and Italian of about thirty, pleasant, agreeable, and good-natured, professor at Bologna, thence obliged to fly with two others. One of his companions was beginning his lecture, when the students called out, 'No lecture, but an improvise upon the liberty of Italy'; as he was an improvisatore. He objected, as, on account of Murat's approach, it might be suspicious. They insisted, and the professors at hand said, 'No harm if not upon present circumstances.' He did it, and the students issued forth to join Murat: they had however made up their minds to do so before. Rossi joined it more openly and loudly, and was obliged to fly. He wrote a memoir to defend himself, in which he said it was only to avoid the Roman dominion, and give it to the Archduke; who told him that he had better write another, as Bologna was already ceded to Pius. When he was ruined thus partially he wrote to the father of his betrothed, to say that he must not (if he chose) think himself bound by his promise, as he was not in the same circumstances as when the promise was given. The father did retract. So far a man of honour. Now how to reconcile his being with Calandion, a magistrate of G violent on the other side? who says he has made a good profession to him, and at the same time professing other opinions to others.

Gave me a letter to Milan, and by him I have been introduced to Saporiti, a good, enthusiastic, ignorant Italian. Talked of the English landing 100,000 soldiers here and there, as if they were so many peas.

Slaneys: the husband jealous of every one – Cambridge degree. When I danced with his wife, he after, when walking with her, came up and gave an arm too. The wife beautiful, but very simple. Galston, Miss, very beautiful.

'Genevan Liberal Society' is a muster of Englishmen for debate on speculative questions. Twice there. Immortality, accomplice's evidence. The members whom I knew were – Lord Kinnul, a most tiresome, long-winded, repeating, thick-headed, would-be orator, Lord Conyngham.

Mr Somers, good head enough. Valence, who I cried to hear; and, meeting me after at Chamounix, the first thing he asked me was, 'Why did you laugh at me?' St Auby, Lloyd, Slaney.

Lloyd, of good Welsh blood, his original name Ap Griffith, rode out. We went out visiting one day, and, in returning in his gig, he touched a horse of a row of carts. The carter struck me upon my back with his whip; I jumped down, and six jumped at me. I fortunately was between a wheel and a hedge, so that they all could not reach. Lloyd, seeing this, jumped down also; then three left me and went to him, and another untied a piece of his wagon with which, while I defended myself from the two (one with a whip), he struck me while fortunately my arm was striking a blow, so that it did but just touch my face. He lifted again; I sprang back, and with all the force of my leap struck him with my fist in his face. His blow fell to the ground, and with his hand to his nose he retreated. They then seized stones to throw, but we closed with them; they could not throw above two, when we saw an English carriage we knew coming. We called, they came, and immediately the boisterous were calm. Some who tried to divide us got blows also.

St Aubyn, an excellent fellow, introduced me to his father at Genthoud: is a natural son, studying for the Church. His father is a good polite man, according to the 'go' school. Keeps a mistress now, though sixty-five years: has many children by different mistresses.

At Dr Odier's – who is a good old, toothless, chatty, easy-believing man – there was a society every Wednesday, where I went sometimes. They dance, sang, ate cakes, and drank tea; English almost entirely, changing every Wednesday. – Went to a concert of Madamigella Coda – the theatre dirty.

When Mr Hobhouse and Davies arrived, we went to Chamounix. The first day through Chesne, Anne-masse, Vetra, Nangy, Contamine, Bonneville (dinner), Cluse, Sallenches (slept). Next day by Chede in two *char-à-bancs*, with each a guide; a fine pine-glen of the Arve, to Chamounix. We went that evening over the Brisson, and to the source of the Aveyron. Next day so bad we left, and returned to Sallenches, taking the fall of Chede in our way; thence to Diodati. Mr Scope Davies played against the marker at tennis: then went, taking Rushton with him.

LB determined upon our parting, – not upon any quarrel, but on account of our not suiting. Gave me £70; 50 for 3 months and 20 for voyage. Paid away a great deal, and then thought of setting off: determined for Italy. Madame de Staël gave me three letters. Madame B wept, and most seemed sorry.

The night before I went, at Madame B's, they acted *C'est le Même* extremely well; a Lausanne girl acting the lady very well. The costumes also extremely good. Wished nobody good-bye: told them, though, I was going. Set off with 47 louis, 112 naps.

Le Valais from Schürer's book, *Description due Départment du Simplon*, 1812, lent me by the Cav. See elsewhere.

16 September   Left Cologny and Lord Byron at six in the morning. Breakfasted at Doraine, 3 leagues. Dined, Thouson, ditto. Evrein, 2. Slept St Gingoux, 4. Passed Meillerie. Saw Lausanne at a distance, right through this part of Sardinian King's dominions. Read Madame Brelaz's verses. Wept – not at them, but at the prose.

17 September   Left St Gingoux at 6. Walked to _____. Took bread and wine. Crossed to Chillon. Saw Bonivard's prison for six years; whence a Frenchman had broken, and, passing through a window, swam to a boat. Instruments of torture, – the pulley. Three soldiers there now: the Roman arms already affixed. Large subterranean passes. Saw in passing the three treed islands. The Rhone enters by two mouths, and keeps it waters distinct for two stone's throw.

From Chillon I went to Montreaux – breakfasted – leaving Charney on my left. I began to mount towards the Dent de Jamanu. Before beginning to mount Jamanu itself, one has a beautiful view, seeing only part of the lake, bound by Meillerie, Roches, and the Rhone. Higher up the view is more extensive, but not so beautiful – nothing being distinct; the water looking merely as an inlet of sky, but one could see the Jura as far as Genthoud.

I entered a chalet, where they expressed great astonishment at my drinking whey, which they give to their pigs only. Refused at first money.

Descended towards Mont Boyon. What owing to the fatigue and hardly meeting any one, sick with grief. At Mont Boyon, dined, and, finding they would not dance, slept immediately after.

18 September   Up at 4. Drank wine and bread. At 6 set off. Passed the Château d'Ox where there was a fair. After that, hardly met a soul. Always on the side of the mountains, each side of a river or torrent; with torrent-bends, pine-forests, chalets, villages without a visible soul – all at work – and ups and downs: so that this road, if I had not had that of yesterday, I should have called the worst in the world. Passed through Château d'Ox; Rougemont, breakfast: Zwezermann, dinner; Gessenay; Lambeck; Reichenstein; Weissenbach; Bottingen, tea and night. The French language leaves off at Gessenay (rather, patois), and they begin their German: found it difficult to go on.

19 September   Got up at 4½. Set off from Bottigen. Went through Obernoyle. Breakfasted at Wyssenbach: refused my money. Went to the Doctor, who charged me a nap. Went through Erlenbach, Lauterbach, Meiningen, to Thun. Splendid scenery; especially the first look at the Lake by the river's mouth, and the pass into a great valley. Took dinner, and then a warm bath. Arrived at 1 o'clock. All the houses are of wood, the foundation only being stone: great cut ornaments between the rows of windows: the wood, fir. Felt very miserable, especially these two last days: only met two persons to whom I could speak – the others all Germans. At Wyssenbach they all said grace before breakfast, and then ate out of the same dish; remarking (as I understood them) that I, not being a Catholic would laugh.

20 September   Got up at 6. Wrote to St Aubyn, Brelaz, father, Vaccà, and Zio, asking letters; to my father, to announce my parting.

Bought fresh shoes and stockings; found no book-seller's shop. The man at the post-office made a good reflection: that he was astonished so many came to see what they who were so near never want to see, and that he supposed that the English also leave much unseen in their own country.

Thun is a neat well-situated town, not large, with arcades – as apparently all the Berne towns. Afraid all day my dog was poisoned; which grieved me so, at seeing it vomit, that I wept. At 2 o'clock went in search of a boat: none going immediately, I walked along the left bank of the lake to Unterseen. The views the most beautiful I ever saw; through pines over precipices, torrents, and sleepers and the best-cultivated fields I ever saw. The lake sometimes some hundred precipitous feet below by feet; at other times quite close to its edge; boats coming from the fair; picturesque towered villages; fine Alps on the other side, the Jungfrau and others far off. The bottom of the lake is especially magnificent. Lost my way, and had two little children as guides back again. One small cascade of seven or eight fountains.

Arrived at 7 at Unterseen: through Nilterfingen, Oberhofen, Rottingen, Morlangen, Neuchaus, to Unterseen. Found two Englishmen at supper: sat down with them. Very miserable all the morning.

21 September   Got up at 6, having determined to go with the two to the Grindenwald in a *char-à-banc*, on account of the state of my foot. I went to the bridge at Interlachen to see the view coming between two beautiful isolated crags. Going, met a man, a maréchal, who had been to Vienna and Bohemia *en roulant* after his apprenticeship, to see the world – stopping a day at one place, a day at another. Returned, breakfasted: and then, after growling at the innkeeper's wishing to take two horses, we went off through a splendid pine-clad craggy valleys through Zweihitschirne to Lauterbrunner; whence to the fall of the Staubach, a bare cataract of 900 feet high, becoming vapour before it arrives – appearing much, and ending in a little stream. The curate of this village received guests: there were the Prince Saxe-Gotha and family. We lunched at the inn, and went back to Lauterbrunner after having looked at the Jungfrau at a distance.

Went from Zweihitschirne to the Grindenwald with the Saxe-Gotha before us, through a more beautiful valley. Saw the glaciers come into it, with the Eiger, Wetterhorn, and other mountains, most magnificent. Walking about, found two girls who gave us cherries and chatted freely. Found that mules were 18 francs a day. A party came in in the dark at 8 with guides, hallooing and making a lively sound. Dined at 7, and talked about mules, hoping to get return ones etc.

22 September   Got up. Could not get mules under 18 francs: my foot too bad to walk. Went with Captain Rice and others back to Interlachen. Got into a boat rowed by two men and a boy. Went by Brientz, Calne, to the Griesbach castle, and then to Brientz – wilder, but not so beautiful as the Lake of Thun. The cascade I did not mount to see on account of my foot. At Brientz an old woman would give us her presence and conversation till one of my companions courted the daughter. Met between Grindenwald and Interlachen LB and Mr H: we saluted.

23 September   Got up at 4. Tired of my company; and, finding the expense more than I could afford, I went to their bedrooms to wish them good-bye. Set off at 5½; and through fine copse-wooded crags, along the Aar, with cascades on every side, to Meyringen; where I breakfasted with two Germans, and old and a young artist – the old, chatty. Bought a pole. Went to see the Reichenbach, a fine cascade indeed. Thence through the beautiful vale of Nachim-Grunden, where for a moment I planned a sovereignty; but, walking on, my plans faded before I arrived at Guttannen, where I dined.

Rode all the way to-day – horrible, only passable for men and mules: it is the way to St Gothard. The road is merely huge unequal masses of granite thrown in a line not the straightest. From Guttannen the road went through the wildest and most sublime scenery I ever read of: vegetation less and less, so that, instead of grass, there was moss; then nothing. Instead of trees, shrubs; then nothing – huge granite rocks leaving hardly room for the road and river. The river's bed the most magnificent imaginable, cut deep and narrow into the solid rock, sinous, and continually accompanied by cascades, and amazing bold and high single-arched bridges. Snow covering in some parts the whole bed of the river, and so thick and strong that even huge stones have fallen without injuring its crust. There are only two houses between Guttannen and the Hospital: one, a chalet wherein I entered; the other, a cow-herd's. Arrived at 6 o'clock precisely, having walked in only 9½ hours 30 miles at least.

The Hospital is an old stone ugly building, consonant with the wild scene, where the poor are lodged for nothing; others, us, an inn.

24 September On account of rain did not get up till 7, set off across the Grimsel, a dreary mountain with snow in every hollow – 5,000 feet above the Four-canton Lake. Descended on the other side to Obergustellen, where I breakfasted at 10. Thence through Verlican, Guesquerman, Munster, Rexingen. Biel, Blizzen; where, out of the dead flat valley, I began to mount, and the scenery began to increase in beauty. One bridge especially over the Rhone, which fell between two clefts' sides, was beautiful. Sinderwald, Viesch, pine-wood; sax along the rocks, and fine path along the mountain. Very fine, though continued hard rain, which drenched me and hindered my seeing a great deal. To Morel, where I went to bed, and ate a kind of dinner in bed at 7 o'clock.

25 September Up at 5; my foot, from having been obliged to walk with the shoe down at heel, very much swelled and too painful to walk. Breakfast. Two students from Brieg, of the Jesuits' College, came in, who had during the vacations been beyond Constance with only two *écus neufs* in their pockets. It costs them ten batsches a year at College. Impudent one: the other modest-looking, but, when I gave him six francs because he had no more money, he asked me for more on other accounts. The Jesuits been restored two years.

At Brieg I sent for the curate, a good old man of sixty. We conversed together in Latin for two hours; not at all troublesome in enquiries, but kind in answering them. The Valaisians resisted two years against the French in 93. It was the only part of the country in which they did so, except Unterwalden, and then it was only the peasants, and in every village there was a French party. The cruelty of the French was dreadful; they stuck their prisoners in a variety of ways like sheep. One old man of eighty, who had never left his house but whom they found eating, they strangled, and then put meat and bottles by him as if he had died apoplectic. They fought very hard and bravely, but such was the power of numbers united to the force of treachery that they were obliged to yield. In 1813, after the French had quitted Brieg, they again attempted to penetrate from Italy by the Simplon; when the Brieg, Kelor, and other villagers, joined by only one company of Austrians, surrounded them in the night, and took them prisoners. In Schwytz and Unterwalden the division was more strongly marked. In Unterwalden (where was the scene) the men divided and fought against each other, some joining the French from Stanz to Engelberg. They were for freedom, and fought as the cause deserved. They killed 5,000 French, more than double their own number; women fought; they were in all 2,100 Swiss. One maid in the ranks, when her comrades were obliged to retreat, seeing a cannon yet unfired, went with a rope-end and fired it, killing thirty French. She was taken; a pardon was offered. She said, 'I do not acknowledge any pardon; my action is not pardonable; a thief pardons, not a just man.' They killed her with swords. The hundred men who came from the higher part of Schwytz, attempting to go to their relief, were through their own countrymen forced to cut their way and march by night; and, when in retreating they came to the other shore of Lucerne Lake, they had again to cut through their own countrymen to arrive at their homes, they refusing them permission to pass. The Austrians, for the help the higher Valaisians gave them, from sovereigns have made them subjects to the lower Valaisians.

The curate came in again, with a description of the Simplon; sat an hour and a half, then left the book. When not here I have written the part of my Journal I missed at the time, and the extract from this book. He came in again about 6 with a basket of prunes for me, and offered to go with me half-way, as he had to go to a church on the way.

26 September   Got up at 5. The curate came, and, my foot being better, I set off. He showed me the bridge over the Massa where was a battle, and the ruins of a tyrant's tower. We came to his church, where he showed me the miraculous figure that was found in the Rhone. He told me the lower Valaisians were ready to join the French in '13, and that, in spite of this, they had given them a majority of voices. Left me in sight of Brieg, telling me he hoped to see me again in heaven. I walked on to Brieg; breakfasted, and then set off along the Simplon, a magnificent road indeed. It is cut in many places through the rocks, in others built up to its side. It has caverns and bridges always wide enough for four carriages; it ascends all the way to the new Hospice, and again descends from it. At its side are houses of refuge (as they are called) where many are kept by government, with privilege of selling food to help the passers-by. There is in each a room with a bed where one can go in case of rain, accident, etc; and, when the time for avalanches etc., these men are obliged to accompany the travellers from house to house. Just where the rising ends the new Hospital was to have been erected, and is half done, but stopped now. A little farther on is the old one; whither I went, and got a dinner in the cell of one of the monks; bread, wine, cold meat, and nuts. He seemed very *ennuyé*; his words slowly fell; said they were St Augustines, not St Bernardites. That St Bernard was a mere reformer of the order. They have been here since 1810 only, in an old castle for which they pay £20 a year. The Simplon was a department of France, and rather well off on account of the quantity of work and money, and not having the *droits* revenues. The Archduke Regnier was there a few days ago incog., and they did not recognise him – which mortified them very much. It is six leagues hither from Brieg, so that I had walked twenty-six miles.

I set off at 2: passed through Sempeln, and through the most magnificent scenery, through the granite galleries. The Italian part is by far the most difficult and splendid. The first boy that I met before coming to Italy, in answer to a question in German, answered, 'Non capisco'; I could have hugged. I arrived after much difficulty at Isella, knocked up. I was ruined in my feet, and it was not till near here that the carriages which parted in the morning from Brieg overtook me. Went to bed immediately in a room where the grease might be scraped from the floor.

27 September   Did not get up till 1 on account of fatigue. Breakfasted most miserably, everything being bad; and then set off, but immensely slowly with red stripes here and there; the men more acute and quicker-eyed. Arrived at Domo d'Ossola at 3; got into a clean though poor inn, and dined well. A gendarme came in to ask how it was that my passport had not been viséd yet; and then, seeing I was a physician, requested a cure for his toothache. It is useless to describe the picturesque: the best page to turn to for it is the memory. After one of the most comfortable fireside-evenings I have had since I left Geneva I went to bed at 7½.

28 September   Set off at 6 o'clock through vine-country, with little hills here and there starting out of the low Alps, highly cultivated, with beautiful little white villas at their tops and sides. Asked a woman what was a house whereon was painted a Democritus, Diogenes, etc. Answered, 'È roba antica' – though evidently modern, but deserted. Indeed the whole of the houses seem too large for the inhabitants – much falling to ruin. From Domo d'Ossola went to Vella; to Vagagna, where I breakfasted and saw the first good-looking Italian girl. The children are pretty, the women quite otherwise. There began to suffer from my feet so much as that to go six more miles took me five hours. No car passed me, or anything.

I arrived at last at Ornavasco. Could get no car, though they kept me half-an-hour in the yard standing, in hopes of getting one. At last agreed with a man that he should set off at 4 o'clock to-morrow to Fariolo for 4 francs. Looked at a bedroom: shrugged up my shoulders, but forced. Dinner: no meat, because 'meagre'. Ate the fruit. The Italian grapes, nectarines, peaches, and pears, I got yesterday, excellent. Two bunches of grapes half-a-franc: two at dinner.

29 September   Up at 5. Got into the char, or rather cart. Passed through Gravellino to Fariolo. Asked 10 francs to take me to Laveno: offered 4 – accepted. Got into the boat. Rowed towards Isola Madre; passed Isola Pescatori; and landed on Isola Bella.

Went over the palace. Many of the floors miserable on account of their being the mere rock. Some good pictures. A whole set of rooms below in the style of grottoes, with windows looking on to beautiful views, close to the lake for *il fresco*. Looked at the terrace: not pleasing the style: and, thinking I should see it all in going round, did not go over the gardens. Went round the island in the boat; magnificently paved, like terrace on terrace.

Thence towards Laveno, intending to go to Lugano and Como; but, hearing that I could go all the way by water to Milan, I preferred this, and accordingly turned round towards Belgirato. Breakfasted on *caffè al latte, uve, and fichi,* 4½ francs. Boatmen proposed my joining a party to Sestri-Calende, which I did. Arona, with the colossus, on my left, Anghera on my right; Monte Rosa; all the bottom part of the lake richly magnificent.

Arrived at an inn – taken for a servant. After some time things got round, when in came two soldiers with swords by their sides, to desire me to step to the police-inspector. I did, and found he could not read the writing in my passport. The boatman came soon after, offering me a plan for to-morrow for five francs, and showing me twelve naps. they got for the boat – which cost only seventy francs. Agreed.

30 September   Up at 5. Off at 6 in a large barge, with yesterday's English party and two carriages, by the Tessino and canal to Milan: at first through a fine hilly country, and rapidly by the Tessino flood. After, slower, and through a flat plain with trees and neat villas and hanging grapes, to Milan. Slept out of town by the canal.

1 October   Up at 7. The boatman came as I had desired, to guide me. Entered Milan by a fine gate with a kind of triumphal arch. The streets are clean but narrow – fine houses. There are two strips of pavement for wheels, and often two for pedestrians. Passed by Santa Maria – fine, all white marble, with many fine statues on the outside. Many palaces. A bad taste shown in plastering the columns and corner-stones of a lighter colour than the body.

Got a letter from Brelaz; well written in composition and in letters, but badly spelled. Got my trunk, after some difficulty, passed. The diligence-keepers asked if they could direct me to rooms: showed two where a man was at that moment going. Got them for 40 lire il mese; a bedroom and sitting-room, second storey, Contrado San Spirito. Sent to the custom-house. Made the men wait – sent them away for two hours, again away for one. More stoppages, and, in centimes, 3 francs to pay. They would not at first

let it (the trunk) go because it was the last day of the month.
Went to dine at a restaurateur's : 1½-franc dinner.

Afterwards put my things into a little order, dressed, and went strolling towards Teatro della Scala. Entered, two hours before beginning, alone. Immense theatre: six rows of boxes, with, I think, thirty-six in a row. *La Testa di Bronzo*, a ballet, and a comic ballet: the ballet the most magnificent thing I ever saw – splendid indeed.

2 October   Got up at 8. Breakfasted on grapes, bread and butter, wine, and figs. Wrote to Lord Byron. Dressed. Went to Marchese Lapone – out of town; Monsignor Brema – not at home. Walked about looking at booksellers' shops. Entered the Duomo – invisible almost, so black and dark. They were putting up drapery for Friday, which is the Emperor's birthday (probably the same as for Napoleon). Returned home, arranged my papers. Took a walk on the Corso; then to the Teatro Rè. The same price for all the places. The piece *Il Sogno di Ariosto*, where Fortune, Merit, Orgoglio, with Mrs Disinganno, were all personified. The dialogue abounded in truths, especially regarding women, which they applauded. The theatre is very small, like the Haymarket. Home to bed.

3 October   Up at 8. Went to a circulating library: read Denina, *Vicende*, all the part on Italy and preface. To the Teatro Scelto di Milano. Enquired about Andricini etc. for my father – not found.

Went to the Teatro Rè; a play of English people in which they kiss the hand, and make more bows than were ever made in a century in England. There were German soldiers in English uniforms present. Home to bed.

4 October   Up at 8 – breakfasted. Went to call on Monsignore Brême – found him. Received me with two kisses and great apparent joy. About to learn English: I promise my help. Walked with me, and invited me to his box.

Left him – came home. Read Denina's *Ultime Vicende*, a poor book. Went to Guyler. Met Caravella – walked with him. Went to dine: where I met his brother, who told me the physician at Florence was dead, and promised to come and take me to the hospital. Met after dinner Abate Berlezi the Crabule. Came home. Read the *Calandra* of Bibiena, and *Sofonisba* of Trissino. Took an ice, and went to La Scala. Feast of St Francis, the Emperor's. When the Dukes went this morning to mass at the Duomo not a hat moved, not a voice of applause: however, when Regnier entered, there was a slight clapping of hands. The theatre was lighted up like an English one, and was magnificent, but showed what the Italians allege – that the scene does not improve by it, but the contrary.

In Brema's lodge there were Monti, Brema's mother, and others. Monti a short man, round face, quick eye; pleasant in conversation, not haughty, modest, unassuming: seemed to take great pleasure in parts of the music and in the dancing.

Brema related that a friend of his, Porro, asked for a passport to Rome: refused, and asked for documents to prove his business. Gave what proved he had business at Maurata, and relatives at Rome. Refused. Went to Swarrow, who told him he could not give it. Porro said: 'Why do the Austrians think the Italians are always making conspiracies?' Swarrow said that they did not know, but, now that they had the upper hand, they cared not; and at last that, if Porro would give his word of honour not to visit any of the foreign embassies, he should have a passport, He had it. Porro was not a revolutionist but had always been against Napoleon, and had belonged to a legislative body by him dissolved on account of obstinacy. Brema and others accompanied me as far as the door, and I went to bed.

From that day I neglected by Journal till this day,
8 December   My residence at Milan lasted till October 30. During that time I had a most happy and pleasant life, Monsignor De Brême taking great friendship for me. My friends and acquaintance were Brême, Borsieri, Guasco, Cavalier Brême, Beyle, Negri, Byron, Hobhouse, Finch, Caravellas, Locatelli, Monti, Monti's son-in-law, Lord Cowper, Lord Jersey, etc.; Lloyd, Lee, Wotheron.

De Brême and I became very intimate, and I believe he is really a good friend. In the morning at 10 o'clock I went to him to help him in English, and towards the end he corrected my Italian translation of *Count Orlando*. We afterwards met at his box every night in the theatre of La Scala. He gave a dinner to Lord Byron, at which were a good many or rather all my acquaintances – Monti, Finch, Hobhouse, two Brêmes, Borsieri, Guasco (translator of Brême was Vicar Almoner under the French Government). A priest came to him to ask leave to confess; Brême, knowing the subject, refused. The Princess was put to move Beauharnais, who sent for Brême and in a very angry mood asked him why he had refused leave. B said that, as he was placed to give him leave, he imagined it was that it might not be granted indiscriminately, that he could not in his conscience give it, but that he was not the chief, and the Almoner, being applied to, might grant it. B asked why, saying that the Princess wished it, and it must be done. De B said he had undertaken the office under the idea that his conscience was to be his guide; if not, the office should be immediately vacant; that he put it to Beauharnais himself whether a man who was buried in the vilest dissoluteness was a proper person to be entrusted with the care of young women's minds. Beauharnais said, 'Right, right; you shall hear no more of it.' This, and another occasion of the same nature, were the only occasions in which he saw Beauharnais privately; he avoided the court, and did not seek preferment. He twice under that government refused a bishopric, and under the new government; giving me as a reason that it went against his conscience to inculcate what he did not believe, and to add power to those who gave them, as he would be expected to side with them. He is violently for the independence of Italy. Christianity he believes not, and gives (I think) a new argument why we should not be holden to believe it. Saul, who was contemporary, who beheld the miracles etc., did not believe till a miracle was operated upon *him*; we at this distance cannot believe with greater facility. He has published an eulogium of Caluro, *Ingiustizia del Giudizio, etc.*, poems, etc. Has written several tragedies; *Ina*, made me weep like a child. He is warm in his affections, and has never recovered the death of one he loved – a young noble lady, of great accomplishments and beauty. His friendship for me was warm: it gratifies me more than any attentions, friendship, or any relation I had before, with my fellow-companions. I cannot express what I feel for him. When parting from him, I wept like a child in his arms. He maintains from principle, not from belief, all the hardships imposed upon him by his tonsure. He would have the world to see that his belief is not swayed by a wish to escape from the bonds of the clerical state. He is charitable, giving away great sums of money in charity; eats only once a day, and studies all day till the hour of the theatre; kind to all who are recommended to him; sacrificing whole days to show them what he has seen a thousand times; a great admirer of English women; has an excellent library, of which I had the use. A great friend of comic, good-natured mimicry. Has an idea of writing *Ida*, a novel containing a picture of the most promising movements of the Milan revolution, and I have promised to translate it. He has two brothers; his father lives yet;

his eldest brother is Ambassador at Munich. The youngest is Cavalier Brême – been officer in Spain; extremely pleasant and affectionate with me. Brême was a great friend of Caluro's, and to him Caluro dedicated one of his opuscules.

Borsieri, a man of great mental digestive power and memory, superficially read; author of *Il Giorno*, a work written with great grace and lightness. He was very intimate with me, Guasco, and Brême. Guasco, a Piedmontese; little reading; but great mental vision and talents. He also was one who attached himself a good deal to me. De Beyle, formerly Intendent des Marchés (I think) to Buonaparte, and his secretary when in the country. A fat lascivious man. A great deal of anedote about Buonaparte: calls him an *inimitable et bon despote*. He related many anecdotes – I don't remember them: amongst other things, he said Buonaparte despised the Italians much.

These four were the usual attendants at De Brême's box.

Monti is a short, roundish, quick-eyed, and rather rascally-faced man, affable, easily fired; talks rather nonsense when off poetry, and even upon that not good. Great imagination; very weak. Republican always in conversation with us; but in the first month, after having declaimed strongly in B's box about liberty and Germans, just as they were going out he said, 'But now let us talk no more of this, on account of my pension.' Under the French government he gained a great deal by his various offices; by this one he has been abridged of half. He translated the *Iliad* of Homer without knowing a word of Greek; he had it translated by his friends, word for word written under the Greek. Easily influenced by the opinions of others; in fact, a complete weathercock. He married the daughter of Pickler, the engraver; a fine woman, and they say an exceedingly good reciter, as he is himself. She has acted in his plays upon the Philodramatic stage. His daughter is married.

Negri – Marchese Negri – a Genoese, not an improvisatore – very chatty; has at Genoa a most beautiful garden which all the English visit. Related to me Gianni's beginning. Gianni was an apprentice to a stay-maker, when one day an Abate, going into the shop, found him busily engaged in reading. Looking at the book, he asked him if he understood it. He said yes, and, on reading, showed it by his expression. The Abate, who was an improvisatore, asked him to see him next morning; when he improvised before him, and observed that the young Gianni seemed as if his mind was full and wished to give forth. He had him sent to school, and introduced him. Gianni in the Revolution, taking the Liberal side, was obliged to leave Rome, and, going to Genoa, Negri heard by letter of it, and went to seek him, inviting him to dine with him. He refused; and Negri, who had promised his friends that he would be of the party, at the hour of dinner went and found him with his nightcap on, deeply reading his favourite Dante; and in a manner dragged him by force to his house, where Gianni pleased much – and stayed a year at Negri's house, teaching him the art of improvisation. Gianni's improvisations were (many) improvised on the spot by an Abate into Latin verse. – Negri came to Brême's box several times, and had the effect of making all except Brême burst with laughter: me he sent to sleep.

Lord Byron came to Milan, and I saw him there a good deal. He received me kindly, and corrected the English of my essay in *The Pamphleteer*. He visited a good deal Brême's box. Mr Hobhouse was with him.

Colonel Finch, an extremely pleasant, good-natured, well-informed, clever gentleman; spoke Italian extremely well, and was very well read in Italian literature. A ward of his gave a masquerade in London upon her coming of age. She gave to each a character in the reign of Queen Elizabeth to support, without the knowledge of each other, and received them in a saloon in proper style as Queen Elizabeth. He mentioned to me that Nelli had written a Life of Galileo extremely fair, which, if had money by him, he would buy that it might be published, – in Italy they dare not; and that Galileo's MSS were in dispute, so that the heirs will not part with them; they contain some new and some various readings. Finch is a great admirer of architecture and Italy. – Wothcron, Mr a gentleman most peaceable and quiet I ever saw, accompanying Finch; whose only occupation is, when he arrives at a town or other place, to set about sketching and then colouring, so that he has of his tour possible. He invited me (taking me for an Italian), in case I went to England, to see him; and, hearing I was English, he pressed me much more. – Locatelli was the physician of the hospital, a good unimpostoring physician. I saw under him a case of pemphizus, and had under my care an hysterical woman.

Jersey, Lady, promised to enquire of her mother, Lady Westmorland, if she would employ me as her physician; but said she thought my having been with Lord B a great objection.

Lloyd; – as I was moving in the pit, found him, and never saw a person so glad in my life. He offered me half of the money he had at his banker's, as he thought I must be much embarrassed. Told me Brelaz and Bertolini seemed to be together, and that the man seemed worked off his legs.

My life at Milan was very methodical. I got up, went to the hospital, breakfasted, came home, studied, dined, and then at 7 went to the theatre. Between breakfast and study went to De Brême to help him in English. It was proposed too, by him, to teach English, which I had intended to do.

I saw only the dome under which is the chapel of St Boromeo – very rich in silver, crystal, and jewels. The body is vested in pontificals, and quite dry. The orbits seem only filled with a little heap of black dirt and the skull etc. is black. There is here the gnometer of Cassini. They preserve here a nail of the cross of Christ. – St Ambrose, the ancient Cathedral. It was at the gates of this that Theodosius was refused entrance. – The Brera library; and the Ambrosian, where I saw the Virgil with marginal notes of Petrarch; some of the pieces of MSS. of the Plautus and Terence, fragments edited by Mai. – Some of the paintings there are beautiful. The Milanese Raphael has some heads expressing such mild heavenly meekness as is scarcely imagined.

When at Milan, I spent almost all my money in books, buying nearly 300 volumes, not being able to resist that thirst for printed sheets, many of which I never shall read. Swarrow, the Governer of Milan, when the Emperor was there, accompanying him to the theatre, saw that one poor man in the pit, leaning against a box, had dared to keep his hat on. Violently enraged, he enters the box, without leave or saying a word; and, leaning over the box with all his orders dangling at his breast, applies two hearty slaps to the poor man's cheeks, and then, rising majestically, leaves the box, and goes to receive the despot's smile. This making a great hubbub, and exciting a great deal of ridicule against the noble police-officer, he insisted with the police-director that not a word more should be allowed to be said.

When at Milan, there came Sgricci, a Tuscan, under the patronage of Monti, who puffed him most egregioiusly, especially his tragic *improvisati*. I accompanied De Brême to Casa Crivelli, where I saw Swarrow and a cardinal; a dried-up ganache with a face of malice that had dried up with the features of the face, but still remained sketched there in pretty forcible lines. The improvisator entered; yellow boots with trousers, blue coat, and a Flemish collar to his shirt. He began *The Loves of Psyche and Cupid*:

commonplace, unpoetic rhymes. *Coriolanus,* a tragedy; such an abominable opiate, that, in spite of my pinching myself and Cavalier Brême rousing me every minute, I found myself, when ended, roused by the applause from a pleasant nap. Heard him again at the theatre; terza rima; *The Grief of Mausolea.* The only bearable parts were those about Aurora, night, etc., which he had beforehand prepared, to clap-in at convenience, from the *Gradus ad Parnassum.* The tragedy being drawn out, first came *The Death of Socrates.* He came forward, saying that, this subject being undramatisable, he would, if the public insisted, attempt it, but that he had rather another might be drawn. *Montezuma* came out. 'Oh,' says he, 'this will touch your passions too much, and offend many probably personally.' The public here stoutly hissed, and insisted he should proceed; he as stoutly called on the boy to draw, which he did, and, there coming forth *Eteocles and Plynices,* he was satisfied, making *olla podrida scenica* of French ragouts, Italian minestras, and Greek black soup. It was reported that Monti's taking him up was by the persuasion of his daughter. An epigram was written upon Sgricci, as follows nearly –

'In questi tempi senza onore e metro
Lavora Sgricci in vano, ha un altro il serto.'

Going one evening with LB and Mr H to B's box, Mr Hobhouse, Borsieri, and myself, went into the pit, standing to look at the ballet. An officer in a great-coat came and placed himself completely before me with his grenadier's hat on. I remarked it to my companions: 'Guarda a colui colla sua berretta in testa' (I believe those were my words), waiting a few minutes to see if he would move. I touched him, and said, 'Vorrebbe, farmi la grazia di levarsi il cappello purch'io vegga?' He turning said 'Lo vorreste?' with a smile of insult. I answered: 'Sì, lo voglio.' He then asked me if I would go out with him. I, thinking he meant for a duel, said, 'Yes, with pleasure'; and called Mr Hobhouse to accompany me. He did. When passing by the guard-house he said, 'Go in, go in there'; I said I would not, that it was not there I thought of going with him. Then he swore in German, and drew half his sabre with a threatening look, but Hobhouse held his hand. The police on guard came, and he delivered me to their custody. I entered the guard-house, and he began declaiming about the insult to one like him. I said I was his equal, and, being in the theatre, to any one there. 'Equal to me?' he retorted; 'you are not equal to the last of the

Austrian soldiers in the house'; and then began abusing me in all the Billingsgate German he was master of – which I did not know till afterwards. In the meantime the news had spread in the theatre, and reached De Brême and L Byron, who came running down, and tried to get me away, but could not on any plea. De Brême heard the secretary of police say to the officer: 'Don't you meddle with this, leave it to me.' De Brême said he would go to Bubna immediately, and get an order for my dismission; on which the officer took Lord Byron's card, as bail that I would appear to answer for my conduct on the morrow. Then I was released.

Next morning I received a printed order from the police to attend. As soon as I saw the order I went to De Brême, who accompanied me to the gate. I entered. 'Where do you wish your passport viséd for?' 'I am not thinking of going.' 'You must be off in four-and-twenty hours for Florence.' 'But I wish for more time.' 'You must be off in that time, or you will have some-thing disagreeable happen to you.' Brême, upon hearing this, immediately set off to Bubna, and I to Lord Byron, who sent Mr Hobhouse in company of Colonel McSomething to Swarrow to ask that I might not be obliged to go. They went. Swarrow received them with a pen in his hand; said it was a bagatelle; that the Secretary of Police had been there in the morning, and that he had told him of it. That it was nothing, that I should find myself as well off in any other city as there, and that, if I stayed, something worse might happen. Hobhouse tried to speak. S advanced a foot; 'Give my compliments to Lord Byron; am sorry I was not at home when he called.' 'But if this is so mere a trifle…' – ' I hope Lord Byron is well'; advancing another foot, and then little by little got them so near the door that they saw it was useless, and left him. De Brême in the meantime had been to Bubna. Bubna received him very politely, and said he had already seen Colonel M., who had explained to him the whole; and that for the mistake of speaking to the officer on guard he thought it enough that I had been put under arrest. 'I am much obliged to you, and am glad then that my friend will not have to leave Milan.' 'What do you mean?' Brême explained. 'It is impossible, there must be some mistake, for I have had no memorial of it. I will see Swarrow this evening about it.' De Brême mentioned with what idea I had left the theatre. Bubna said that German soldiers had one prejudice less; and at the theatre in the evening I heard many instances of the officers of the Austrian Army acting meanly in this respect. Amongst others, Bubna's son, being challenged for insulting a lady at a public ball, accepted the challenge, but said there were several things he had to settle first, and that he would appoint a day for the following week. He left Milan the Saturday before. A young Italian had a dispute with a Hussar officer, and challenged him, for which he was brought before the police and reprimanded. Some days after, the officer, standing at a coffee-room door, asked him if he wished to settle the affair with him. He said yes, and they immediately entered. The officer, spoke to several of his companions in the room, and they all struck the young man, and pushed him out. He could get no redress.

30 October   Got up early next morning, packed up my books and things; then went to seek for a coach that was parting for Lodi. Found one, and fixed that a vetturino, who was going to set off next day for Florence, should take me up at Lodi. Went to see De Brême. He told me he had been to Bubna's, but that he had found him out at a council of war, and that he had left an order none should follow him. I took leave of De Brême, and wept in his arms like a child, for his kindness and friendship had been dear to me. I took leave of LB, H, and Guasco. The last offered me his services in any way, and said he should take it as a favour the oftener he was applied to. I got into the coach with only 5 louis in my pocket, leaving my books in the care of De Brême, and left Milan with rage and grief so struggling in my breast that tears often started in my eyes, and all I could think of was revenge against Swarrow and the officer in particular, and a hope that before I left Italy there might be a rising to which I might join myself. I arrived at Lodi; wrote to Lloyd to ask him to lend me some money, and went to bed exhausted.

31 October   Up at 9: breakfasted. Went to see the Duomo and other churches without feeling interest; the hospital, which is a magnificent building. Returning to the inn, I met the vetturino. I found in the coach a Prussian student of Heidelberg who had made the campaigns of '13 and '14 with the rest of his companions, and who was banished Heidelberg for slapping a Russian in the face. Growled against his king for not keeping his promise; hated the French, and gave me an interesting account of the way of spending the winter evenings in his part of Germany, Pomerania; the young working at some pursuit of hand, the old relating their tale of youth. A Milanese woman and son. We went that evening to Casal

Panterlungo. Supped and went to bed, I and the Prussian in the same room.

2 November   Up at 4. Across the Taro to Parma. Went, in spite of my having so little money, in search of books – Boccaccio's *Fiammetta*. The Cathedral and Bapistery. From Parma to Reggio, a beautiful town with fine palaces and porticoes, though, on account of the few inhabitants, appearing a huge sepulchre. To Rubiera: supped and slept.

3 November   Up at 4. Through Modena, where I saw the Duomo, and the Tower which contains the Lecchia porticoes – palaces of the Duke – four orders heaped one on the other. Here they examined my box, and were going to send it to the dogana on account of books; when, upon my saying I was a physician, they let them pass.

At Bologna supped with the Prussian. To the opera. Saw a ballet, extremely ridiculous: barbarian dances with astonishing powers of limbs forming in the air out and in on their feet.

4 November   Up at 9. Went to see the churches and private gallery. After dinner roamed about the town in a most melancholy mood, entering the churches and sitting in the dark for an hour, etc. Went to the Theatre of Cento Cavalli: beautiful Greek architecture. To bed – a play.

5 November   At 10, expecting to have been called before, the vetturino came, saying he would not go, since I had hindered the Prussian from setting off on Monday, without security; and that he would go to the police to gain it from the Prussian that he should be paid at Florence. After a good deal of disputing I gave it, in a promissory note that I would pay if he could not. Found afterwards it was only to get time.

Went to see the churches, the public place, San Propero, the Neptune. After dinner to Madonna Santa Lucia. Along the portico 'Questo è da vendere' was written on portions of the wall. The public cemetery. Saw a coffin, when dark, brought into the church with torches. The poor are separated from the rich, and have only the turf upon them: the rich groan under the weight of marble. The priests, monks, nuns, etc., all in separate squares; a cardinal's hat covering a death's head.

Returned to Bologna. Went to the theatre. Saw *Agnese*: wept like a child: the acting of the madman inimitable. Went to bed.

6 November   Up at 11. Set off with the Prussian and an Italian officer across the Apennines. Oxen in continual use. Misty, so could not enjoy the view. Dreadful winds to Pianoro. That evening the officer related all the services he had been in; French liberty, Consulship, Emperor. Refused by the Austrians; went to Murat, and now going to offer himself to the Pope; if not accepted to America. For which side? 'Spanish or Creole.' He had the unfeelingness to joke upon his father's being killed in the time of the liberty-rows, saying he got that for not changing; on which I felt so nettled that I spoke for half-an-hour upon the ruin the fickleness of the Italians had brought upon themselves. He felt, I think, ashamed; at least he gave up that kind of light talk.

Forgot to say that at Modena I presented my passport so that the '24 hours' were invisible; and left at Modena one who had accompanied us from Piacenza, telling the most barefaced lies about boats, dogs, and thieves, that were ever heard.

7 November   At 4 up. Arrived at night at Fortebuona. Dreadful wind and rain. Supped and went to bed.

8 November   At 5 walked a good part of the road. Arrived at Florence by the Porta San Gallo, through the Arch. The custom-house officer, when we told him, if he wanted to look, he might open 'Che? Un servo del sovrano? Ci sono dei facchini.'

Florence, on entering, disappointed me, as we were obliged to go round on account of the road being mended. Went to the inn. Dressed – not having changed linen since Milan. Went to the post: no letters. In despair, remaining with only four scudi. Walked about the town, – Arno: into the Cathedral and Baptistery.

Went to seek Cavalier Pontelli. Knocked at his door, along Arno – both before and behind. Could not make any one hear. One who lived near (Lecchini), upon my asking how to get in, said he was thankful to say he was not Pontelli, and did not know. Returned home. Gave the Prussian a missal I had bought at Bologna. He broke my pipe. Went to bed. Wrote to Pontelli and Brême.

9 November   Got up; went to seek Pontelli. Found he had a villa at Porta San Gallo. Went thither, knocked; saw his head pop out of the window in a greasy night-cap. On my announcing myself, he descended, opened the door, and received me with welcome. Found him at breakfast, sausages, caviare, etc. Sat down; told me his housekeeper would not show herself; invited me to come to his house instead of the inn. Went into town; took a peep at the Gallery – at the precious vases, Venus, etc. Went to the inn. Put up my things, paid; and, seeing the Prussian envied me my desk, I gave it him, on condition that, if we ever met again, he would paint me a picture he sketched in my album. Went to Pontelli; dined; accompanied him to town. His servant took a porter to carry my things to the Arno house, and then we went to pay visits.

In the way he told me he lived very retired, and very economically that he might not want; that the people now looked upon him with a good eye; that the Government also did not prosecute him; and that he in fine thought that a revolution would be general – trying to persuade me that his avarice was mere policy.

Went to pay a visit to Cavalier Tomasi, a Cortonian. Found many in the room, who all sat upon me about English politics. Left them when they were going to play. Thence to Abate Fontani, Librarian of the Riccardi Library. Talked of Madame de Staël, Finch, etc.

Returned home. Found I was in the house of capponis, Pontelli having the lower storey.

19 November Up at 9. Dressed in black silk, etc., the housekeeper going to mass; and, Pontelli apparently not being willing that I should accompany her, I went out a little after, and went to the same church, where I spoke with her. Looked at the church; and then went to San Lorenzo, Santo Spirito, where I saw the tomb of Galileo, Machiavelli, Alfieri, Cosmo de'Medici, etc.

Returned, and went with a letter from De Brême to the Countess of Albany. Found there several. Presented my letter: 'Very like your father.'

Conversation became general. Republics being brought upon the tapis, I took to defending them, especially against a gentleman near me. After some time he went, and I gathered he was brother to the King of Prussia.

Took my leave, and came to dinner, after going to the caffé to wait for Pontelli. Rain hindered him from keeping his appointment, so that I went at last alone to San Gallo, he having the custom of staying the Sundays only in town. Was presented by him to Lecchini, the Inspector of Police, who recognised me as a

Tuscan, and the domiciliary communication was made out as such.

11 November   Tried to stay at home. Forced by Pontelli's long-in-vain repeated hints to go out; jealous of his young housekeeper, though she is hardly worth it. Roamed about, dined and went to bed.

12 November   Same. Dined with him at a restaurateur's.

13 November   Got up at 7; tired of Pontelli, and set off for Arezzo, with a shirt in my pocket and with my dog. When at Incisa it began to rain; walked on through Feline, Monte Varchi, to Arezzo. Thunder and lightning excessive, with violent rain. I was at last so numbed that when roused I seemed to be wakened; my dog could not stand it, but at 7 miles from Arezzo fell. I did not perceive it, but walked on. Arrived at 8, having walked 45 miles in 12 hours, having stopped once at Incisa to eat and rest. Found my uncle's house; knocked. The servant, hearing I was his nephew, flew up-stairs, and I met a tall, stout, slovenly woman, my aunt. On the second storey, where they lodged, they made a fire. I changed my things for my uncle's, and while changing he arrived – a tall, stout, handsome, mild-looking man. Put myself to bed; ate, and they left me to sleep.

14 November   Found myself well; no cold, only my left groin stiff from a wound in my foot. Saw my two cousins, Pippo and Teresa; put myself to study. After 6 went with my uncle to Signor Gori, where I heard music. Four or five girls wanting husbands, two priests, whitewashed walls, and several young men, were the entertainment.

While at Arezzo, my life was quiet enough; study till I went out at 6, when I went to play at cards and talk at Signor Gordi's. Saw the prisons. One of the descendants of a true Lombard family walking about in a dirty sailor-looking jacket. Signora Onesti and daughter the most abominable scandal-talkers I ever heard, though she was a Pitti. Library always shut. The School of Ignatius a fine building. Churches fine: the Chapel of St Mary, the Cathedral with the basso-rilievo altars, the church with the altar painted by Vasari, etc. – I recovered my dog.

21 November   Set off to return to Florence with half-a-scudo in my pocket; having refused to accept from my uncle, not being willing to let him know how it stood. Frost on the ground: hurt my foot. Lost my dog again at Montesarchi. At Feline got into a carriage, not being able to do more on account of my foot. Met a physician, a cavaliere and his wife. Arrived at 7; Pontelli lent me a scudo to pay.

22, 23, 24 November Stayed at Pontelli's on account of my foot, though Pontelli tried to send me out under pretence that I should see the town. But, not being able, he stayed at home till 6, when he told me I had better go to bed – which I generally did to quiet him. No letters according to servant.

25 November Tired of Pontelli. That I might go to Pisa, I issued out intending to sell my watch-chain; but as a last chance looked at the Post Office, and found two letters from Lloyd, who, as soon as he had received my letter, set off from Venice to see me. On the road he lost his purse with 36 louis, and, having no letters at Florence, he could only give me 20 scudi. Received me with great kindness, and assured me that, while he had money, I should never want. Dined with him and Somers. They advised me to settle in Florence as physician to the English. I however determined to see Vaccà first; wished him good-bye, as he was obliged to got to Rome for money.

26 November Went to seek the Naviglio, to go by water to Pisa. At going out, stopped by the gate-officer, who, on hearing me enquire where the boat was, would not let me pass without proofs of my being *originario Toscano*; so I went to Lecchini, and got him to write me a declaration. The boat could not set off to-day, so returned to Pontelli and went to bed.

27 November At 7 set off in the boat on the Arno for Pisa.

29, 30, November, 1 December Stayed in my room, copying *Osteologia* of my grandfather.

2 December Up at 9; went to see Vaccà; still at hospital. While waiting for him, saw an Austrian colonel, who, in the excess of his gratitude to Vaccà, called him the Dio della Medicina. Vaccà expressed great joy to see me; told me to make his house my own;

to dine there when I chose, and often: to begin to-day; not to use ceremony. Left me, and I returned home: went to dine at V's. Introduced me to his wife, a pleasing pretty French-woman, the former wife of his brother; he had just obtained the Pope's dispensation to marry her. Spent the evening there.

3, 4, December to 21   Went to the hospital in the mornings when Vaccà was not ill; three or four times to the Library. Studied in the mornings; went to dine either at Vaccà's or at eating-house; always evenings at Vaccà's. Corsi, a well-informed lawyer, cav serv to V; Mario ex cav serv. Cecco Castanelli, Pachiani, etc.; chess with the English; with Vaccà. For the various information I obtained there see notes.

21 December   Went in the evening to the Countess Mastrani's. Ices, iced people, prepared poetry, music. Went to the theatre, in the days past, several times. Saw Goldini's *Bugiardo*, with Harlequin etc.

22 December   As usual.

23 December   Same.

24 December   Ditto.

25 December   Christmas-day. Walked along Arno. Spent the evening and dined at Vaccà.

26 December   Up at 7. Went with Vaccà to Leghorn, a neat, regular, well-built town. The first thing I went in search of was the sea, and I stood gazing some time on the waves. The Public Place and Strada Maestra fine. Saw Vescali's collection of alabasters. Returned by 3. Dined with Vaccà. Went to the theatre with Mrs Vaccà, who introduced me to Signora Bettina Franciuoli.

27 December   As usual. Up at 4 – dined at Vaccà's – went to theatre, and to B's box.

28 December   Went to hear nella Chiesa dei Cavalieri (after a ride with Mrs Vaccà) Nicolini play a sonata upon the organ, which is perhaps the finest in Italy. There were the Prince Villafranca, the

Countess Castelfiel, Princess della Pace, and other nobles. At Vaccà's and theatre.

29 December   Up at 3½. Dined at Vaccà's: theatre. English etc. as usual.

30 December   Up at 1. Reading Sismondi. Got up – went to Vaccà to dine. After English, to the Casa Mastrani: all evening with Sofia. The others – Biribro, Dionigi.

[This is the last entry in the Journal.]

from *Letters of John Polidori*

(1816–1817)

To Francis Polidori

Brussels, 2 May 1816

My Dear Fanny,
I shall see Waterloo in a day or two – don't you wish to be with me? But there are many more things that I have seen which would have given you as much pleasure. Shakespeare's Cliff at Dover, the French coast, the phosphorescent sea, Bruges, Ghent, Antwerp, and Brussels, have all got more than is in any of Feinaigh's plates to excite the memory to bring forth its hidden stores. The people amongst whom we are at present dwelling is one that has much distinguished itself in the noblest career, the race for liberty; but that tends little to the ennobling of a people without the sun of literature also deigns to shine upon them.

I am very pleased with Lord Byron. I am with him on the footing of an equal, everything alike: at present here we have a suite of rooms between us. I have my sitting-room at one end, he at the other. He has not shown any passion; though we have had nothing but a series of mishaps that have put me out of temper though they have not ruffled his. The carriage, the new carriage, has had three stoppages. We are at present at Brussels merely to have the carriage-part well looked at and repaired.

The country till here has been one continued flat; and, except within this neighbourhood, we have not seen a rising ground on which to feast our eyes. Long avenues paved in the middle form the continued appearance of our roads. The towns are magnificently old, such as England cannot rival, and the state of cultivation is much greater than in England: indeed we have not seen a weed or a foot of waste ground all our way. The people in the country show no misery; the cottages comfortable, white-washed, large windowed, shining with brass utensils internally, and only having as many heaps of dirt as there are inhabitants – who certainly throw away all their cleanliness upon the house, fields, roads, and windows. But I will not fill my letter with this, as some time you will either see my Journal in writing or print – Murray having offered me 500 guineas for it through Lord Byron. LB is going to give me the manuscript, when done printing, of his new cantos of *Childe Harold*.

How are you all at home? Papa, Mamma, Meggy (have you heard from her?), Charlotte, Bob, Henry, Eliza, and Mr Deagostini.

Remember me to all, and to all who enquire about me not merely from curiosity – telling me in your next letter whether they exceed the number 0. I am very well, and wrote Mamma from Ostend.

I remain, my dear Fanny,

Your affect. Brother,

J. Polidori

Write to me – Dr Polidori, à Genève, poste restante – and soon, as I shall be there in 12 days.

To John Hobhouse, Whitton Park, near Hounslow

Coblentz, 11 May 1816

Dear Sir,

As we are at last some way on our journey, I take a sheet of paper up, in despair of filling it, to tell you we are both well and hearty. Lord Byron's health is greatly improved, his stomach returning rapidly to its natural state. Exercise and peace of mind, making great advances towards the amendment of his *corps délabré*, leave little for medicine to patch up. His spirits, I think, are also much improved. He blithely carols through the day, 'Here's to you, Tom Brown': and, when he has done, says, 'That's as well as Hobhouse does it.' You and his other friend, Scrope Davies, form a great subject of conversation.

God! Here I am at the end of all my thoughts. Oh no! Waterloo was ridden over by my Lord on a Cossack horse, accompanied by myself on a Flemish steed; Lord Byron singing Turkish or Arnaout riding-tunes, and your h[umble] s[ervant] listening. We had a very day of it. Lord Byron visited Howard's (I think Colonel) burying-place twice. We have had two days by pre-eminence in our tour – to-day and Waterloo. To-day we came from Bonn hither through the finest scenes I ever saw, modern and ancient; the 13th and 18th century forming an *olla podrida* with the bases given in the year 1. Towers and towns and castles and cots were sprinkled on the side of a ... But here I am on poetic stilts, cut short for prose ones.

They boast – the Ministerialists and others – of our being the happy land. I should like to carry John Bull to Flanders and the Rhine: happiness, content, cleanliness (here and there), husbandry, plenty without luxury, are here bestowed on all. War has had no effect upon the fields; and even at Waterloo no one (except for the glittering button or less brilliant cuirass in beggar's hand) would imagine two such myriaded armies had met there. No sulkiness is seen upon the face here, and no impudence. On the Rhine and in Flanders there are hardly any beggars. To-day we had nosegays given us by little girls for centimes. But the other day, coming to Battice, we met the best beggars: three little girls, pretty though not well dressed, ran along our carriage, crying out – 'Donnez-nous un sou, Monsieur le Général en chef'; and another, 'Chef de bataillon.' Having given some, a boy followed, pulling faces comic enough to make such grave dons laugh, and crying out, 'Vivent Messieurs les Rois des Hanovériens – donnez-moi un sou.'

As I fear I have tried your eyes, and lost my pains after all on account of the illegibility of my accursed pen's scratches, I must end – assuring you at the same time I am with esteem

Yours etc.,

J. Polidori

We count upon being at Geneva in ten days at best. Excuse the bad writing, etc., for I am in a fever of digestion after my ride. – J.P.

To John Murray

Brussels 6 May 1816

Sir,

By Lord Byron's advice I wish you would take this heap of trophies under your care passing for us what is due for Customs etc. – We had a wonderful ride over Waterloo on a Cossack horse and a Flemish steed. We are well in health etc.

Yours, J. Polidori

PS

Lord Byron will account to you for it, he would pay yourself but cannot ascertain the amount. Lord Byron will write in a day or two.

To John Murray

Villa Diodati, 18 June 1819

Dear Sir,
We are at Campagne Diodati, near Geneva. Has a Mr Gordon remitted into your hands the spoils of Waterloo – we should be much obliged to you if you would send us Kubla Khan and Christabel and other poems of Coleridge Esq.

To his Father, Gaetano Polidori

20 September 1816

My Dear Father,
You judged right with regard to my writing. I had written twice since your letter announcing *The Pamphleteer*, and was anxiously waiting yours. Your letter gave me pleasure; and I was indeed in want of some just then, for I was in agitation for my parting from Lord Byron. We have parted, finding that our tempers did not agree. He proposed it, and it was settled. There was no immediate cause, but a continued series of slight quarrels. I believe the fault, if any, has been on my part; I am not accustomed to have a master, and therefore my conduct was not free and easy. I found on settling accounts that I had 70 napoleons; I therefore determined to walk over Italy, and (seeing the medical establishments) see if there proves a good opportunity to settle myself, so that I hope I am still off your hands for nine months: perhaps Lady Westmorland, who is at Rome, is desirous of having an English physician for longer, I having a letter for her from Mme. De Staël. I shall write to-day to Vaccà and Zio [uncle] for letters to Milan to physicians, in your name; and at present, till I think they and my trunks can have arrived, will wander amongst the Alps, – in which course I am now at Thun, almost in the centre. I have seen Mont Blanc and its glaciers, and will see the Jungfrau, Grindelwald, and Grimsel. Then I will go by the Simplon to Milan, whither direct to me poste-restante, only putting my Giovanni etc. names in full, as there are Polidoris there. I am in good health and spirits; I hope this won't hurt yours, for assure yourself I will do all I can not to allow you to feel any inconvenience on my account.

Remember me to my mother, who I know will feel deeply this disappointment; to Mary, Fanny, and Charlotte, to Signor Deagostini and Signor De Ocheda, and to all.

If you could get me letters of introduction, they would be of great use. In the meantime, my dear father, believe me

Your affectionate son,

John Polidori

To Lord Byron at Campagne Diodati, Geneva

Milan, 1 October 1816,

My Lord,

From the date of my letter you will perceive I am already in Italy – I have been here 2 days after many fatigues but no perils thou they say there are robbers and that between Varese and Milan a chain of English Carrriages was stopt by not gallant cavaliers. I learnt it from a party who came in the same boats by the Lago Maggiore, the Sesino and the Canal as myself to Milan which they did with carriages and all packed into a barge on purpose to avoid the fatal spot – which I did to avoid the perchance on my left foot which is sorely mangled by the new shoe of Mr Brightstone of Geneva.

My route has been throughout accompanied with the most magnificent scenery, I shall not describe any part both because your Lordship I believe hates description and because you will also, I hope, tread the same road into this once happier land – I do not know whether you went to the Grimsel it is a scenery of its own kind…

To Gaetano Polidori

Arezzo, November 1816

Dear Father,

I fear you must be in much anxiety at not having heard from me for so long; but the reason was that I did not wish to write before having seen my uncle – to whom I went the day before yesterday, and who received me with great affection and pleasure. I wrote to him from Thun. Thence I went to Grindelwald and Lauterbrunner; hence to Interlachen, and, by the Lake of Brientz, to Meyringen; by the Grimsel in the Valais to Obergasteln; thence to Brieg; and then by the Simplon down to Farinoli in the Borromean Islands. Thence I embarked to Sestri Calende; thence to Milan – where, meeting the poet Monti, Lord Byron, Monsignor De Brême, and others of my acquaintance, I remained some weeks. Thence I went to Florence, by Bologna, Modena, Parma, and Piacenza, and crossing the Apennines. In Florence I stayed two days, and saw Cavalier Pontelli, Abate Fontani, Dr Frosini, and others. Thence I went on foot to Arezzo, where I found my uncle, my aunt, Pippo, and Teresa, all well; and they received me with great cordiality into their house, where I now am.

Seeing, by your letter to my uncle, in how much trouble you are on my account, I determined, after learning whether Lady Westmorland will employ me or no – if yes, to go to Rome; if no, to go straight from Leghorn to London, to the bosom of my family. I shall soon hear from Lady Westmorland, as Lady Jersey undertook, at the instance of Monsignor De Brême, to ask her mother whether she wants me or not, and she is now in Florence, *en route* for Rome.

I wish that in your next letter you would send me enough money, in a bill on Florence, for paying the passage from Leghorn to London, for the chance of my not having enough remaining…

When I see you again I shall have much to tell you about, but will not put it into a letter. Suffice it that I have found that what you told me about Italy is but too true. I am in good health…

Your affectionate son,
John Polidori

To this letter the uncle Luigi Polidori added a few lines concerning Lord Byron: 'I became indignant at some references [made by John Polidori] to the strange conduct of that Lord Byron with whom he was travelling: but *he* kept his temper well – I envy him for that. All these people are hard: Patience!'

Gaetano Polidori to His Son, John

Addressed to; Il Signore Doctor Giovanni Gulielmo Polidori
Ferma in Posta, Milano, Italy.

London, 30 September 1816

My Dearest Son,
Your letter produced in me a two-fold and opposite sensation:
gratification at your having quitted a man so discredited in public
opinion, and sorrow at seeing you almost a vagrant, and at the
uncertainty as your lot. But at all costs I should have liked to see
you in London, where at least bread and roofing would not have
you wanting... so long as I could divide the two with you. I hope
however that mishaps, if this can be called one, will open your eyes,
and that you will recognise the error of following over much the
dictates of a warm fancy. I recommend you to be at least cautious
in your travels... I will see to you getting some letters of
introduction for you; and meantime I send you one for Lord
Cowper... he is a liberal and courteous gentleman, and Lady
Cowper an excellent and beneficent lady. I am sure they will do
you any service they can. At Pisa I am sure that Vaccà will receive
you as a son, and will make you acquainted with all the best people
in that city... If I can, I will procure you a letter of recommendation
from the Duke of Sussex to the Grand Duke of Tuscany. In short I
will do everything which a father should do for a son whom he
loves; a father who forgets everything else when he sees his son in
need or in danger.
    Your most affectionate Father

Draft Letter to Messrs Sherwood and Neely

3 April 1819

Dear Gentlemen
I see in the title page of a tale purporting to [be] by Lord Byron the
Vampyre that you are the publishers of it, I therefore take the liberty
of addressing myself to you –
    Lord Byron is *not* the author – I who am referred to in the letter
of the Magazines am that author, I was the '*Gentleman*' who
travelled with his Lordship and who wrote the whole of that trifle

– I therefore desire that you will account to me for it as by your having entered it at Stationers hall before the publication of the Magazine. I am deprived of all copyright therein and cannot any longer take advantage of my own work – if I have not an immediate answer I shall immediately procure an injunction from Chancery to stop its further sale for I will not in any manner allow myself to be deprived of what is mine – I shall at the same time if the title page is not cancelled & my name inserted instead of Lord Byron, immediately publish in all the papers there this a mistake in the author.

Yr &c

J Polidori MD

To Lord Byron

Pisa, 11 January 1817

My time here is perhaps the most valuable that I have yet passed in the study of my profession – Vaccà the first surgeon in Italy undoubtedly an ancient school fellow of my father has received me like a son & old friend – he is a man with all the fire of his nation & judgement of a northern knowing exactly the limits between the uses of these two faculties & with few if any prejudices not only in religion &c but what is more difficult in his profession – I thought myself very free from medical prejudice but by his instruction by his demonstration of how much is thought fact in medicine which is merely a rash induction. My presumption is much diminished & I have put myself to study again what I thought I knew.

I divide my time between the hospital reading medicine & Italian literature till 4 when I dine with him & afterwards accompany his wife to the theatre – so that from 7 in the morning when I go to the hospital to 11 when I return home I am always occupied for the conversation of Vaccà is perhaps more useful than a book to me.

Indeed, if my mind could but rest with regard to the future I should be very content but that is so uncertain & promises so badly that I cannot bear to think about it – Lady Westmorland I know nothing of yet – I was thinking of settling in Florence but the only person who could be of use, the Countess of Albany, is engaged to a French physician who cures especially the Cytherean complaints.

I have one brilliant prospect before [me] the Bresil, Vaccà has exerted himself very much for me & upon one of his greatest friends, Olindo Giusto, being appointed by the Danish court, in consequence of his marrying the first minister's daughter, to the general consulship of Denmark at the Brazils he has seen him & induced him to take me along with him & do all in his power in the Brazils to my advancement in my profession being thus sure of the Danish practice & having a probability of the English from being so my fortune they assure me would be made – he has even offered me a room &c in his house & having set off for Copenhagen two days ago will on his arrival write to me where I am to meet him at Lisbon or London to go with him in July. But I don't think I shall be able. I would not indeed, it would be absurd to go without 2 or 3 hundred pounds & my father being unable to advance it me I have only one hope that he will consent to raise it in some way or other but this is so weak that I fear I shall have to struggle it out with out hope in Europe.

To Lord Byron

Pisa, 17 January 1817

I have arranged the observations I have made upon different subjects in Italy but especially medicine & surgery into the shape of a journal and I think I have got some interesting information upon the state of these two last sciences and I have at least in my own eyes put it upon paper in if not an accurate at least a clear style might I ask your Lordship to recommend to Murray[?] I have also a play, *The Duke of Athens*, but I fear at this you will be more inclined to laugh than any thing else, but as I wish to go to the Brazil and I do not think my father will help me, might I ask your Lordship to read & judge it. That the information in my journal (medical) is accurate I can assure you from having read it to Vaccà who has corrected it where any thing was mistaken. I feel very anxious about this Brazil plan and if I did not fear troubling you I should wish to ask you that if you could you would give me some means of getting recommended to some one of the English who have influence at the Portugese court. For it would be too late after having gone there & not succeeding to come back & try to settle in any other place.

I fear I ask too much of your Lordship, as in return I can only assure you that I am affectionately your obliged and humble servant,
John Polidori

– would you remember me to Mr Hobhouse – would you also tell me if Mr Shelley is in London.

Lord Byron to his Publisher, John Murray

January, 1817

Dr Polidori as I hear from him by letter from Pisa is about to return to England – to go to the Brazils on a medical Speculation with the Danish Consul – as you are in the favour of the powers that be – could you not get him some letters of recommendation from some of your Government friends – to some of the Portugese settlers – he understands his profession well – & has no want of general talents – his faults are the faults of a pardonable vanity & youth – his remaining with me was out of the question… but I know no great harm of him – & some good – he is clever – & well accomplished – knows his profession by all accounts well – and is honourable in his dealings – & not at all malevolent. – I think with luck he will turn out a useful member of society (from which he will lop the diseased members) & the college of Physicians… He has kept a medical journal under the eye of Vaccà (the first Surgeon on the Continent) at Pisa – Vaccà has corrected it – & it must contain some valuable hints or information on the practice of this Country. – If you can aid him in publishing this also – by your influence with your brethren – do – I do not ask you to publish it yourself – because that sort of request is too personal & embarrassing. – He has also a tragedy – of which having seen nothing I say nothing – but the very circumstance of his having made these efforts (if they are only efforts) at one & twenty – is in his favour & proves him to have good dispositions for his own improvement.

Appendix: Four Letters about Polidori

Louis de Brême to Luisa Stolberg D'Albany, Florence[1]

Milan, 30 October 1816

Madame!
You would not have forgiven me had I not given a letter for you Madam, to M. Polidori, spirited and knowledgeable young man with whom I have been friendly since my trip to Switzerland. He's an Anglo-Italian whose father without a doubt has the honour of being known to you as he was the secretary of our Count Alfieri. The young Polidori is the friend and the long time companion and appointed doctor of Lord Byron; because he is doctor of the University of Edinburgh in that sad and useless faculty. I have taken great interest in him which he deserves because of all these things. He also comes highly recommended by Mme. De Staël.

Mr Polidori will tell you about the accident that obliges him to quit Milan earlier than he had previously planned. When you have listened to all that he has to say, I beg you to give him the best advice to obtain support from the Minister of his government in Florence.

Madam,
Your most devoted, obedient, and obliging servant
L. de Brême, son

Louis de Brême to Madame de Staël at Chateau du Coppet, Switzerland

Milan, 7 October 1816

Madame!
Dr Polidori has arrived; I will be doing my utmost to ensure that he mixes with the greatest of his Italian counterparts. In the meantime to fill his spare moments, he wants to compose a dozen Italian tragedies and then it will be the English ladies turn.

---

1 Translations of the following three letters are the editor's own.

He's a really nice chap. He very sincerely offered to teach me English. I am expecting Lady Jersey who Brougham calls our 'Queen of the Opposition.' I wrote to Come in order to let the good Lady know that I have reserved an apartment for her at the Hotel Royal. According to what Brougham has communicated to me from Florence, she'll be here on the 10th. Is it true, as Polidori says, that all those people when they return to London, don't remember us anymore than they remember Collin Tampon? This could only be true up to a certain point. I would be inconsolable if the Lansdownes were to forget me.

Louis de Brême

Louis de Brême to Madame de Staël in Paris

Milan, 30 October 1816

Madame,
Lord Byron is very kind. An opportunity recently presented itself to demonstrate his 'good heart' to Polidori, and he seized it with simplicity and eagerness. Also I shall tell you that I think there are some men who aren't valued at all because of what one calls their 'behaviour' whose souls are a treasury of real qualities; their souls are maybe not 'sociable' but they are eminently human. Lord Byron is gifted with a variety of qualities for which his compatriots and his family do not give him credit. This is quite natural as he is missing the qualities that are normally valued. We spend most of our evenings together and many of these we spend at the Theatre.

Polidori left this morning for Florence. Don't believe anything that you might hear about him or about the reasons of his hurried departure[2] from here before I am able to inform you about it; which I will do on the first occasion that presents itself. In the meantime, if you have the opportunity to in Paris, could you please help him with all your influence with the minister of his government in Florence; whilst it is possible for one to be more careful than he is, and one could also be less unhappy, generally it is not possible for one to be a more honest, naïve, and well-meaning man. You see

---

2 The opportunity which presented itself was when Lord Byron intervened in favour of Polidori after the doctor had been arrested by the Austrian police during an altercation with an Austrian official he provoked at La Scala.

Madam, I feel I am obliged to retract the too superficial judgements that I made of him at Coppet when I thought to see only vulgarity in character and moreover in spirit, it is simply a matter of lack of knowledge, of deep discernment and of a real feeling for beauty. You'll have judged him at the same time according to the truth. I am only speaking well of him in order to reconcile myself about him.

Dante Gabriel Rossetti to William Allingham

21 March 1855

In Medwin, in Moore, and in Leigh Hunt, and elsewhere, I have seen allusions to him [John Polidori] which dwelt on nothing except his faults... I have met accidentally, from time to time, with persons who knew him, and he seems always to have excited admiration by his talents, and with those who knew him well, affection and respect by his honourable nature...

FyfieldBooks

Two millennia of essential classics

The extensive FyfieldBooks list includes

For more information, including a full list of Fyfield*Books* and a contents list for each title, and details of how to order the books, visit the Carcanet website at www.carcanet.co.uk or email info@carcanet.co.uk